Parting Shots

Parting Shots

Freda Bright

LITTLE, BROWN AND COMPANY
BOSTON   TORONTO   LONDON

To Joan and Bayley Silleck
London, New York, and various places in the heart.

ISBN 0-316-10839-1

Published simultaneously in Canada
by Little, Brown & Company (Canada) Limited

Printed in the United States of America

Part One

1

". . . DIVORCE!"

The word wafted up toward the ceiling, echoed faintly, hung in the air for a second or two, occupying a kind of no-man's-land until Dani (who made a point of never being the first to mention it) seized it and brought it down to earth.

"Ah . . . yes," she said. "Divorce. Well, naturally that's an option. But first, I want to impress upon you, Mrs. Gessner, that divorce can be hell."

It was a statement of fact, brisk and nonjudgmental, after which she switched to a more intimate tone. She was talking now woman to woman, your friend, your confidante, the dispenser of common sense and wholesome advice.

"Divorce is such a drastic measure, Mrs. Gessner. A major upheaval that will affect every area of your life. So before we get down to cases, I'd like you to ask yourself: Are you sure you want to go through with it? You've put in all those years of marriage . . . thirty-five, did you say? Practically your entire adult life. So let's take a little break now to reflect, reconsider. What's a few minutes more compared to all those years? Try to think of the good times you and your husband have had together, the happy years, the children. Then consider what other options are open. Because once the legal mechanism gets under way, once you push the green button, the going gets rough and it's hard to turn back. I regret to say there's no such thing as a painless divorce."

That said, Dani Sloane swiveled her chair toward the window and pretended to be absorbed in the view. She'd give her client time enough to wipe her eyes, collect her thoughts and maybe, just maybe, ponder Dani's message.

Except for the hum of the air conditioner and the sound of Mrs. Gessner's breath coming in quick, uneven gasps, the office was silent. Dani folded her hands and let her mind drift.

Even in repose, Dani Sloane (or Danielle Sloane, Esq., as it read in neat brass letters on the door to her office) emitted an aura of warmth, of goodwill and unflappable calm. Her voice was low, her expression invited confidence. *You can talk to me*, the tilt of her head implied. *So place yourself in my hands and I'll know exactly what to do. I can solve all your problems. Trust me.*

Clients did trust her, and to good effect, for Dani always played scrupulously fair. She never lied, never cheated, didn't pad bills or encourage useless litigation. "Firm but fair" was one of her mottoes; "short and swift" was another.

(It's that sort of thing, one of her colleagues kidded, that gives lawyering a bad name. More likely, it was that sort of thing that had kept her from making partner.)

At forty-one, she was an attractive woman: tall, slender, with alert blue eyes and a warm smile. The thick brown hair that had begun showing traces of gray was swept back off her face in a casual cut. She was wearing her office uniform: a tailored suit, silk blouse, pearl button earrings and low-heeled pumps (it didn't pay to loom large over clients or judges, experience had shown). The total effect was that of the New York career woman, par excellence.

Furtively, the New York career woman par excellence glanced at her watch. It was 4:38. *I'll give her a few more minutes*, she thought, after which they could get on with the business at hand. With luck Dani would be out by 5:30, grab a cab and get home before 6:00. Mrs. Gessner was the last client of the day.

Today's appointment was primarily a chance for lawyer and client to get acquainted. Dani would determine a few basics, establish the ground rules and discuss fees. Mrs. Gessner would decide if she and Dani were compatible. Only then would the real work begin.

As was her practice, Dani had opened the meeting with her

"divorce can be hell" proviso. The speech was standard procedure, the first of several set pieces delivered to each new client, issued more for form's sake than out of any conviction that it would trigger second thoughts. But Dani felt it had to be said.

CAUTION—she ought to post a sign on her office door. Nothing fancy. Just a neat boxed rectangle, like the Surgeon General's warning on cigarette packs.

> ## CAUTION
> DIVORCE CAN DAMAGE YOUR HEALTH.
> PHYSICAL. FINANCIAL. EMOTIONAL.

Or maybe even blunter:

> ## PROCEED AT YOUR OWN RISK.

Not that it ever made a whit of difference. By the time the newcomer had opened that door, crossed the threshold, settled down across the desk within easy reach of the ever-present Kleenex box—by then, the die was cast. Divorce was what they'd come for; divorce was what they got—and who was Dani to knock it? It was how she earned her livelihood.

Nonetheless, she felt obliged to fire this brief salvo before getting down to cases. It was a way of covering her ass. Then later, as often happened, when the warring parties went ballistic, she would be indemnified from any charge that "You never told me it would be such hell." Sure, she'd told them. Right at the start. They just never listened.

"A useful specialty," Jack Pruitt said when he'd first interviewed her for the job, though his upturned nose implied *a necessary evil*.

The firm had never before had a matrimonial lawyer on staff, but its managing partner hated the thought of losing potential revenue.

"More and more of our clients are asking for the service and I don't like to see them take their business elsewhere. Time we got into the act. What the hell, divorce is a basic commodity these days. Like undertaking."

Seeing Dani's raised eyebrows, he continued with a smirk. "Better, in fact. Funerals are strictly a one-shot deal. I mean, how many times can a client die? Whereas divorce! A nice juicy divorce can generate a shitload of other income for the firm. Divorcées sell their houses . . . write new wills . . . dissolve partnerships . . . then get prenups so they can go ahead and make the same dumb mistake twice. Stick around long enough, my bet is, and you might even get repeat business."

Dani had smiled, a wry, pained smile that said: For this I sweated out three years of law school? To set asunder what God—or at least a justice of the peace—has joined?

She'd been psyched for a job in corporate law or international, something clean and prestigious. Instead, she was being invited to hire on as a souped-up social worker. Jack Pruitt must have read her face, for he immediately shifted gears. A short burly man with the dark quick eyes of a ferret, he was accustomed to winning arguments one way or another.

"Okay, matrimonial's not the most glamorous specialty, but it's varied, interesting. Loaded with all kinds of opportunity. You'll be litigating, writing contracts, honing your negotiating skills. What more could a first-year associate ask for?"

Moreover, he wanted a woman for the slot. That decision, he assured her, had nothing to do with affirmative action; it was a judgment call. Matrimonial law demanded special qualities, Pruitt felt. Feminine qualities.

"Sensitivity . . . tact . . . all that jazz. You'll be dealing with clients at the most emotional juncture of their lives. Besides," he continued, "a lot of women don't want a male attorney handling their divorce. It's a question of trust. They probably feel they've been fucked around enough by men already. Who knows? Maybe they're right. In any case, this job will be right up your alley. You're a smart lady. Pragmatic. Plus—and please don't take this amiss—" He looked her over and gave a knowing nod, like a judge at a cattle show. "Plus you've got a nice face. *Simpatica*. That never hurts."

Her first instinct was to say no. The sexism behind his reasoning offended her. And as specialties went, family law was a backwater: low profile, low paid, lacking in status. She'd probably never make partner.

But beyond that was her own sense of distaste. Was this how she wanted to spend her waking hours—mucking about in other people's dirty laundry like a chambermaid in a tenth-rate hotel? Dani was inclined to agree with the Boston law professor who stated that "Divorce is to law what proctology is to medicine."

"I'll think it over," she'd said, then went home and thought it over. A week later, she had joined the firm.

As it had in every major decision of her life, common sense carried the day.

Dani was thirty-five years old at the time, with the ink still wet upon her law degree and money owing to the bank. In a crowded job market, she was competing against an army of fresh-minted lawyers, many of whom enjoyed political clout or family connections. Dani had neither. A "nice face" didn't count for beans on a résumé, and *simpatica* for rather less. She was not a "hot property," as the term was defined by the big downtown firms.

In any case, the fast track was closed to her.

Dani was willing to work hard and work "smart." She was not willing to work the eighty-hour week. The corridors of law school had echoed with horror stories (at least horrible to her) of life on the fast track; of the pace in the Wall Street megafirms where big bucks and big law went hand in hand, where "starting salaries" nudged the six-figure mark, where lights were proudly burning at three A.M., where newcomers survived, if they survived at all, on a diet of black coffee and Pepto-Bismol, where you always kept an overnight bag at the ready and your private life on the back burner; firms that held you fast with "golden handcuffs."

Exciting stuff if one was young and single and childless and driven. Dani was none of the above. She was a lawyer, yes, but a lawyer second. First and foremost, she was a married woman.

Who intended to stay that way.

Thus, Pruitt-Baker filled her bill of particulars. The firm was medium sized, medium wattage. Sharp but not earthshaking. Hustling, but not hysterical. The midtown location meant she could be home each night at a reasonable hour. The money was . . . Alas! There, Jack Pruitt wouldn't budge.

Well, money isn't everything, she reminded herself. All life was compromise. And though the pay was piddling by Wall Street standards, it made for a healthy second income. She resolved to stick it out for a year or two and, if the work proved too tacky, then either move up or move elsewhere. Dani Sloane wasn't married to the job. Thank God!

Nevertheless, here she was, six years later, on a brute-hot summer afternoon, occupying the same utilitarian office, sitting behind the same fake-walnut laminated desk, facing the same cramped patch of sky. The only change of decor was the doughty oak armchair she'd insisted upon, her clients needing something firm to grip, and, on the opposite wall, a print of Hicks's *Peaceable Kingdom* with its recumbent lions and lambs. The picture had a soothing effect.

Six years. Six years of doing business at the same old stand. Not yet a partner, apparently never destined to be. No glittering triumphs to boast of in the alumni rag, no famous names to drop at dinner parties. But had you forced her, on pain of perjury, to confess the truth and nothing but, Dani would admit being happy with the status quo.

She was good at her craft. Her clientele had grown. She was a modest but steady earner for the firm, though you wouldn't think so whenever she requested a raise.

"You're just providing a service," Jack Pruitt would say, "not greasing the wheels." He perpetually nagged her to hustle up more business. "Volume. What I want from you is high volume."

On the books, a fast turnover meant more money for the firm, a bit more clout for Dani. But she was satisfied: She had carved out a comfortable niche and was as busy as she wanted to be. Sometimes—today, for instance—even busier.

As her boss had foretold and a glance at her calendar confirmed, divorce was indeed a basic commodity.

From the start, the work had engrossed her, comprising, as it did, the emotional spectrum.

First, the feverish phone call, the unfamiliar name in the desk diary; then a total stranger walking into her office. She could never quell the flutter of anticipation, the sense of a drama about to unfold. And what dramas they were!

Heartbreak, incest, desertion, abuse, adultery, perversions that would have set Freud's hair on end. Dani had seen man at his most venal. Woman at her most vulnerable. And often as not, vice versa. Oh! the tales she could tell you, were she less than discreet. Each case had its unique set of fierce secrets, of dark struggles, tattered passions, broken hearts.

And into this chaos, Dani could bring sanity, a sense of order. With luck, perhaps, even justice.

"But you don't understand," a client once reproached Dani when she had counseled moderation. "You can't, unless you've been through it yourself."

Not so, she was tempted to answer. After all, does a criminal lawyer have to commit murder in order to do his job? Is a cardiologist required to have a heart attack?

She was a professional. Objective, as every true pro must be. Able to make the distinction between her clients' lives and her own, between heart and head. Yes indeed, one should be feeling, caring, *simpatica*. But one must never, never overstep the line.

As for the implication that the success of her own marriage had blinded her to certain insights, nothing could be further from the truth.

Quite the contrary. Domestic peace had made a better lawyer out of her; it had given her judgment, comfort, perspective, stability, strength, above all, a clarity of vision that enabled her to swim through a sea of other people's tears without ever losing sight of the goal. And that goal, simply put, was to get the best deal possible for her client.

A "good divorce," if that weren't a contradiction.

Or none at all, if the client so chose.

"So . . ." Dani swiveled her chair back and faced Mrs. Gessner. "Shall we talk?"

Mrs. Gessner opened her mouth and nothing came out. Instead she began gasping for air like a beached whale.

She was a well-coiffed middle-aged matron with the gloss of suburbia upon her, plump veteran of ten thousand home-cooked dinners, dressed in a "nice" linen suit that was both expensive and dowdy. Ordinary looking in every respect, except for the eyes, which were frozen in a catatonic glaze.

"He left me!" she finally blurted out. "My husband moved out and left me. Would you believe? He left me for another *man!* Can you imagine?"

Dani nodded sympathetically. "Oh, I'm so sorry."

But Mrs. Gessner scarcely heard. "You don't believe me, do you?" she said, herself apparently unable to believe such an enormity, for she felt called upon to clarify. "Another *man!* He left me for a . . ." Her mouth contorted as she struggled for expression. *Gay, queer, fag, queen, homosexual:* such terms were clearly alien to her, at least in connection with her husband. ". . . for a . . . a *faigele!*" she whispered. "Who ever heard of such a thing?"

Dani nodded again, patted her hand, then reached for a legal pad. Go tell the poor thing that her predicament was not unique. That would be cold comfort indeed.

"I see," she hummed. "And we'll get to that, I promise. First, though, how about a little background. . . ."

Linda L. Gessner [she scribbled on the pad]
Occup. Housewife, Glen Cove L.I.
Married 1954.
Three kids, 2 grown sons, married daughter.
Husb: Ira G., 59 yrs.
Assets????? Income???? $$$?

There they were—the magic words: Assets. Income. Money. Time to zero in on the issues.

"About your husband, what line is he in?"

Linda Gessner drew a breath. Then—

"Ira is a prominent-Park-Avenue-dentist."

The words tumbled out in a seamless cluster, a catch phrase iterated so often over the years that each element had long since melded together into an indivisible whole.

Dani cocked an eyebrow. The locution was familiar. Her mother employed it all the time as a kind of shorthand. There was her uncle Jack-who-plays-the-ponies. Her brother Kevin-the-baby, though Kevin was now thirty-nine. Her sisters were always identified as Sally-the-pretty-one and Anne-the-born-athlete. She herself was Dani-the-smartest-of-the-bunch. Thus in three or four words, one's role in life was determined forever. No further analysis required.

Dani experienced a swift insight into Linda Gessner.

She was Mrs. Prominent-Park-Avenue-dentist. There it was. The grand total of a lifetime's investment. In that package of words lay Linda Gessner's identity, her image of self. She was Mrs. Dr. Ira Gessner, wife of the prominent-Park-Avenue etc.

Who was gay, worse luck.

And had dumped her for a *man*.

And nothing was ever going to be the same again.

Poor thing! Dani thought, and inched the Kleenex box closer, waiting for the flood. But when it came it was words, not tears.

The catchphrase had done the trick, for Mrs. Gessner suddenly rediscovered her tongue and, before Dani could squeeze the next question in, had embarked on a breakneck litany.

Grievances, memories, trivia and turning points: they were pouring out unstemmed, unedited. She was transfixed by a compulsion to state the situation over and over, then over again, to tell the story of her life, her marriage, her husband's astonishing lapse as if, through dint of repetition, it would somehow make sense.

"Three years of Tufts I put him through . . . I worked, I struggled. My husband left me for another man . . . our children, our gorgeous children . . . left me for another man . . . thirty-five years in the same bed . . . left me for another man . . . adjacent plots in Mount Hebron . . . left me for another man . . . second honeymoon in Barbados . . . left me for . . . left me left me left me. . . ."

Little of it was pertinent, but Dani could not stop the flow. She checked her watch, this time openly. Already it was 5:10. She was going to be late.

"Mrs. Gessner!" Dani tried to make eye contact, but it was hopeless. Linda Gessner was in shock.

Stage One.

Dani recognized the symptoms. The glazed eye. The deaf ear. The mindless babble. It was the start of a drawn-out cycle that was par for the course when a long marriage died.

"Like undertaking," Pruitt had joked. And so it was. She was presiding at the death of a marriage. The similarities were profound, given minor variations. For divorce imposed its own version of the five stages of mourning.

There was Stage One: shock. One had but to glance at Mrs. Gessner for an example.

Stage Two: denial—He/she couldn't do this to me!

Stage Three: pain—I wanna die I wanna die I wanna die.

Stage Four: hatred—I'm gonna get that bastard if it's the last thing I do. That was the worst stage, the toughest for lawyers to deal with. And often, the most profitable.

Then, finally, Stage Five: grief and acceptance.

Mercifully, not every client underwent each stage of the process. On the other hand, not every one made it through to Stage Five. And therein lay the difference between death and divorce. In divorce, "that bastard" was still alive and kicking. Maybe even having a wonderful life. Laughing, loving, partying.

Without me!

For that was the cruelest twist of the knife. That the author of one's misery should dare, should have the nerve, the gall, the insensitivity to be happy! At least the dead had the good grace to stay put.

Some clients never gave up the struggle, staying locked in Stage Four forever. Such lives they led! Consumed by bitterness. Mired in fantasies of revenge. Drained by endless litigation. It made you sick.

To Dani's mind, that was the real tragedy of divorce. The refusal to accept reality and cut your losses.

Certain attorneys encouraged clients in this folly. "Why not?" their rationale went. "The meter's running."

Dani, however, was not one of those attorneys. Firm but fair.

"Mrs. Gessner! Ahoy there!"

She rapped the side of her desk with a pencil, but Linda Gessner was still trapped in the loop. "Left me . . . left me . . . left me for a man . . ."

Christ! 5:20 already. Desperate measures were called for.

As a matter of policy, Dani didn't discuss her private life with clients, but this once, perhaps a touch of the mundane would break the spell.

"Mrs. Gessner." She raised her voice, in despair of getting through. The woman was cocooned in misery. "Please listen. I know you're in pain and I hate to cut you short, but my daughter's leaving for college tomorrow morning and I have to get home early, help her pack. You know how it is. . . ."

"Oh?"

The flood stopped. The tactic worked. Kids . . . college . . . luggage . . . the small change of daily life. These were concepts Linda Gessner could grasp, a message from a saner world. Out of reflex, she responded politely.

"Oh? How nice. Which college?"

"Oberlin. It's her freshman year."

"Our Geoffrey went to Antioch. That's also in Ohio."

"Practically neighbors." Dani smiled. There! She had her client's attention. Time now for Dani to deliver the second set piece of the day.

"Mrs. Gessner, as you probably realize, most divorce suits are largely concerned with the division of assets. Who gets what . . . custody of the children . . . a fair and equitable"—she stressed the word—"distribution of property . . ."

"But this is different. My husband le—"

"Yes, I know. And I'm sorry. However, whether or not one is the injured party matters rather less than you might think in law. Perhaps less than it should, but there you are. In the old days, before the current law was enacted, divorce was pretty much about the past—who did what to whom. But nowadays, it's about the future. It's about who's going to get what, about starting a new life. The court essentially doesn't concern itself with sexual misbehavior. These are permissive times, Mrs. Gessner, and besides, there are limits to the kind of relief the law can provide."

She went on briskly to explain the matter of legal fees, methods of payment. Had Dr. Gessner retained a lawyer? Yes? Leo Margulies? Splendid.

"I know Mr. Margulies. I'll give him a ring in the morning and we can have a preliminary chat."

"But what do I do now?" A note of panic had crept in.

"First go home and get a good night's sleep, then tomorrow . . ."

Dani handed her a printed questionnaire, covering the essentials: stocks, bonds, bank accounts, real estate, investment properties. Was Dr. Gessner incorporated? Did he have a pension plan?

". . . then tomorrow start filling this in."

But Mrs. Gessner could grasp none of this.

"I mean, what do I do with my life? What do I do? Where do I go?"

Dani gave a *simpatica* sigh. "Mrs. Gessner,"—well, here it comes, another of her set pieces—"I'm a lawyer, not a psychologist. I don't have those answers. I wish I did. You might want to seek some counseling. . . ."

She went on to observe that, on an hourly basis, therapy was cheaper than legal advice. And for certain problems, far more effective. Briefly, she weighed the wisdom of another suggestion: that Mrs. Gessner get herself tested for AIDS. But that would have to wait for another time, when the shock had worn off.

Dani then rose and offered her hand.

"So if you would like me to act on your behalf"—Mrs. Gessner nodded numbly—"fill this form out as best you can. Also, if you can manage it, I'd like copies of your husband's income tax returns for the last five years. Okay?"

"You're asking I should spy on Ira, go through his desk? I couldn't. What would he say if he found out?"

"Mrs. Gessner," she said gently, "you've got to stop thinking of your husband as your partner and start thinking about yourself for a change. You'll need that kind of distance in the weeks to come."

But Mrs. Gessner was shaking her head. "But you don't understand," she said. "My husband left me for another man."

Twenty minutes later, Dani was wedged in crosstown traffic, pondering dinner and a nice cold drink. The thermometer atop the Equitable Building read 92°. The humidity even higher was her guess. She peeled off her jacket. Just her luck to get an un-air-conditioned cab.

At the corner of Fifth Avenue and 57th, traffic ground to a total halt.

Oh shit!

Dani scowled. As if the heat wasn't bad enough, it sounded as though every driver within a twenty-mile radius was going bananas. Smart! Like leaning on the horn was going to get traffic moving again! *Sometimes* . . . , she thought. *This city* . . . !

Now the sirens were joining in.

"What the hell . . ." She leaned out the window. "An accident? What's happening?"

Maybe she should get out and walk.

Then she saw it, a block away in front of the Plaza Hotel. One of the Central Park carriage horses had broken loose—God knew how!—and was rearing wildly between the cars.

Dani sucked in her breath, felt a surge of adrenaline. It was a nightmare, an urban horror movie. The creature had gone berserk, driven crazy by the noise and heat. Above the blare of the horns, she could hear it whinnying. See the froth on its mouth. Practically smell the creature's fear. It was panic. Pure blind panic.

Her heart skipped. Where the hell was the hansom driver responsible? How could such things happen? Someone could get killed. . . .

She rolled up the window, just in case.

A few minutes later, the situation was under control. Somehow or other, the beast had been calmed down and led away. Traffic resumed its normal snail's pace.

It was close to seven by the time she got home.

"Good evening, Dmitri." She smiled at her favorite doorman.

"Evenin', Mrs. Sloane. Hot enough for you?"

"I'll say."

She stepped inside. The lobby was cool. Ted would have checked the mail already. Anyhow, nothing but bills. She headed straight for the elevator.

Frank Wilson was standing there with his apricot poodle.

"Hi, Frank," she greeted her downstairs neighbor. "How are you holding up in this heat? Hiya, Mimsy." She patted the dog, then pushed the buttons: 14 for Frank Wilson, then 15 for herself.

She fished the key out of her bag and opened the door. The cleaning woman had come, she noted with satisfaction, sniffing the scent of lemon oil. Everything gleamed. The mahogany table in the hall reflected the silver bowl filled with marigolds. The air-conditioning was going full blast. Bliss.

Just inside the door stood two bulging suitcases and a flight bag, with a portable Olivetti atop the pile.

"Hi, Mom!"

Samantha poked her head out of the bedroom. Beneath a bushel of wild-flowing dark hair *à la* Cher, her hazel eyes were bright with anticipation. Her skin glowed with health.

"Hi, toots." Dani grinned back. "Tonight's the night."

In the kitchen, a shirtsleeved Ted had the blender out on the counter and was making margaritas. To be precise, the world's greatest margaritas. His with salt on the rim, hers without. "Be with you in a min," he sang out above the buzz of the Waring blender.

Dani stood on the threshold, freeze framed, and absorbed the scene. The familiar rooms. Familiar furniture. Familiar faces. Pruitt-Baker, Linda Gessner, runaway horses—at this moment, nothing could be further from her thoughts.

And standing there, she felt a surge of wild joy.

My home. My husband. My child.

2

DANIELLE SLOANE had every right to be pleased with herself, with her accomplishments, with what life had put on her plate.

"The sun shone on the day you were born," her father was fond of saying. Excepting the occasional transient cloud, it had really never ceased shining.

Dani was the third of four children born in quick succession to Ralph and Mary Fletcher of Hupperstown, New Jersey. Like many another ex-GI, her father was making up for lost time in the boom following World War II.

Ralph Fletcher had had a "hard war." A glider pilot with plenty of action behind him, he was forced down over Normandy shortly after D-Day and spent the final months of the conflict in a POW camp. The experience marked him for years to come.

"Don't tell me about war," he'd say, though inevitably it was he who raised the subject. "You're talking to a veteran of the Hundred and First Airborne." Then he'd fold his arms, cross his long rangy legs and add the kicker: "I was a POW in Germany."

In latter years, he cultivated an RAF mustache in deference to what had been the greatest adventure of his life.

During the months of his incarceration, Mary Kellogg waited patiently on the home front, as she had been waiting since that night in 1942 when Ralph had pinned her at a fraternity dance. (No, she was not one of *those* Kelloggs of snap-crackle-pop fame, though she never actively disclaimed the connection, preferring to let people think what they chose.) A determined young woman with a profound belief in destiny, she never doubted Ralph's safe return. He must return. Her future hinged on it. She had the china picked out, the silver pattern selected, had even put a down payment on the living room suite.

The day of his homecoming, which was an event of considerable local note, Ralph being Hupperstown's sole POW, Mary was at the head of the deputation. She looked fetching in a bouffant cotton dress and white gloves. Ralph looked haggard but interesting. "My hero!" she breathed, and the high school band struck up a Sousa march. Then she kissed him in full view of the crowd.

Before the year was out, the erstwhile warrior was married, mortgaged, and had taken over his father's insurance business (fire, life, auto, liability) on Main Street. The pattern of his life had been set. In due course, he joined the American Legion, the Kiwanis, the Cross Brook Country Club, the Chamber of Commerce, Veterans for Eisenhower (followed later by Veterans for Nixon, Goldwater, et al.) and the board of trustees at St. Matthew's Episcopal Church. He played golf with the mayor once a month and bought a new Buick every other year. In his spare time he read memoirs and history books.

Mary Fletcher's life was equally full.

Had Dani chosen the path of domesticity, she could hardly improve upon her mother's example. Mary was a wonder. Helpmeet, homemaker, cook, chauffeur, hostess, clubwoman, she was also the arbiter of what was "done" and "not done" in local society. An aggressively cheerful woman, her sole complaint being "Why don't they ever print the good news?," she drew strength from the doctrines of Norman Vincent Peale.

"You are what you think," she impressed upon her children, "so you may just as well think positive."

Whining was forbidden in the Fletcher home; optimism was the law of the land. The youngsters were expected to be chipper, study hard, and work out their differences in a reasonable fashion. Fletchers didn't make scenes. Fletchers were self-reliant. Above all, Fletchers were prudent: moderate in the consumption of alcohol,

circumspect in language, conventional in habits and keeping a good
five miles under the speed limit on all occasions.

The family attitudes had been largely shaped by the nature of
Ralph Fletcher's occupation. Like many a salesman, Ralph had
wound up his own best customer, philosophically speaking. "Life"
was a condition you insured against, he informed his children. In
a world fraught with dangers, risk must always be hedged.

"When I was a POW in Germany," he once reminisced, "we
had an 'escape artist' in our ranks. Stanley Weinstein, his name
was, one of those clever New York Jews. Every time you looked
around, there was Weinstein trying to go over the wall, under the
wall, you name it. Just reckless. Well, no one had ever escaped
from Minderhausen, but old Stan—you couldn't hold him down.
He kept trying to bust out, the Krauts kept bringing him back.
Well, one night he snuck up to the top of the water tower. Must
have been thirty feet high. I guess he figured if he jumped, he might
clear the outer wall."

"So did he jump?" Dani asked.

"Yup. Jumped. Landed in the woods and broke his back. The
irony of it was, Dani, our camp was liberated three weeks later.
So the great escape was all for zilch."

Dani found the tale disappointing. She adored her father, thought
him the most imposing of men and silently wished that he, rather
than Mr. Weinstein, had been the hero of the piece. Though without
the broken back.

"But isn't it an officer's duty to try to get away?" she asked. She
had read that in a novel.

"It's your duty to survive, honey. To know your limitations. So
Weinstein wound up paralyzed from the waist down, poor slob,
whereas yours truly came home in one piece and married your
mother."

And lived happily ever after, it went without saying.

The World According to Ralph and Mary was a simple and
orderly place. Within the family, the division of labor was complete,
the role of the sexes sharply defined. Boys were expected to grow
up and become men. Girls were expected to grow up and be—
girls.

"Imagine that," Ralph Fletcher commented upon reading a story in *Time* magazine. "This girl Muriel Siebert just bought herself a seat on the stock exchange. What next? They'll be running for president, I suppose."

Dani giggled. Not at the word *girl*, which at the time seemed a suitable appellation even for a forty-year-old banker, but at the idea of being the sole female on the stock exchange. It sounded neat.

"I want to be in Hupperstown when the world ends," Dani liked to say, "because everything happens there twenty years later."

New York City was an hour and a half away by turnpike, light years away by all other criteria. You went there once a year around Christmas to see the Radio City Music Hall show.

Her childhood was busy but uneventful, largely notable for her reaching adult height (a self-conscious 5'8") by the time she was thirteen.

A good kid, enormously bright and hardworking, a member of Future Homemakers of America, she was nonetheless given to vague amorphous daydreams, dreams in which Hupperstown played no role. Someday, she fantasized, she would be a Distinguished Personage—admired, envied, glamorous, with a page-long entry in *Who's Who*.

Precisely what the nature of her accomplishment would be that would catapult her to these heights (brain surgery? aviation? politics? theater?) had yet to be determined. Nonetheless, it was bound to be something fine and triumphant, entailing a huge corner office and marvelous clothes. After which, although pursued by many men, she would marry either Paul Newman or Steve McQueen and live forever in a state of wedded bliss.

For, as fiercely as she wanted to place first in everything, she also wanted to be loved. It never occurred to her that these might be mutually contradictory aims.

In her senior year, Dani ran for class president only to be trounced by Central High's biggest jock. "That numb-brain," she muttered, wiping her eyes in the girls' washroom. "That make-out artist." She was twice as smart as Robbie Mitchell and far more deserving. Her credentials were outstanding: Honor Roll student, active in the Drama Club, the French Club, the Chess Club, captain of the girls' softball team; whereas Robbie's greatest achievements were accomplished on Saturday nights in the backseat of his father's Chevy.

She would love to have punched him in the kisser, but protocol demanded the gracious handshake.

"The better man won," she congratulated him.

"The only man won," he grinned back. Dani grimaced.

The defeat was painful. Positive thinking hadn't helped one whit. "There's no justice," she groused.

"Now now," Mary Fletcher chirped cheerfully. "Nobody likes a sore loser. We can't all be chiefs, Dani. There have to be Indians too."

Was that supposed to make her feel better?

A few months later, however, it was her turn to chirp when the yearbook chose her as Most Likely to Succeed. And that "numb-brain" Robbie Mitchell got turned down by all the good colleges, whereas Dani had been accepted at Smith, Wellesley and Barnard.

"We can't all be Indians"—she reported to her mother with a smirk. "There have to be chiefs, as well."

Dani loved her parents, her sisters, her kid brother, Kevin. Loved the big white frame house with its Victorian trim and bar-becue pit out back. Loved the neat lawns and placid streets and dear friends of her childhood.

When she gave the valedictorian speech at Central High that June, there was a catch in her voice.

"Hupperstown will always . . . always be close to my heart."

The sentiment was sincere. And she couldn't wait to leave. To get into the great world and become a renowned something-or-other, a Distinguished Personage who went Everywhere, knew Everybody. And then to marry Paul Newman or Steve McQueen or a combination of the two. Or whatever . . .

World, she whispered. I'm on my way.

3

DANI FELL IN LOVE TWICE during her years at Barnard: once with New York, then later with Ted Sloane. In both cases, it was love at first sight—and for keeps.

"Capital of the world" she inscribed in her diary, though, in fact, Dani's New York was but a portion, a sliver of the whole. Her "capital" consisted of a rectangle bounded by the Columbia campus on the north and Greenwich Village on the south, a few square miles crammed with shops, theaters, concert halls, coffeehouses, bookstores, restaurants and jazz joints, with Central Park as its core. Within these hundred odd blocks, Dani believed, the choicest offerings, not just of America but of the globe, the best of the best, had been boiled down, distilled, condensed and were now being served for her delectation.

That there were other New Yorks—indigenous enclaves of the poor and ethnic, neighborhoods where the orderly grid of numbered streets and avenues gave way to such apposite names as Flatbush and Sheepshead Bay and Hunter's Point—scarcely entered her consciousness. Such locales were as remote as Siam or, worse, as boring as Hupperstown. Even their roaches were second-class citizens.

She glommed onto Manhattan with the fervor of the true provincial, devouring all the entertainments on offer, determined that

she would live, work, marry and thrive here within the magic
rectangle; grow savvy, sophisticated and urbane; and that when she
died people would say, "Now there was a true New Yorker."

On occasion, she would pause on the steps of Barnard, watch
the crowds, scan the skyline and suck the hot fetid breath of the
city into her lungs. It tasted of grime and sweat and auto fumes.
Of youth and hope and freedom.

Never trust anyone over thirty, the cry went up. If you could find
anyone over thirty! For the world was younger in those turbulent
closing years of the sixties than it had ever been before or since.

By decade's end, a new vocabulary had sprung up to service a
new way of life, and old words acquired different meanings. Hip-
pies, yippies, flower children and Jesus freaks took turns in hor-
rifying their elders as they engaged in love-ins, be-ins, acid trips,
happenings, getting busted and getting laid with unprecedented
frequency.

"I know," Ralph Fletcher said to his daughter on the eve of her
departure for college (Not "I hope" but "I know," such was his
confidence), "that you have better sense than to get involved with
those . . . those beardniks." The nightly newscasts had instilled
in him an aversion for all facial hair, his own RAF mustache excepted.

To which tirade Dani made the proper noises. Her father was
a darling, she felt, but a bit of a dinosaur. Mary Fletcher's advice
was more specific.

The occasion was a shopping trip to the Villager Shop in Princeton where Dani was kitted out with a full complement of "suitable
clothes": John Meyers skirts, Fair Isle sweaters, six pairs of leather
pumps and enough white cotton underwear to send the commodities
market up by two ticks. God forbid Dani should get run over by
a taxi and have some New York cop make snide remarks as to the
state of her underwear. White was safe, white was reputable. Cotton
was best. That her daughter might one day forgo the full complement of lingerie (bra, panties, stockings and slip) was too monstrous
even to be discussed. By Mrs. Fletcher's lights, any girl so depraved
as to prance about braless probably deserved to be run over by a
taxi. Virginity—and the appearance of virginity—were matters of
paramount importance.

"The world doesn't respect girls who don't respect themselves, Dani. You hear?"

Dani heard, but didn't listen.

Within weeks of her arrival at Barnard, she had swapped her sweaters and skirts for tie-dyes and blue jeans, traded her horn rims for granny glasses, and learned to iron her wayward hair until it lay perfectly flat. The following year, she divested herself of her virginity. The recipient was a violin student from Juilliard. The sex was okay. Not great, but okay, and when it was over, Dani's feeling was one of accomplishment rather than guilt.

God, she thought with a quiver of delight, *if my parents could see me now!*

By her senior year, Dani could look back upon a half-dozen such "accomplishments." Moreover, she could lay claim to having sung folk songs in Washington Square Park, wiggled her toes in the mud of Woodstock, marched against the war in Vietnam, subscribed to *Ramparts* and *Screw*. She had also learned to curse, to smoke pot, to give head.

In moderation.

For despite Ralph Fletcher's fears that his daughter was turning into a "hippie or worse," despite her perpetual cry of "God! If they could see me now!," Dani remained true to the family genes. By contemporary standards, she emerged as a sensible and ambitious young woman, absorbed in Jacobean theater and tending to see things in historical perspective. In short, a poor excuse for a radical.

"Let's discuss this reasonably," she said at an SDS meeting on the eve of the march on Columbia's Hamilton Hall, only to be hooted down and booted out. She never went back. Carrying an antiwar placard was one thing. Getting your head smashed in, quite another. Thus, she burnt no bras, built no bombs and always turned in her assignments on time.

Which was more than could be said for Kaycee Carlson.

"Before you utter another word"—Dani would fly to her roommate's defense—"I'll remind you, not only do Kaycee and I bunk together, but we're best friends. So watch it."

This public show of loyalty masked a deep-seated ambivalence. Dani adored Katherine Courtney Carlson (who styled herself Kaycee), envied her, pitied her, resented her, usually all at once.

Sharing quarters with quite the loveliest creature in Barnard was tough on the ego. How could you not deem yourself a lesser being, a kind of human satellite alongside the girl who had everything?

When it came to feminine assets, Kaycee had cornered the market: tawny blond hair, classic features, a lean sexy body capable of accommodating oceans of beer and mountains of junk food without paying the price in zits or flab. It was too much. That she should also be possessed of money and chic (Kaycee's mother had been a fashion model who married often and well) only added to the sense of injustice.

Kaycee was spoiled but generous. She had a car, a sporty red Morgan convertible, which was available on demand, like everything else she owned. "Borrow my earrings," she'd insist when Dani was dressing for a date. Or "This Spagnoli sweater looks better on you than on me"—a blatant lie—"so do me a favor and take it."

Though her clothes were fabulous, the pick of Bendel's and Bonwit's, she treated them with throwaway chic. Her trademark was scrunching up a Hermès scarf to wear as a jeans belt. She was also quite bright.

"Bucks, beauty and brains," as one classmate put it. "How's not to hate?"

And Dani couldn't help wondering in such a friendship, where was the equity? What could a mere mortal such as Dani offer by way of exchange?

Yet like the princess in the fairy tale whose birth was blessed by all the fairies but one, Kaycee labored under a curse, haunted by a sense of worthlessness. In her own eyes, she was neither as beautiful as her mother, nor as brilliant as her father nor as talented as her art teachers, as clever as Dani: the list went on forever.

Only with men did she feel complete. She lived for their admiration. "Boy crazy," as Mary Fletcher might say.

Given Kaycee's looks, her charm, her way of peering into a man's eyes that said "You are wonderful beyond all others," the attraction was mutual. Kaycee could pick and choose, and did so with great frequency. Columbia University was right next door, aswarm with men men men, all of whom seemed to have her number.

The phone in their room never stopped ringing. "It's for you," Dani would say, routinely handing over the receiver with a shrug. And when Kaycee wasn't there to take calls, Dani felt herself besieged.

"Do you know where she is?" "What time'll she be back?"

"Well, tell her Hank from Med School phoned," one exasperated fellow said, "for the fifteenth fucking time this week."

"The sixteenth fucking time," Dani said.

"Who is this anyhow?" he asked.

"Just the message center."

Most of the callers sounded attractive: budding writers, lawyers, doctors, MBAs. The list was daunting and Dani, who had been reasonably popular in high school, felt like Typhoid Mary alongside Kaycee's Belle of the Ball. Envious didn't begin to describe.

Yet smart as Kaycee was, Dani observed, that's how dumb she could be when judging men.

If she liked a man, she went to bed with him right off, bed being the place where like turned to love, or so she hoped, for her life was a quest for grand passion, high romance. She yearned to be "swept away," rendered senseless by love, believing in the image so totally that she was swept away every few weeks by a new Mr. Wrong. In this regard, she had a knack amounting to genius.

Kaycee could walk into a room packed with available men and, purely on instinct, batten on to the one born loser. Give her a blowhard, a Don Juan, a latent homosexual, a married man with kids or, best of all, one of those macho student radicals who believed with Stokely Carmichael that the place for women in the movement was on their backs—and Kaycee was enthralled. She claimed to see properties in them that others did not.

"I'm in love," she would announce with manic exuberance, the morning after a night with some new Galahad. "I'm so happy I could die."

A short time later, the bottom of the world had dropped out, and Galahad would be rechristened Louse of the Month.

In the years they roomed together, Dani saw Kaycee through three abortions, one D and C, and half a dozen false alarms.

"I swear to God," Kaycee told Dani, "I can get pregnant just by looking at a guy. It's a scientific phenomenon. When I die, I'll will my body to Harvard Medical School."

Why not? Dani was tempted to crack. *Everyone else has had a whack at it.* Instead, however, she launched into her big-sister diatribe. "Why don't you take precautions, like any normal person? Remember the old Girl Scout motto and Be Prepared."

"I never joined the Girl Scouts," Kaycee replied, "not being big on single-sex activities. Besides which, I was in love."

"You can be in love and still exercise normal prudence."

But Kaycee argued that normal prudence would rob the affair of spontaneity. "One of these days, Dani, you'll meet some guy and know what it is to be swept away, to throw caution to the winds. And when you do, I'll be there for you, I promise. So just stand by me this once. You know," she added, "you're the only friend I have in this joint. I'd be lost without you. I trust you, Dani. I need you. Forgive?"

Dani forgave.

And therein lay the equity between Kaycee and Dani, the quid pro quo that made friendship possible. To be needed, to be looked up to and leaned upon, to know you were essential to someone else's well-being and capable of solving all problems—to Dani, that proved an irresistible appeal.

Yes, Kaycee might be prettier, richer, more popular and all that jazz. But Dani was the stronger of the two.

On a February afternoon of their senior year, Kaycee phoned to ask a favor. From the breathy voice, interspersed with giggles and whispers, the circumstances were easily deduced.

"Be a lamb, Dani, and save my life. I'm supposed to be meeting a guy named Ted Sloane in twenty minutes at a restaurant in Harlem. We were going to the Skinks concert. Well, something's come up . . ."—more giggles, a masculine snort in the background—". . . and I can't make it. I'm, like, otherwise engaged. I'd call and cancel, but the thing is, I forget the name of the restaurant. Though how many Chinese restaurants can there be on 125th and Broadway?"

Would Dani go there, meet Ted and explain—no, not that Kaycee was in bed with another guy, but some kind of reasonable story. Then the two of them could catch the concert. The tickets were on her dresser . . . cost a bundle . . . shame to let them go to waste.

"You'll like the Skinks," Kaycee promised. "That British group. They used to be the Dead Letter Office." Then she added as an afterthought, "You'll probably like Ted, too."

Dani had no trouble spotting Ted Sloane, even in the mole-hole interior of the Szechuan Palace. He was in a back booth drinking Chinese beer and nibbling on noodles with half an eye on the door. Kaycee's description was accurate: sandy hair, short beard, horn-rimmed glasses, mid-twenties . . . "a big guy, six-two, six-three, built like a football player." He was wearing a floppy Irish sweater over the regulation blue jeans. He was also the only Caucasian in the place.

Dani's first reaction was: Kaycee must be out of her skull to let this one get away. Her second reaction, unalloyed pleasure. She smothered a triumphant smile.

"Hi!" Dani hovered over him, uncertain of how to begin. He looked up, his face bright with expectation. "I'm Kaycee's room-mate, Dani. Unfortunately, Kaycee couldn't make it tonight, so . . . ummmm . . . ummmm . . . she sent me instead."

"Oh?" The face collapsed. The man had been expecting a hot fudge sundae and was being served plain vanilla instead. Then he crossed his arms in a show-me gesture. "I see . . . she just couldn't come. May I know why?"

Dani reddened, embarrassed on Kaycee's behalf as well as her own.

"Exams." She said the first thing that came to mind.

"In February?"

"Well actually . . ." Dani hadn't expected to be cross-examined. She switched alibis, offering excuses on a rising scale of improb-ability—dental appointments, flu symptoms, out-of-town visitors, the total collapse of the New York subway system—while Ted Sloane's face registered an equally rising tide of disbelief.

"Plus," she concluded limply, "she's got an absolutely splitting headache. Anyhow, I have the tickets and if it's okay with you, we could catch the concert together."

Dear God, she prayed. *Get me off the hook*. She could like this man, wanted him to like her. Damn Kaycee Carlson anyhow!

He looked dubious, apparently trying to decide whether good manners required that he accept this massive fiction or whether he should tell Dani to piss off. Then he stood up and motioned her into the booth.

Stood up, mind you! Dani's heart swelled with relief. Stood up like a proper gentleman and pretended he was "pleased to meet you," though he himself had been "stood up" in the more disagreeable sense of the term. Who said chivalry was dead?

"You left out beriberi," he said when they were both seated.

"I beg your pardon?"

"And tidal waves and plagues of locusts." Then he laughed, a what-the-hell laugh from the depths of that barrel chest. "You're a lousy liar, Dani what's-your-name. Don't ever try to make it as a lawyer."

"I'm sorry."

"About Kaycee not coming or about being a lousy liar?"

"Both."

"Yeah . . . well."

The waiter brought them grease-stained menus the size of a small-town phone directory. Nothing looked familiar, no spareribs or shrimp with lobster sauce.

"You like Szechuan cooking?" he asked.

"Don't think I've ever had it."

"Then you're in for a treat. It's the greatest . . . wave of the future. Cantonese is dead, Shanghai is on the way out. Take my word for it. What say we start with some sesame noodles? If you like, I'll do the ordering."

She liked. She liked everything about him: his looks, his confidence, his air of sophistication, the aplomb with which he threaded his way through the menu. What he didn't know, he asked. When the waiter answered, he listened, ear cocked, filing away data for future reference. Yes, he knew how to listen. She liked that too.

"And two more of these babies!" He tapped his beer bottle with a plastic chopstick. Then he leaned back and studied her with a good-natured air.

"So, Dani Fletcher, other than the fact that you are a Barnard senior, a loyal friend, an easy blusher and weigh in at about a hundred and twenty pounds, I know nothing at all about you."

Dani giggled. "You're a veritable Sherlock Holmes."

"Nope. Just a journalism student with a lively curiosity. Tell me something about yourself. Where are you from? What do you want to do when you graduate? Do you prefer the Mets or the Yankees? And why?"

Dani took a deep breath. "I'm from a place called Hupperstown," she began, and by the time the noodles arrived, she had handed up a near complete life sketch, though even to her own ears it sounded uneventful.

Yet he listened with interest and smiled, not too often, but in all the right places. By her second beer, Dani was in full flow.

"So I'm hoping for a career in theater, maybe working behind the scenes—production or artist management. My mom says maybe I should go to Katie Gibbs and learn shorthand."

She stopped short. Her mom had also said, "When you're interested in a boy, get him to talk about himself. It's what they like best."

"Well, that's enough about me." She turned to Ted with a smile. "Now it's my turn to play Sherlock. Because other than the fact that you're a terrific listener, I know absolutely zilch about you."

Ted came from Cincinnati, she learned, where his father was a marketing executive at Procter and Gamble. He had gone to Dartmouth, majoring in language ("French, Russian, the whole catastrophe"), and was currently doing graduate work at the Columbia School of Journalism. This information was conveyed in a modulated baritone. A wonderful voice, Dani thought. Like a news announcer's. A voice of authority.

Yes, he liked New York with reservations. It compared favorably to Cincinnati, which was, he declared, "the most boring town in the USA."

"I'll challenge you on that," Dani said. "The loser gets to spend two weeks in Hupperstown."

Ted, however, had broad grounds for evaluation, having already sampled a good chunk of the world. He had backpacked across Europe, worked one summer in a kibbutz, done a junior year abroad, had actually been in Paris when another Dani—Dani Cohn-Bendit—had captained a student revolution.

"That was some zoo, let me tell you. Cobblestones flying, riot cops swinging. They put lead in the lining of their capes, you know. From there I went to Rotenberg, which was a whole 'nother ball game."

Dani was spellbound. "God! You've been everywhere."

"I like to travel. Itchy feet."

By the time the hacked chicken arrived, she believed him to be as knowledgeable in every area of life as he was about Chinese cookery.

She asked the obvious question: "What about Vietnam?", men his age having either served or sought student deferments or fled the country. Where did he stand?

"I'm Four-F, thank God," he said with a grimace. "Saved by a perforated eardrum. Though if I'd been called up, I don't know what I'd have done. One half of me says, burn my draft card. The second half says, head for Sweden. And the third half . . ." He furrowed his brow. "It's that third half that's the bitch. I like to picture myself behaving in some heroic capacity. Theodore Jay Sloane, Scourge of the Establishment, idol of *Ramparts* magazine, beloved of Jane Fonda, you know the routine. But that third half of me would probably knuckle under and do my duty. The curse of a bourgeois upbringing."

Of course he was opposed to the war. What caring, thinking person was not? "But because I could cop out, someone else had to serve in my place. Some ghetto kid is my bet, without half my privileges, and getting his ass burned in the bargain. That really sucks."

The inequity troubled him. He felt morally obliged to do something of value, an act of restitution if you will. He owed as much if not to the U.S. of A., then at least to himself and to the poor bastard getting shot up on his behalf in some rice paddy.

"So I signed up for a two-year hitch with the Peace Corps after graduation. Ecuador most likely, my Spanish is pretty good." First, he'd spend four weeks in training in St. Croix. "Digging latrines, learning double-entry bookkeeping, how to raise chickens . . . whatever's useful." After which he'd ship out. The prospect was exciting. He'd never been to South America before.

"The plan is, I'm to set up schools, organize literacy programs, plus anything else that comes to mind. Kind of pay my dues as a human being."

He leaned forward by way of emphasis. The glasses slid down his nose to be pushed back by an extended index finger. He had broad, powerful hands, like Michelangelo's David.

Dani studied the planes in his face and thought. "Theodore J. Serious." His attitudes surprised her. This was 1970, fella! No one joined the Peace Corps anymore. Certainly not grad students at Ivy League colleges. That kind of activism had suffered a mortal blow one November day in Dallas and been interred soon after in Southeast Asia.

Ted must have divined her skepticism, for he gave a self-conscious shrug.

"Yeah . . . I know. The Peace Corps went out with Jackie Kennedy's pillbox hat. It's passé. Even worse, it might be—God forbid!—truly productive. The hip thing to do is storm the steps of Columbia, right? and bury automobiles in Pismo Beach and throw bladdersful of pig's blood at the fuzz. Well, as far as I'm concerned, that's theater, not action. Who does it benefit? Anyhow, I saw enough bloodshed in Paris. I don't like watching things go BOOM!"

"I'm with you there," Dani said, "But after the Peace Corps, then what?"

"Then I become rich, famous, and all that jazz. My dream is to write a book about the political impact of the Peace Corps, or at least some major articles. Foreign affairs, the effects of U.S. policy—fascinating! And the experience itself should be priceless. With luck, I'll come back and land a job with a good paper. Maybe get a column eventually."

His ultimate goal was to become another Walter Lippmann or James Reston, a guiding force in American journalism. As he spoke, parlaying dreams and hopes and fantasies, Dani listened entranced.

The waiter brought the beef with orange sauce and another round of beer. They were both a little drunk. The conversation turned general: movies, books, theater. Dani was astonished at how often their tastes jibed.

Yeah, Ted too preferred Joseph Heller to John Updike, favored Garbo over Monroe, baseball over football. Agreed emphatically that most creative writing courses were a waste of time. Psych courses, too, for that matter. Oriental mysticism, the wisdom of the East? Terrific, if you happened to be oriental. He himself loathed the Moonies et al. just a tad less than he despised Richard Nixon. Dani nodded, chatted and thought, *What a find!*

The talk turned to music.

"Speaking of which . . ." She glanced at her watch. The concert began in twenty minutes.

Ted Sloane leaned across the wasteland of dirty dishes, brace-leting her wrist with his thumb and forefinger. His touch was electric. Dani pictured his hands around her waist.

A spate of words sprang to mind: Ted Sloane was so mature . . . sensitive . . . virile . . . urbane. By this time, she had en-dowed him with a dozen attributes to account for a violent surge of physical attraction. He looked so see-ree-ous!

"Look, Dani. Do you really want to hear . . . what's the name of this group, anyway?"

Her heart thumped up against her rib cage. Was he coming on to her so soon? You bet! Why else forfeit tickets to the hottest concert in town? Dani was flattered. Flustered. They'd only known each other a couple of hours; she couldn't possibly hop into bed with him at this stage of the game. Maybe later, after the concert, when they were juiced up by the music, the crowds. Probably later. Almost definitely.

She uptilted her head, like a flower toward the sun, then gave her warmest smile.

"The Skinks. They used to be the Dead Letter Office, which is probably what you know them as," she said. "Only now that Derek Sly's joined them, they changed their name."

"Ah. . . . The Skinks." Ted released her hand and made a face. "Listen, there's something you ought to know about me. I'm not a rock fan. Fact is, loud noise drives me bananas. Maybe it's the perforated eardrum. Anyhow, it's an ordeal. Dylan, Baez . . . yeah, okay, I can handle it, though personally my taste runs to classics and jazz. But Dead Skinks or whatever? Would you mind passing it up, Dani? We could catch a movie instead. To tell you the truth, I was only going to the concert because . . ."

He stopped, at a sudden loss for words.

"Because . . ." Dani stiffened. One needn't be a mind reader to complete that sentence. "Because you thought you'd be going with Kaycee Carlson, right?"

He had the decency to look mortified, but Dani couldn't let it rest. Four years of being runner-up, of playing second fiddle, goaded her on. She felt shattered to the core. "And instead of the . . . the prom queen, you got stuck with the consolation prize. Tough!"

"You misunderstand," he blurted.

"I understand perfectly." Oh yes, she understood that, eardrum and all, Ted Sloane had been willing to endure this "ordeal" for Kaycee's sake, but not for hers. She felt demeaned, humiliated. The first so-called mature man she'd met in months, and here he was slavering over Kaycee just like the rest of those sophomoric morons.

She didn't know where to direct her anger: whether at Kaycee for being callous and beautiful, or at Ted for rubbing it in. Ted was easier, and he was right at hand. Besides, she had to live with Kaycee.

"Look, Sloane." She fought down the impulse to say, *Fuck you*. "Let's call it a night. You're not obliged to me in any way." She opened her bag, fished out a ten and a five. "This should more than cover my share. Good-bye. It's been real."

She flounced out, without looking back, and headed down Broadway choking with rage. Damn damn damn damn . . . !

She was fuming still when, minutes later, Ted materialized on the pavement before her.

"Hi, Dani," he panted.

She could hardly believe her eyes. He was walking backward, like a character in a slapstick movie. His arms were raised for balance, his face mere inches from her own.

"We have to talk." He backpedaled, as she tried to step around him. "There's been a terrible misunderstanding. I hardly know you, Miss Dani Fletcher of Hupperstown, but I sure as hell want to if you'll give me a chance. It's not every day I meet a Mets fan who reads Heller and has fabulous legs. But seriously, how can you and I have any kind of meaningful relationship if you insist on disappearing before the fortune cookies? Yours was terrific, by the way. It said you're about to fall in love. Plus which, you have change coming. Two dollars and ninety cents."

She couldn't shake him. He wouldn't shut up. Just kept on jabbering all kinds of nonsense, from Edward Lear limericks to Abbott and Costello routines—determined to make her laugh or at least crack a smile. And all the time walking backward, breaking into a jog trot when they came to a curb. And making, Dani thought, a thorough spectacle of himself.

Dani was mortified. "Leave me alone," she wanted to cry, but refused to give him the satisfaction of a reply. Let him trip. Let him fall into a manhole. Let him send a Valentine to Kaycee Carlson. Dani Fletcher had a concert to catch.

By now, passersby were noticing. Some giggled. A cabby honked his horn and hollered encouragement.

"You want to hear the Skunks?" he persisted. "Okay, we'll go hear the Skunks. Go anywhere you like. Name your poison. All I ask is you talk to me. One little word, but more is better. Lady won't talk to me," he confided to the chili-dog vendor on the corner.

"Talk to him, honey," the vendor said. A woman pushing a baby carriage amened: "Yeah . . . give the guy a break."

Ted did a knee-bend and tipped an imaginary hat.

By now Dani was buffaloed. This was Mr. Theodore J. Serious of a half hour earlier? The Peace Corps Straight Arrow? The future Lippmann—soft-shoeing down Broadway with a fan club of kibitzers in his wake?

At the corner of 118th, Dani made a sharp turn and started across Broadway against the light, heading for the subway. It had begun to snow.

Without looking, Ted stepped off the curb and plunged into traffic. "We can't go on meeting like this," he sang out while angry motorists divided around them. Suddenly, there was a screech of brakes. A pickup truck shrieked to a halt, missing him by inches.

"For Christ's sake!" she yelled. "Watch where you're going!"

"You can talk!"

"You lunatic!" Her heart stopped, started again, as she realized what was happening. He was doing it—crossing Broadway blind— for her.

It was idiotic, but thrilling too. Never before had any man risked life and limb in pursuit of Dani Fletcher. Shown such perseverance on her behalf. For her sake, he was undergoing a true ordeal, far more dramatic than merely sitting through a rock concert.

"Asshole," she said, then grabbed his arm and tucked it into her own. "Now behave! I don't want to be responsible for your early death."

They crossed the street in the conventional fashion of young lovers, arm in arm. A handful of onlookers cheered.

"Where'd you learn that stunt, anyhow?" she asked when they'd achieved the safety of the pavement.

"Old Ritz Brothers shorts. I used to run 'em backwards on my dad's Moviola."

"Well, you sure scared the bejeezus out of me. What got into you, Ted Sloane?"

"Impulse," he said. "Comes over me every now and again."

Then Theodore J. Serious resurfaced briefly. "I know it was dumb, but I didn't want to lose you. So accept my apologies and if you want to hear the Skunks . . ."

"The Skinks," she said. "And actually I'm not crazy about mob scenes either."

"In which case, I know a nice quiet piano bar down the street."

It was impulse that brought Dani to his room a couple of hours later, impulse and three tots of Hennessy. They either made love or had sex, she wasn't sure which.

She awoke in the small hours with a raging thirst, a pounding headache and a stab of anxiety. Ted was asleep, his arm across her belly. It weighed a ton.

"Hey, Ted." She struggled free, then switched on the bedside lamp. "Wake up."

"Yeah . . . what . . ." He sat up and rubbed his eyes.

"I've got to know. I won't hold it against you, but it's crucial to me. Tell me, did you ever go to bed with Kaycee?"

Ted propped himself up on one elbow, leaned forward and devoured her face with hungry eyes. "Kaycee who?" he said. "I don't think I know any Kaycee. Now let's make love."

4

SWEPT AWAY.

Had not Kaycee Carlson so thoroughly preempted the term, Dani would have confessed to being swept away. Instead of which she admitted merely to be "madly crazy head-over-heels in love."

From that first night on, the new lovers couldn't get enough of each other. The days weren't long enough. Neither were the nights spent in Ted's grubby furnished room.

Most mornings, Dani would stumble back to the dorm in a semi-stupor: bleary-eyed, lips swollen, neck covered with hickeys, happier than she'd ever been. She would change clothes, collect her books and check if her parents had phoned. Her alibis were getting better all the time.

"It isn't just sex," she was swift to assure Kaycee. Ted was—she sang his praises—warm, intelligent, decent, funny, thoughtful, generous, delightfully free of cant. In short, everything she wanted in a man, in a husband. Paul Newman and Steve McQueen rolled into one. And, considering that whimsical streak that she had first glimpsed in his death-defying waltz across Broadway, a touch of Mel Brooks for good measure.

Best of all, he was crazy about her.

"No one will ever love you as much as I do," he once whispered in her ear, a declaration all the more moving for having been issued not in bed, but while they were combing the secondhand-book

stacks at the Strand. She had to kiss him then and there. Dani too
was convinced she would never, could never love anyone as much;
that every place they went together was sacrosanct. She kept a pair
of chopsticks from the Szechuan Palace hidden in her dresser drawer.

"Look who turned out to be the hopeless romantic!" Kaycee
would tease. "Remember, I saw him first."

The only cloud on the horizon lay in the direction of Hupperstown. Dani's parents would be outraged had they known she was
living with a man. That she was twenty-one years old and entitled
to a life of her own—such reasoning would cut no ice with the
Fletchers. Yet despite Dani's prevarications, they sensed that some
sort of hanky-panky was going on.

"You never come home weekends," her mother complained.

"Just busy, I guess."

But Mary, too, had once been young and ardent. "It's a fella,
isn't it?"

Something to that effect, Dani mumbled.

"Well, bring your young man down here, so Dad and I can look
him over. We won't eat him, I promise."

Dani dodged the issue. It was a ticklish proposition.

First, there was the question of Ted's appearance. Given Ralph
Fletcher's knee-jerk view of "beardniks" and grown men in blue
jeans, of anything that bore a counterculture air, her father was
bound to disapprove. But beyond that lay the larger question. For
even if she could induce Ted to shave his beard for the occasion,
wear a suit and tie, and refrain from all discussion of politics, even
so, what was the point of subjecting him to family scrutiny? She
and Ted had no proper future. That was the reality. He would
soon be off to Ecuador for a two-year stretch. As far as Dani was
concerned, it might as well have been Vietnam.

"What's going to become of us?" she would ask, heart on hold,
waiting for him to utter that word of all words: *marriage*. She wanted
to be married, desperately. To become Mrs. Ted Sloane. It was a
goal alongside which all her juvenile dreams of worldly triumphs
now paled. Later was soon enough for a career. In a first-things-
first agenda, what could take priority over immediate personal
happiness?

Yes, she considered herself a feminist, a thoroughly contemporary young woman who had passed many a late night with her classmates in the dorm, decrying the traditional role of the female in society. But that was before Ted Sloane entered the picture and turned her life upside down.

However, marriage required two willing parties, and Ted never brought the matter up except in a roundabout fashion.

"How could I possibly ask you," he said, "to scrap your plans, let alone forfeit all the things you love here—theater, movies, concerts, friends? For what? To rough it with me in Ecuador? You're a city person, Dani. Anyhow, what would you do there—work in the fields? No no, it's too much of a sacrifice. Maybe when I get back . . ."

"Yes?"

"Well, maybe then we'll work something out."

Dani tried to figure out if Ted's circumlocutions added up to a proposal of sorts, though the word *marriage* had yet to be mentioned. And even if he asked, the idea of a long engagement was laughable. Ted himself always poked fun at rituals and formalities, saying they were against his irreligion. Besides, a ring and a promise wouldn't make the separation less real. Two years was an eternity. They couldn't keep their hands off each other for two days.

"You could change your plans," she suggested.

"And not go?" His incredulity was patent. "Oh, honey, I couldn't back off at this late date."

What was more, he didn't want to. For all his sweetness and good nature, Ted could not be budged on this score. Dani alternately sulked and simmered.

If only he would grow up, settle down! If only he could be more like her father—a comfortable family man with a doting wife. Was that so awful a fate?

"Typical male," Kaycee Carlson analyzed the situation. "No matter how much they care about you, their careers always come first."

Dani was prone to agree. And even if they got engaged, what would she do while Ted was gone? Four years of college, while pleasant, had done nothing to define the thrust of her life. Maybe she had a future in theater, maybe not. She was certain she had a future with Ted. Provided, of course, that he proposed. And even if so, then what?

Although in theory she would follow the man she loved to the ends of the earth, in reality she loathed the prospect of leaving Manhattan.

Conceivably, she might exert emotional blackmail and force him to shelve his ideals, but what basis was that for a marriage? He'd wind up hating her. She'd wind up hating herself. Besides, he was entitled to his dream. Yet she was wretchedly unhappy, and as summer neared, panic set in.

"Please stay," she pleaded, snuggling up against him in bed. They had just made love for what seemed perilously close to the last time. "I'll go nuts if you leave."

"But I can't shift gears at this point," he replied. "I'm committed."

"More committed to the Peace Corps than to me, that's for sure!"

"Look," he said reasonably. "If I were the kind of guy who welshed on promises, you'd probably want no part of me. Well, I've made a promise—to the Peace Corps, to myself. You knew that when we met. I want to go to Ecuador, I want to write this book, and by God, Dani, I intend to do both."

"And what you don't intend to do is"—she drew a breath—"is to marry me."

The word stopped him short.

"Wow!" He jerked to attention. "You never said you wanted to get married. You never once mentioned it."

"Well, of course I do!" She burst into tears. "What sentient decent human being who is wildly in love doesn't want to get married? Except maybe you," she sniffled.

For once in his life, Ted was totally flustered.

"Is this a proposal?" he asked.

She nodded, eyes streaming.

"That's not right," he mumbled. "The man's supposed to do that." Then, stark naked, he climbed out of bed and knelt on the floor amidst a welter of dirty coffee cups and pizza wrappings. "Okay, here goes. I love you, Dani. I want to be with you always. And so I'm asking you—on bended knee, I'll have you observe— to be my wife. Does that do it?"

Dani wiped her eyes on the corner of the sheet. "I accept. And you come back to bed now."

Ted clambered in with a bound. Then he hugged her.

"Good! That's settled. We'll get married. Yeah . . . why not? Next week, if you like. All it takes is two bucks and ten minutes at City Hall. No fuss, no muss. People do it all the time, I suppose."

"I only intend to do it once," Dani said. Yet the offer was in hand, hard and concrete. Ted had scarcely sweated.

"Now that you've gone so far, Ted, maybe you'd consider some kind of compromise."

"Like what? And don't say giving up the Peace Corps. Jesus, Dani. I'm giving up my bachelorhood. Isn't that enough of a compromise? Okay, let's take it that my going to South America is the given. But maybe there's some kind of quid pro quo I can give you. Ask me something that's within my power."

She promised to think about it. The next day she came up with the answer.

"Okay, love, I'll go wherever you want. Ecuador, ends of the earth, same difference! But now I demand my pound of flesh. No City Hall. No two-buck special. I want a proper wedding, not just for myself but for my family. I know how you feel about ritual, I know you're going to say it's an obscene waste of money, but this is important to me. My folks are not going to be delirious about my marrying some guy in the Peace Corps and going off into the bush. After all, they've had me for twenty-one years, they've got some expectations, too. So let's do it right, a proper send-off. I want the ceremony to take place at Saint Matthew's in Huppers-town. That's where my parents got married, both my sisters. I want to have an engagement ring, bridesmaids, an ice sculpture in the shape of a swan or whatever. I want my father to give me away. I'll wear white and carry orange blossoms, you'll wear a morning coat and striped trousers."

"And the beard?" Ted felt he had to draw the line somewhere. His integrity was at stake. "Will your father give you away to a man with a beard?"

She paused for a moment, then grinned. "The beard can stay. That's you, Ted, and I'm not about to change you. Only marry you. So what do you say? Is it a deal?"

"That's all?" Ted seemed relieved, as if he'd been expecting stiffer demands. Then he confessed that his own parents were sure to be pleased at the prospect of a proper wedding. He suspected the Sloanes and the Fletchers had much in common. "That's all," she said. "Except for one small request. I want us to be supremely happy, love each other forever and stay married for about one zillion years."

5

SAMANTHA SLOANE had selected Chez Jacques for the *grande bouffe* (her locution for pig-out) that was to mark her final evening in New York. Samantha loved everything French: French lit, French history, French movies and, to her mother's dismay, French food.

Samantha also liked Italian food and Chinese food and Mexican food and double cheeseburgers washed down with a chocolate malted. But French food was her absolute fave.

Granted, which both parents did, that Sam was a good kid, a terrific kid, all you could ask for in a daughter. Granted that she was smart, observant, articulate, blessedly unrebellious (though what she had to be rebellious about, Dani couldn't imagine. The girl had been cuddled and coddled from birth). Granted that she was a wonderful student who had shone at Dalton and been accepted by all her first-choice colleges. Granted that her parents looked into those alert hazel eyes and envisioned the future doctor or lawyer or diplomat. That Samantha should also be endowed with a tart, if self-deprecating, sense of humor was but frosting on the cake. ("My daughter could make it as a stand-up comic," Ted boasted to his colleagues, though naturally both parents predicted a loftier future.)

Granted all those merits, Samantha gave Dani a hard time. Mother and daughter were at constant loggerheads.

For Sam's sense of humor did not extend to even the faintest comment touching upon personal appearance. On that score she was painfully sensitive. At the merest whiff of criticism concerning clothes or hair or posture, she would recoil like a clam in a vinegar bath. As for any discussion of weight, she'd cut your head off.

Sam was on the chunky side. Not exactly fat, but getting there meal by meal. It was the prevailing factor of her social life. Other girls—plainer, duller, slimmer girls—had more fun on Saturday nights.

Ted made light of the problem. There would be scads of nice guys in his daughter's future, once she went off to college. Anyhow, why the great rush to maturity? He dismissed the surplus pounds as "mere baby fat. She'll grow out of it, Dani. She's only seventeen."

"Nearly eighteen," Dani replied. "Not Daddy's little girl anymore. Sam's overweight, Ted, pure and simple. I'd say by twenty pounds. And what's going to happen when she gets to Oberlin and gains the proverbial Freshman Fifteen? Christ, she'll be devastated. The poor thing's self-conscious enough as it is."

"All teenagers are self-conscious about everything," Ted remarked equably. "It goes with the territory. It'll pass. Just sit back and let nature take its course. After all, she's only a kid."

But if nature took its course, Dani feared, Sam could wind up weighing two hundred pounds.

In a sense, Ted was right. Samantha was only a kid. Seventeen, but a very young seventeen, insecure and easily hurt. For months Dani had lain awake nights worrying about her daughter's ability to cope with campus life. Drugs, booze, promiscuity, cults, date rape, drunk drivers—the causes for alarm were infinite. The only hazard Dani didn't lose sleep about was anorexia. Sam Sloane was not one ever to pass up a square meal, let alone a hot fudge sundae.

Food food food. The topic wouldn't go away. For who would put a lock on Samantha's appetite, once her mother wasn't around to play "enforcer"?

Routinely, Dani took defensive measures. At home, the kitchen cupboard had long since been stripped of cookies, crackers, ice cream and the like. The upshot of this stringent regime was that Samantha would stuff herself at the local Häagen-Dasz while her parents dutifully starved. In addition, Dani tackled the problem with tactics ranging from the subtle to the suasive to the strict.

First came flattery. ("You've such a lovely face, Sam, such wonderful bone structure. And you'd be absolutely stunning if you lost a few pounds." Which elicited the wounded response "You think I'm gross, fat, obese, humongous, a mountain of blubber . . ." and so on until Samantha ran out of synonyms.)

Next, Dani switched to a sisterly approach. ("I'm thinking of joining a gym and working out for an hour every morning. How about keeping me company? What do you say, Sam?" "Nope!")

The gentlest hint that Sam might discuss her weight with a therapist was enough to send the girl into near hysterics. "What am I, some kind of nut? Thanks a lot!"

In despair, Dani sought out the school psychologist for a confidential chat.

"Girls that age are highly sensitive," he said. "Particularly the daughters of successful women. Most likely Sam feels she's in a losing competition."

"Oh please!" Dani protested. "I'm not one of those powerhouse females who get written up in *Fortune*, just a run-of-the-mill nine-to-five lawyer."

"Who happens to be clever, capable, self-assured"—Dr. Krantz smiled—"and slim, which is doubtless the unforgivable attribute. However, I'd be happy to have a chat with Sam and sound her out."

"But make it casual," Dani cautioned. "God forbid she thinks we're conspiring behind her back."

"I'll be discreet," he promised. But clearly, not discreet enough, for a few days later Sam came home from school in a white rage.

"I feel humiliated!" she seethed. "Half the kids in my class saw me coming out of his office. You set me up!" Then she stomped off to her bedroom and turned the stereo up to the max. End of discussion.

Yet Dani never threw in the sponge. Instead, her tactics grew more arcane. Last night, for instance, when the subject of dinner reservations arose and Samantha placed her bid for Chez Jacques, Dani tried a strategic counterploy.

"French is boring," she said. "How about Japanese for a change?" Then, gauging the lack of reaction, shifted gears rapidly. "Even better, how about us going up to Thwaites for fresh boiled lobsters? Now there's something I bet you won't find in Oberlin."

Samantha saw right through her. "They don't have decent French there either. We looked, remember? You said all they seemed to have was health-food restaurants. That plus McDonald's. Besides, I love Chez Jacques. It's so romantic."

So it was, by a teenager's definition. Dani made the reservations.

Chez Jacques was a landmark, like Lindy's or Mama Leone's. One of those old-fashioned French restaurants that believed in huge portions and the divinity of sauce. Dani's parents had discovered it on a visit to New York and taken Samantha there for her fifteenth birthday. It was that sort of place: overheated, overpriced, beloved by out-of-towners, reeking with manufactured "ambience" from the red plush banquettes to the pictures of Montmartre to the team of strolling violinists playing "C'est si bon."

The moment Dani picked up the menu, her spirits sank. It was pure time warp, like that forty-year-old tune!

Every dish was *à la crème* this and *au beurre blanc* that. No one dined like that anymore. Certainly, not health-conscious New Yorkers. In vain, she searched for a piece of broiled fish.

Samantha, too, was rapt in contemplation of the menu, brow furrowed in a chevron of doubt.

"I'm torn between the *pâté de campagne* and the *escargots bourguignon* for openers." Her voice was questing, anxious. "Or maybe the *saucisse toulousaine*. What are you guys going to have? Mom? Dad? Help me out."

Dani felt a lump in her throat. Their big girl, this "young woman," still required confirmation for the simplest decisions: snails or pâté? Out of reflex, Dani took charge.

"Well, let me see," she said, mentally calculating as to which had fewer calories. Maybe she should push the smoked trout instead. How wrong could you go with smoked trout? Across the table, Ted shot her a five-alarm glare.

Don't nag, his look said. *This is Sam's last night*. Dani clammed up. Ted took over.

"Tell you what, honeybunch," he said. "You order the pâté, I'll get a dozen snails—that way, you can have your pick of both. In fact, Sam, why don't you do the ordering? Your French is way better than mine. Well, Dani, what are you having for starters?"

And Dani, who knew a cue when she heard one, said, "The *saucisse* sounds pretty good to me."

Samantha ordered, making concessions neither to calories nor cost, while Ted chose the wine. What the hell! Dani thought. Calories don't count, not when it's your last night together as a family.

Already, empty-nest syndrome was threatening to become something more than a woman's magazine cliché. She and Ted had discussed the problem thoroughly.

"Don't think of it as losing a daughter," her husband had said. "Think of it as gaining a lot of closet space." Yet despite this stab at levity, he also found the prospect bleak. Was there a male equivalent of "empty-nest"? Dani wondered. Probably.

The hors d'oeuvres arrived, reeking of garlic, along with a bottle of St. Emilion. The musicians struck up a medley of show tunes. The restaurant was filling up. Above the bustle of the waiters, there rose a happy hum of conversation. Only their table seemed exempt from the general glow. Dani's depression was contagious.

They ate the first course in near silence. "The Last Supper" kept echoing in Dani's head. It was a dreadful phrase. There was a qualitative difference, she reminded herself, between a child's leaving for college and a crucifixion. The former was supposed to be a joyous occasion.

The small talk had run out with the last of the snails. Packing, finances, tomorrow's flight—all had been covered ad nauseum. Dani fished for something to say.

As for the message that mattered most—We love you, we'll miss you, you are the light of our lives—if Samantha didn't know as much by now, she never would. Anyhow, this was supposed to be a festive occasion.

Dani caught her husband's eye. Ted forced a smile and ordered a second bottle of wine.

He was drinking more than usual tonight, but comment was pointless. Ted knew when to stop. Bad enough being the family Calorie Cop, Dani wasn't going to play Booze Warden in the bargain.

The waiter arrived with the entrées. By unspoken accord, all three Sloanes fell into animated chatter.

"*Les escalopes de veau, c'est pour madame?*"

Dani nodded. Overcooked, she could see. And at thirty bucks a plate, they garnish with canned *petits pois*.

"Yes, wonderful," she crooned.

"*Et pour moi, le steak au poivre,*" Samantha said.

The waiter plunked down a two-inch-thick slab of beef drowning in sauce. Ted was having duck.

"*Bon appetit,*" said the waiter.

"*Merci bien,*" Samantha replied.

Silence again descended on the table, broken only by the occasional inquiry. "The steak tender?" "Yeah, how's yours?" "Fine. You want a taste?" "No thanks."

Munch, crunch, clatter of silver.

After a while, Ted pushed his plate away, the duck scarcely touched.

"About my Visa card . . . ," he said.

Samantha put down her fork and looked appropriately somber. "I know, Dad. Only for emergencies."

"Well, use your judgment," he said. "I don't want you to . . ." The sentence trailed off. He returned to the scrutiny of his wineglass.

A brief pause. Munch, crunch. Dani forced down the last of her *escalope*. "Mmmmm . . . that was delicious."

Glumly, they waited for the busboy to clear away. Every now and then, a roar of laughter went up from a group seated a few tables away.

"Sounds like they're having a good time," Samantha said with a cheery smile, then lowered her eyes, embarrassed.

Dani felt close to tears. My baby! She wanted to put her arms around Sam and hug her. Then do the same to Ted. He looked wretched, poor man. Losing a daughter.

"Oh listen," Dani said. "Did I tell you about this carriage horse that went berserk outside the Plaza?"—then remembered that she had. Oh well . . .

"That must have been scary," Samantha said politely.

"Yeah . . . was. I hope the horse is okay."

"They won't shoot him, will they, Mom?"

"Of course not."

Christ, what a topic! She scoured her mind for something interesting, more anecdotal. Mrs. Gessner and her dentist husband sprang to mind. Now there was a conversation piece! But although the kind of story that could be amusing second hand, it hardly seemed suitable tonight. Besides, Dani never discussed clients in public. No telling who might be listening.

"How about dessert?" she asked. Who knows? They might whip up a lively disputation on the relative merits of *marrons glacés* and chocolate mousse. After which, they would settle the bill and slink off.

Ted signaled the waiter. A moment later, as if in answer to a summons, a large balding man who had been sitting with what Dani had come to think of as the Fun People detached himself and shambled over to their table.

"Teddy Sloane . . . Well, I'll be damned." He shot out his hand in greeting. "I thought it was you. It's been . . . Jesus, what? . . . twenty years?"

Ted wobbled to his feet, looking pleased.

"At least that. Colin Stevens . . . my wife, Dani . . . our girl . . ." Then he pulled out a chair. "Collie and I were in grad school together. How about a drink?"

Collie hesitated. "Well, maybe a quickie. I'm with a bunch of people."

The two men couldn't have been close, Dani realized, or she would have recognized the name, but Ted seemed glad to see him. Or perhaps merely relieved to have found something external to focus on.

"You in town for the ASNE convention?" Collie asked.

Ted shook his head. "We live here."

"What's ASNE?" Dani asked.

"The American Society of Newspaper Editors," Ted explained. "It's a trade association."

"Pretty good convention," Collie said, "though they could've picked a better town. I can't believe how much New York has changed. This place is a piss, isn't it?"

"Tell me something," Ted said. Both men laughed.

There followed a quick rundown on the old days: who married whom, who went where for what. Collie was managing editor of the *Sausalito Bugle*, it turned out. "It's a good little paper," he said. "We were one of the first to blow the whistle on the S and L's. How 'bout you, Ted. What have you been doing with yourself?"

Ted didn't skip a beat. "I was working overseas for the *Times* . . . Afghanistan, Burundi, Albania. . . ."

Samantha tittered. Collie looked puzzled.

"I understood that no American newsmen were allowed into Albania."

"Meet the exception," Ted replied. "You see, I'm one of a handful of journalists who not only is fluent in Grllog, which is High Albanian, but also Pflatzlog, which is Low Albanian, the language of the mountainfolk. Seven years in lovely Tirhana, mosquito capital of the world. In fact, you're looking at the only American ever to get close enough to Enver Hoxha to smell his breath. The man ate whole garlic three times a day."

Collie grinned. "You're kidding, right?"

"Right. I'm kidding."

"So what have you been up to, seriously?"

"Public relations."

Collie laughed, and relaxed. "Yeah, smart. My wife is always telling me I should go into PR. I kind of envy you guys. That's where the bread is, she says. What company you with?"

"Globexx." Ted bit the word off.

"Holy shit!" Collie gave Ted a sneaky smile. "Big bad Globexx! And here I was, all set to make a pitch for your job. What's he like, by the way? Have you met him?"

"What's who like?" Ted feigned innocence.

"Morton Ketchell, who else! Man of the Hour."

"El Swino!" Samantha broke in with a giggle. "Dad actually

writes some of his speeches," she added. It was half boast, half apology.

"Sam!" Dani's jaw dropped. But remarkably Ted took the gaffe with aplomb.

"Now, sweetie," he pretended to scold. "Watch your language. You are speaking to a member of the working press concerning the beloved chairman of our firm." Then Ted grinned, the cockamamie grin of a drunk enjoying an intensely private joke. "What is the Great Man really like? Ignore my daughter, Collie.' Those were the ramblings of an innocent child. As for the real Mort Ketchell, a glimpse at the inner essence? Get your notebook out, pal, because I'm giving you this insight for direct attribution. 'Morton B. Ketchell is the kindest, warmest, bravest, most wonderful human being it's ever been my privilege to know.' And when you quote your source, remember it's Sloane with an 'e.' "

Collie gave a belch of laughter and rejoined his friends.

"That 'kindest, warmest' bit," Dani said when they were getting ready for bed. "Isn't that a line from some movie?"

"*Manchurian Candidate*." Ted groped his way to the bathroom. "Where do you keep the Pepto-Bismol these days?"

"I think we're out. Try the Maalox. You eat too much?"

"Drank too much. Thanks for the euphemism. My mouth tastes like the bottom of a bird cage."

She heard him fumbling in the medicine cabinet, then the dull thud of something falling on the tiles.

"Why the fuck do you always leave your talcum powder where it's going to get knocked over? Goddammit to hell!"

He kicked something, cursed some more, then appeared on the threshold, his feet dusted with a fine layer of L'air du Temps powder. For a moment he stood there, haggard, eyes full of misery.

"Jesus, he wasn't even one of the hotshots."

"Who are you talking about?" But she knew.

"Collie Stevens. There were a hundred guys there who could write rings around him." Ted's voice was thick with envy. "Me included. But he's done well. Made a life for himself. Affected people in a positive sense."

"In Sausalito?" Dani rolled her eyes. "Well, if you want to be a big fish in a suburban swimming pool . . ."

Ted looked at her oddly. "You would say that." Then he backtracked. "I'm sorry. This is not my day to be gracious."

"Well, climb into bed, honey, and I'll get something for your stomach. It's late. You want to be fresh in the morning."

On her way to the kitchen, she heard the familiar sound of rock music coming from the dark of Sam's bedroom. *Can't you sleep, baby?* Dani mouthed the words. Then answered her own question. *Probably not.*

"It's like I'm going off into the great unknown," Sam had kidded a few nights earlier when they were packing. "Beyond this point there be monsters."

But Dani had read the fear beneath the flippancy, and tried to reassure her. "You know something, Sam? I was petrified when I went away to college," she said, "nervous as a cat. And Hupperstown was only sixty miles away. It was like leaving the womb second time around. I thought, I won't know a soul at Barnard. I'll be totally surrounded by strangers, probably all these sophisticated New York types. What if I don't make any friends? . . . Which was one scary proposition. My first night in the dorm I was ready to take the morning train back to Jersey. But you know what? Every other freshman in my class was just as nervous and apprehensive as I was—even Kaycee, would you believe! Well, within a couple of weeks, I was so busy with new people I could barely remember to phone home. You'll be fine, love. And Oberlin seems like such an intimate place. You meet kids from all over the country, make lots of new friends . . ."

And Sam had nodded with false bravado. "No problem."

Now, outside her daughter's room at midnight, Dani listened to the grumbling voom-voom of classic rock. She put her hand on the door, wondering whether to pop in for a final goodnight kiss–cum–pep talk when the music switched off. Dani sighed, then went into the kitchen and made a cup of herb tea.

How quiet the apartment had grown without the muffled sound of Sam's stereo. It would be switched off from now on, Dani realized. Empty room, empty nest. Notwithstanding Ted's quip about not losing a daughter but gaining a closet, they were losing a daughter.

By the time she returned with the tea, Ted had fallen asleep. She slid into bed beside him, her ears attuned to the silence. Already she missed Sam, and it was a long haul until Thanksgiving.

Well, at least—she took off her nightgown and snuggled up against her husband's back—at least she and Ted had each other. She lay her cheek against his shoulder. He smelled faintly of booze and bath powder. But a nice smell, she decided. Sexy. How well they fit. How seamlessly their bodies joined together. Mortise and tenon. She rubbed up against him, wallowing in the familiar warmth.

Ted stirred. Grumbled something. Perhaps he wasn't so fast asleep after all. Dani felt a sudden lurch of desire. Lightly she drew a line with her fingers from the base of his throat down the length of his chest till her thumb came to rest on his navel.

"Sweetheart?" she whispered moistly in his ear. "Are you asleep?"

But Ted Sloane was dead to the world.

A pity, Dani thought. Tonight of all nights, they should have found consolation in each other's arms. Though for some time now, their lovemaking had become—perhaps *jaded* was too strong a word, but listless. And, on more than one sweated occasion, disturbingly incomplete.

"I'm sorry," a frustrated Ted would apologize, adding that he was tired or stressed out or had too much on his mind. And Dani would be sympathetic. He was a man, after all, not a machine. Inevitably, over the years, the first hot flush of sexuality had subsided into a kind of pleasurable routine. And lately, sometimes, not even that.

These occasional bouts of impotence troubled her, not least of all because she knew how much they preyed on Ted's mind. He would be miserable for days afterward.

"Maybe you ought to see Dr. Hendricks for a checkup," she'd suggested at one point, but he dismissed the idea out of hand. "Why? So he can tell me I'm not twenty-five anymore?" Then he'd softened. "It's only a phase, Dani. It'll pass."

But now, with their daughter's departure, they would be entering yet a different phase of their marriage. Life without Samantha.

Suddenly, in the back of her head, Dani could hear her own

mother's injunction: *Look on the bright side. No cloud so dark it doesn't have a silver lining.*

Dani sat up in bed. Why not look on the bright side? From that perspective, a new scenario swam into view. One phase was passing; another, about to begin.

After all, if Life Before Samantha had been a glorious age of romantic discovery, why shouldn't Life Without Samantha prove the same?

Freedom. Privacy. A recapturing of youth for the first time in years, it would be just Dani and Ted, alone and together, enjoying the bliss of a second honeymoon. A time for emotional repairs, replenishment. For self-indulgence. Minor pleasures.

Starting tomorrow, they would (a 100-point bonus) be able to keep ice cream in the freezer. Gallons of it. The Calorie Cop would opt for early retirement and on nights like this, she and Ted might hop into bed with a pint of Heavenly Hash, eat themselves silly, then make love for hours without giving a damn about how much noise they might be generating. Just like in the old days. And nights.

Dani sighed. Not only nights, for that matter. Mornings. Lovely Sunday mornings. A Loaf of Bread, the *New York Times* and Thou.

Or matinees. Lunch hours. In fact, whenever the spirit moved them, business permitting. Love in the afternoon. Such a delicious phrase. Why, they hadn't had that kind of rendezvous in years.

Eighteen years, to be exact. Since Ecuador.

Such bliss, she thought back fondly. Those torrid siestas in Ecuador when the whole world was asleep—people, ducks, chickens, even the flies—except for Ted and Dani Sloane, fucking themselves blind every afternoon on a canvas cot in a two-room shack.

Life Without Samantha. It would be even better than Life Before. Freer, easier. Because the hard years, the years of struggle, were mostly behind them.

Dani Sloane, World-Champion Optimist. Ted used to call her that. Well, she had a lot to be optimistic about.

Seconds later, she fell asleep, nuzzled against her husband's shoulder, smiling faintly in anticipation of the thousand nights to come.

6

"PARADISE," as defined by Peace Corps volunteers, "is a hot shower and a cold beer."

Yet in retrospect, Ecuador was paradise. The passage of time had endowed the experience with a magic glow. People, events, hardships both small and truly awful, the daily frustrations, the occasional heart-lifting triumphs—all had long since been glossed over by the patina of years to become the stuff of anecdote, of romance. Moments to be recalled (though less and less often) with a moist eye and unblushing affection.

"Remember?" Ted would say, and offer a few key words, thereby triggering a host of memories.

The "showerhead" that consisted of a yellow plastic bucket punched with holes; the variety and voracity of local insect life; getting drunk on chicha on Christmas Eve and praying for death the morning after; the sound of nose flutes at dusk; the tang of woodsmoke from the village; their pet parrot, Moses, whose sole vocabulary consisted of the phrase "Let's go, Mets"; the equatorial sun that plopped behind the horizon with a breathtaking suddenness; the three-legged dog that had hobbled into their bungalow and ate up a year's supply of Ortho jelly; the cantankerous blue jeep that only started if you kicked it; their pal Josh Kaplan from Baltimore who'd married a Quechuan Indian and gone native; those long sweated "siestas" on the canvas cot when all creation held its breath.

It was a dream, made more dreamlike by the thinness of the air, the beauty of the countryside, the timelessness of peasant life, the sense of being cut off from all that was familiar. From the fruit in the trees to the stars in the heaven, nothing was as they had known it. The only constant in Ted's and Dani's lives was each other.

The dream came to its close one night as they sat on their veranda gazing up at those unfamiliar constellations, and Dani told her husband that she was pregnant.

"Ahhh . . . ," Ted said. "I thought so."

And, she said, she didn't want to have their baby in the clinic at Cajabamba. She'd worked there long and hard enough to have no illusions about its quality. Nor would she go to the hospital in Guayaquil, some two hundred miles away. It was not as if they were truly Indians. A new set of responsibilities had come into play.

Ted lay his head on her lap. "Let me think about it."

He was silent for so long she wondered if he'd fallen asleep. Then he stood up, stretched and stroked his beard.

"Well, love," he announced. "Looks like it's time we joined the real world. I'll give my notice."

"But your book?" she said. It was still unfinished.

"Oh, the book," he scoffed. That too was a dream, as elusive as smoke from the Indian villages. "Who'd want to read the self-serving memoirs of some Peace Corpsman in the outback? I've done most of what I set out to do, Dani. Paid my dues to the world at large. Now it's time I paid them to you. We'll go home. I'll get a job, something suitable for a married man"—he broke into a grin—"and expectant father. On a newspaper, God willing, but if not, I'll take what I can get. Advertising, public relations, promotion, whatever's out there. Gotta make us three a living." He leaned over and pulled Dani to her feet.

"I'll never forget this place, these people. It will stay with me always. Paradise Lost. But that's how it has to be. Rat race," he announced to the stars, "here I come."

*   *   *

"Hot water! New movies! Yikes!" Dani said their first day home. It was great to be back. Ted agreed.

Within a matter of weeks, the Sloanes had retrieved their wedding presents from the attic in Hupperstown and rented a tiny apartment in Greenwich Village. The beard that Ted had refused to shave for his father-in-law now came off for prospective employers, though he continued to draw the line at pinstripes.

Luck was with him. He soon found a job in the public relations department of Samarand Inc., an international petrochemical firm that manufactured paints and industrial coatings. Hired, ostensibly, on the basis of his South American experience, Ted was plunked down in a glass-and-steel building on Park Avenue where the closest he came to utilizing his command of Spanish was the occasional lunch at Rincon Madrid.

The salary was good though not earth-shaking, his colleagues convivial, and the work (to Ted's surprise and Dani's relief) enjoyable. Mostly it entailed the writing of press releases and articles concerning new products for the trade papers. "The *New York Times*'s loss"—he would say—"is Industrial Coatings' gain."

By the time Samantha was born, there seemed to be no trace left of the bearded khaki-clad Peace Corps volunteer. That Ted Sloane had been replaced by a clean-shaven young man in a Brooks Brothers suit and neat tie.

Even Ralph Fletcher, once so sourly critical of his son-in-law's "Ecuador adventure"—even counter-counterculture Ralph Fletcher was mollified.

"Like father, like son," he said to Dani, while a few paces ahead of them, Ted pushed a baby carriage across Washington Square Park.

"What's that supposed to mean?" Dani asked, though the intent was clear. It meant her father was finally satisfied that Ted Sloane had stopped gallivanting around the world pursuing God-knows-what quixotic ideals, and had settled down to become a company man, a family man, a "credit to the community." Not so different from the senior Theo J. Sloane, still toiling in the vineyards of P&G.

Thus a generational peace obtained.

Every August Ted put in a month of hard labor to produce a

piece on the Industrial Paints and Epoxies Division for the company's annual report. His effort was invariably acknowledged by a substantial end-of-year raise.

Though never substantial enough, it turned out. New York City continued to gobble up his paycheck in its entirety. Only millionaires and those with large rent-controlled apartments ever seemed to get far enough ahead of the game to raise a proper family.

At first, when Sam was an infant and they were absorbed in the minutiae of parenthood, they talked a good deal about having a second child. "Only children, lonely children," they both felt.

"But later," Dani said.

"Definitely later," Ted concurred. "When we have more space and more money."

Yet money pressures aside, he was content with his lot. Marriage suited him. He liked his work. He adored his wife and baby daughter. He played tennis every morning, was home by six every night. He and Dani lived happily amidst a pleasant clutter of books, magazines and furniture you could put your feet up on. They were a popular couple in a city where life never grew stale.

When Samantha entered first grade, Dani returned to college, in keeping with the spirit of the times. She spent a semester working for a masters in English lit before concluding that the time for intellectual dalliance had passed. She would do better learning a profession. The following year, she switched to NYU Law.

In the long run it proved a shrewd move (lawyers rarely starve), but in the short term it was sheer chaos: baby-sitters, tuition fees, scheduling hassles, never enough hours in the day, enough days in the week, the whole ménage being kept alive by take-out pizzas and Chinese food. The simplest tasks required complex arrangements involving everybody from dry cleaners to school teachers to Ted's secretary to Dani's parents, who could be depended upon to pinch-hit in the clutch.

In her life, Dani swore, she'd never been pushed so hard. Was this a preview of years to come?

And when, a few weeks shy of her thirty-fourth birthday, Dani passed the bar, she marked the event by falling asleep over crab cakes during a celebratory dinner at Gloucester House. The next morning, she was out looking for a job.

For a while, she and Ted talked about having another baby, but once she started working at Pruitt-Baker, the subject got lost in the shuffle. Who had the time, these days? The energy? Then Dani turned forty, and that was that.

No matter. Their lives were so full already. So busy busy. Busy with friends, theater, concerts, dinner parties; busy with so many goodies to buy and see and eat; busy with their burgeoning careers, their growing daughter; busy juggling lunch dates and court dates and squash dates; busy dashing from client meetings to condo meetings to the weekly meeting of the 79th Street Society for the Preservation of Penny-Ante Poker.

Had you told Ted and Dani Sloane that they had evolved into quintessential New Yorkers, they might have paused for a moment, just long enough to give a breathless nod of assent, then scooted on, just a tad late already, to the next item listed in their Filofax.

Ted's ancient dreams had dwindled to a stack of *Foreign Affairs Quarterly* (largely unread) in the bottom of the bedroom bookcase. As for Ecuador? Why, Ecuador was little more than a pleasant haze, a memory, a few dozen snapshots, some native pottery and a large woolen tapestry woven by the Otavalo Indians that hung on their living room wall above the TV.

7

THE S.S. *FAIRWEATHER FRIEND* was a thirty-one-foot
sloop encompassing a mass of lesser statistics: 4 sails, 16hp auxiliary
motor, 4'10" draft, 5'9" headroom ("duck everybody!"), sleeps 6
("six midgets," Ted quipped), with $18,500 still owing to the bank.
It was the joint property of the Sloanes and their good friends
Kaycee and Barney Feldman.

In season, the boat was moored on City Island to be taken out
for day sails when the weather was fine.

The Sunday following Samantha's departure, the Sloanes and
Feldmans assembled there before nine, armed with picnic baskets
and plastic coolers. The day was exceptionally warm, perhaps the
last such for a while, and thus an opportunity not to be missed.

Once the *Fairweather* had battled its way clear of dockside traffic
and attained the freedom of Long Island Sound, the voyage subsided into a familiar routine.

The men handled the sails, drank beer and made nautical noises,
more so since boating was a novelty—not just to Ted, raised so far
inland, but to Barney, who made a joke of it. "We Jews are not
exactly a seafaring folk. Unless you count when my grandfather
came over steerage."

He liked to tell the story of a Brooklyn boy who, having grown
rich in the rag trade, bought a yacht and kitted himself out in an
officer's uniform. Then he invited his parents aboard to admire the

effect. When asked how he looked, his mother replied, "By me you're a captain, by your poppa you're captain. But tell me, by a captain, are you a captain?"

Yet Barney took to sailing like a Norseman. He had a natural feel for the craft and the sea. "By me you're a captain," Ted said with awed respect.

While their husbands grappled with the elements, Dani and Kaycee (née Carlson, ex Burke) stripped down to bikinis and stretched out on deck to snooze and gossip for an hour or two. After which, according to the same routine, "the girls" would set out a picnic lunch accompanied by a semidecent bottle or two.

"A totally sexist division of labor," Kaycee said with approval. "Everything we didn't go to Barnard for!"

At forty-two, she was still lovely, though that breathtaking freshness that had made her the envy of the dorms—and of Dani—had been lost, left behind in such places as Mykonos and Santa Fe and Southern California.

"All those years of following my bliss and what did it get me?" Kaycee would say, examining herself in the mirror. "Cellulite and crow's feet."

Since graduation, the two classmates had kept in touch sporadically, staying friends despite divergent lifestyles. By the time Dani returned from Ecuador, Kaycee had got herself married and divorced. While Dani was nursing her baby, Kaycee was in New Mexico learning t'ai chi from her latest mentor. A year later she was in Oregon studying batik with a guy she'd met in Santa Fe. Then followed a stretch in Steamboat Springs where she met Jerry and went through her Indian jewelry phase.

Well before Dani entered law school, the pattern of Kaycee's wanderings was set: love 'em, lose 'em and leave for someplace else. The men she lived with usually dwelt on the fringes of the art world. Some were marked by the paranoia of the failed and secondrate, though all of them, she claimed, were magnificent in bed.

Thus Kaycee shared her body, soul and modest trust fund with, among others, an underground filmmaker, a primitive painter, a Chicago commodities broker ("my sole aberration"), a Haitian poet who believed in reincarnation, a West Coast performance artist who worked in the nude.

Where Kaycee's heart was committed, her aspirations tagged along. Thus she painted, constructed collages, threw pots, learned to make exquisite hand-dipped endpapers. Had she persisted in any one craft, stayed in any one place, she might, conceivably, have enjoyed a measure of success. But she remained a dabbler, a decorative hanger-on of men who themselves were hangers-on. Her true career was romance.

Periodically, she would descend on the Sloane household in a cloud of perfume, fresh from the latest Eden, to recount tales of instant rapture, of sexual abandon and stormy scenes, of couplings in Greek caves and unfurnished lofts. "Men are such shits," she would say with glee. "If I'd been smart, I would have hung on to good old Ted."

A sly dig, Dani inferred, coming from a woman whose life was packed with glamour. But Dani bore no malice. She would listen to these erotic adventures, envy mixed with disbelief, then go about her own mundane business. Kaycee was as good as a pop novel, she declared.

By the time Dani passed the bar, Kaycee had moved to London and was living with a fashion photographer. For the next several years, she tried her hand (more accurately, her face) at modeling, but by then her beauty had peaked. The girls who beat her out for jobs were younger, fresher, prettier. When Derek dumped her (for someone younger, fresher, prettier), Kaycee had yet another abortion and beat a low-keyed retreat to New York.

"He was fabulous in bed," she told Dani. "Hung like a stallion, though not exactly prime husband material. If I'd married him, it would have just been throwing more business your way." She grew thoughtful. "I sometimes wonder if I didn't make my initial mistake years ago. I should have married some guy like Ted, a Mr. Straight Arrow, and had children. I like kids, you know. I might have made a terrific mother, don't you think?"

For an instant Dani wondered—was Kaycee jealous? But that was absurd. As so often, her friend was talking to hear herself talk.

"Come on," she said mildly. "If you'd really wanted a baby, you'd have had one. There are plenty of single mothers around."

Kaycee shook her head. "Not me. I couldn't go that route solo. Plus, the finances aren't right—I've pissed away most of my trust fund. Well, no matter. The right man will come along one of these days. Here in New York, let's hope."

"And if he doesn't? If he doesn't exist? Then what? You going to sit and hold your breath till it's time to collect Social Security? Be realistic, Kaycee. You don't need another man. What you need is some meaningful work, a career. An alternative life plan, if you will . . ."

"I recall our having had this conversation in college. You were always telling me to Be Prepared. Only then, you were pushing Planned Parenthood. Now, it's Planned Life, no less! Talk about inflation. I know what you're going to say. I ought to go back to school, take classes, learn skills. . . . Well, I've been taking classes all my life, everything from aerobics to Zen, with three years of est seminars thrown in. And as for learning a useful trade, like law or accounting, it's too late. I lack your self-discipline. I can't move mountains on my own. You know me, lovey. I don't function unless I'm with a man. I feel . . . no, it's more than lonely. Incomplete. Unfinished. The world is made for twosomes, Dani, going back to Adam and Eve. You can rattle on about careers and independence and living in some studio apartment with only roaches for company, but you've never done it, to be honest. All these years you've had this fucking great marriage, this wonderful kid. You can go home every night and crawl into the sack with Ted and tell him what a lousy day you've had at the office, and he'll say, 'There, there!' and then whatever went wrong doesn't matter anymore. You Sloanes are such a tight little island. Always have been. I envy you that perfect felicity."

"Whoa," Dani broke in. Kaycee romanticized everything. "Don't confuse us with Ozzie and Harriet. Ted and I have had our shouting matches too, believe me. And when we're not screaming at each other, we're screaming at Sam."

Kaycee looked skeptical.

"Yeah . . . sure. Anyhow," she said, "you're right about one thing. I've got to get a job. I can't expect any help from my mother. Did I tell you what she's up to, that beautiful old dame? Seems she got this bug, she wants to visit every country in the world before she dies, have 'em all stamped in her passport. And now for the really wild part. She wants to do it in alphabetic order, no less.

She's in the B's now, Botswana. Did you ever hear anything so
daffy?"

Dani smiled. "Following her bliss, I expect."

Within weeks of returning to New York, Kaycee found work as a
photographer's rep. Within months, her life had undergone a complete turnabout.

The work suited her admirably, calling as it did for a smart
appearance, a persuasive tongue, a penchant for gossip and a grasp
of technical problems. Her major client was a glossy-haired young
fashion photographer named Bo Antonelli who, Kaycee declared,
"will sleep with anything that moves. We're talking major-league
tomcat here." Theirs was a strictly professional relationship.

Thus Kaycee spent her days beating down the doors of New
York advertising agencies, and it was behind one such door that
she met Barney Feldman.

Barney was fiftyish, twice divorced, with grown children, Bronx-
talking, street-smart, a no-nonsense art director at Marsden Inc.
who appeared unimpressed by the Waspy blonde with the black
portfolio. He listened to Kaycee's spiel, told her Antonelli's stuff
was putrid, then invited her to lunch at Palm Too.

"What's wrong with Bo's work?" Kaycee asked over steaks and
salad.

"He hates women."

Kaycee was struck by the insight. Once articulated, it explained
so much. How shrewd Barney was!

He then proceeded to divest himself of other opinions, largely
uncharitable, concerning Lite beer, I Ching, Werner Erhard, brown
rice, Norman Mailer, aroma-therapy. In one hour, he trampled
over half the credos Kaycee had subscribed to. His pragmatism
bowled her over. Such manliness, she thought. Such assurance.

Two months later, the couple was standing up before a judge
in the Municipal Building, though Barney would have preferred a
Jewish wedding, while Kaycee's friends breathed a collective sigh
of relief.

"I'm so happy, I keep having to pinch myself," she gushed to
Dani who had drawn up the prenuptial agreements. "I can't believe

it's really happening. Barney's so different from other guys I've been with."

"Yeah . . . he's a grown-up," Dani replied. Then she flung her arms around Kaycee's narrow shoulders. "Welcome to the real world. Be happy, love, and no mo' blues."

As for Barney, who used to call himself a two-time loser, he declared that "Three's the charm. This is it! This time I'm marrying for keeps, and that's a promise."

Those events had taken place some three years before this hot September day aboard the *Fairweather Friend*. By now, Kaycee considered herself "an old married woman."

"Hey!" She tapped Dani on the back. "You're getting fried. Think we should do something about lunch?"

Dani blinked her eyes open and sat up on the towel. "I must have dozed off," she said.

In the prow, Ted and Barney were sitting with their heads together, deep in conversation. Shop talk, was Dani's guess. Either that or baseball. She and Kaycee exchanged complicitous smiles, smiles that said, *How nice our husbands have hit it off so splendidly*.

A gust of wind ruffled the calm. Ted hoisted himself up to let out more sail. Dani watched him as he worked, a tall good-looking man, freckled, barefoot, wearing an old T-shirt and khaki shorts. Perhaps it was the outfit, perhaps the shimmer of heat, but he looked scarcely different from the young Peace Corpsman who had stood on a hilltop in Ecuador and declared undying love. A bit thinner on top, a bit thicker about the middle, but otherwise the same.

She willed him to turn toward her, to catch her eye and wink, maybe wave, but Ted was absorbed in his task.

Kaycee was studying him, too.

"Ted's growing a beard," she observed. "Didn't he used to have one when he went to Columbia?"

"Didn't everyone?" Then Dani lowered her voice until they were down in the galley.

"About the shrubbery," she confided, once they were out of earshot, "he started growing it last week. This may sound weird, but it's Ted's form of protest. His declaration of independence or whatever. Globexx is such a buttoned-down place, I think he's half hoping they'll notice the beard and can him. Though how you live on unemployment insurance beats me." She began unpacking groceries. "It's ironic, really. Right after the takeover when everyone was being let go, we suffered agonies. Agonies! Ted was convinced he was next on the hit list. And I don't have to tell you it's no picnic for a guy his age to be on the street. PR is a young man's business, you know. He's lucky to have a job at all these days. And now, this fucking oil spill. . . . It's too much!"

"Go tell me about it," Kaycee said. It was a rhetorical aside. What was left to say that hadn't already been reported ad nauseam in the press? Except for its impact on the Sloanes.

The previous year, in the largest merger since Nabisco-RJR, Ackland Oil of Texas acquired Samarand Inc. The resulting conglomerate was named Globexx.

It was "a perfect marriage," according to the new CEO, Morton Ketchell, though it proved less a marriage than a forcible rape. Ketchell was a tough lean Texan with a reputation for building tough lean companies. He showed his hand early. Within months of the merger, Globexx began selling off the less profitable divisions. Among the first to go was Industrial Coatings.

"There will be no unnecessary firings," the interoffice memo read, "merely the trimming of flab. Where possible, personnel will be subsumed into other divisions of the corporation. A tighter Globexx is a better Globexx."

The memo was the opening gun in a reign of terror. Each morning, Ted went to the office not knowing which familiar face would have vanished (when Globexx fired you, you left within the hour) or if that day would be his last. Soon the phones stopped ringing. The typewriters fell silent. Technically, his department was defunct. Clusters of employees huddled in corridors or behind closed doors, trading rumors and horror stories in hushed tones.

Like everyone else, Ted sent his résumé to the headhunters and began making the rounds, but decent jobs were tight in a city still reeling from the '87 crash, and relocation was out of the question. Move? How could he? He had a daughter in her junior year at prep school. There was his wife's career to be considered. The new boat, the apartment and hardly any money in the bank. Reasonably, how could a man his age be expected to uproot his whole family? Equally preposterous, how could he take a journeyman's job at thirty thou? The Sloanes were accustomed to living well: nice vacations, theater tickets, dining out two or three nights a week.

He felt cornered, depressed. Daily, Ted would leave the office at 5:00, go home, have a drink, then make dinner and await Dani's return. He'd always liked puttering in the kitchen, but now his efforts grew more ambitious, more elaborate. After eight hours of forced inactivity, he ached to use his hands.

"They fired Dave Droesch today," he might greet Dani when she arrived. Or "Janie Walsh is in Mount Sinai with a bleeding ulcer. I thought women didn't get ulcers."

They did at Globexx.

This unnatural state ended abruptly with the Friday Morning Massacre. By closing time that night, only six in a department of fifty were left standing. Miraculously, the Angel of Death had passed over Ted Sloane; he found himself transferred to International Corporate Affairs.

"I survived!" he said, gray with relief, but puzzled as to the relevant factors. Age, merit, salary, pension rights, appearance, or simply the luck of the draw? He hadn't a clue.

"Perhaps quality had something to do with it," Dani said, but Ted was dubious. Too many fine people had fallen. Later he learned that he had been spared because his file read *Bilingual Spanish*. "Dear God! I haven't spoken it in nearly twenty years."

With the transfer, life in the doldrums gave way to life in the hurricane's eye. Ted was absorbed into a group of writers and information officers whose function was to sanitize the corporate image. It was an impossible task. Globexx had become the company everyone loved to hate.

Globexx defiled. It polluted. It engaged in checkbook lobbying at home, wholesale bribery abroad. Its pipelines fouled the inland waterways; its offshore dredges scarred the California coast. As for the company's relation with the environmentalists (Sierra Club, Audubon Society et al.), according to Mort Ketchell, "They can all take a flying fuck." The sole concern was bottom line.

And the bottom line looked terrific.

On April 7, the Globexx tanker *Gargantua* ran aground off the coast of Maine, depositing twenty-three million barrels of oil. The slick spread from Old Orchard to Bar Harbor, its impact spread around the country. What brought the scope of the tragedy home to Main Street America was a photo snapped by a photographer in Kennebunkport. In the foreground lay a pile of dead seabirds. In the background, the president's front porch.

The Monday after the spill, an emergency meeting was called in the main conference room to discuss damage control. Everybody who was anybody at Globexx attended: lobbyists, political advisers, senior staff from the department of Cultural Affairs, experts from Consumer Relations, Advertising, Promotion and Corporate PR. Towering above them all was Morton B. Ketchell.

Ted had never before seen his CEO in the flesh; he didn't like what he saw. Ketchell looked older than he had on the cover of *Fortune:* a taut, wiry man with arctic blue eyes, the drawn facial lines of the dedicated jogger and a skull-hugging haircut that denoted the ex-Marine.

"What we have here," Ketchell began, "is not an ecological problem. It's a public relations problem and should be treated as such. Your job is to draw attention away from the events of April seventh and focus on the positive. What a great company we are, the good we do, the vision, the vastness of Globexx. I don't want to hear about a couple of dead birds on a beach. I want to hear how you're gonna alter basic perceptions. Tell you one place I'd like to begin and that's by stringing up that fucking photographer by the balls."

There were some polite titters from the paid courtiers, which Ketchell acknowledged with his death's-head grin. Then he placed his watch on the table, folded his arms and glared down the length of the room.

"So much for the humorous portion of the meeting. I'm ready to entertain ideas from all over, no matter how off the wall. They might be something we can build on. But ideas, not bellyaching, got me? I've had it up to here with negative thinking." He pushed a button on his watch. "You have ninety minutes."

How about cleaning up the mess in Maine for openers? was on the tip of Ted's tongue. But he kept his mouth shut. Neither he nor anyone else was dumb enough to utter the forbidden word: *pollution*. Onward and upward was the order of the day.

Suggestions poured in, ranging from the canny to the fanciful. Globexx should announce a major donation to the Olympics Committee. To the Cancer Fund. To the president's wife's favorite charity.

They should spread a rumor that the spill was caused by sabotage. Whose? Russian, maybe. The Maritime Unions. Better yet, the lobby for natural gas. Guffaw guffaw.

Hey, bright idea! Why not fund a year of *Sesame Street* on PBS? Sponsor the Miss America contest? Better better! Hands flew up. Why not a documentary featuring the all-American guys who run Globexx service stations? Call it *Meet Your Neighbor*.

Brainstorm! Hire a famous spokesman to tour the country. Yeah, famous but wholesome. Loretta Lynn. Charlton Heston. Bill Cosby. Awed silence. You couldn't top that. Jesus! . . . Cosby would be beautiful. Get him going for us on all the talk shows.

"Hey hey," someone yelled. How about buying time on Fox TV for a profile of Mort Ketchell with wife and kids? "Plus a dog," Ted's boss piped up. "A nice shaggy dog. Airedale, maybe. They poll high for warmth and compassion."

Ketchell took it all in, nodding now and then, sometimes tagging specific ideas for development.

As the afternoon wore on, Ted slunk lower and lower in his seat. He wished he were dead. He wished Mort Ketchell were dead. Not just dead, but executed in a manner befitting his crimes. Ten days in the electric chair. That seemed about right. What a farce this meeting was!

"Why don't they just give the fucking tanker a new name," Ted muttered to the woman on his right. "Call it the *Good Ship Lollipop* with Shirley Temple at the helm."

"You there!" A long bony finger waggled in Ted's direction. "What's that about a new name? Speak up, man."

(Later, recounting the incident to Dani, Ted would say, "You know how people faced with hanging are supposed to have their lives flash before their eyes? That was me. For about two seconds, all I could think of was mortgage payments, boat loan, four years of college fees.")

Instantly, his mind went into overdrive.

"I thought"—he began improvising—"that it might make sense to rename the tanker, sir. I mean . . . like, we've got a ship here of Liberian registry flying the Panamanian flag and mostly crewed by nonunion Filipinos."

"It's un-American? Is that what you're saying?"

Ted paused. Was he breaking the rules by voicing a negative? *Think mortgage, boat loan, tuition.*

"Well, it could be advantageous to sound a bit less foreign. Take the name, *Gargantua.*"

"Gargantua means big," Ketchell said, eyes narrowed. "What could be more American than that?"

Mortgage, boat loan, tuition. Ted drew a deep breath and forged ahead.

"Very true, sir. However the term originated in a satire by Rabelais. *Gargantua et Pantagruel.* Gargantua was a wild man, a bit of a buffoon. Not an image we'd want to project. And French," he added for extra fillip.

"I see." The narrow eyes narrowed further. A tense silence obtained while Ketchell deliberated, then—"Good thinking. What alternatives did you have in mind?"

Ted fought down a flash of panic.

"I haven't had time yet to work out specifics."

"Who'd you say you were, fella?"

"Ted Sloane, International Corporate PR."

"Okay, Sloane. I want a hundred new names on my desk by eight tomorrow morning."

Ted worked late that night, coming up with a hundred and five suggestions (but not including the *Good Ship Lollipop*), then came home and threw up.

"I don't think I can hack this, Dani."

"It's two A.M.," she said. "You're tired." The optimist in her sought out the bright side. "Remember how last year you were beefing you had nothing to do? Well, better busy than bored. Right? And at least you're in a position to score some Brownie points. Sounds like Ketchell was quite smitten with you."

Ted glared. "Are you suggesting I suck up to that motherfucker?"

"Of course not, sweetie. It's just that you may as well look good until something better turns up. To quote a very savvy guy named Ted Sloane, it doesn't hurt to think mortgage, think tuition."

"I'm thinking ducks," he said. "I'm thinking of those goddamn ducks dying on the beach at Kennebunkport."

8

THE ONLY THING WORSE, Ted discovered, than being on Mort Ketchell's shit list was being in the great man's favor. You couldn't hide, escape or transfer out.

His days were now spent in an atmosphere of constant crisis, unabated tension. He began suffering from stress headaches and indigestion. Worse yet, he couldn't even see the results of his labor. "If I'm going to be a whore," he griped, "at least let me be a good one." But his most strenuous efforts all went for nothing.

There was the time Ketchell's secretary had him paged in the men's room to inform him that the Great Conglommerateur had consented to be interviewed by Barbara Walters on *20/20*. Drop everything, Ted was instructed, draw up the one hundred questions (Mort Ketchell liked round numbers) Walters was likely to ask, then devise appropriate responses.

For the next few days, Ted worked around the clock: running tapes of old broadcasts, analyzing Walters's style, consulting with Ketchell's third and fourth assistants to check tone and content. Then the night before the interview, Ketchell backed out. No explanation. Does the royal family explain? Does God offer alibis?

In idle moments, Ted drew up lists of epithets, mostly obscene. "El Swino" was among the mildest. One night, he came home with a six-inch voodoo doll from a novelty shop. What the hell, he said. Maybe the Haitians had it right.

All that spring there was no living with the man. "Is this what
I busted my ass for at journalism school?" he would growl. "So I
could write press handouts on the joys of pollution? Fuck and
double fuck!"

Nor was Globexx the only target of his wrath. In a remarkably
short time, Ted's view of the world had skewed 180 degrees. In
every conceivable aspect, life had gone wrong, turned sour.

The apartment, for instance. Their terrific (okay, small but still
terrific) two-bedroom apartment on the fashionable East Side that
they'd gone in hock up to their eyeballs for. All of a sudden it had
become, in Ted's vocabulary, "a shoe box," "a sardine can," "a file
cabinet," "an air-conditioned coffin," "the armed fortress."

"What sane person would pay a premium to live in Sing Sing?"
he asked.

External noises drove him up the wall, and, this being Manhattan, they were ubiquitous. Ghetto blasters. Car horns. Sirens
en route to New York Hospital. Neighbors.

"You'd think for two hundred and forty-nine thousand dollars,
the builders could have put in some soundproofing. Christ! Not
bad enough we get the racket from the street, I have to hear every
time the goddamn Speyers flush their john!"

"Ssssh!" Dani put a finger to her lips. "They'll hear you yelling."

His frustration peaked one night when he kicked in the television
set in the midst of a Globexx commercial. Dani was livid.

"If it makes you happy to be miserable," she yelled, "fine! Be
miserable. Only don't take it out on me. Or on the furniture either!"

Did Ted Sloane think he was the only person in the world who
lived with stress? she lashed out, Dani lived with it, too, she reminded him. By the caseload. Day in, day out, she took her licks
from cranky clients, lousy judges, bad rulings. Pruitt-Baker was
no picnic either, she'd have him know; it was sexist, rife with office
politics. "Why do you think I never made partner? How does that
make me feel? But I don't go around behaving like a maniac. I
cope. I roll with the punches. Which is more than you're willing
to do."

As for his constant bitching about the apartment, she was sick
and tired of it. What did he expect? she asked. That they could
live as peacefully and spaciously as when Ted was growing up in

the suburbs? But this wasn't Crescent Park, or Hupperstown, either. This was New York, dammit! Manhattan. The Big Leagues. The greatest, most exciting city in the world—and you paid for the privilege of living here by forfeiting certain minor creature comforts. And if you couldn't cut it, Bud, you either shut up or got out. You didn't vent your spleen on a defenseless TV.

She stormed out of the room, coming back a minute later with a dustpan and brush for him to clean up the mess, but one look and her anger turned to panic. Poor Ted! He had buried his head in his arms, his body wracked by wrenching sobs. In the face of such despair, Dani felt helpless.

"Poor babe!" She hugged him close. "I didn't mean to come down on you so hard."

After what seemed like an eternity, he staggered to his feet. "Sorry. Not your fault," he said. "I'm just bushed." Then he lurched into the bedroom and fell asleep fully dressed. He slept for fourteen hours.

"Look," she said when he got up. "We have to talk. All this anguish is raising hell with our marriage. Let's see if we can't work something out."

They talked. That day and the next and the next: long, civilized, reasonable conversation that explored options, examined alternatives, and resolved nothing. Maybe a bang-up vacation was in order. Or a leave of absence. Or perhaps Ted should simply up and quit. No job was worth killing yourself over.

"And what'll we live on, Dani?"

"Well, we could sell the apartment," she said dubiously.

"We'd take a bath. This is the worst possible time. Don't you know how depressed the real estate market is these days?"

"Not as depressed as you are, Ted. I'm worried for you. Would you consider some counseling? Your health insurance covers psychotherapy."

"Yeah, but it's a company policy. Which means I'd have to stay on at Globexx for the benefits." He laughed. "Company drives me crazy, then pays the shrink bills so it can drive me crazy all over again."

His dissatisfaction with New York came to a head again a week later when he had his wallet lifted on the subway.

"What was it doing in your outside pocket?" Dani asked.

"So now it's my fault? And don't tell me I should've known better than to take the subway. Well, I'm sick and tired of living defensively. This goddamn town."

"Now now . . ." Dani was mollifying. "There are thieves all over, including the suburbs, so don't blame New York. Try and look on the bright side, hon, the compensations. After all, you didn't have a subscription to the Met Opera back in Crescent Park, or your pick of Broadway shows."

"We didn't have muggers or panhandlers, either. We had trees. You remember trees? They're green? They have something called leaves? You know, I find it extraordinary that on an income of six figures a year, we can't afford to keep a car and get into the country weekends."

"You know what garaging costs. Be reasonable."

But by his lights, Ted was being reasonable. It was reasonable to be unhappy in a wretched world. However, after that blowup, he made an effort to keep the domestic peace. He grew sad, rather than angry. He began seeing a therapist. It didn't seem to help.

One night he came home ashen and fell deadweight into his favorite lounge chair. Dani was certain he'd been fired. She poured him a drink and waited.

"I did something today I've never done before," he said, studying the bottom of his glass. "And never thought I was capable of. I crossed a picket line."

The line was composed of several dozen environmentalists who had assembled in front of the Globexx Building.

"They were college kids mostly, some older. Good people. Caring. They had these signs that said 'Clean Up Or Shut Down.' 'Globexx Must Go'—that kind of stuff. I averted my eyes and walked right past 'em, like the company fink that I am. And all the time I could feel their contempt, their opprobrium. How could I do such a thing? What kind of man have I become? I should have grabbed a sign and joined their ranks. Ten, twenty years ago, I would have." His eyes were bright with pain. "It ain't working, Dani. We've got to get out of here . . . out of this city, out of this life."

Dani was at a loss for words. She began flailing wildly in search of a solution, no matter how radical. Anything was better than this despair.

"Fuck the money," she declared. "If you've really had it with New York, we'll sublet the apartment and get a place in the suburbs. Southern Westchester, maybe. One of the easier commutes. They say Pelham is nice and rents are half what they are in Manhattan. Why not?" She tried to talk herself into it. "We'd have some space. You could keep a car, plant a garden. . . ."

But Ted didn't even consider the proposal. "What difference would that make, Dani? I'd still have to go in to the same fucking office every day, the same fucking city."

"Then quit the job. It's not the end of the world. We could manage for a while on one salary."

"Ted Sloane, house-husband? No thanks, Dani. Anyhow, I meant really out. Away from the rat race."

Dani didn't understand. "But where could we go? Be specific. I have my job to consider, after all. We have to eat."

He sat for a long time without answering, then raised his eyes to the Indian tapestry on the wall.

"Ecuador," he said with an odd quaver in his voice. "I want to go to Ecuador. Will you come with me?"

Dani's jaw dropped. Was this his idea of a joke?

Then he looked at her and smiled. It was an ineffably sad smile, yet still a smile.

"But what would you do in Ecuador, eh, Dani? It's a Catholic country. Not much call for a New York divorce lawyer, I shouldn't think."

She heaved a sigh of relief and poured him another scotch. Thank the Lord he was only kidding.

"Of course he didn't mean that literally, about leaving New York," Dani explained to Kaycee as they fixed lunch in the galley. "He's too much of a pragmatist. Besides, he's as much of a city person as I am. Ted would die if he didn't have his opera subscription, let alone daily delivery of the *New York Times*. Honestly, can you picture either of us in the boonies?"

"People do live there," Kaycee insisted.

"Not people like us. That was just his way of letting off steam.

Anyhow, things seem to have settled down at Globexx lately. Ted seems . . . well, I don't know if *happier* would be the word exactly, but more resigned, more at peace with himself. I think the shrink has helped. It's as though he's arrived at some kind of decision."

She uncorked a bottle of Beaujolais, letting it breathe. It was an excellent vintage. Then she smiled.

"Plus now that Ted's a member of the Crisis Management Committee, there should be more money involved. They have a very strict job-classification system at Globexx, you know. Like the army or civil service. Ted'll be an E-six, and as I understand it, that's worth another eight or nine thou next year. We'll know definitely after the annual review. My idea is, once we're out of the woods financially, I'd like Ted to have his escape hatch. He deserves it. A little weekend place in the country, maybe."

"What country did you have in mind?" Kaycee asked. "Ecuador?"

Dani wheeled around, astonished. Honestly, Kaycee could be so dense at times.

"When Ted was talking about Ecuador, he was using it as a metaphor, Kaycee. A way of saying he'd like to be young and free again. Well, who wouldn't! Oh great!" She unwrapped a plastic container. "The deli put in some of those fantastic cracked olives. Did you remember to bring the chèvre?"

Lunch was served on deck, and the balance of the day was notable for an abundance of sunshine and a lack of incident, though Dani couldn't help noting that both men were unduly quiet. Barney in particular looked dour. Dani's antenna went up. Trouble in the Feldman paradise? But she didn't have a chance to ask discreetly.

By sundown, the *Fairweather* was back in its mooring. The four friends crowded in a taxi and headed for Manhattan.

"You free for lunch this week?" Kaycee asked Dani.

That confirmed it in Dani's mind. Trouble in paradise. She wondered if Kaycee was getting restless. Or having second thoughts about the prenups, that clause about no children. Maybe she wanted some advice.

Dani's mind skipped to the week ahead. "Let me see. . . . Ummmm, tomorrow I'm at court in White Plains. Tuesday, there's a staff meeting. The next day I have to schlepp out to Long Island, new client. Thursday's out. I tell you, Kaycee, some days I'm lucky to find time to put on fresh lipstick. Busy busy busy." So were they all. Busy busy busy. That was the basic condition of their lives. Still, Dani hoped, never too busy for old friends. And if she couldn't find the time, she'd make it. "Yes, sure. I'll have to check my office Filofax, though. Give me a ring midweek and we'll fix up something."

"Will do."

But Kaycee never called.

9

"YOUR PLACE OR MINE?" Leo Margulies had asked.

Dani opted for his, preferring the Greenwich Village ambience to Pruitt-Baker's. Leo's office, on the ground floor of a Horatio Street brownstone, exuded an amiable scruffiness. So did Leo.

Leo had a reputation for being tough that Dani found misleading. Maybe it was the combination of a nasal Brooklyn bark and Brillo Pad hair that created the image: Leo had the style of a disputatious terrier.

Dani, who had dealt with him before, knew better. She had found Leo both fair and reasonable. Not exactly a marshmallow (negotiating with marshmallows was no fun—where was your sense of victory?), but certainly no "bomber."

The term tickled her. *Bomber*: It was one of those jargon words, a kind of verbal shorthand that court buffs adopted and that had filtered down to the general public as signifying the more flamboyant members of the matrimonial bar. Thus Raoul Felder was a bomber. Marv Mitchelson. Richard Golub. The ultimate bomber had to be Willi Shannon, whose white Rolls-Royce bore the license plate SPLIT.

Dani had seen the car, but not the man. Like everyone else, she followed his exploits in the popular press, yet it was a hypothetical curiosity, it being doubtful she would ever grapple *mano a mano* with Shannon or any of his ilk. Her clients lacked both clout and wallet for such encounters.

Bombers represented movie stars. They represented real-estate tycoons, show girls who'd married up, socialites who'd married down, the rich and famous, the rich and infamous. Some had become celebrities in their own right, outshining their clients. Bombers enjoyed seven-figure incomes, yacht club memberships, press agents, private planes. Bombers received invitations to all the best dinner parties, where, if they were feeling expansive, they might regale their fellow guests with war stories worthy of a four-star general.

For combat was the mark of the dedicated bomber. Armed combat. Fierce, prolonged, costly, merciless, take-no-prisoners combat. His battle cry was *every last cent!*, though whether that last cent would wind up in the pocket of client or attorney was sometimes subject to dispute. And when the struggle was over, when the smoke of litigation had cleared, you could tell where he had been by the body count.

Dani had no desire to join their ranks, and if she had, it wouldn't have mattered. Bombers were universally male.

She did, however, wish to do well by her clients, which had brought her to Leo's door today. Leo was representing that "prominent-Park-Avenue-dentist" and gay deceiver, Ira Gessner.

"Welcome to Castle Dracula," he greeted her. "You ready for some coffee and horse trading?" Then he ushered her into his shabby conference room.

Two Styrofoam cups had been set out amid a welter of documents, along with a carafe of instant coffee, a jar of Pream and a bag of Dunkin' Donuts. Dani stifled an impulse to test the surface for dust before pulling up a chair.

"That's what I love about coming here, Leo. You put out such a fabulous spread."

"Better than that decaf crap at Pruitt-Baker."

"Our coffee may disappoint," she conceded, "but we give good Danish."

The two lawyers exchanged conspiratorial smiles. They were comfortable with each other and, within the clubbiness of the matrimonial bar, considered themselves friends as well as occasional adversaries.

Dani sipped her brew, munched a cruller and considered giving Leo a nice set of mugs for Christmas. They finished their coffee, then Leo spread open a folder on the table. Dani opened her brief-case and followed suit.

"*In re Gessner v. Gessner,*" Leo began, "this one should be a quickie. My client is willing to pay your client's legal fees—within reason, of course—plus he's offering her a magnanimous settlement. Far exceeding my recommendations, I might add, but the good dentist just wants out of there fast. Your Mrs. G is one lucky lady."

Dani shrugged. "That depends on your definition of luck. Okay, Leo. Let's get on with it. I've got a net worth statement plus a list of joint assets. Let's see how it stacks up against yours."

They began comparing notes.

As usual, Dani's first order of business was the quest for hidden funds. She never ceased to be amazed at the ingenuity of wayward spouses when it came to making money disappear. Brokerage ac-counts under dummy names. Secret safe-deposit boxes. Undeclared tips, fee payments taken in cash. So-called creative accounting.

"You mean to tell me," she charged a garment industry exec, "that you support two homes, a girlfriend and a Mercedes 300SL on an income of forty thou a year? What's your secret?"

"Careful management," came the reply.

That case had been a lulu, requiring private detectives, a flock of CPAs, the services of the firm's tax department and extended litigation. "A genuine money spinner," Jack Pruitt had conferred his approval. "More of those."

Gessner v. Gessner held out no such promise. Far from concealing his financial situation, Dr. Gessner had laid himself bare. Every nickel was accounted for, every last share of stock. As Leo had said, "a quickie." In and out, short if not sweet, which was fine with Dani who worked on straight salary. And afterward, no blood on the ground. Nothing but the "lucky lady's" tears.

"A lot of money here," she remarked, "but let's try and keep it simple. One from Column A, one from Column B, so to speak. I don't want to drag this out. My client's hurting."

"Fine with us," Leo said.

They began assembling figures. At one point, Leo put down his calculator, noted a subtotal and scratched his head. "Maybe I should give up all this law shit and switch to root canals."

"Dentist to the stars, his wife tells me. Gets a thousand bucks a crown."

Five cups of coffee later, the broad outlines of an agreement began to emerge.

"Let's take a break," Leo said. He stood up, stretched, touched his toes ten times in quick succession, then sprawled into his chair.

"So what do you think, Dani? Is this pretty much what your client had in mind—halvesies, plus she gets marital home and contents?"

"Jesus," Dani groaned, thinking of Linda Gessner's blitzed-out eyes. "She doesn't have anything in mind. My bet is she'll do what I advise her."

"The ideal client."

Dani frowned. "Would you believe she didn't have a clue about her husband's sexual proclivities? Not a clue! She's such a conventional soul, poor thing. Even now, she can't bring herself to say the F-word."

"F for fairy or F for fuck?"

"Whichever," Dani replied. "The whole thing came down on her out of the blue."

"Oh c'mon, Dani. You know better than that. Nothing ever happens out of the blue. She must have figured some kind of hanky-panky was going on. I mean, what kind of dentist has office hours at three in the morning? What did she think her Ira was doing? Filling cavities?"

Dani couldn't resist. "Well, he was, wasn't he? Filling cavities of a sort?"

Both lawyers laughed. Then Dani shrugged.

"You're probably right, Leo. She had to have an inkling. None so blind and all that jazz. Well, as they say, the wife is always the last to know. Still it's sad. Also weird. Gessner is pushing sixty, which is a little late in the day to come out of the closet. Is it male menopause or true love or what?"

"A bit of both, is my guess. And if you're thinking that Ira's been seduced by a black-leather hunk, you couldn't be wronger.

The new boyfriend is a middle-aged gent, thin on top. A city official, no less. He came to Ira for bridgework last winter, their eyes met over the dental tray and bingo! The earth moved." Leo gave a good-natured grin. "The two of 'em were here Wednesday, holding hands. It was kind of sweet."

"Well, it beats me. Here's this guy married thirty-odd years, good husband, good provider, respected in the profession. What made him jump the tracks?"

"Do I know?" Leo thunked the back of his hand against his forehead in a limp-wristed gesture. "I have the soul of a woman trapped in the body of a man. . . . Or however that line goes. I represent 'em, Dani. I don't psych 'em." He poured fresh coffee. "Okay, back to work. Basically, what does your client want?"

"She wants," Dani said, "to continue being Mrs. Ira Gessner. But since I gather that ain't in the cards, what say we start with the mutual funds. . . ."

A half hour later, they had roughed out a settlement. Leo was correct. The dentist had been liberal, handing over the lion's share of the estate. Half his pension plan. The house in Glen Cove. Plus, after some nominal wrangling, virtually all the household goods. She gets the Mercedes, he gets the Chevy. Yeah okay, she can keep the condo in Florida, he'll settle for the cottage in Maine. . . .

Jesus, Dani thought, *how desperately the son-of-a-bitch must want out of there*. In which case, she might winkle out a few more concessions. It was worth a try.

"We want a guaranteed annual income," she said.

Leo shook his head. "Share of earnings. We'd agreed."

"Well, I'm having second thoughts. Suppose Gessner decides to chuck his practice and take up batik or beachcombing? This is a guy who's already changed his lifestyle radically. If he does it again, what'll she live on?"

"For Chrissakes, Dani. Gimme a break! A, he loves his work. B, he can't afford to quit. And C, Linda Gessner is coming out of this with nearly two million dollars in assets. You want blood? If things are so tough, she can do what a million other women do in her situation. She can get a job."

"Oh yeah? What did you have in mind, Leo? Brain surgery? Formula One racing? Come off it, pal. This woman's only business skills are running raffles for the Sisterhood at the Temple. No way she can earn any kind of decent living. You know that's shit."

"You know it's shit and I know it's shit. But the court doesn't know it's shit. The court would say that we've made your client a spectacular offer. If anything, they'd knock it down by a third. I wouldn't play hardball on this if I were you, Dani. What are you gonna do—litigate?"

"Conceivably. We might seek divorce for fault. Cruel and inhuman et cetera."

"Sure." Leo nodded sagely. "Your little lady is going to stand up before a bunch of total strangers and testify . . . to what? That her husband got caught with his dick in the wrong aperture? That she's been living with a fag all these years? This from a woman who can't even handle the F-word? Be reasonable. Nobody wants to get into a pissing contest. . . ."

Leo was right, of course. And he had offered a nifty settlement, though she wouldn't give him the satisfaction of saying so.

She packed her briefcase, put on her jacket.

"Okay, Leo. Reasonable is my middle name. Naturally, we'll want our appraiser to evaluate his practice, but in the interim I'll put your proposal to my client. Chances are she'll go for it. It's very fair. Funny though, isn't it? All that structure, the home, the social life, the whole schmear. They raised three kids together and now it's all right out the window, just because some middle-aged guy gets caught up in a dream."

"Never underestimate the power of fantasy," Leo said, escorting her out. "It's the most potent fuel in the world."

He stopped, lobbed an imaginary baseball toward an equally imaginary home plate at the end of the hall. "You know what my pet fantasy is? To be relief pitcher for the New York Yankees and save their ass in a World Series playoff. Forty-eight years old and still clinging to the dream."

Dani laughed. "The way the Yanks have been playing, they need all the help they can get. Don't despair."

"How about you, Dani? What's yours?"

She put her hand on the door. "My pet fantasy? Don't know as I have one."

"Balls! Everybody's got one. You mean to say you're the one

person in creation who has everything they want out of life? There's gotta be something eating away at you, something wacky and wild."

Dani racked her brains. Her wish list included any number of items. A second bathroom. A holiday in Bermuda. An Armani suit. That Ted should find a new job. That Samantha should lose twenty pounds. But those were wishes, not fantasies.

"To make partner at Pruitt-Baker . . ."

"By you that's a fantasy?" Leo broke in.

". . . without working the hundred-hour week."

Leo considered. "Yup, that's a fantasy."

She emerged in the late-afternoon sunshine, bumptious with success, having just cut a doozy of a deal. It being too early to go home, too late to go back to the office, she decided on a stroll through the streets of the Village.

Once upon a time, she and Ted had lived in this neighborhood. Their first apartment had been a third-floor walk-up on Christopher Street, notable for its cockroaches and ten-foot ceilings. She missed those ceilings.

Remarkable, she thought, how the area had kept its character. Leafy streets where nothing rose above four stories, little bookstores crowded with youthful browsers, craft shops, small cafés. It looked essentially unchanged. More expensive, of course, but what wasn't these days? Yet the landmarks had hung in there. She fought down a sense of déjà vu.

With a spring in her gait, she strode past the Circle in the Square, Minetta's Tavern, the good old Peacock Café. What a treat that place used to be! If she hadn't coffee'd out at Leo's, she would have popped in for espresso and cannoli. For old time's sake.

Instead, she turned down 8th Street and peered into shop windows. Maybe she'd buy a little something to celebrate.

FELINDA'S FANTASY

Now there was a stopper. Lingerie—but such lingerie! Fragile wisps of chiffon and sequins, peekaboo panties and bras. Who wore such stuff? she wondered. Hookers? Yet the boutique bore none of the tackiness of the Times Square emporia. It had an elegant air.

Who wore this stuff? Dani answered her own question. Those who indulged in the occasional fantasy. Never underestimate its power, Leo had said.

He was right. The world was full of fantasists, ordinary folk succumbing to fervid private dreams. Dr. Gessner, remaking his life on a romantic impulse. Kaycee's mother (currently in China) hotly pursuing passport stamps. Even Ted, still mooning over a tropical paradise that had never really existed except in his head. Yes, even Ted.

She looked in the window and furrowed her brow.

Imagine Ted's reaction if he came home tonight and found her waiting for him, togged out in nothing but a half ounce of see-through chiffon and a couple of pasties! Especially after a day with El Swino. Why, he'd love it! He'd laugh and love it. The lingerie was so erotic, so off the wall. So very un-Maidenform! She stepped inside.

"I don't normally do this sort of thing," she was about to explain, but the saleswoman—a tall, athletic creature who looked as though she belonged in the social notices of the Sunday *Times*—let Dani browse in peace.

Gingerly, Dani picked up a bikini set and held it against the light. Never had she seen its like. A whisper made of peacock feathers and satin ribbon, the iridescent minimum. A swirled feather barely covered each nipple, while a single peacock "eye" concealed the pubes. Sixty dollars for the bra, forty for the panties. Dani gasped. Good fantasy didn't come cheap.

But these weren't articles of clothing. They were aphrodisiacs. Love potions for the weary male eye.

The saleswoman came over. "Gorgeous, isn't it? We just got that in this morning."

"Gorgeous!" And unspeakably sexy. "You don't think . . . ?"

Dani paused, thrilled and faintly embarrassed. "Question is, how do you care for a garment like this?" She couldn't picture bringing it in to her dry cleaners.

The woman smiled. "Well, they're not constructed for everyday wear. I predict that once the man in your life sees how fabulous you look, he'll have it off you in thirty seconds flat."

Dani left the shop a hundred dollars poorer, then compounded the crime by splurging on a cab.

All the way uptown, she rode in a state of pleasant anticipation, feeling soft and feminine. Tonight when Ted got home, she'd be waiting at the door, freshly bathed and scented, peacock-feathered, irresistibly sexy. By God! she couldn't wait to see his face. Thirty seconds. After which, they'd tumble into bed. Like in the old days.

Shrewd old Leo was absolutely right. Everybody needed a touch of fantasy now and again.

To her chagrin, he was home when she got there, sitting in the big black Barcalounger. Suit jacket on, striped tie still tied. He looked tired and pale and endearing and curiously formal.

"What's up?" she asked. "El Swino let you out early?"

So much for her big surprise, she thought, faintly annoyed. Worse yet, his eyes seemed fixed on the little lavender bag. No chance of keeping Felinda's Fantasy a secret.

"So how was your day?" she asked. "I know, I know . . . hot and hectic. I thought you had a staff meeting at five."

He was still staring at the idiotic package, mesmerized. Dani blushed.

"You won't believe what I just bought, sweetie." She clutched the package, trying not to sound foolish. "But don't call me nuts until you see it on."

He raised his head and almost, but not quite, met her eyes. "Please sit down, Dani." You'd think he hadn't heard a word she'd said. "I've something to tell you."

His voice was hoarse, strained. She wondered if he'd been drinking. She sat down on the sofa opposite, Felinda's Fantasy beside her, and waited politely for him to begin.

Something was wrong here. The way he was perched on the edge of his chair like a bird poised for flight. His fists were clenched, she noticed, the knuckles white. There was a fine band of sweat across his forehead. Why didn't he take his jacket off if he was hot?

The stance was familiar, yet unfamiliar. Ted, yet not Ted. Like one of those trick pictures on cereal boxes: Find twelve things wrong with this drawing. Only Dani couldn't put her finger on what was awry. *Relax, honey,* she was tempted to say. *Make yourself at home.*

He pursed his lips, but didn't speak, didn't move. He simply sat there immobile, eyes focused at some distant spot behind her shoulder. Dani turned to see what had engaged his attention, but nothing looked out of place.

She could no longer endure his silence.

"Ted, honey . . . tell me what's the matter. Did you lose your job? Are you sick or something? You look so peculiar."

His mouth began working, but nothing came out. She felt a wave of nausea.

"Did someone die? Oh my God!" she cried. "Something's happened to Samantha!"

His mouth formed an *O.* No.

"Thank God!"

Her mind flew all over the place. Did this, conceivably, concern Barney and Kaycee? Maybe they were splitting up. But would Ted take that so hard? Of course he would; he was so close to them both.

"Does it have to do with the Feldmans?" she asked. "I saw Barney confiding in you the other Sunday. I gathered something was amiss. What is it, Ted?" She started to yell. "For Christ's sake, talk to me!"

He cleared his throat, twice in fact, though he avoided her eyes. And when he spoke, his words came from across a great distance.

"No," he muttered. "Barney wasn't confiding in me. I was confiding in him. I told him. . . ." He cleared his throat again. "It's over, Dani. Finished. I hate this life. I hate my work. I hate this city. . . ."

The words were coming faster now, in an uninflected drone. So fast that Dani could hardly keep up with them. They scudded by her at the speed of sound, then disappeared in a mysterious void far beyond.

"I want out . . . ," that muffled voice was saying. ". . . can't live this life . . . can't stand the lies . . . sorry. . . ."

Dani's ears shut. Her mind froze. She felt herself being enveloped in a sea of cotton wool. Everything was happening a thousand miles away. To somebody else. In a movie. A play.

". . . don't want to hurt you . . . unendurable . . . sorry . . . God, sorry. . . . Gotta get out. . . ."

He's gone crazy, Dani thought. Ted Sloane has gone and had himself a nervous breakdown. He was talking gibberish. Get out? Out of what?

Out of work! That's it, he'd been fired. Only that didn't make sense. El Swino adored him. He must have quit. Yes! that was it. Ted had quit Globexx on an impulse and now he was petrified. She struggled through the layers of cotton wool trying to grasp his meaning, but she could only catch the odd word, the isolated phrase.

". . . waited . . . Samantha went off to college . . . sorry. . . ."

Now that made no sense at all. Of course Samantha had gone off to college. Everybody knew that. What did her going have to do with the price of beans? There was nothing to be sorry about. Kids went to college all the time.

Yet on and on the man rambled, spewing out disjointed nonsense, one absurd sound bite after another.

". . . can't go on this way . . . had it with everything . . . live in Mexico . . . a kibbutz. . . ."

Jesus God! How did Mexico get into this? They didn't have kibbutzes in Mexico. This was all—preposterous. Too unbearable to think about.

Her mind refused to cooperate; her thoughts scattered in a dozen different directions. That suit should go to the cleaners. His beard was coming in gray. Funny she hadn't noticed it before. Maybe they should send out for pizza tonight. Pizza was so comforting, like nursery food.

". . . utterly wretched . . . didn't want to do this. . . ."

Do what? Okay, Ted was unhappy. Well, she knew he was unhappy and was trying to help. Always had. Done everything within her power. Just spent a hundred bucks on peacock feathers, for Christ's sake, which was probably unreturnable.

". . . coming on for a long time. . . ."

She tried to focus, but how do you focus on such wild talk? Okay, she thought. He's unhappy. Confused. Maybe if they got that weekend place in the country he'd feel better. Or a dog. Or if he took up a musical instrument. Now there was a neat idea!

Music soothes . . . calms! If only he'd stop this idiotic babble. It was making her dizzy.

". . . fifty-fifty . . . hate hurting you . . . never want to hurt you . . . thinking about leaving for months. . . ."

Leaving? Leaving? What the hell was that all about? He couldn't possibly leave. He had books out on loan from the library. You couldn't leave New York unless you'd returned your library books. Leaving? Would someone tell her where? When? Good Lord, they had six people coming for dinner on Saturday night, including the Damaceks and that couple from Rye he liked so much. She was making bouillabaisse. Maybe she should cancel. No . . . no . . . Ted'll be fine by Saturday. And next Wednesday—well, next Wednesday they had tickets for chamber music at Lincoln Center. No way he'd miss the opening of the concert season—not after having paid for orchestra seats.

Funny, though, his expression just then. An uncanny mix of the strange and the familiar. She couldn't figure it out.

". . . hate myself . . . end of the tether . . . forgive . . . new life . . . start all over again . . . divorce. . . ."

His voice trailed off.

Divorce?

Dani sat up. At last—a word that registered, a term she knew. "Divorce?" she yelled. "What the hell are you talking about? Who's getting divorced? We have six people coming to dinner Saturday night. What's the matter with you?"

Then suddenly, she had a revelation. She knew. She knew in her bones why the look of him had puzzled her so. Why she'd found it familiar and strange all at once. Familiar because it was her husband. Strange because that look had no place in this house. In this room. Had nothing at all to do with Ted Sloane.

She recognized the look. By God, she knew it well. The glazed eye, the white-knuckled clench, the tension etched around the mouth. She had observed those stress signs a hundred times, but not here. Never here. She had seen them in her office, in the pale faces across her desk.

But this was no client sitting before her, no fee-paying stranger. This was the man she loved. Her Ted. Her sad, crazy, darling Ted who was more wretched than she'd ever imagined. This was Ted Sloane, the best of the good guys, and he was having a breakdown.

That knowledge ripped through the web of cotton wool, restoring Dani's voice, her clarity.

The poor man. My poor poor darling! What a state he must have fallen into, even to think such dreadful things. She felt an adrenaline jolt.

"Oh God, Ted. I'm sorry. I had no idea you were so . . . so miserable, so distressed. Let's try and work this through sensibly. I realize you've been going nuts at Globexx, all that pressure. And believe me, I feel for you. Maybe you should change therapists. Or if you want, we could both go to a marriage counselor, although I'm not convinced that's where the problem lies. But I'm willing . . . whatever I can do to help you. As for any talk of divorce, what can I say? Don't even mention the word, even as a joke. We've got a good marriage going here, you and I. A wonderful life."

He didn't acknowledge a word she'd said. Didn't meet her eyes. He had moved into a separate world.

She leaned forward, wanting to seize him, to grab him by the shoulders and shake some sense into the man. She wanted to slap him. Hit him. Anything to provoke a reaction.

She put her hand on his sleeve. He recoiled at her touch. Then, finally, his eyes met hers.

"Maybe you call it a good marriage, Dani. I don't. Maybe you were happy. I wasn't. Can't I get it through your head? It's over. We're through. I'm leaving."

He said more, much more that night. Bombarded her with charges, revelations, complaints, apologies, but Dani blocked the words out, neither hearing nor grasping. Her brain had shut down in protest.

Part Two

Part Two

10

JACK PRUITT ambled past her office, peered inside, did a Marx Brothers "take," rolled his eyeballs, checked his watch, rolled his eyeballs again.

"Do I have the wrong day or am I hallucinating? If I didn't know better, I'd say that was Dani Sloane actually gracing our humble premises on a—yes, by God, a Saturday afternoon. You led me to believe that working weekends was against your moral principles."

Dani looked up from the papers piled on her desk and glared back. "Ha Ha," she said.

He sidled in and plunked down in the vacant chair.

"I hardly ever get to talk to you, you keep such a low profile. So, Dani, what's on your plate these days? You making money for the firm? Fill me in." He riffled through the stack of files, picked one at random, wrinkled his nose. "*Jehanger v. Jehanger.* Am I pronouncing that right? What's the story?"

"Husband wants to take the kids to Pakistan, says they're his under Islamic law. She wants sole custody."

Jack frowned. "Do these guys have any money?"

"He runs a newsstand. I'm applying for Legal Aid."

"Terrific. *Bowes v. Greist?*"

"That's a funny one. Ms. Bowes is suing her live-in boyfriend over possession of a lottery ticket. He won six grand, she's claiming it's communal property. Not a lot of dough involved, but an interesting question of law."

"I'm sure the Supreme Court can't wait to make a ruling. Moving on, *Lockney v. Lockney.*"

"We represent the husband. The guy's been on the street since Drexel folded; I've filed to get his maintenance reduced. The hearing's Thursday."

"If he can't pay for his kids, how's he gonna pay his legal fees, or shouldn't I ask? You sure do pick 'em. What have we here? *Gessner v. Gessner.* Oh yeah, the dentist fella. You know what the five most expensive words in the language are? 'These teeth can be saved.' " Jack laughed at his own joke. "And they say lawyers are bloodsuckers. Actually, my wife's been going to Gessner for years. He fixed her bite, cost me a fortune. Is this our chance to bite back?"

"Yup. We got the retainer up front. It'll be easy money."

Pruitt nodded. Nothing soothed his chronic dyspepsia like a swift and profitable settlement, except, perhaps, the prospect of prolonged and even more profitable litigation.

"What'd the good drillmeister do, by the way—get caught with a tootsie?"

"Something like that," Dani said, then seized the chance to grab some credit where due. "I managed to cut Mrs. Gessner one beautiful deal. The house, the furniture outright, plus fifty percent of all other assets. She's going to walk away a wealthy woman."

"Good good. And let's hope she spreads the word among her galfriends in Glen Cove. You could do with a few more rich-bitch clients. So you took him to the cleaners, did you?"

"Yeah, well . . . she's entitled."

"Ah, *les girls, les girls!*" Jack made a sound halfway between a snort and a snicker. "Nothing like watching the female establishment gang up against the wandering male. A veritable spider's feast."

Dani considered throttling him, decided against it.

"The woman's in her fifties," she said between clenched teeth. "Hardly one of *les girls.*"

"Jesus, aren't we the sensitive creatures!" he slapped the folders down on her desk with a crisp smack. "You know what your problem is, Dani? You can't take a joke."

No—she scowled at his departing back—*that isn't my problem.*

Dani buckled down to work, though it was increasingly hard to concentrate. Being in the office on Saturday was like visiting a foreign country. She felt ill at ease, disoriented. The air-conditioning was off, the switchboard unmanned, voices echoed down the corridor. The place even smelled different.

Notwithstanding, there were a dozen or so bodies about. The jobaholics (Jack Pruitt among them), assorted yuppies on the partnership track, paralegals putting in for overtime, a secretary, a kid from the mail room. Who says the work ethic is dead?

Or maybe it wasn't the work ethic. Granted, it was a rotten afternoon, wet and cold, prime time for clearing up paperwork, but still . . . ! *Don't these people have anything better to do? Don't they have private lives?*

Then it struck her. These Saturday journeymen—so busy filing, photostating, researching—were largely making work where none existed. They were fugitives. Displaced people. Just like her. For if, as the saying went, home is where you go when there's no place to go, then conversely, the office is where you go when you didn't want to go home.

Dani's coming in was an act of cowardice. It spared her having to cope with the phone. Friends, family, acquaintances—no telling who would ring up on weekends, not one of whom knew about the sudden change of circumstances. Thus far, Dani had kept Ted's departure a secret, but the prospect of making small talk was terrifying.

"So what's new, Dani?" The most routine question in the world. How could she answer? And God forbid people should call asking for Ted. It was all so—humiliating!

The morning after Ted's "panic attack," as she had come to define it, Dani canceled the week's social engagements. Excuses ranged from "a touch of flu" to "the old tennis elbow acting up." She took pains to avoid anything so serious as to encourage drop-in visitors bearing chicken soup. Just enough to keep friends at bay.

Her Saturday night dinner guests were told that Ted had been unexpectedly called away on business. (Which was true in a way, since the monstrous Globexx was more or less directly responsible for the status quo.)

"Yes, I'm sorry too," she told Nancy Damacek. "I was planning to make the most gorgeous bouillabaisse. We'll do it another time, promise." Then she phoned up Rosedale's Market to cancel the fish order. It was her last outgoing call.

There was no reason to sound the alarm over what was nothing more than a nasty incident, a temporary glitch. Instead, she took the advice she tendered clients: Least said, soonest mended.

Maybe later, when things blew over, she'd confide in a few select friends—"Ted and I had a wee crisis last fall"—and the "wee crisis" would enter the realm of anecdote. At present, however, she didn't feel like talking to anyone who mattered. Didn't feel like talking to anyone, period.

Not to Kaycee, who had phoned repeatedly, leaving a slew of cryptic messages. Definitely not to Kaycee. That Ted should have divulged his (their?) most intimate secrets to Barney Feldman, and by extension to her closest friend, was bad enough. That he had done so without consulting Dani was mind-boggling. The whole business smacked of disloyalty, though whose she wasn't sure.

And the last person she wanted to speak to was the author of all this misery. Talk to Ted Sloane? Hell, she didn't even want to think about him. He had phoned half a dozen times since Hell Night, leaving a number where he could be reached. A hotel, she presumed. Who cared?

The first time she heard his voice, deep and disembodied, on the answering machine, it spooked her. Dani fled to the bathroom, hands clapped over her ears. Afterward, she went for a long walk, in case he phoned again.

"Let him worry," she muttered as she marched down Second Avenue. The man had behaved abominably. He could sweat it out until she was good and ready. Meanwhile, it was easier not to pick up the phone.

The one caller she dared not hide from was Samantha, who might worry if no one answered. Fortunately, however, her daughter, full of herself as only a raw freshman can be, let the days slip by without ringing home. "Once they go to college they never phone except for money," friends had warned her. Dani was grateful for the lapse. Still, the prudent course was to be out of the house as much as possible.

So here she was on this Saturday afternoon, pushing papers when by rights she should have been scrubbing clams, deveining shrimp and preparing for a dinner party.

Well, cleaning seafood was grunt work anyhow, she told herself. The smell got under your fingernails and lingered for days. Yet a sense of disappointment prevailed.

Now that she did it so rarely, cooking was no longer a chore but a hobby, like tennis or sailing, a means of physical release. The bouillabaisse recipe, clipped from *Gusto* magazine and pinned to the refrigerator door, had teased her for months. Everything about it was a challenge. The hunt for ingredients (a fishmonger who stocked sea eel and rockfish), the strategic decisions (blender or mortar and pestle?), the ultimate plunge into the unknown: all required planning, concentration, nerve and verve.

From midday on, in the normal course of events, the apartment would be fragrant with Provençal herbs. Then, around six, she and Ted would pull out the dining table, put in the extra leaves, polish glasses. Out would come the best china, the wedding-present silver. She was always a bit nervous just before dinner parties, like an actress on opening night.

Then curtain up, as the guests arrived, festive and hungry. The apartment would grow hot, happy, noisy with drinks and small talk, leading up to that dramatic moment when, amidst a chorus of approval, Dani produced the steaming bouillabaisse in that lovely Portuguese tureen Ted's parents had given them for Christmas last year.

And it would taste as good as it looked. In her mind's eye, she could see herself basking in compliments, dishing out seconds. In all the world, was there a more civilized pursuit than the dinner party? Good food, good talk, good friends. The sense of being beloved.

Dani sighed. It had killed her to cancel. No, not cancel, she corrected herself. Postpone. For Dani was determined to view recent events in a positive light. Ergo:

It was a relief (a) not to have to cook today and (b) not to have to clean up the mess tomorrow morning. Dinner parties were a helluva lot of work whereas being temporarily single—well, it was like being let out of school for the summer. No more homework. You're on vacation, kid.

The notion of a holiday had first surfaced Wednesday morning as she sat in Superior Court waiting for the judge. He was late; Dani couldn't care less. She sat there doodling, drifting, mood poised between the freewheeling and the irresponsible. She was on vacation, kid. A vacation from marriage. The more she thought about it, the more sense it made.

After a zillion years of living in each other's pockets, in each other's hair, of never spending a night apart (except when she was in the hospital having Samantha, and that didn't count), after two decades of Siamese twinness, of unbroken tandem, Mr. and Mrs. Ted Sloane had decided on a brief respite from each other.

There was nothing untoward about it. Indeed, separate vacations were as much a civilized institution as, say, the Saturday night dinner party. Many couples enjoyed them on a regular basis, and their marriages fared none the worse. Probably better, Dani ventured, since everyone alive had to come up for air on occasion. In which case, the savvy course would be to relax and enjoy it.

That first night on her own—not Hell Night (which she steadfastly refused to remember). That night had been a disaster, with Dani weeping buckets, Ted storming out of the house with a flight bag. No, not Hell Night, but the following one. To repeat, on her first full solo night, Dani's mood had been almost euphoric.

She had soaked in the tub for an hour, then climbed into bed with a box of Cheezits and watched *The Razor's Edge* on cable TV. What a movie! Tyrone Power seeking mystic fulfillment, Gene Tierney seeking Tyrone Power. Paris, the Riviera, those slithery gowns by Adrian. Dani wallowed in it. Had Ted been there, he would probably have made snide remarks from the sidelines. Okay, so it was a woman's picture. She was a woman, wasn't she? Did every movie have to be in French with subtitles?

"Bliss," she mumbled with a mouthful of Cheezits, "and let the crumbs fall where they may."

Which happened to be on his side of the bed.

Dani stayed up until two-fifteen, riveted.

The following evening, she stretched out on the living room sofa with an ancient Agatha Christie. ("How can you read that crap?" Ted would have said), then at midnight sent out for pizza—"with pepperoni, anchovies, mushrooms, the works." The pizza was lovely, greasy, a cholesterol high. Dani devoured it straight from the carton, licking her fingers as she ate.

My self-indulgence knows no bounds, she said to herself, mightily pleased.

On Friday, she drew up a list on a legal pad: Benefits Of Being Single. The number astonished her.

To begin with the obvious: The place was hers, every inch of it. She could bunk down in either bedroom or on the sofa if she pleased. Could hog all the blankets and the hell with you. Conversely, she could stay up all night watching junk.

Oh, this brave new world teemed with unforeseen "coulds" and "why-nots," mostly pleasant. She could (she noted):

Put her feet up on the coffee table.

Do her Linda Ronstadt imitation full voice.

Make a face. Pick her teeth. Bite her nails.

Leave hair in the sink, leave the ironing board out, leave the cap off the toothpaste, which drove Ted nuts. Dry her pantyhose on the living room radiator. So there!

Not that Dani would, necessarily, make that comfy descent to total slobdom. Years of cohabitation told against her. But the point was, she could. She was entitled.

As she was entitled to watch *Good Morning America* over breakfast or run the dishwasher at two in the morning. Sure, kid. And no question as to who would get first crack at the Sunday *New York Times*. Not only the crossword, you bet. The Arts and Leisure section too. All the way, baby! She could hardly wait for Sunday to roll around. Life Without Samantha and Ted.

On the debit side, come Sunday, there'd be no Sam to ooh-and-ah with over the fashion ads. No Ted to trot to the corner for bagels. But bagels were dispensable. Or she could buy a few and keep them in the freezer.

So you see, she argued, not all negatives were bad. Indeed some were positively beneficial. She jotted down those items whose absence constituted a boon.

No rock music emanating from Sam's bedroom. No Monday night football on TV. No mention of that boring Mort Ketchell. No listening to Ted grinding his teeth at three A.M. And that's just for openers.

By the time Dani had finished her accounting, all detailed memory of Hell Night had been banished. She and Ted were taking separate vacations. She intended to enjoy the freedom while it lasted. And maybe score a few Brownie points at work.

Dani stayed at the office until six that Saturday, grabbed a bite in a coffee shop, then headed for the discount ticket booth in Times Square. A lot of good plays were on twofers.

Twofers. Dani grimaced. A silly word! As though no one ever went to the theater alone. Still, there was no law against buying a single ticket at half price. Or full price. What the hell, even if she had to pay top dollar, she'd see a good show tonight and damn the expense. She was on vacation, right?

Her first impulse was to seek out something that Ted wouldn't care for, but that presented a problem. Their tastes were basically similar. Then she noticed that seats were available for *The Piano Lesson*.

Ted was dying to see it; he was a huge August Wilson fan. Fine, Dani thought. She wouldn't wait for His Nibs. She'd see it on her lonesome, best seat in the house. Then later, when this self-imposed vacation was over (another week or so at most), she'd manage to let drop that "I saw the Wilson play while you were doing your number. It was great! Well, how was I to know when you'd be coming back?"

And oh! wouldn't he be pissed off.

But when she got to the box office, she couldn't bring herself to do anything so petty, so damn mean. Instead, on impulse, she paid $100 to a scalper for a seat at *Phantom of the Opera*, secure in the knowledge that Ted loathed Andrew Lloyd Webber and if she didn't see it now, she never would.

Wrapped in the darkness of the theater ("a hundred dollars for a theater ticket. I must be nuts"), alone, anonymous, Dani gave herself over to the moment. It was grand fun, and she left whistling the tunes.

She got home to find all the lights in the apartment were blazing.

Dear Dani—the note on the coffee table said.

I just came by to collect a few things. Tried to phone but can't seem to reach you. Call me. We have to talk.

No signature. He had left a number. That was all.

In the bedroom, the closet door was ajar. Dani inspected the contents, gingerly opened dresser drawers, then checked the desk, the bathroom.

Ted had taken, not everything to be sure, but enough to be worrisome. Most of his good clothes, his laptop, his tennis racket, the two large suitcases. His terry-cloth robe from behind the bathroom door. He'd left his books, though, she observed with relief. The Ted she knew would never embark on a major life change without taking all his books and records. Never never never.

She shut the door and went into Samantha's room. Everything there was so neat, so orderly; the dresser cleared, the night table bare. So unnatural! Only a life-sized poster of Sting above the headboard gave testimony that this room had once been inhabited by someone she loved.

Dani turned off the light and stretched out on her daughter's bed.

The silence was oppressive. Never in Dani's life had she felt so alone. So lonely. She lay there aching, keening. She missed . . .

Oh yes, she missed the familiar clutter, the endless bustle, the banging of drawers, the clatter of Sam's little Olivetti typewriter, the mutter of late-night phone conversations carried on under the covers. She even missed the goddamned rock music. She missed—Sam!

"Oh baby!" Dani blinked back a tear. "What a ride you and I are in for."

Then she switched on the lamp and fetched a tattered pink terry robe from the hook in Sam's closet. It was a thoroughly disgraceful garment. ("I hope you're not going to take that antique with you to Oberlin," Dani had cautioned. And Sam had laughed. "It's all yours, Mom. Use it for dusting.")

Dani wrapped the robe around her, pulling the cord tight. It smelled faintly of Sam's favorite Charley cologne.

Then she lay down her head and fell asleep at Sting's feet.

11

THE BARBER CHAIR that dominated the den of the Feldmans' Central Park West apartment had been variously described
as an eyesore, a household joke, a charming bit of Americana, and
a high-priced antique.

"What a witty piece," a decorator friend once commented, stroking the worn red leather headrest. "And I love the brass fittings.
Where on earth did you get it?"

"It belonged to my father."

"Ah . . . was he a collector?"

"Nope. A barber on Tremont Avenue. I keep it around to remind
me that I still can make an honest living should the ad business
ever turn sour."

Having come up the hard way at Marsden Inc., Barney made
his mark "creating"—a word he loathed—a campaign for a line of
lingerie that became an instant classic. The first ad pictured a plump,
lovable grandma clad in a torrid red satin slip, staring into the
camera, arms akimbo. "So there!" she declared. "I did it and I'm
glad." Follow-ups featured a nun in a bright yellow teddie, a woman
cabbie showing a flash of peach pantyhose. Real Underwear for
Real People was the theme.

Like their originator, the ads were warm, funny, human, slyly
sophisticated. "And full of bullshit," Barney would add. He refused
to take the business seriously. "It's not as though you're designing

the Sistine Chapel." You could count on Barney to be the first to point out that the emperor was bare-assed, even if the "emperor" was chairman of the board. As a result, clients either loved him or hated him.

Ditto ex-wives, of whom Barney had two.

When in his teens, he had married his high school sweetheart. He and Ada stayed together for over twenty years and raised three children, the youngest of whom was a senior at Amherst. If asked what had gone wrong, Barney maintained a gentlemanly discretion, but Kaycee analyzed it as a classic case of "he grew, she didn't." The divorce had been bitter.

The second Mrs. Feldman was a top fashion model: "face of an angel, mind of a gnat." Both attributes were topped by a mass of golden hair requiring constant attention. Rowena Rance's self-absorption was complete.

"That hair!" Barney would laugh in retrospect. "Her life was an uphill struggle against split ends."

Their two years of marriage was almost devoid of conversation. "I couldn't make myself heard above the roar of the hair dryer. Would you believe I was out of the house for three weeks before she noticed?"

Then, by way of compensation, the gods had sent Kaycee knocking on his door. This, Barney said to himself, is the woman I want to grow old with. He loved her kookiness, her sense of adventure, the raggedy way she'd stumbled through life and not succumbed. He loved her Waspy good looks, her vulnerability, her way of looking at him as if he were the greatest guy who ever came down the pike.

With this third marriage, life started afresh. Barney overflowed with plans. He and Kaycee would stick it out in New York a few more years, work hard and get some money together (two divorces and three sets of college tuition having exacted their toll), after which he would kiss Madison Avenue good-bye and collect the rewards of a lifetime's labor.

"We'll travel," he rambled happily. "Sail the islands, take up golf, enjoy the good life, make love in the afternoon. Free as the birds, God bless 'em. I can hardly wait."

His only request, noted in their prenuptial agreement, was that Kaycee forgo children.

He had gone that route, he argued. "The whole bit, from the diapers and Pablum to tricycles to adolescent acne to putting three children through college. God knows I'm crazy about my kids, but enough's enough."

Kaycee was in no mood to quibble. She was pushing forty; motherhood scarcely seemed in the cards. She'd settle for Barney and "happily ever after," which was how things had turned out thus far.

One day, in the second week of her "vacation," Dani left the office to find Barney waiting in ambush.

"I have orders to take you home to dinner." He seized her arm. "Kaycee's waiting for you. Let's go."

"You should have called," she spluttered.

"We did, plenty. You should pick up your phone."

Dani was instantly suspicious. "If Ted's sent you as some kind of designated hitter . . ."

She couldn't think how to end the sentence, but Barney shook his head. "No one else will be there, just us three. Nothing fancy. Kaycee's making meat loaf."

That said, he half dragged, half pushed her out of the building and into a cab. Dani went without a struggle. Why not? She had nothing on for the evening beyond the video shop and a Stouffer's Lean Cuisine.

The last few days, she had been growing bored, restless. She missed Ted. In a way, it was a relief to let Barney carry her off. Making decisions, even ones as trivial as which movie to rent, had become a strain.

Kaycee's meat loaf was warm and comforting as nursery food. They washed it down with a couple of bottles of Beaujolais. Throughout dinner, the conversation had been bland, but Dani sensed a hidden agenda. Thus she wasn't surprised when Barney suggested coffee in the den. "Unless you'd rather have brandy."

"Will I need it?" she asked tentatively. "Coffee will be fine. Technically, I'm here under duress."

She settled into the couch, tucked her legs up under her. On the wall, a blowup of the gray-haired red-slipped grandma winked at Dani. "So there!"

Her host had taken the barber's chair and was trying to look avuncular, while Kaycee brought in a tray. Dani braced for the ordeal. Then the Feldmans exchanged glances and Barney, given his cue, cleared his throat and plunged in.

"Like Rimsky said to Korsakov, I suppose you're wondering why I've asked you here today."

His attempt at humor sank without a trace, followed by an awkward silence. He began again.

"What I'm trying to say, Dani, is Kaycee and I have been worried about the way you've been ducking, hiding out. It's not healthy. We've both been through this kind of situation ourselves and . . ."

"All we want to do is help," Kaycee piped up.

"Did Ted ask you to speak to me?"

Barney had the decency to look embarrassed.

Dani moistened her lips. "Thank you, I will have that brandy after all. And a little more coffee, please?"

She used the break to marshal her thoughts; foremost among them was resentment. True, the single life had begun to pall and she was ready to take Ted back into the fold. To forgive if not forget. She was lonely. She missed his company. It was no good saying "Wow! Did I have a day at the office!" to the image of Tom Brokaw on the Seven O'clock News. Besides, not thinking about Ted, her goal the past two weeks, required too much emotional energy. She loved her husband. She wanted him back. That was that.

What stuck in her craw was this third-party intervention. What was she—a child? An idiot? It was humiliating. Fond as she was of the Feldmans, they had no call to intervene in what was a strictly private dispute between the Sloanes.

Well, Dani was too old to run home crying to "father," which seemed to be Barney's self-appointed role. As for Kaycee, the idea of taking counsel from that source was absurd, given her friend's lifelong symptomatology of "man troubles." She couldn't help but feel resentful.

"I appreciate your concern, but I really don't require either a shoulder to cry on or a helping hand. In fact, I prefer not to discuss it. What's been happening is nobody's business but our own. However . . ."

As a courtesy to her hosts, she launched into the now familiar rationale: the Sloanes had had a minor tiff, a misunderstanding, they were taking a brief vacation from each other. As Kaycee and Barney made no comment, Dani quickened her pace. "However," she concluded, "when Ted's ready to talk, I'm ready to listen. He doesn't have to recruit any friends to run interference. All he has to do is phone me direct."

This time, the glances Kaycee and Barney exchanged were laced with alarm.

"Or drop a note," Dani said crisply. "Or come around to the house. He has feet, he has keys. It's not a federal case. And now I think I'll pop along home. Thanks for the dinner, it was super."

She tossed off her brandy and started going for her coat, when Barney jumped up, bellowing like a seal.

"Siddown!" he hollered. "Just siddown and stop lying to yourself. What is it with this vacation crap anyhow?"

Dani went white.

"I mean, please siddown, for Chrissakes." He lowered his voice to lecture-hall pitch. "You're going to have to hear this sooner or later, so you may as well hear it from people who love you. Do you have a clue about what's going on in Ted's life? Do you even know where he is?"

For a moment Dani had the crazy notion that the Feldmans had stashed Ted away in a back bedroom, that he was going to venture forth any second, like a character in those ditsy movies she'd been renting. Tadaaaa! Music swells . . . hearts beat wildly . . . then across a crowded room . . . Fred and Ginger. Hepburn and Tracy. Dani and Ted.

"Darling!" "Sugarpuss!"—the scenario plunges them together, as they embrace to a round of applause.

She looked at the Feldmans. Far from applauding, the pair looked grim as ghouls. She sat down.

Hold it! she wanted to tell them.

Hold everything while she ran away. Vanished into the last reel of the movie, that glossy land where all journeys end in lovers meeting, while the music plays on. Credits. End titles. Lights up.

"Well, Dani?" Barney was waiting for an answer.

"No." She blinked. "I don't know where Ted is, but you're

obviously going to tell me. And I'm sure I won't like what I hear. Let me spare you the agony. Ted's involved with some woman." The brandy had left a bitter taste. "You can tell me straight out, Barney. I'm a big girl now. He's been having an affair. Am I right?"

Barney nodded, relieved that she was being so sensible.

"That's very mature of you, taking it this way."

"I'm a very mature person."

Kaycee swiped at her eyes. "Actually, it's more than an affair, Dani. The thing is, he's fallen in love."

"In love," Dani said. "I see."

In love! IN LOVE???

The idea was obscene. Preposterous.

Naturally, the idea of Ted caught in some kind of amorous web had crossed Dani's mind. He might conceivably have said something about it That Night. Who could remember? Whenever the notion surfaced, she had struggled to suppress it as unworthy of Ted. But some nights, alone in the dark, she could almost admit the possibility. Almost.

Ted was a married man. Married men had affairs. Ergo, Ted was conceivably having an affair. She could grant that.

But in love? IN LOVE??? No way.

Had Ted been in love, she would have known it. You couldn't fool Dani. Hell, on the subject of Mr. T. J. Sloane, she happened to be the world's greatest living authority. Go ahead. Haul her up on some quiz show—only it wouldn't be Twenty Questions, more like Twenty Thousand Questions. You'd never stump her. Dani knew the topic inside and out.

She knew his belt size, his inseam size, his favorite songs, his corniest jokes, the way his eyes glazed over at family gatherings and the name of his fourth-grade teacher. She knew that aspirin made him break out in hives and how he liked his hamburgers (medium rare with a slice of Monterey Jack) and the kind of noises he made in the act of love. She could reel off his precise positions on every issue from the works of J. D. Salinger to the Shining Path rebels to big-league baseball salaries to what was the right way to mix a margarita. She knew his most trivial thoughts, his deepest convictions, his most heartfelt complaints. She knew the smell, the taste, the look, the touch, the length and breadth of the man. She knew where he'd left his keys when he himself hadn't a clue. That's how well she knew Ted Sloane.

So how, pray, could he fall in love without Dani's catching on? Falling in love was a spectacular act. It entailed pain, joy, emotional turmoil. You couldn't disguise such things from your wife. Not if you were Ted Sloane, who happened to be the least artful of men.

Unhappy, yes. She'd known he'd been unhappy for quite some time. It had been the subject of endless discussions last spring. But in love? IN LOVE???

Gimme a break!

What had happened was this. Simple. Ted Sloane had "put his dick in the wrong aperture" as Leo Margulies had remarked of Dr. Gessner. He had "shacked up with a tootsie" in Jack Pruitt's lexicon. He was—choose your terms—having a roll in the hay, a bit on the side; getting his ashes hauled, his rocks off, his meat massaged; doing the dirty; discharging his overload; indulging in hanky-panky; enjoying a fling, a quickie, a flier; grabbing some nookie; involved in an extramarital adventure. Couch it in vulgarisms or euphemisms, it came down to pretty much the same thing. Ted was in the grip of a temporary aberration. Dani supposed she could live with that fact till it blew over. But in love? IN LOVE???

The earth opened beneath her feet.

"I see," she said. "Fallen in love. When was this?"

"Quite a while ago"/"Very recently" came the simultaneous answers.

"Mmmm . . . mmmmh!" Dani nodded. "And how long have you two known about it?"

This time there was no answer at all.

"Terrific." She took a deep breath. "Well, I may as well hear the gory details. Look"—for Kaycee was crying—"let's just get it over with. I promise not to froth at the mouth or get hysterical. I'm familiar with these situations. There's nothing you can tell me I haven't heard a million times. I happen to be a divorce lawyer, remember? So . . . who is she? How did they meet?"

Ted had noticed her one morning on the picket line at Globexx. A young woman, pert-faced and skinny with red flyaway hair, bundled up against the April chill in a ski jacket. She was carrying a placard almost as big as she was. I WEEP FOR WHALES, it said. Cute, he thought. The girl, not the sign. She was still there, half frozen, when he went out to lunch. She must have smiled. He smiled back.

"What's a nice guy like you doing working for a lousy company like this?" she teased.

"I keep asking myself the same question."

They both laughed and wound up having lunch at a nearby coffee shop.

Ted had no mind for a flirtation, not at first. Jen—her name was Jen—struck him merely as a nice young person who cared keenly about the environment. But she was sweet, appealing. "Fresh" was the word that sprang to mind. She laughed at all his jokes, which made him feel worldly. And though lunching with a picketer meant consorting with the enemy, the experience had charmed him sufficiently to repeat it the following noon. Soon, they fell into a routine.

"I missed you yesterday," she said one Friday morning.

He wanted to say, *I missed you, too*, which was absurd on the face of it. Already this "girl" had got a clutch on his heart. "I was in Washington writing a speech for El Swino."

"Oh, I thought maybe you'd been canned."

"No such luck."

"Well, if you feel that way, why don't you just up and quit? After all, it's only a job."

He smiled, "Life's not that simple, Jen."

"Oh, but it is." She placed her hand on his. "Life is as simple as you want to make it."

The day they became lovers was a revelation, a watershed in Ted Sloane's midlife.

As a first-time philanderer, he had anticipated being riddled with guilt, shame. But his relief was greater than his guilt, as though a hundred-pound weight had been lifted from his shoulders. *This is what it's like to be born again*, he thought. To be the man he once was: young, ardent, hopeful, passionate. To be free.

During those pre-Jen months of depression, of suffocation and despair, an old Peggy Lee song kept running through his head. Is that all there is? Only this? Nothing more? He'd resigned himself to that reality, but he had been wrong. There was more. Better. And though he suffered the intermittent twinge of conscience, he found solace in the notion that Dani didn't need him; Jen did. Nearly as much as he needed her.

In her arms, he rediscovered that part of him that he had mourned as lost forever. The prime part, the quintessential Ted Sloane. In her bed, he shuffled off the company hack, the conformist, the cut-from-cardboard straight man, and rediscovered that vision of himself he had left behind in Ecuador.

How glorious to find a woman who divined the romantic soul beneath the three-piece suit. A young and pretty woman, too. Who admired him, found him savvy and exciting. All this, plus sexual chemistry. How glorious to be crazy in love once more.

And yet . . . and yet. All that summer, Ted wrestled with his demons. "I can't just walk away from everything," Ted the Husband argued with Ted the Dreamer. "I have obligations. Responsibilities."

"But you've met them," his alter ego was quick to reply. "You've been a faithful husband, a conscientious father, a good provider. You've kept your nose to the grindstone, your shoulder to the wheel. You've paid your dues for twenty years, so what's holding you back?"

"There's my wife."

"She's an independent woman."

"And my daughter."

"She's off to college in the fall. Don't you see, they don't need you anymore? Time's running out, old buddy. You may never have another chance. Smarten up. You think you're gonna live forever? You think being happy is a cardinal sin?"

All those months, those years when he had felt himself drowning, dying, going down for the last time, he had accepted his fate. And here he was, being granted a reprieve. Freedom. Suddenly, a second chance at life was within his grasp. Every instinct said, "Grab it!"

Why, a man would have to be mad, blind, self-destructive to choose despair over joy. No, he told himself. This wasn't a second chance, it was his last one. Now or never.

"Choose life," Jen had pleaded. He chose life.

*   *   *

"So there we are," Barney concluded.

He had sketched out the bare bones. Dani had filled in the emotional blanks. It all made a kind of ghastly sense. "The thing is," Kaycee wept, "Ted's so happy. They both are, happy as clams."

"You mean you've seen them together?" Dani reared back in disgust.

"We went sailing."

"Aboard the *Fairweather*? My boat? Our boat? For God's sake, Kaycee, you're my oldest friend!"

Barney flew to his wife's rescue. "Blame it on me. I'm sorry, but Ted's an old friend, too. We can't just dump him. We love you, babe, we're on tap if you need us, but don't ask us to take sides. You'll be okay. Hell, you'll be fine. You are one strong capable resilient lady. If anybody knows how to roll with the punches, that's our Dani."

"Did Ted ask you to say that? That I was strong, capable, all that shit? No. Don't bother to answer."

Somewhere, down around her toes, a white hot ball of rage began to form. She fought it down. Later. Later there would be time to cry, to shriek, to curse, to howl with pain. Not here in front of Barney and Kaycee. Besides, she was (it said right there in the lifetime warranty) one strong capable resilient lady with a fierce sense of pride. All she asked was to be alone with her misery.

"Okay, Barney, be a messenger. Tell Ted I need a day or two to absorb all this; at the moment I'm reeling. Then he can call me and we'll talk. Now I really must go. I'm wiped out. Plus I'm drunk. No, lovey . . ." She rejected Kaycee's suggestion to spend the night with them. "I'll just grab a cab. One thing about this whole business, though, that absolutely flummoxes me. This girl, this Jen-person . . . With all the thousands of men who go in and out of the Globexx Building every day, what made her latch on to my husband?"

"She recognized him from a photo on your desk," Kaycee said. "It seems she used to be a client of yours."

"Red hair . . . big blue eyes? Oh my God, Jenny MacDougall." For a moment, Dani was too choked with anguish to think straight. *No more body blows*, she wanted to cry. *Let me up!* Instead, making a herculean effort (she was a strong, capable woman, right?), she managed a grisly smile. "Well, thank you, Kaycee. That makes my day complete. And thank you for dinner. Now I must be going. Please please . . . no scenes."

Kaycee stared in open-mouthed admiration.

"You're a wonder, Dani," she marveled. "You truly are. The way you're taking this, so . . . so graciously. If it were I . . ."

"But it isn't you, is it?"

12

WELL, HOW ABOUT THAT!

Dani stretched out on the bed feeling like a fish on a marble slab: gutted and bleeding and raw.

"How about that!" she said to the ceiling. "Am I blind or dumb or both or what? Unbelievable!"

Two people, one she loved and one she liked. Two people who hadn't so much as known each other one year ago had somehow met and conspired to destroy her. Correction: had met, "fallen in love" and conspired to destroy her.

Big Papa Bear Ted. Fragile little Jenny. Sober solid middle-aged Ted. Fluttery young Jenny-Jen-Jen. A couple so odd, so disparate, they might have come from different planets, for Christ's sake. Why were they doing this to her?

Dani tried to picture Ted and Jenny in a single frame. Couldn't. Then, after a while she could. Could envision them together, Ted's firm strong fingers cupping Jen's small pert breasts in an enveloping embrace. See the tan of his skin against the porcelain white of her flesh, the roughness of his beard against her cheek. He would slide his hands down her body past that tiny waist, over those narrow, delicate hips till they encircled her ass, then Ted's mouth would close about her nipples, licking . . . sucking . . .

Dear God! Dani sat up in bed. Don't even think of such horrors. Better, far better, to conjure up the lone pathetic image of Jenny

MacDougall when she had first walked into Dani's office, a little lamb, meek and lost.

She had been twenty-three then, going on fourteen. A pretty thing, small-boned and waiflike, with enormous blue eyes and milky skin—the kind that showed all the bruises.

One look and Dani waived her Surgeon General's warning. In this case, divorce appeared to be just what the doctor ordered.

"My husband will kill me if he finds out I've come here" were the first words out of her mouth.

Dani observed the marks on the throat, the tremor of the hands, the eyes like those of a trapped animal.

"It looks like he's been doing a pretty good job of it already. Well, that stops right now. You're safe here. Now take your time and tell me everything."

What followed was a tale both familiar and sordid. Wide-eyed secretary from the sticks, dashing investment banker, a courtship out of a fairy tale. But no sooner were they married than Prince Charming revealed his violent side. Dani noted it all for the record: the beatings, the sexual abuse, the torment. There were no children, thank God. Just this fragile Beauty and that Beast.

"He can have the money, the furniture, the apartment." Jenny had wept. "All I want is my freedom."

But Dani, fueled by moral dudgeon, was tenacious. "If you're not going to bring him up on criminal charges, at least hit him where he lives, in his wallet. Let him know he can't do this sort of thing with impunity."

Dani had fought tooth and nail in that case, though there were moments when she wondered who the opposition was: that scumbag MacDougall or the self-effacing Jenny. Sweet, soft, vulnerable Jenny who read Harlequin romances in the anteroom and wondered where she'd gone wrong.

"Stand up for your rights!" Dani insisted, though it took endless clucking and mothering until Jenny finally agreed. "Get what you're entitled to. Don't reward him for beating up on you. Once you show him you're not a professional victim, you'll feel better about yourself, believe me."

In the end, Dani prevailed to the tune of a two-hundred-thousand-dollar cash settlement.

"Take it." She thrust the check in Jenny's hand. "Go to college, start over, make something good of your life. This is your declaration of independence."

But it was easier filling Jenny's purse than mending her psyche. Even now, two years later, Dani could recall their final talk.

"I'll never marry again," Jenny had said. "I'm through with men. They're not worth the pain." It was the cry of the walking wounded.

"Oh now, Jenny . . . ! All men aren't like Alvin MacDougall, thank heavens. There are plenty of wonderful guys around."

Had Dani smiled at that point? Had she beamed down upon Ted's photo on her desk as living proof of manly virtue, an advertisement for marital bliss? She didn't recall, though she did remember ending the session on an upbeat note.

"Listen to Momma," she crooned. "Have I ever steered you wrong? You're young, Jen. Your whole life's ahead of you. When you're ready, you'll find someone else. Someone really nice."

And so she had. Jennifer MacDougall had found Ted Sloane.

How could you? Dani raged at the empty room. *You owe me!* she yelled into the void.

Waves of misery engulfed her. You couldn't suffer this much, she thought, and survive. Wherever she looked, the image of Jenny's face—big blue eyes, milky skin—illuminated the darkness, supernatural and full of menace. *How could you do this to me?*

Such duplicity. Such cruelty! Dani had been a rock, a shield, a second mother to that girl. One might honestly say she had saved Jenny's life.

Not that she'd expected any reward other than legal fees, but she had gone beyond the professional realm. She had offered her friendship.

The cynics were right. No good deed goes unpunished in this world.

For by now it was clear that Jennifer MacDougall had planned the seduction of Ted Sloane, and with more skill than Dani would have credited her for. She had staked out her victim, batted those big blue eyes and, in a single blow, destroyed a hitherto happy family.

That Ted had permitted himself to be caught in the trap was

also disgusting, but more comprehensible. Even bright men can be suckered.

In love? Infatuated was more like it. "Infatuated," Dani said to the ceiling. "Bemused, besotted, bewitched, like a goddamn schoolboy." A classic case of middle-aged angst. "Male menopause," she yelled at the mirror, "and don't you tell me there's no such animal!"

How could it be otherwise? How else explain that the man who knew Dani better than anyone else in the world, who had lived with her on terms of unparalleled intimacy, should now turn his back? How else account for such brutal, total rejection?

Was she a leper, a pariah? Was she some slimy creature, repellent to sight and touch, that had crawled out from a rock to befoul his landscape? She was the same old Dani. And he was bewitched.

To view Ted's action as anything other than temporary insanity was to grow limp with self-loathing.

Dani fell asleep exhausted and dreamed of being set upon by a pack of small feisty dogs with huge blue eyes.

When Ted phoned two days later, she started to blubber at the sound of his voice.

"How could you . . . !"

"Please," he said. "Don't cry. We can't talk if you cry. Shall I call back later?"

"I am not crying and fuck you!" She slammed down the receiver.

He called the next evening. They wrangled. Once more she hung up in a fury, disgusted both with him and herself.

And yet he persisted.

"Listen," he said, "we have to consider Samantha. She phoned me at the office yesterday, I didn't know what to say. Now I think the best way to deal with this is, we make a joint call to Oberlin and break the news together. Show her we're behaving like sensible adults."

"You break the news," Dani lashed out. "It's your news, not mine. Tell her you've moved in with your bimbo."

That time, Ted was the one who hung up.

He called back an hour later.

"Be reasonable," he said.

"I should be reasonable?" Her voice shrilled to supersonic. "Am

I the one who's been behaving like an asshole? Am I the one chasing after teenage tootsies?"

Slam! Bang!

He didn't phone over the weekend, but Monday he called. He sounded chatty, conciliatory. He talked about the weather and current events before coming to the point.

"So Dan, how're things going with you?"

"Okay," she said cautiously. "Dan," he had called her. The diminutive of a diminutive. Did she detect a pleading note therein? A tinge of longing? Was this the same old, good old Ted? "I'm surviving. What's on your mind?"

"I thought it would be nice if we had lunch later this week." He sounded downright friendly. "How about Thursday at Veneziano's on Fiftieth Street. You ever been there?"

"Nope." His request had caught her off balance.

"Me neither, but I understand they do great lamb. We're set then, Thursday at noon."

"What do you think it means?" She had phoned Kaycee the moment Ted got off the phone.

"He wants to get back together is my bet. Why else ask you out to lunch? Not that I've been privy to Ted's secrets lately. I've hardly seen him. To tell you the truth, I'm too pissed off at the way he's behaved. What a schmuck!"

"Yeah. . . ." Dani grew thoughtful. "I suppose so. So you think it bodes well, his calling like that?"

"Well, you'll find out soon enough, won't you?"

Dani hung up to spend a good hour parsing every word of Ted's invitation, like a scholar mulling the Dead Sea Scrolls. It was a text dense with mysteries.

Why lunch? She wondered. Because lunch was a civilized meal? Because lunch implied a time limit? Because lunch was usually a one-drink affair? Because Blue Eyes couldn't spare him for dinner? Or because Ted didn't trust himself to be alone with Dani in the apartment?

Anyhow, what kind of lunch did he have in mind? Business or social? Either way, his preference for lunch over dinner was significant.

So too was Ted's choice of restaurant. Not one of their usual haunts, but neutral territory, a place devoid of personal overtones. It could hardly have been a random decision, but did that augur ill or otherwise? And what was the deeper significance of his choosing Veneziano's, which was large and reputedly fancy? They had talked of going to Italy next summer. He knew she loved lamb. Did that signify? Or did the choice of a new restaurant indicate the desire to make a new start?

That last interpretation made sense, Dani thought. By now, Ted must have begun wearying of his dalliance. Blue eyes and all, Ms. Jennifer MacDougall was not the world's most fascinating creature. Not only was she closer to Samantha's age than to Ted's own, she was miles beneath him in intellect. I WEEP FOR WHALES. How sophomoric could you get!

What did the two find to talk about? Rock groups? The care and feeding of motorbikes? The complete *oeuvre* of Jackie Collins? *The Simpsons*, for Christ's sake? Dear God, could you picture Ted watching *The Simpsons*? You had to laugh! Well, one thing for sure, from now on he'd have the Sunday *Times* puzzle all to himself. While Jenny settled down with a copy of *Seventeen*.

Cheap shot, Dani chided herself. Totally unworthy. Yet the whole business kept coming down to what George Bush might have called "the age thing."

Above all else, the generation gap rankled. Jenny was undeniably young and cute, and while Dani considered herself reasonably attractive, forty is forty. And forty-one, even worse.

She dragged herself before the full-length mirror and turned up all the lights for an on-site inspection. Not bad, not good. A little gray in the hair, some flab on the upper arms. Suck in her gut and she might pass for thirty-nine. With a faceful of makeup, thirty-eight. Put on her good beige suit and it was back up in the forties again.

She had never been one of those women who did clever things with scarves or spent hours agonizing over the right shade of nail polish. True chic had always eluded her, for unlike Kaycee, she had never deemed it worth the effort. Dani preferred to think she had achieved her own style.

Now, however, she wondered if that wasn't a euphemism for

laziness. When she and Ted were home alone together, she rarely bothered to put on lipstick, let alone sexy duds. Theirs was a sweats-and-sneakers household.

Well, this Thursday she was going to look terrific for him, make him realize that his wife was not a woman to be taken for granted. While Dani couldn't compete with Jenny MacDougall in the youth-and-innocence sweepstakes, she could surely pull herself together with more aplomb. With true wit and sophistication.

"Who does your hair?" she asked the office receptionist, a creature of such staggering chic as Dani could never aspire to. Then she called for an appointment. "Today," Dani pleaded. "It's an emergency."

Later that afternoon, she strode out of Maison Panache, oddly gratified and two hundred dollars poorer, although baffled that an underpaid receptionist was willing to spend that kind of money on herself.

"Of course you want to get rid of the gray," Mister Paul had said. "Of course." "And I'd suggest some frosted streaks by way of highlights." Dani paused but a fraction of a second. "Do with me what you will," she replied.

Hair gleaming, she headed for Saks and, with the help of a personal shopper, blew another wad on a silk jersey dress with proper accessories. Then over to the Feldmans' for an expert opinion.

"Great!" Kaycee nodded approval. "You should have colored your hair years ago."

"And you think Ted'll like my outfit?"

Kaycee adjusted the collar, undid an additional button. "Yeah—if he's got eyes in his head."

"It's not too seductive? I mean, it's only a lunch."

"Seductive is the whole idea, Dani. You're gonna come on like gangbusters and get him back! That's an order."

"I don't know, Kaycee. I can't figure him out anymore. I haven't been this scared since I took the bar exam."

She spent most of Wednesday crafting scenarios. What concessions she would make, what terms she would demand, how best repair existing damage.

If Ted was fed up with life in Manhattan, Dani could deal with that. Like most items, it was negotiable. They could move to the suburbs. He could find another job. She would support him for as long as the changeover took. She had told him that before. "I was willing to try," she could say with honesty. "Now let's both try." A marital crisis was no time for false pride.

Of course Ted would have to give up the girl. That was not negotiable, that was her quid pro quo.

And if he couldn't? Dani shuddered.

A few years ago, Dani had had a roving male client hot for divorce and remarriage. But his wife, clever woman, had waited him out. He tired of the romance and returned to the fold for a happy ending. European women behaved like that all the time, she understood. Maybe Dani, too, would be wise to turn a blind eye for a while.

The more immediate problem was the one Kaycee raised. Should Dani try to seduce Ted on Thursday afternoon? Would the afternoon conclude with their making love? Did she want to? She was unsure.

But this much she knew: she wanted Ted to want her. She wanted to arouse in him the old hot, urgent passion as proof that her attraction was still paramount. Sex was power, influence. It was the hold wielded by Jenny MacDougall. Dani would have to regain that dominion. And while she wasn't feeling the least erotic these days—nothing like being dumped on by your husband, she reflected, to squelch the libido—she hoped that once they touched, the old chemistry would assert itself. But even if not, even if she continued to feel sexless as a fish, should Ted make a move, she'd encourage him. They had made up squabbles in bed before. It was a step, a start.

It wasn't, however, a strategy, for who knew what Ted had in mind. She would have to play it by ear. Whatever happened, though, Dani resolved in advance to remain cool and ladylike throughout. There would be no hysterics, no tears, no chewing the scenery. If this lunch were truly to mark the end of their marriage, let there be dignity.

Thursday morning, she phoned in sick to the office, then went to the Face Place to be made up.

"Nothing theatrical," she explained. "I'm a lawyer. It's for an important business lunch."

"We do a lot of lawyers," the beautician said.

At a little past twelve, newly glamorous, nervous as a cat and supremely self-conscious, she entered Veneziani's. Ted had chosen a formal ambience for their reunion: starchy white tablecloths, black-clad waiters, an elegant maître d' who ushered her across the marble floor to the table where her husband was waiting.

Ted sprang to his feet, the perfect gentleman, brushing her cheek with his lips. "Don't you look nice, Dani. I like what you've done with your hair." The compliment was merely polite. There was no attendant sparkle in his eyes. Dani's heart sank.

"You're looking well, too, Ted."

She sat down stiffly. He ordered cocktails, inquired about business, killing the time till the martinis arrived.

Dani nibbled on a breadstick, feeling nauseated. "I could sure use that drink," she said.

"Couldn't we both?" He had a tight frozen smile. "Waiter, pronto!"

The drinks came. Ted took a hearty swig, then launched into what Dani instantly recognized as a prepared speech. It might have come from the PR department at Globexx. It probably did, beginning with the Feel-good introduction.

He was glad she was well, she certainly looked marvelous, he'd thought about her a great deal and was delighted to see that she was thriving.

Dani couldn't miss the valedictory undertones. It reminded her of her high school graduation speech, fulsome and insincere. She leaned back in her chair. There were to be no fumbling kisses or sweated sheets on this Thursday afternoon. Romance was the farthest thing from Ted's mind. All she wanted now was to get the meal over with and go home to collapse.

"You're looking good, too, Ted," she broke in. "That's a new tie, isn't it? I've never seen it before."

Reflexively, Ted adjusted the knot.

The gesture infuriated Dani. While it was perfectly understandable that she had made herself over head to toe for this occasion, spending a fortune in the effort, it rankled that Ted should be wearing a new tie. That tie argued his other life.

"I suppose she got it for you," Dani said.

Ted refused to be rattled. "You know I always buy my own ties, Dani. I still do. Shall we look at the menu?"

"You look," she said miserably. "I'm not hungry."

He ordered a rack of lamb and another round of drinks. Then he launched into Part Two of his discourse.

They were both grown people, intelligent adults. She knew from experience that refusing to deal with realities only aggravated matters. There were so many details that had to be settled promptly. The mortgage. The boat loan. He should make arrangements for picking up the rest of his gear. Not least of all, they must discuss Samantha's future. Her welfare was paramount in both their hearts. Samantha seemed, he thanked God, to have taken the news well. Smart, she was. Mature. Perceptive. His guess was, she understood what was what.

Mature? Perceptive? Dani stared in disbelief. If her own talks with Sam were any indication, the poor kid hadn't begun to grasp the truth.

"What's going on?" Sam had called her mother more in puzzlement than in panic, just as Dani was gearing herself to call and break the news. "You guys have an argument or something?"

Momentarily caught off guard, Dani fumbled for words. "No, it wasn't an argument, exactly. A good deal more serious, I'm afraid. It was more like a . . . a . . ."

It struck her that Ted might not have laid the facts on the line. "What exactly did Daddy tell you?"

"He said he's living in Greenwich Village at the moment, he needed to be by himself for a bit, that you were both fine and I was absolutely not to worry. Everything'll be okay."

Dani listened with astonishment. *Fine? Okay?* What was going on here? Apparently Ted had made no reference to anything as concrete as separation or divorce, let alone any mention of his involvement with Jen MacDougall. Perhaps he planned to release the news in stages, perhaps he had just chickened out. But in his attempt to mitigate the painfulness of the situation (*fine? okay?*), he had succeeded only in making it sound trivial.

Dani drew a deep breath. "I wish I could say that it was only a spat, darling, but it looks like this may be permanent. I'll do my best to help you understand . . . ," she began, but Sam, riding above her mother's words, refused to hear.

"It's just some dumb argument, right, Mom?" Sam kept insisting. "You two'll work it out. I mean, like all married people argue. I don't want to listen to this stuff."

"We'll talk again tomorrow," a distressed Dani said at last, "and I'll try to make things clearer then." But when she called the following day, the first words out of Sam's mouth were a hopeful "You and Dad patch it up yet?" Dani winced. In Sam's plea she heard the same note she herself had struck a few weeks earlier: a mixture of denial and wishful thinking.

"I wish it were so simple, sweetie. . . ." She once more tried to broach the reality, but the pattern of denial repeated itself.

Then Monday—miracle of miracles!—Ted had called, sounding conciliatory, proposing this lunch, and Dani's heart flipped. Almost like the cavalry to the rescue. How could she help but nourish hope? In which case it was just as well that Samantha had refused to credit the seriousness of the situation. Because if there was even a chance that Dani and Ted could make it up after all, then Sam had been spared unnecessary suffering.

"I'll be seeing Daddy tomorrow," she informed her daughter cautiously. "We're going to talk."

"Great!" Sam's voice swelled with relief. "I'm glad you guys are finally getting your act together. See, Mom? It's like he said, everything will be just fine."

"I'll let you know what happens," Dani said cautiously, but when she hung up, she crossed her fingers. *I wish I wish I wish . . .*

Now, a dozen hours later, wishing was futile. There would be no good news to impart, and Ted had known it all along.

Dani stared at him, her heart overflowing with bitterness. The man traveled in a different orbit. So Samantha was mature? Perceptive? She knew what was what? Naturally Ted preferred to think so. It let him off the hook.

You weren't honest with Sam, Dani thought. *You left the hard stuff for me.* It was a continuation of old familiar roles: Good Cop, Bad Cop. She didn't trust herself to speak.

Ted must have misread her silence as a kind of accord, for he leaned across the table toward her. Mr. Sincere in an unfamiliar tie. For the first time that afternoon, his eyes engaged hers.

Whatever else happened, he wanted Dani to know, "I'll always be there for you."

The phrase jarred. *There for you.* What crap!

Coming from Ted, it sounded positively mealymouthed, with its facile sentiment and pop-psych ring. Ted didn't speak like that. He used to claim such clichés made him barf. Besides, how the hell could he be "there for her" when he was living with somebody else?

"How dare you patronize me!" Dani burst out.

At the next table, three businessmen turned their heads in inquiry, then looked away, embarrassed.

Dani lowered her voice. Dignity, dignity! Now she knew why Ted had chosen this restaurant—for its gentility. Well, she had no intention of making a scene in public. She wasn't a wild woman.

"Okay, Ted. Let's cut the platitudes, and get down to basics. What do you want to tell me? Forget the written speech and just give me the outline."

Ted shifted in his seat, "Okay."

He was quitting his job after Christmas. He planned to move to the Caribbean and make a new life.

Dani's bitterness spewed over. "You and who else?"

"Don't start that, Dani." Cool as ice, the man was.

"I'm not starting anything. Not a fucking thing."

She ached to rattle him, slash away at his abominable reserve. It was intolerable that he retain the upper hand.

"May I point out, Ted, that you're the one who set off this chain of events, so don't accuse me of starting anything. I was simply wondering if you plan to take Miss Junior Jailbait to the Caribbean with you, or perhaps she's financing the jaunt on the money I got her. Money *I* got her, Ted, when Baby Blue Eyes didn't know enough to come in out of the rain. Jesus!"—Dani couldn't resist—"She's young enough to be your daughter!"

"That's unfair and you know it!" he snapped, affording Dani the faint satisfaction that she had hit him on the raw at last. A moment later he recovered his sangfroid.

"Be honest, Dani. The zip had gone out of our marriage well before I cut out. Jennifer may have been the catalyst, but she sure as hell wasn't the cause. Anyhow, I don't intend to discuss her and I sure don't want to get into rehashing twenty years. What's done is done, so let's calm down, talk reasonably."

"Reasonably"—Dani swallowed her bile. She was beginning to hate the word—"what the hell are you going to do in the Caribbean? How will you earn a living?"

"That's still up in the air. I've been thinking of maybe looking for work as a journalist. As you know, I've always wanted to be a foreign correspondent."

"You never wanted to be a foreign correspondent."

"Don't you tell me what I wanted to be. I must have talked about it a hundred times when we were in school, unless you never listened, which is also possible."

They were circling each other now like fighting cocks, Dani hot and increasingly frantic, Ted cool and controlled.

"You never wanted to be a foreign correspondent," she jeered. "That is bullshit and you know it. A journalist, yes, but not a foreign correspondent. Never!"

"Right! I didn't want to be a foreign correspondent and I never bought my own ties. Now are you happy?"

"Besides which"—she refused to let it go—"what makes you think you could land a job as a, quote, foreign correspondent? You're not even a fucking reporter. You're a PR man, for Christ's sake. A flack."

"I never said I was going to get a job as a foreign correspondent." Ted ground the words out between clenched teeth. "I said I would maybe look for one. And then again, maybe not. I don't know."

"Forty-four years old and you don't know what you want to be when you grow up?" Her voice rose with each word.

This time, the businessmen did turn and stare.

Ted recoiled. "That's right, Dani. I don't know. Could be I'll write a novel. Or buy a boat and run charter fishing cruises. Or teach English. Or just sit on the beach and watch the tide roll in. Now are you satisfied?"

"No, goddamnit, I'm not satisfied." Tears of rage rolled down her cheeks, dragging streaks of mascara in their wake. "And who's going to fund this little fantasy? Or do you plan to live off your girlfriend?"

"I have some money," Ted reminded her. "There's the boat, the apartment, my profit-sharing. You know the law, Dani. Who better? I'm entitled to half our net worth."

"To hell with the law!" Her composure was slipping fast. "And the hell with you, Ted Sloane! Is this why you wanted to meet in a restaurant . . . because you think I'm too much of a lady to make a scene?"

"Because I hoped we could talk like civilized people."

"Civilized people don't walk out on their wives! They don't . . . they don't . . ." But she was too choked with tears to continue. She began sobbing, out of control.

At that moment, Danielle Sloane, Esq., was on the point of becoming everything she dreaded in her clients: messy, weeping, helpless. A public spectacle.

Ted jumped to his feet. For a moment, she had the wild hope that he would take her in his arms and comfort her. That he would make all this ugliness vanish. *Let's go home.*

Instead he handed her his handkerchief. "Hopeless," he muttered. Then he threw down a pile of bills and fled. Their reunion had lasted less than twenty minutes.

Dani lay her head on the table praying for death. The waiter tiptoed over.

"Will you be wanting the lamb now, madam?" he whispered.

She wiped her eyes and stared at Ted's handkerchief. Pressed into the white linen folds was a disgusting hairy creature. A black widow spider? Dani's stomach lurched.

Ted Sloane was plotting to kill her. He was insane. Homicidal. It was the ultimate nightmare. Numbly, she peered at the instrument of death only to discover upon closer inspection that it was nothing more than a set of Face Place eyelashes. She wanted to weep, out of sheer humiliation.

"Please," she implored the waiter, "call me a cab."

By nine that evening, Dani had pulled herself together sufficiently to make the promised phone call to Sam.

"I would give my soul," she said, "not to have to tell you this, my love, but I feel you've got to know the truth. Your father and I have separated—"

"I don't believe you!" Sam burst out.

" . . . by mutual consent." She bit her lips and lied—not to let Ted off the hook, but to gentle the blow. "No one's to blame. You know, when people are married as long as we are, even with the best intentions in the world, they sometimes grow apart . . ." She continued in this vein a few minutes longer, softening the contours, dulling the edges, yet leaving Samantha no room for doubt or fantasy. "So you see, it's over. I know this comes as a terrible shock, Sam, and it's a major change. But some things never change, I promise. We both love you dearly, nothing can alter that. Sam?"— for there was silence at the other end—"Are you there?"

"I can't believe this is really happening," came the outraged howl. "No way. Not to me. I want to speak to my father, then I'll call you back."

An hour later, a stunned Samantha was on the phone again, her voice thick with strain.

"You didn't tell me he had a girlfriend." It was an accusation. "He says he's sure I'll love her, too. What's she like, Mom? He says you know her."

Dani shuddered. How far was she expected to go on defending Sam's cherished image of her father? Surely this was too much, too awful. All the rage of noontime came winging back. *Your father is a no good son-of-a-bitch*, she yearned to cry out, *who's deserting us both for some bimbo*. But much as she ached to unburden herself, she ached even more for her daughter.

"Jen's . . . um, very nice . . ." Dani forced the words out. "A very sweet person . . ."

Long sigh. "Yeah, that's what Daddy says." But a worried Samantha hungered for detail. What did Jen look like? What kind of work did she do? Were they going to get married? Dad had sounded so cheerful.

Dani winced beneath the barrage.

"Look, I really can't say what your father's plans are."

Sam burst out in an anguished cry. "Why does everyone insist on treating me like a child? You could've told me about it before. Like I have a right to know what's going on."

"Indeed you do, sweetie, and we should talk. Why don't you get on a plane tomorrow, come here for a few days . . ."

"No!" Sam bit the word off.

" . . . or I'll fly out Saturday morning. . . ."

"No!" Even more emphatic. "I want to digest this by myself. I'm not a baby. I don't need to have my hand held."

"Well, I hate the idea of your being alone at such a time." Dani paused. From experience, she knew better than to suggest a chat with the school psychologist, yet she didn't want Sam to nurse her wounds in private. "Is there someone there you can talk to? Your roommate Nancy? Your housemother? Some special friend . . . ?"

"Yeah, I suppose . . ." Sam dragged it out. "But right now I'm just bushed. Can we deal with it another time?"

"Sure. I'll call tomorrow. I love you, Sam. Whatever else, remember that." She swallowed, whispered: "We both do, Daddy and I."

That night, Dani couldn't sleep. It had drained her to cover up for Ted, make amends for Jenny. Life was so fucking unjust.

After a wretched hour, she switched on the light and looked for something to read. The new Marquez book lay on the bedside table. Ted had bought it last summer and left it out for her perusal. "You'll enjoy it," he had said. They both cherished Marquez.

Yet no sooner had Dani picked it up, than she felt a shudder of revulsion. This was Ted's book! He had held it in his hands a dozen times, savored it, chuckling here, frowning there, occasionally moistening his index finger with the tip of his tongue as he turned the pages.

Gross! The thought of his spittle on the margins, of his invisible fingerprints on every page turned her stomach.

Ted Sloane had touched this very volume with those same familiar conjugal hands that were at this very moment wrapped around the flesh of Jenny MacDougall. Dani hurled the book across the room.

Ted had poisoned it for her. This book, this innocent book, had been despoiled by his touch. It was infected, contaminated, like the bedside clock he switched off every morning. And the water carafe. Like everything else on this night table. In this room.

Not enough that he betray his wife and daughter. He had to defile their possessions in the bargain.

Suddenly everything in the apartment struck her as filthy, befouled by Ted Sloane's lying, adulterous touch. She hated him. She hated him for having left her. For having married her. For the way he moistened his fingers when he turned the pages of a book. For having watched her make a fool of herself in the restaurant. For making her feel unloved and unwanted. She hated everything about him.

In the morning, she would send him a registered letter advising when he could collect his things, then she'd change the lock on the door. Once his possessions were gone, she would hire a bonded cleaning service (not her weekly Mrs. Palchuck, but a whole team of pros) to wash, clean, scour, sterilize, sanitize, fumigate until the premises were once again safe to the touch. She would have the rugs sent out. The windows washed. Put all the dishes through the dishwasher—twice. Buy new sheets. She would have the place repainted. Exorcised. Not a trace of him must remain.

At the crack of daylight, Dani dressed, went to a coffee shop for breakfast, then headed for the office. She was the first person in.

This venue, at least, was untouched by Ted. Except for the photo, the one Jenny must have glimpsed. Dani dumped it in the bottom drawer unceremoniously, then went over to the metal file cabinet. There was the Gessner file.

In the silence she could almost hear Mrs. Gessner's wounded bray. *My husband left me . . . left me . . . left me!*

Men! Goddamn 'em. They were all the same. No judgment. No self-restraint. They shattered lives left and right, simply so that they might indulge in their whims, their vile little urges. And left women to pick up the pieces.

Dani pulled out the Gessner folder, then slammed the drawer shut with a harsh metal clang.

Nothing like watching the female establishment gang up on the wandering male, Jack Pruitt had said. Indeed there wasn't.

13

DANIELLE SLOANE had always thought of herself as a married woman. Other terms might flesh out the picture—*mother, daughter, lawyer, liberal, American, brunette*—but they were ancillary qualities. It was the married state that defined her above all else.

As a newlywed, she had taken pride and pleasure in being introduced as Mrs. Sloane. Long after the novelty palled, she continued to refer to herself in that manner when dealing with butchers, plumbers and such. The building staff addressed her as Mrs. Sloane. Most of their Christmas cards plus much of their junk mail were sent to Mr. and Mrs. And while Dani would never have been so egregious as to have Mrs. Theodore Jay Sloane imprinted on her credit cards (she was a product of the '60s, ergo, a feminist of sorts), the Mrs. part of that configuration was embedded in her soul.

She had always liked being married, being a Mrs., a woman possessed of husband and household. And though she would never confess to such a biased sentiment, at heart Dani felt faintly superior to those women who had been unable to find or keep a mate.

Good men were thin upon the ground. You couldn't escape that conclusion. It was confirmed daily by a river of books, by talk shows, singles ads, by the discussion that went on endlessly in the Pruitt-Baker typing pool.

"Cheer up," she told Marie, who answered the phones in her

department. "Single's not so bad. If you heard all the misery that goes on in my office, you wouldn't be in such a rush to get married."

Yet while Dani's head announced one thing, her heart declared another. "Mrs." was still the supreme accolade, and marriage the ideal institution.

Yes, a good man was hard to find, and in a society marked by an acute dearth of eligible males, she had found and married one of the best.

Who had upped and left her for a younger woman.

After the ruckus at Veneziano's, it was impossible to continue the pretense.

Her husband had left her, that was the fact. He had cut her loose from her moorings, set her adrift in an infinite void. How extraordinary that a hitherto gentle man should be capable of inflicting such emotional violence. Nonetheless, people would have to be informed.

It killed her. How could she admit that she, Dani Sloane, smart, capable, the woman everybody envied (well, some people, anyhow), the dispenser of advice, had suddenly been cut down to size? That she was no different, no better, than the army of unhappy women who filed into her office?

She didn't trust herself to say the right thing, not without weeping and cursing. Were explanations required? Was there a formula? Perhaps she should send out cards.

> *Mrs. Danielle Sloane announces the*
> *sudden death of her marriage.*
> *Please omit flowers.*

She felt possessed of a thunderbolt, an instrument capable of shattering the illusions of almost everyone she knew, after which they would perceive her in a different way. It was awesome. The best approach was the simplest. She would break the news in a single truthful statement, neither more nor less. Not "Ted and I have split up" or "We've decided to call it a day." Why should she lie on his behalf?

Her first test came shortly after Ted cleared out his things.

"The locksmith was by this afternoon," the doorman said. "He left you a new set of keys."

Dani looked into Mikhail's sad Romanian eyes and assumed he must know that her husband had gone for good. Still, she felt called upon to clarify.

"Aaah . . . well . . ." Dani fumbled for the words that would minimize embarrassment all around, then said simply. "My husband has left me."

Surprising how the sentence had slid out of her mouth, slick as grease. Mikhail nodded gravely and Dani was conscious of having made her official debut as an abandoned woman.

My husband has left me. It had a rhythm, a ring. It was a phrase that became easier with practice.

Now when the phone rang at home, Dani knew what to do. No more ducking or faking. "My husband has left me," she said to friends and neighbors and telemarketers and wrong numbers alike. Straight up front, no fancy business.

Within a week, she had the routine down pat, allowing for minor variations as circumstances demanded.

Hello. No Ted's not here. My husband has left me.

There was a distinct if awful pleasure in the thrust of the words, like probing an abscessed tooth with your tongue.

"My God! I just heard," Ellie Johnson said. "Pat and I couldn't believe it. How're you doing? Can we help?"

Dani's reply was "My husband has left me."

Gravely, a Tom Brokaw of grief, she broadcast her story everywhere as though announcing some great natural disaster: to cab drivers, strangers in the checkout line at the supermarket, the kid who delivered the *Times* each morning. When feeling particularly low, she varied the wording.

My husband has abandoned me.
My husband deserted me.
My husband left me on September ninth.
My husband left me for a woman half his age.
My husband left me and it'll be five weeks on Monday.

It all came down to the same thing: *left me left me left me.* It was the vast monumental fact of her existence. Her waking thought each morning, her lullaby every night. As for the effect this would have upon Sam, she could only imagine.

Thus, absent, Ted assumed an even larger presence than in the years they had lived together. Mechanically she went through the motions of shopping, dressing, eating—her inner eye fixed only on him. She grew absentminded, stupid.

Often she would begin some routine activity and have it slip her mind a few seconds later, with the result that she burned out the coffee maker, scorched her best silk blouse, and locked herself out of the apartment on four occasions, necessitating a lavish tip to the doorman each time. She forgot where she put things, from phone numbers to groceries, the most grievous loss being the jacket of her good black wool suit. God knew where she left it. In a taxi? In court? Wherever, it was Ted's fault.

As it was equally his fault when Dani rode right past her bus stop, or crossed the street oblivious to traffic. "Hey, lady, you crazy?" a truck driver yelled. Yes, she was. Crazy, obsessed, consumed.

The day she found a box of Tampax in the freezer, Dani sat herself down and delivered a mental lecture on self-discipline. This zombie stuff must stop, she resolved. She was a person, a cogent human being, a woman possessed of friends, neighbors, family. A fortunate woman, in the grand scheme of things. How dare she wallow in self-pity at a time when millions, nay billions, of women in the world were far worse off. Diseased, starving, brutalized, homeless—women who would mortgage their souls to be in Dani's fine Italian shoes. Her attitude bespoke the crassest self-indulgence.

True, most of those millions and billions of women were married, they had husbands! but marriage wasn't everything, Dani kept telling herself. Faithful husbands weren't everything. She must view this in perspective. The surest picker-upper was to take the advice she offered clients: Get out and do something positive.

Accordingly, a few nights later, having been assured that Ted wouldn't show, Dani went to their poker club, where she was greeted by a raft of old friends, all of them warm and supportive.

"I don't expect you'll be seeing the late Mr. Sloane"—Dani said; it amused her to designate him thus—"since he's found a more titillating way to spend his evenings."

Over the next three hours, amidst the clatter of chips and beer steins, Dani provided her fellow-players with a detailed account of Ted's delinquencies. "And then he said . . ." Horror upon horror. "Half his age . . ."

Bruce and Marian Barstow walked her home.

"I know what you're going through," Bruce said with feeling. "I went through the same thing myself."

"You did?" she snapped in disbelief, finding it presumptuous of Bruce to compare his own first marriage, a dinky affair that only lasted a couple of years, with the great and intricate structure of Dani's own.

To all who asked and many who didn't, Dani set her friends straight on the facts. She was performing a public service. The people in their circle ought to know the kind of person Ted Sloane really was, she stressed. (For *person*, read *rat*, *swine*, *psychopath*.) "Not that I'm pressuring you to take sides . . ."

Everyone was sympathetic, though her tales of treachery often triggered a can-you-top-this? kind of response. "You think that's bad" was a typical rejoinder. "You should hear what happened to my cousin Alice!"

Some world! Dani thought. Everybody has to be one-up.

She invited six people to dinner one Saturday and made bouillabaisse. The dish was superb, the party a disaster. Dani never shut up. By ten o'clock, the guests had fled.

"Christ!" She threw a mess of clamshells down the garbage disposal, which responded with a gratifying bone-crunching noise. "I am so fucking boring, I am beginning to bore myself. I am worse than my aunt Helen with her boring boring hysterectomy, and I am going to button up about Ted once and for all while I still have a few friends left." Easier pledged than done, she discovered.

Kaycee bore the brunt of it, enduring hour after hour of Dani's grievances, until one tearful midnight, she threw up her hands and begged for mercy, crying, "No More!"

Only at the office did Dani employ a measure of self-restraint, managing to function tolerably well. Other people's problems provided therapeutic relief, and she was grateful for some kind of intellectual challenge. Work helped fill in the yawning holes in her life.

"You've been putting in a lot of hours," Jack Pruitt observed, finding Dani hunched over her desk one night.

"Yes . . . well, my husband has left me. On September ninth." She almost added: *A day that will live in infamy.*

"Ouch!" Jack clapped a paternal arm around her shoulder. "I'm sorry to hear about that, Dani. Genuinely sorry." He went on to make the usual noises—his support, sympathy, blah blah blah. Then he said something that made Dani wince. "You gotta admit it's ironic, though."

"What is?"

"The divorce lawyer getting divorced."

Dani admitted nothing of the sort. And when her next-door neighbor thought to console her by saying, "It happens to everybody," she blew up. The hell it did! What had happened to her was unique in the history of human woe.

"Read this!" she said, handing a letter to Chris Evans, who occupied the next office. "Go ahead, read it aloud."

In fact, it was no different from dozens of letters she sent out routinely.

"Dear Danielle Sloane," Chris read. "Your husband has consulted me in regard to your marital difficulties. Please have your attorney contact me as soon as possible. Yours truly, Whittaker Rollins, Esq."

Chris handed it back. "Short but sweet."

"Can you beat that!" Dani burst out. "My sleazeball of a husband has gone and got himself a lawyer. Coward! He's too chicken to talk to me direct, some attorney has to do it for him. I find that incredible! What should I do, Chris?"

Chris was bright and never minced words.

"Give you two alternative courses of action, Dani. One, get yourself a good matrimonial lawyer . . ."

"I am one, remember? The other?"

"Or two, hire a hit man and really settle his hash."

"Very funny," Dani said. "And don't think the idea hasn't occurred to me."

Chris shrugged. "Them's the choices, although I'd recommend the former course of action."

Her response to Chris's advice was to jam the letter into the bottom drawer, alongside the photo of Ted.

Of course she didn't wish her husband dead. That was talk, hyperbole. She was a gentle peaceful law-abiding citizen, not some character out of a gangster flick. Yet anger was building within her to an unbearable pitch. If she didn't vent it soon, she would burst.

When Dani did explode, it was in an unforeseen fashion. The target wasn't even Ted Sloane.

"Sorry, pal." Dani pushed the draft of the Gessner settlement across the desk to Leo Margulies. "I'm afraid this has to go back to the shop for repairs. My client and I have had second thoughts. We want the house in Maine, too."

"Wha' house?" Leo blinked in surprise. "For Chrissakes, it's a cottage . . . a fisherman's shack. Worth maybe thirty thou at most."

"Linda tells me they spent their honeymoon in Maine and it has sentimental value. The idea that her husband's new . . . um, companion might have access to the premises causes her extreme mental anguish."

Leo unleashed his you-gotta-be crazy look.

"Well, she ain't gonna get it. This is outrageous and you know it. If Linda Gessner's that hot for the place, she can offer to buy it at full market price, presuming he'll sell. Lord knows she's got the bread. Or—tell you what—she can give him back half the house in Glen Cove as a trade-off."

Dani's face was stone. "No trade-off. Linda wants Glen Cove and the Maine place, both outright."

"She can want all the land west of the Mississippi, as far as I'm concerned, but that means zilch. What's with you, Dani? We had an agreement."

"Nope. A proposal. Sorry, Leo, but it's no more Mr. Nice Guy. The way we see it, Linda Gessner has been fucked over enough for one lifetime and she is not about to underwrite the drill-meister's amorous career. If the good dentist wants to think with his dick, he'll have to pay for that privilege. So here it is, Leo. Read it and weep. We want the cottage, in fact all the real property, plus all the mutual funds plus a guaranteed income of one hundred thou a year." She handed him the laundry list.

Leo glanced at it and gave an uneasy laugh. "Nice try, Dani."

"The hundred thou net after taxes, of course."

"I'll come back when you're feeling serious."

"Things don't get more serious than this. Try me."

Leo got up. "See you in court, counselor."

"Oh no you won't." Dani's voice rose, resonant with passion, conviction, rage. "Now hear this, because I'm tired of wasting breath! If you think Gessner is just going to pay out a few bucks and walk away clean, you've both got another think coming. This is a woman who's been totally betrayed. Linda Gessner wants justice. Retribution. And I want it for her. She's entitled."

Dani caught her breath. She was about to embark on the first unethical action of her career. But had Dr. Gessner behaved ethically? Had Ted? Who had struck the first blow? What she was doing was little more than evening the score.

"We've got hold of his patient list," she said, "fresh from the computer. The name and address of every man, woman and child who's ever opened wider for the guy. Well, I wouldn't put it past Linda to get on the horn, phone each one and warn them that they're being treated by a man who could have AIDS. And it's good-bye Doctor Dentist."

"AIDS?" Leo shouted. "He doesn't have AIDS!"

"Do you know that for a fact? Prove it! Here's a guy who left his wife, his loyal trusting wife, to indulge in his sexual fantasies. You gonna tell me this fella he's shacked up with is Ira's debut on the homosexual scene? Bullshit. I know the type. My bet is Ira-baby has been leading a double life for years—picking up young boys in Forty-second Street peep shows, the gay bathhouses, God knows what he's been up to on the sly! I'm going to let this man put his hands in my mouth? No way. My boss's wife happens to be a patient of his. If Muriel Pruitt had a clue about his life-style . . ." Dani rolled her eyes. "Read about the gay doctor in Seattle? Bitch of a case. He's on the receiving end of a hundred lawsuits. My God! once this kind of thing gets out, Ira's finished. Destroyed."

She caught her breath. "So! The house in Maine, the mutual funds . . ."

"Is that a threat?"

"I prefer to think of it as a scenario."

"I don't believe this." Leo looked sick. "And I can't believe you're encouraging her in this lunacy. It won't wash. A, if Linda Gessner does make those calls, we'll sue her for criminal slander. And B, why should she? Bankrupt men can't pay maintenance. Anyhow, there isn't a judge alive who would tolerate such behavior. She'd be cutting off her nose to spite her face."

"Could be, but she'd do it, all right. She's just crazy enough with grief to go for broke. Because she doesn't care, don't you see? She has nothing left to live for. Nothing. Nada. Zilch. So what's it to her if she destroys him in a kind of Götterdämmerung? When Ira left her, he ruined her life. He might as well have shot her and got it over with." Dani was yelling, her eyes afire. "She doesn't give a flying fuck about the money, Leo. She wants this guy's balls on a spit, and who can blame her!"

"Well, goddamn talk her out of it!"

"I can't, I won't even try." With effort, Dani regained her self-control. "Hell hath no fury and all that jazz."

"I ought to haul you up before the bar association."

Dani looked mock-shocked.

"*Moi?* For being unable to gag a client? You wouldn't dare. Publicity's the last thing the good dentist wants."

"Maybe if the four of us sat down together . . ."

"No way. She doesn't want to be on the same planet with him, let alone the same room." Dani got up to indicate the meeting was over. "I'm off to Florida this afternoon. I'll be back Monday. I expect your answer by the fifteenth."

Leo stalked out of the office while Dani held her breath, stunned by her own audacity. Only when the door was safely closed did she realize her hands were trembling.

14

SOME FOUR YEARS EARLIER, on his sixty-fifth birthday, Ralph Fletcher put his house and business on the market.

"I'm retiring too," Mary announced. "I say, the heck with housework and long Jersey winters. It'll be a relief not having to take care of that old barn. What's to keep us in Hupperstown anyhow?"

Not their daughters, who were happily married and dispersed all over the country, nor their son, Kevin, who worked for a think tank in Palo Alto where, according to family legend, he led a rakish bachelor's existence. Their obligations fulfilled, it was time Ralph and Mary lived for themselves.

Accordingly, they sold the house, the furniture, gave their Irish setter, Jiggs, to a neighbor. Then they bought a condominium in a dazzling white high-rise in Naples, Florida, complete with patio and swimming pool, which they proceeded to furnish from scratch in what the decorator called "Gulf modern."

The area teemed with golf courses and it was Ralph Fletcher's plan to play every day that weather permitted, before entering that Great Nineteenth Hole in the Sky. Mary set about constructing a new circle of friends and took up ceramics and *t'ai chi*.

By now, they considered themselves proper Floridians. Their conversations were peppered with references to the awfulness of northern weather ("a foot of snow in Syracuse, I see!"), the quality of the local markets ("You can't buy fruit this fresh in Jersey"), the ease of life ("We're hardly ever up before nine") and the Great Move South, which was "the best thing that ever happened to us."

These constant paeans made Dani suspect that her parents were secretly homesick for Hupperstown. They were perennially parched for news and secondhand gossip.

Dani dreaded the trip. She had saved her parents (spared them, she preferred to think) until decency forbade further delay, then flew down for a weekend. Hers wasn't the kind of bomb one could drop over the phone.

Her father met her at the airport.

"Just you? No Ted?"

" 'Fraid not," Dani said, blinded by the sun. "I'll explain over dinner."

Ralph looked at her shrewdly. "Your mother doesn't cook anymore, you know. She's become a 'liberated' woman."

They dined that night at a fish house overlooking the water. Throughout the first course, Dani was regaled with the list of complaints that came with the territory. Except for the waiters, Dani was the only soul in the restaurant under sixty. God's Waiting Room.

"Try the grouper, dear," her mother insisted. "I don't think you can buy it up north. It's a nice fish."

When the main course arrived, Dani remarked, "It's delicious. We had grouper last Christmas when we came down, I remember. Which brings me to the subject of Ted."

Mary Fletcher dipped her napkin in ice water, intent on removing an invisible stain on her skirt, while Ralph studied the mounted marlin on the opposite wall.

Seeing that they anticipated some dire assault on either their emotions or their finances, Dani strove to make it as painless as possible. Already, she could hear her mother's familiar plea: "Why don't they ever print the good news?" Dani gritted her teeth and began.

"Ted and I have decided"—it was a struggle to keep from crying. Suddenly she coughed. "Sorry, I seem to have got a bit of bone caught in my throat." She coughed again, wiped the sweat off her face, then produced a bowdlerized version of the breakup. Omitted was all mention of ugly scenes thrown in restaurants or redheads with enormous blue eyes, let alone the unbearable pain of daily life. Go tell them that she was an open wound, that the slightest stimuli—a Cole Porter lyric, a Technicolor kiss, a stray whiff of after-shave lotion—could reduce her to jelly. What for? Why spread the misery?

Instead, she stressed Ted's distaste for New York, coupled with his desire to start life anew elsewhere. Put like that, the rupture sounded like a stroll in the country.

"So there we are, folks. Samantha knows all about it, she's taking it in her stride. I'm getting used to it, too. We'll probably file for divorce one of these days."

Her father looked stern and chewed his lips a great deal; but her mother seemed shaken to the core. Throughout Dani's recitation, Mary had been torturing her napkin into knots, agitated and fretful as a baby.

"Surely," she pleaded, giving the napkin a vicious wrench, "if it's just a question of jobs or geography . . ."

Dani shook her head. "It's over, believe me."

"Well," Mary Fletcher burst out, "all I can say is I'm glad I'm not living in Hupperstown anymore! We were always so proud of you! You were such a good, well-behaved child."

"What on earth is that supposed to mean?"

"In all our family . . ."—Mary's voice was trembling—"both families, the Fletchers and the Kelloggs, not one single person has ever been divorced. Never! Aunts, uncles and Lord knows how many cousins—every one of them manages to get along fine. And it's not as if we were Catholics, either. No ma'am! We don't simply throw in the sponge. We make an effort to work out our differences, and that's a lesson you and Ted could learn. What am I supposed to tell people, Dani?"

"Tell them I'm a pioneer."

"Is that supposed to be witty? Well, it's not. Everybody had such respect for you, we gave you such a beautiful wedding. Six bridesmaids, two more than we gave Sally. I suppose I should be thankful you waited till we moved to Florida to drop this bombshell. At least here we don't know anybody. I mean, not real close friends like the Keilers and Mayor Pierce."

"Now, Mary . . ." Ralph sought to keep the peace, but Dani

drowned him out. She was furious, feeling that she had flown from one domestic nightmare to another.

"For God's sake, Mother! My life lies in ruins, and all you're worried about is what the folks in Hupperstown will think? Who gives a crap?"

"You didn't say your life was in ruins, Dani. You said nothing of the sort, you said it was a joint decision and all I said was, Why don't you get back together again? Anyhow, must you use such revolting language! I've heard quite enough." Mary dipped her napkin in ice water and dabbed at her eyes. "I will not be yelled at, Dani. There's no respect for anything anymore and that's the truth. No proper values. No discipline, no self-control. When I was a child . . ."

"Sweet Jesus!" Dani groaned. "Let's not turn this into a social tract. Times change."

"Some things never change!" Mary shot back. "I don't understand you, Dani. Why must you go to extremes? Divorce . . . ! That's such a terrible step!"

Dani winced, half expecting to hear her "Surgeon General's warning" to clients flung back at her from this unlikely quarter. The worst of it was, she agreed with much of what her mother had said. The proud daughter laid low.

"Now, Mary . . ." Ralph was patting his wife's blue-veined hand with a there-there gesture, calming, comforting. "It's not the end of the world."

Dani watched in amazement. Who was the injured party here anyhow? Inexplicably, it seemed to be her mother. Then she softened. What had she expected? Indeed, some things never did change. Her mother, for instance.

Mary Fletcher remained what she had ever been: a narrow, conventional, basically good-natured soul, neither as clever as her husband nor as venturesome as her children, living in a tightly defined miniworld, a stranger to turbulent emotion. Easy does it!

"I apologize, Mom. I didn't mean to snipe. But divorce isn't such a big deal these days, honestly. There's no stigma attached. Perfectly respectable people get divorced, and I'm speaking from professional experience. Look," she reasoned, "there are divorcées in Hupperstown, too, maybe not in our immediate family but . . ."

Dani named half a dozen offenders. "Kids I went to school with, people from your country club . . ."

"Excuse me." Mary Fletcher got up. "I have to go to the powder room and then, Ralph, I'd like you to take me home. I can't discuss this anymore tonight."

They drove home in silence.

Dani hid in the guest room until her parents had gone to bed, then she stepped out onto the balcony. The night was silky dark, the air was soft and smelled of jasmine. A few minutes later, her father joined her.

"Couldn't sleep." He lit a cigarette.

"Should you be smoking?" Dani asked.

"At my age, who gives a damn?" Then he sighed. "Your mother didn't mean to hurt your feelings, Dani. That's just her manner. She'll come around."

"Yeah. . . . I know."

They stood for a while without talking. She watched the red glow of his cigarette, listened to the croaking of the bullfrogs. New York and Ted seemed far away.

Then Ralph said, "There's another woman, isn't there? Ted's involved with a girl."

Dani considered. "Yup."

"I thought so." He took a pull of the cigarette. "In fact I knew it! I never really liked Ted, you know that? I never trusted him."

"I know."

"I never liked him from the start. I never liked his politics, that hippie beard of his—"

"Oh, Dad! You're talking twenty years ago."

" . . . or the fact that he's left my daughter in the lurch. Selfish bastard. Who is she, Dani?"

"The girl? A girl. Young . . . pretty . . . a former client of mine, not that it matters."

Even in the dark, she could feel the force of her father's wrath. Had Ted been here, Ralph would probably string him up southern-style. The idea pained. How odd, Dani thought. Given five seconds lead time, she would damn Ted Sloane in the most excoriating terms to anyone willing to listen, to total strangers. Yet hearing her father badmouth him was intolerable.

"Look, Dad, these things happen every day. Besides, he's still Samantha's father. Anyhow, what's done is done."

"You always did stand up for him, Dani. He doesn't deserve it. The man's a fool. A lovely loyal wife, a wonderful daughter who adores him . . . I don't know why he couldn't just soldier on."

"Soldier on?" It struck her as an odd turn of phrase.

He ground out his cigarette. "I mean, show some spine. Stick it out. Like I did."

Startled, Dani held her breath, awaiting revelations.

"Why, you think your husband's the only fella ever lost his head over some attractive woman?" Ralph continued. "Happens all the time."

"You?" she murmured.

"It wasn't officially what you'd call an affair," her father was quick to assure her, then his tone mellowed. "But almost. Very almost. You remember Steffie Wilcox who used to do my books?" Dani didn't, but held her tongue. "Lovely creature with honey-blond hair and the prettiest smile in the world. There was a time I would have gone to the stake for her." He laughed gently at the memory. "Or California, even better. But I didn't. That's the point. I stayed. I soldiered on. I was a married man with responsibilities, you among them." He seemed pleased with his disclosure. "Your dear old dad is full of surprises, huh?"

Dani tried to picture her father in the throes of romantic rapture, couldn't.

"Did Mom know?" she asked.

"Your mother makes a point of not knowing what she doesn't want to know," he said mildly. "It's a great gift. To change the subject, what kind of financial arrangements did Ted make?"

"Oh God," she mumbled, "I haven't even begun to cope with the money end. This has all been so traumatic."

"Well, at least you've got a lucrative profession. I'll help you if I can, Dani, but as you know I'm nearing seventy and the way the stock market's been going . . ."

"Please, Dad. I didn't come to put the touch on you."

"Though if New York is too expensive, you might consider moving down here to set up shop. Not that there's much call for divorce lawyers in Naples, I shouldn't think, this being a retirement community, but you could do wills, real estate, that sort of thing. And you'd always have a roof over your head. We're still your parents, honey. Fact is, I'd rather enjoy having someone intelligent around to shoot the breeze with."

"Thanks, Dad." She tried to make light of it, lump in her throat notwithstanding. "Who knows, I might take you up on it."

"Ah, you'll be fine, Dani. You're strong, resourceful, a born survivor. And Ted you say is moving . . . where?"

"The Caribbean. To watch the tides roll in or something equally ambitious. Though he did make some noises about looking for a job as a foreign correspondent. He now claims it was his childhood ambition, which presumably I thwarted."

"Yes, I remember his saying something to that effect when you got married."

"You do?" Dani said. "I don't."

But her father hadn't heard her, for he went on. "Ah, youthful dreams . . . youthful dreams!"

Then he harrumphed. Or so it sounded to Dani, who couldn't tell if he was angry or wistful. The moon came out behind a cloud and she could make him out now. He was leaning against the balcony, absorbed in the faint horizon. A frail old man, silver-white to the point of transparency.

"When I was a POW in Germany," he mused, "there was this fella in our compound who'd been a barnstormer in civilian life, one of those pilots who did commercial air shows. I don't think they have 'em anymore. Well, our great dream was that after the war, I would get my pilot's license and Ben and I would start a little air run up in Alaska. Carry mail, cargo, fly in medics to the hinterlands. There wasn't much oil drilling then, it was virgin country, vast, full of adventure. Beautiful, too, according to Ben. We talked about it constantly. . . ."

"And . . . ?"

"And I came home from the war and all of Hupperstown turned out. There was a brass band and there was your mother waiting, both our families in fact, and everybody expected certain things of me. We were Ralph and Mary, old high school sweethearts, the all-American couple. She'd even had the silver engraved. And that was the end of Alaska."

Dani sucked in her breath. Did her father realize what he was saying? That he had gone from one prison camp to another. Only the form of his captivity had changed.

"Not that I regret it, mind you. Your mother and I have had a wonderful life."

He cleared his throat. In the moonlight his eyes looked rheumy.

Why didn't he swoop up his bride and start the airline anyhow? she was tempted to ask, but she knew the answer. Her mother was not a woman to take a flyer, in any sense of the word, and her father, poor dear, had spent the rest of his life rationalizing his abject surrender.

"You could still take a cruise there," she said. "It would be a lovely trip in summertime."

"To Alaska?" he laughed. "What for? It's probably as built up as everywhere else. Oil spills, fast food, the whole catastrophe. It was a pipe dream anyhow. No, love, your mother and I are here to stay. What's that expression? See Naples and die?"

He took a vicious swipe at his arm. "These goddamn Florida mosquitoes. They're worse than the Jersey variety."

She returned to New York depressed, amazed, relieved, disheartened. Were there no happy marriages anywhere? Diogenes might have done no better looking for the perfect couple than for his proverbial honest man. Perhaps there was a link between the two ideals.

Once home, she did her duty by informing the rest of her family.

"Oh, God! That's awful," her sister Anne consoled from her home in Richmond. Anne had married early and well. "I think Ted's behaving like a total shit. It's a good thing you're such a strong woman. If it were me, I'd be climbing the walls." Her sister Sally in Denver echoed the sentiment.

Next she phoned her brother, Kevin, in Palo Alto.

"How did the folks take it?" was the first question out of his mouth.

"Well, it was a shock, naturally. Mom was disappointed, to put it mildly, but I think Dad was secretly gratified. I was convinced he was going to say, 'I told you so.' He never did care for Ted, you know. By the time I left, they'd both come round a bit."

"Interesting," Kevin said. "Mucho interesting."

Dani poured herself a scotch and dialed her final call of the evening.

In a few days, her daughter would turn eighteen. A proper adult, at least in the eyes of the law.

In the past, birthdays had always been family occasions, celebrated with gooey cakes, silly and serious gifts, commemorated in home movies and campy Polaroids. But now that the Sloanes had ceased to be a family, Dani felt it more important than ever to make the day special and avail herself of the opportunity for a heart-to-heart.

Lately, her daughter's talk had acquired a macho quality, a kind of hollow jauntiness: *Everything's super. Working my butt off. Went skating yesterday. Doing great in French lit!*

Dani was afraid that Sam was building barriers, erecting a carapace of empty words to hide her true emotions. And those emotions must be (what else *could* they be?) pain, rage, terror, anguish. In short, the very feelings that ravaged Dani night after night.

Yet any suggestion that Sam unburden herself met with the flip reply that "I'm one hundred percent totally fine."

Dani felt frustrated. Reach out and touch somebody, the phone company sang. But only touching was touching. Only seeing was believing. And only face-to-face would suffice. Two people in a room. With the barriers down.

Thus far Sam had ducked all invitations to come home. Dani decided to try another tack. If Sam felt so uncomfortable *receiving* sympathy, she might feel better dispensing it. To see, for once, that her mother was vulnerable too.

"I'm Fed-Exing you a plane ticket for the weekend," Dani told her over the phone. "We'll have fun, shop for birthday presents. I'll make your favorite dishes. . . ."

"But, Mom!" Sam went on instant alert. "It's midsemester. . . ."

"Please, honey. We've never spent a birthday apart. It's important, especially now," she added. "I need you, Sam."

"You *need* me? For what?"

Dani sighed. "Well, I wish I could say *I* were a hundred percent totally fine, but no such luck. It's lonely here. I miss you. I wish you'd come home and hold my hand for a bit."

"Oh, gee . . ." Sam was perplexed. "Well, yeah . . . in that case, sure."

"Wonderful!" Dani replied. "I feel better already."

Which was, in fact, nothing less than the truth. She yearned for Samantha's company. Indeed, *only* Samantha's. No one else need apply.

Dani's recent frenzy of activity—the collaring of total strangers, the buttonholing of casual friends, the agonized howl to all who cared to listen (and to many who did not) that her husband had left her left her left her—that passion had burned itself out. In retrospect, a kind of temporary insanity.

She could still picture the pained expressions on the faces of her instant "confidantes": the averted eyes, the uncomfortable pauses, the furtive peeks at the clock. The memory made her wince.

Doubtless, her most intimate friends took her behavior in stride. But that larger amorphous circle of acquaintances—the neighbors, tennis partners, dinner companions, members of their poker club, their theater group, their gym—would Dani ever have the courage to face those people again? Especially among those people the Sloanes had befriended as couples, Dani felt herself becoming Odd Woman Out.

The embarrassment, clearly, was mutual, for the phone rang less often of late. Which was all right, for at this point Dani asked little more than to lick her wounds in peace.

Were it not for anxiety about Samantha, she would have been content to climb into bed, pull the covers around her and disappear from the world.

But now, with something to look forward to, she set about planning their weekend.

Saturday, they would go fun-shopping in the Columbus Avenue boutiques, then Sam's serious present. A leather bomber jacket? A portable TV? It was better not to think about the cost. Then lunch at Sarabeth's or The Gingerman, and maybe the latest Neil Simon comedy.

Throughout the day Dani would be loose, easygoing, ready to chat about the past, present or future as the situation warranted, giving her daughter plenty of cues.

Then, Saturday night, dinner at home, by candlelight. By which time, ideally, Sam would have opened up.

Tomorrow first thing, she made a mental note, pick up plane tickets. Call the courier service. Order a cake from Eclair. Phone her ticket broker. Orchestra, tell him. Best seats. Better not to think about the cost of that, either. Because once you started worrying about money . . . ! Dani's heart thudded. Money money money. The magic word.

Her father's mention of finances had struck her on the raw. To think about money was to panic. Thus far, she had put off thinking about it, but now she succumbed to a wave of anxiety.

For two presumably "smart people," Dani and Ted had been lousy managers, with the result that their total wealth came down to a heavily mortgaged apartment, half of a secondhand boat and a few thousand bucks in the bank. The only prudent step they'd ever taken was setting up a trust fund for Sam's college education, and that barely covered the first two years.

Beyond that, their way of life had been predicated on boundless optimism. These two "smart people" earning two goodish salaries functioned on the theory that next year would be even better, time enough to get ahead of the game.

Well, next year a carefree Ted would be lounging on a beach in the Caribbean squishing sand between his toes while Dani would be grappling with a mortgage that devoured half her income.

All that night, she lay in bed dreaming up worst-case scenarios. She would sell the apartment for a pittance (the market being dreadful at the moment) and move to a dingy one-bedroom in Flushing where the halls reeked of cabbage and none of her friends would visit her and she would be mugged on the subway when she went to work. She would lose her job, go on food stamps. Welfare. Become a pariah. A bag lady. It could happen. She'd had a preview.

Only a short time ago, Dani had collected some old clothes that Ted had left, jammed them unceremoniously into a shopping wagon and, leaving the house without combing her hair or putting on lipstick, took the lot to a thrift shop a few blocks away. The day was warm; she was wearing a ratty jacket and jeans, sweating as she dragged the wagon. All the way up Second Avenue, fellow pedestrians averted their eyes and gave her wide berth. It took Dani but a few minutes to realize—they assumed she was a crazy lady! *No no!* she wanted to clutch their arms and cry. *I'm a respectable member of the middle class—just like you!*

Suppose it really did work out like that, though! It was possible. All the familiar assumptions—that she and Ted were going to work, save, retire, and be happy together for ever and ever—had proved false. The greater likelihood was that she would prove to be yet another example of downward mobility.

Never again would she live, as the divorce briefs often put it, "in the style to which she was accustomed."

But of course the style to which she was accustomed was marriage.

Late on the afternoon of the fifteenth, an embittered Leo Margulies called to inform her that Dr. Gessner had caved in on every particular. "Against my advice, I want it known for the record. I think you're a disgrace to the bar."

Dani was jubilant. "Everything, everything!" she crowed as soon as he got off the phone. She sat there for a moment, feeling the power surge through her veins. By God, she was good and smart and tough and turning into one helluva lawyer.

Then she zoomed into Jack Pruitt's office to drop a copy of the agreement off on his desk ("Look upon my works, ye Mighty, and despair"), after which she phoned Linda Gessner.

"You're going to be a very rich woman," she gloated. "I got you everything, the moon on a stick, even the cabin up in Maine."

"The cabin?" Linda was baffled. "What would I want with the cabin?"

"You want it, believe me. Why? Would you rather Ira had it?"

"Noooo . . . I just don't remember ever asking for it."

What Linda had asked of Dani was far broader in scope: that Ira Gessner rot for a hundred years in hell, after which he be drawn and quartered and thrown to wolves, the dentist's wife having progressed from total zombiedom to full revenge mode at a rapid pace. Viewed in that wise, securing the cabin was well within Dani's mandate.

"Anyhow, you own a place in Maine for what it's worth. We've got a splendid settlement here, one for the record books. You can go out and celebrate."

"You mean that's it?" she sounded disappointed. "It's all over?"

"Linda, there's nothing left to take. The battle's finished. We've won."

She sighed. "I guess you're right. But tell me, Dani, what did you say that made him give in so quickly?"

Dani laughed. "Believe me, you wouldn't want to know!"

That evening, she left the office feeling better than she had in months.

Maybe she wouldn't become a bag lady after all.

15

SAMANTHA DULY ARRIVED Saturday morning, looking neither fatter nor slimmer, merely different, though Dani was hard pressed to put her finger on what had altered other than a stylish haircut. The long wild locks favored throughout high school were now neatly clipped in a blunt cut that fell just below the ears.

"Quite a change," Dani remarked.

"You don't like it," Sam said. "I knew you wouldn't."

"Well, you're wrong, pet. I like it very much. It's trim and smart. Makes you look quite sophisticated."

"It's not so short." Sam primped the ends defensively. "There's a girl in our house who keeps her head shaved like Sinéad O'Connor, so don't say mine's short."

"I didn't say short, sweetie. I said trim. It was meant as a compliment."

One thing that hadn't changed, Dani silently observed, was Sam's hypersensitivity. It was an inauspicious start for what she hoped would be an intimate weekend.

Dani's tack was already charted. She had made a mental list of dos and don'ts, noting which topics required exploration (Sam's feelings about the separation, for instance) and which were not to be touched upon (Dani's feelings concerning the same). There would be no bitching, no partisan pleas for sympathy. Dani's role was to provide a patient ear and helping hand. For whatever her personal sentiments about Ted (he should roast in hell) or about Ted-and-Jennifer (they should both roast in hell, but separately), Dani resolved to swallow her anger—choke upon it if necessary—in her determination to present a United Front.

She was as good as her pledge. A dozen times during the day she dropped casual lead-ins to hot topics. "Your roommate Nancy . . . aren't her folks divorced?" Or, "Did you see El Swino's picture in *Time* last week? Daddy really needed to leave that place." Or, "The three of us should work out our plans for Christmas. Any ideas, lovey?"

But Sam wouldn't rise to the bait. Clearly, all substantive discussion would have to wait till dinnertime, with Dani plunging in head first.

It was guaranteed to be painful. Awkward to boot. By comparison, that first Facts-of-Life lesson, delivered when Sam was in grade school, seemed a snap. Easier to explain how Mommy and Daddy made babies, a fundamentally benign proposition, than to say how Mommy and Daddy had come to this pass.

On Saturday evening, Dani set the stage for a confidential talk: a lovely dinner at home, candle-lit if you please, with Sam's favorite beef bourguignon and a Death-by-Chocolate cake from Eclair. This once, calories be damned!

Throughout the meal, Sam had been polite but withdrawn: small talk about school, compliments on the food, avoiding her mother's eyes whenever possible, avoiding any mention of her father. Dani waited patiently for the opportune moment.

Over coffee, she decided, while the candles burnt low. Then she would begin her piece. But Sam must have sensed what was in the wind, for the moment her plate was clean, she sprang to her feet, geared for flight.

"I'll load the dishwasher, then I'm going to hit the sack. It was a terrific meal. Thanks, Mom."

"No!" Dani rose in chagrin. "No, honey, please! We have to have a serious talk."

Reluctantly, Sam shambled back into her chair, eyes down.

"When you were an infant," Dani began tentatively, "I'd sometimes wake up suddenly in the middle of the night, all ears. The house would be totally silent, not a peep, yet I knew instinctively that in a few seconds, you were going to awaken and cry. And sure enough, you always did. It was as though the umbilical cord was still there and I could sense your feelings even before you did, we were so close. Your father used to say I was psychic. Of course, that was a long time ago. I'm not psychic anymore, Sam, and you're not an infant. You're eighteen, a grown woman. So I have to ask you in words, you have to tell me in words how you feel about what's happened this last month."

Sam drained her already empty coffee cup.

"I don't want to talk about it," she mumbled.

"I don't either, Sam. It's painful all around, but it's a topic that won't go away." Her throat grew tight. "Your father and I may have our differences but—"

The phone rang.

"I'll get it!" Sam leaped up with a saved-by-the-bell expression.

"No, I will!" Dani said, annoyed. "Whoever it is can call back."

An unfamiliar baritone materialized at the other end.

"Is Samantha there, please?"

"May I ask who's calling?"

But before Dani was vouchsafed an answer, the instrument was snatched from her hand.

"I'll take it in my room," Sam said. Dani poured herself a scotch and regirded her loins.

"Who was that, lovey?" she asked when Sam emerged twenty minutes later.

"A friend."

"Does your friend have a name?"

"Everybody's got a name, Mother."

"He has a nice voice," Dani said. "Very manly. Is he someone you met at school?"

She took Sam's noncommittal grunt to be a yes.

"So have you been dating him?" Dani encouraged. "One of the boys in your class?"

"His name is King Kong," Sam shot back, "and he wants me to costar with him in his next movie, okay?"

"Okay!" Dani threw up her hands. "Sorry I asked. Anyhow, getting back to what we were discussing—"

"What *you* were discussing. I wasn't discussing anything in par-

ticular. All day long, you've been fishing around in my head . . .
what do I think, how do I feel, all that stuff. Well, how I feel is
my business. Private. Personal. You think you guys are the only
ones entitled to secrets?"

"What secrets, Sam? I'm doing my best to be open—"

"You and Dad ship me off to college like nothing is wrong when
all the time you both knew you were splitting up."

"It was nothing like that, Samantha—"

"Oh no? You told me it was mutual, that it was all la-di-dah. I
must have heard that a dozen times today. And never once did you
mention he was *living* with his girlfriend. I learned it by accident
when she picked up the phone one night. What am I, the fifth
wheel in this family? An outsider? But that's okay!" Samantha
fought back tears. "I can handle it. I'm an adult now, right? That's
what you said when I cut the cake tonight. You made this speech
about what an important birthday this is. Well, if I'm an adult,
that means that I'm free to do what I want. I'm old enough to vote,
get married, join the army—and keep my own counsel. You can
have your secrets, I'll have mine. I want you to respect that,
Mother. . . ." (*Mother.* Dani picked up on the formal usage, the
second time Sam had used it tonight.) "I'm not your baby anymore."

With that, Samantha escaped to her room, shut the door and
turned up the stereo.

So much for tonight's heart-to-heart talk, Dani thought, watching her prospects vanish. Then suddenly she felt weak-kneed with
misgivings. *Idiot*, she told herself too late.

She had hoped to do the right thing by suppressing her anger,
downplaying the circumstances of Ted's departure. Yet all her cant
about "mutual agreement" and "no hard feelings," an approach that
only yesterday seemed to make sense, had simply muddied the
waters. Sam had seen through the lies and euphemisms, and Dani
found herself wondering if she had embarked on this course in
order to spare her daughter useless anguish, or merely to spare her
own wounded pride.

Maybe her mistake had been in taking the advice she tendered
clients ("Don't badmouth the other parent"), but taking it too far.
Or maybe Sam had sensed her true feelings.

"Samantha?" she rapped at her daughter's door. "Can we talk?

I'd like to clear things up." But all Dani's knock got by way of response was a cry to "Just leave me alone!"

Sunday morning, Sam breakfasted with her father and "that woman," then came back for her gear. Her mood was thoughtful.

"I'll call a cab and ride to the airport with you," Dani said, hoping for a last-minute rapprochement, but Sam forestalled her. "Please don't fuss. I'd rather you didn't."

"You sure? Well, anyhow, I'll see you in a few weeks at Thanksgiving. You want to place your order now—turkey or duck?"

Sam frowned. "Dad said I didn't have to come out on Thanksgiving. He said Christmas would be okay."

Oh he did, did he? Dani fumed inwardly. We'll see about that! But for Samantha's sake, she swallowed her bile. United Front. That was the ticket she was determined to present to her daughter. Your parents are a united front at least where you're concerned.

Monday morning, she called Ted at the office, ready to give him holy hell.

The receptionist answered. "May I ask who's calling?"

Dani paused. They hadn't spoken since the fiasco at Veneziani's. "Tell him it's his daughter."

He was on the wire a second later. "Sam, honey?"

"I want to know who gave you permission to tell my daughter . . ." Dani launched a nonstop tirade, concluding with "Well? What do you have to say?"

At the other end came the shuffle of papers. Then—"Whit Rollins informs me that you never answered his letters," he said.

"Who the fuck is Whit Rollins? That lawyer of yours? What's he got to do with this conversation? I'm talking about Thanksgiving."

"He says he sent you three, on the eighth, the sixteenth and the twenty-first. The last two were registered."

Ted sounded remote and businesslike, which enraged her further. She had the sense of fighting phantoms.

"Well, what do you care if Sam doesn't come home? You've got your girlfriend to keep you company, you don't need a daughter. You're not the one spending Thanksgiving alone over a TV dinner. I thought we were going to handle these things together!"

"Look, Dani. I'm not getting involved in this one. Sam didn't want to come and she's old enough to make her own decisions.

We'll see her at Christmas. Anything else you want to say to me, get in touch with Whit. That's what he's there for. Got to dash!"

"Wait!" she hollered. "I haven't finished!" but she was talking to the dial tone.

Lawyers! Dani kicked the bottom drawer where Rollins's letters moldered, along with the photo of Ted. She hadn't even opened the last one, though she could guess at its contents. "If I fail to hear from you or your lawyer within five business days, I will begin legal action on Mr. Sloane's behalf." Or words to that effect. The next move would be a summons to appear in court.

Then she kicked the drawer again. I can't deal with this, she thought. Not in my present state of mind. But of one fact she was certain: *Over my dead body will he get a divorce to marry Jen MacDougall.* It was a pledge as solemn as her marriage vows.

16

IN NEW YORK ADVERTISING CIRCLES, Barney Feldman's turkey dinners were famous.

Each year the art director threw a catered At Home for "New York's homeless." The idea had originated one lonely Thanksgiving between marriages and quickly became an institution. To be sure, Barney's Hundred Neediest Cases bore no resemblance to the shivering masses huddled over grates in Grand Central Station. His guests were designers, artists, TV producers, copywriters, account executives, culled from every reach of his professional life, people who—for the most part—led vibrant social lives but had no place to go on that most domestic of holidays, the fourth Thursday in November.

At Barney's, you might encounter up-and-comers newly emigrated from the provinces, veteran bachelors, recent divorcées, single men and women who lacked a "significant other" at this juncture.

For Barney, it was business entertaining, and the guests assembled there as much to talk shop and meet prospects (both romantic and professional) as to feast on turkey and Beaujolais nouveau.

"Come join us," Kaycee had said. "Who knows, you might meet somebody or at least make a few contacts. But do me a favor—promise not to bitch about Ted. It's a party."

"Scout's honor, best behavior. Not a word about that scurvy louse shall pass my lips. So, what should I wear?"

"Anything you like, as long as it doesn't show gravy. It's basically informal. By the way, my mother will be there. We've caught her for a week on the fly, between Fiji and Finland. She looks great."

"When does she not?" Dani laughed.

Deirdre Carlson Spence Greaves was timeless, a kind of monument for the ages like Mount Rushmore. She had been a beautiful woman when, in her words, "there really were beautiful women. Bettina, Lisa Fonssagrives and me. Diana Vreeland called me 'the face of the decade.'" And though Deirdre never specified which decade, Dani took it to be the '40s when she had been a regular on the covers of *Vogue* and *Bazaar*. After which, she shelved modeling for marrying, an even more lucrative career.

When Kaycee and Dani were rooming together at Barnard, Deirdre would sometimes swoop down en route between Bar Harbor and Palm Beach, arriving unannounced in a haze of Arpège, exquisitely groomed and dressed. Invariably, she would declare the dorm a pigsty, then take both girls out to an expensive meal. Then off she would fly like some migratory bird, to return only with the change of season.

One morning, calling early at the dorm, she found Dani alone. Dani had answered the door wearing a plaid robe over a long flannel nightgown. Deirdre sniffed as though she smelled something bad.

"You'll never get a man like that, dear," she said. "Good Lord, didn't your mother teach you anything about clothes?"

Dani laughed. "Only that I should always wear clean white cotton underwear; she said that way I couldn't go wrong."

"And nobody else will go wrong with you, more's the pity! First of all, silk is ever so much nicer than cotton. . . ."

Then, settling down to await her daughter's return, Deirdre offered insights into the beauty regimen that had landed her three wealthy husbands. Years later, Dani could still remember the conversation.

"Don't ever let a man see you with your hair in rollers, that goes without saying. Or sitting on the john or picking your teeth. And never eat spaghetti in public or lobster in the shell. There isn't a woman alive who can maintain elegance under such circumstances. Always put on fresh makeup before going to bed. . . ."

"You mean, remove your makeup, don't you?"

"I mean put on. Not a lot, just a light base, blusher, a touch of eyeliner, enough to preserve the illusion. And perfume, of course."

Each morning, Deirdre said, she arose a half hour before her mate to put on her eyelashes and prepare for the day. None of her husbands had ever seen her naked face. "I'm beautiful, duckie, but not that beautiful."

Each afternoon, Deirdre repaired the ravages of the night before. "Skin care, set my hair, manicure, tweeze, you know—the basics. Then I lie down and cover my face with veal cutlets and take a one-hour nap. . . ."

"Veal cutlets?" Dani suppressed a giggle.

"They're wonderful for preventing those nasty little pouches under the eye. I see you find this funny," she said sharply, for by now, Dani was doubled up. "It happens that a great many people put beefsteak on a shiner. With good reason. Fresh beef is very effective for healing broken capillaries and tightening the skin, though I prefer a thin medallion of veal."

The last time Dani had seen her was at Kaycee and Barney's wedding, looking blond, skinny and fabulous. By then the famous visage had undergone several face-lifts, and Dani, who disapproved of cosmetic surgery on principal for all but the severely deformed, couldn't help but marvel.

To any suggestion that Deirdre should submit to the passage of years and "grow old gracefully," she might well have replied, "I *am* growing old gracefully. Have you ever seen me more elegant?"

By the time Dani arrived at the Feldmans', the place was a zoo. Fifty, sixty bodies, packed in as though it were the last soup kitchen in America.

"Welcome!" A harried Kaycee greeted her at the door. "Now the gang's all here. We've got tons of food so be sure to glutton up. Otherwise Barney and I will be eating this garbage for the next three weeks. So grab a plate and circulate, that's an order."

"This garbage" ranged from platters piled high with oysters and smoked salmon to every conceivable variety of pie. Behind the buffet, an imposing Jamaican in a starchy chef's hat carved turkey and roast beef to order.

Dani took a plate, then, remembering the second half of Kaycee's injunction, smiled cheerfully at the set of shoulders ahead of her in line.

"Hi."

Shoulders turned. They belonged to a tall outdoorsy type in a Harris tweed jacket.

"Hi. I'm Andy Banks of Tribec Productions and you're . . . ?"

"Dani Sloane."

"You with Marsden?"

"No, Pruitt-Baker."

"Sounds familiar," Shoulders said. "That one of those downtown design boutiques?"

"Actually, we're one of those uptown law firms." She had the decency to sound embarrassed. "I'm not in the ad game, just a family friend."

"Nice meeting you." He turned back to the buffet.

Dutifully, she piled her plate with goodies, then looked around for a familiar face. Except for her hosts, the only person she recognized was Kaycee's client Bo Antonelli of the big black eyes and little black book. The photographer had poured himself into the tightest pair of jeans Dani had ever seen (was he wearing a codpiece, she wondered, or was he that superbly endowed?) and was chatting up the two prettiest women in the room. He saw Dani and winked. With Kaycee's description in mind ("He'll fuck anything that moves"), Dani decided to forgo the pleasure of his company and instead made her way to a vacant seat at one of the little tables placed throughout the apartment.

"Hi," she said, wedging herself in between a fox-faced man in his early forties and a woman in a mink polo shirt.

"Hi," they returned.

"Looks wonderful, the turkey, I mean."

"Yeah," said Mink Polo. "We were just talking about the Chiat-Fallon merger. What's your take on it?"

Dani gave a noncommittal smile.

"You ask me," said Fox Face, "I think Minneapolis is out of its league. What do they know from International?"

"They know, they know," Polo said. Mr. Suede Pants leaned over from the next table. "I heard Burt Rogers took a forty-thou cut to go there from Scali."

"To Minneapolis or International?" Dani asked politely.

"The hell he did," said Fox Face. "Burt was canned."

"No shit!"

"Yeah . . . account of the Volvo fiasco."

"I hear Frye Gibson's going to Y and R for one twenty."

"One ten, but they gave him stock options."

"Excuse me." Dani got up. "This turkey's so good, I'm going back for seconds."

"Hi," said the portly gentleman in the dessert line.

"Hi," Dani murmured.

"I haven't seen so much food since my son's bar mitzvah. It looks wonderful."

Dani turned to him and beamed. A man with children, bless him, an emissary from the real world.

"Normally, I wouldn't be here myself," she explained, "except my daughter couldn't get home from college. You know what airports are like Thanksgiving weekend. I'm Dani Sloane."

"Lou Morrison. Can I get you some coffee?"

They sat down and talked about their kids for a bit. He was very sweet, warm, fatherly, and so fat he overflowed the narrow chair. His "bar mitzvah boy" was now in Rome studying architecture. His wife had "passed away" the year before. He was, Dani noted, the only man at the party wearing a proper suit and tie.

"Are you a civilian?" she asked. "I mean, everyone here appears to be in advertising."

"Myself I'm in the rag trade. I happen to be Barney's oldest client. Riviera Nights Lingerie," he cued. "Slips, panties . . . Maybe you've seen our ads."

"Of course! The little lady in the bright red lace. Real Underwear for Real People. That's you?"

"That was my sister-in-law Bessie in the ad, but the company— that's me."

They chatted awhile longer, then Lou asked if he might have dinner with her some evening. "That would be nice" was on the tip of her tongue, when suddenly warning bells went off.

Dinner? With him? Where was her head? The man was in his sixties, bald as a bagel. He had wattles. Suppose Ted, that rat! (for by now, Dani thought of him exclusively in epithets: he was Ted,

that rat, that scum, that louse, that swine, etc.) should see her in
his company! Worse, suppose Ted, that scuzz! was with his young
lovely Jenny. She could picture them exchanging patronizing glances.
Pathetic, they would think. Pathetic she would look.

"Oh my!" Dani exclaimed. "There's someone I haven't seen in
ages. Kaycee's mother, in fact. If you'll excuse me . . ."

She wriggled loose and made her way over to the window seat
where Deirdre, sublime as ever in a soft gray woolen dress, was
picking away at a plate of carrot sticks and smoked salmon. Dani
remembered Kaycee's saying her mother hadn't eaten a piece of
bread in fifty years.

"My dear!"—she half rose to brush Dani's cheek with papery
lips. "How kind of you to keep an old woman company. And how
nice to see a familiar face in all this mob."

Dani smiled. "I couldn't agree more."

Deirdre put down her plate. "Kaycee told me all about what
happened with Ted. Such a pity. Such a loss."

Dani, half expecting her to say that this was the result of going
to bed without makeup, prepared to mount a heated defense, but
Deirdre patted her knee with a blue-veined hand. "I was referring
to Ted's loss, not yours, my dear. Men are such children, they
haven't a clue about self-preservation. No matter, you'll meet someone new. Marrying well is the best revenge, I always say."

Dani nodded. "To change the subject, how was Fiji?"

"Divine. An earthly paradise. I could have stayed there forever,
gathering shells."

"Then why didn't you?"

"Because I'm off to Finland next week. Oslo will be pitch dark
when I get there, and bitter cold. A night at the Hilton should
suffice. Then France, thank God—and a week in Paris."

"But what's the rush, Deirdre? Why can't you linger in the nice
places and avoid the rotten ones? I don't get it."

"My dear Dani, I'm seventy-five, although if you dare bruit
about such a nasty untruth I shall sue for slander. Nonetheless,
being ancient, I don't have the luxury of time. It's taken me four
years already getting to F."

"But what I don't understand is why do it at all! You can't see
anything in such a short time."

"It's not about seeing, Dani. It's about accomplishing. This is something I promised myself centuries ago."

On her eighth birthday, Deirdre explained, her parents had given her an inch-thick coloring book. *Boys and Girls of the World* it was called, with the countries in alphabetical order, each illustrated by a boy and girl in typical native dress. "Kilts, saris, lederhosen, djellabahs. The Siamese children were twins, I remember. It was so exotic."

Deirdre adored the book, poring over each illustration hours on end. "Right then and there I knew that's what I wanted to do in life. Someday, when I'm old and rich, I told myself, I'll visit every one of those places. That was my childhood dream. Well, I'm old and rich now, although it took me three marriages to get there. Of course, many of those countries no longer exist or have different names—Siam is Thailand, for instance, and there are a number of new ones like Namibia. I use Rand-McNally as my guide. On the other hand, there are certain of the old countries I had written off as dead and gone that may be making a comeback. Lithuania, for example. As you can imagine, the logistics are a challenge but that's half the fun of it. The down side is jet lag, of course. I work with this marvelous travel agent. . . ."

With a sense of awed delight, Dani listened to her rattle on. Leo Margulies was right. Never underestimate the power of fantasy. Or of money, either.

By seven the hordes had gone, the caterers were clearing away, Barney was cat-napping in his barber's chair, Deirdre had retired to the guest room, presumably with a pair of veal cutlets, and Kaycee had changed into sweater and slacks.

"Let's walk off some calories," she said to Dani. "I could use a breath of air."

The two women headed down Central Park West at a leisurely pace. The side streets were empty, the whole city having gone into turkey overdose.

Their relations had altered over the past two months, subtly yet irrevocably. Dani suspected she had lost status in Kaycee's eyes, merely by the fact of being a deserted wife. She felt herself bested in an undeclared contest.

Indeed, far from seeking Dani's advice these days, Kaycee was inclined to dish it out. "I mean it kindly," she would begin, then go on to insist that Dani was doing herself no good by surrendering to grief. Instead, she should smarten up her wardrobe, lose five pounds around the hips. "You'll feel better about yourself." And the best cure of all was a new romance.

"Believe me, I understand how these things work. I've been dumped often enough to know the ropes. What you ought to do is book a ski holiday or try a dude ranch for a week. Some place where the male-female ratio is right."

The idea of taking counsel, about men of all things! from Kaycee Carlson struck Dani as ludicrous. A happy marriage had made her old friend smug.

But tonight, Kaycee was in a quirky mood. Maybe it was all that champagne.

"So?" she asked routinely. "You meet anyone eligible?"

"They may have been eligible," Dani said with a sigh, "but I'm not. Not yet. Maybe not ever. Still, I'll have you know, I was an obedient guest. I didn't breathe one solitary word about Ted. Not that I had a chance to. All anybody wanted to do was talk shop. Shop and money. They could have been speaking Chinese, for all I knew. Are ad people always so insular? I suppose lawyers are, too, when you get them in groups, though Ted and I made a point of not mixing business with pleasure. He disapproved of socializing with colleagues. Said it was too much like fouling your own nest."

"Ted Ted Ted . . . ," Kaycee muttered.

They walked for a couple of blocks in silence, both women differently preoccupied, when Kaycee piped up with a question that took Dani aback.

"How binding is a prenuptial contract?"

"Depends," Dani replied. "They can be renegotiated at any point, if both parties agree. Why do you ask?"

Kaycee bit her lips.

"As you know, Barney doesn't want more children and I signed off on that when we were married. Well, now I've changed my mind and he hasn't. In fact, he's adamant."

"Good Lord, Kaycee! You're not pregnant, are you?"

"No, but I want to be. Desperately. And I don't have much time left, Dani. It's now or never."

Dani mulled this over, trying to picture Kaycee changing diapers in her Anne Klein separates.

"Not that it's any of my business, but what brought this all on?"

Kaycee pursed her lips. "It's like this. Suppose Barney leaves me, takes up with someone else—what'll I have that's my very own? It's like . . . well, you have Samantha, my mother has me, but I'll have zilch."

"But why on earth should Barney leave? The man's happy as a clam, he thinks you're the greatest thing since felt-tipped pens. Do you have any reason to suspect he's fooling around?"

"Did you have any reason to think Ted was? Well, did you? No. He was the model husband, for God's sake, the picture of fidelity. Face it. He blindsided you all the way. But when Ted did his number, it was like some awful truth coming home to roost. Shocked as I was, it proved what I knew in my heart: They're all cut from the same cloth, the lot of them. You know Barney cheated on his first wife, he told me once. . . ."

"I understand it was a long unhappy marriage."

"My mother thinks I married down," came the non sequitur. "She always refers to him as 'my Jewish son-in-law,' though she usually goes on to say they're supposed to make good husbands." Kaycee brooded for a moment. "He dumped his second wife, too— so much for good Jewish husbands."

"From what I hear, she was a total airhead. Besides, they only lived together a year or so. Come on, Kaycee, lighten up. Barney's a pussycat, not a mean bone in his body."

"Why are you defending him, Dani? If Ted could do it . . . ! Or are you defending Ted as well?"

"Are you kidding?" Dani burst out. "After the suffering he's caused?"

Kaycee nodded. "I feel the same way. Barney says I should forgive and forget, but I can't. That's some sleazy example your husband set! Especially to Barney, who spends his entire working day surrounded by women—models, secretaries, cutesy young

art directors eager to sleep their way up. Why should I assume
he's a pillar of virtue any more than Ted was? Whereas if I had a
baby . . ." Her voice trailed off.

"You think that would help you hang on to him?"

She shook her head no. "If I do this, it won't be for Barney's
sake, or even for our marriage. It'll be for me, for my future. I saw
my gynecologist last month. He was quite encouraging. He says
I'm in great shape for forty-two."

Dani blinked. She tried to picture being the sixty-year-old mother
of a rambunctious teenager. Bad enough being one in her early
forties. Did Kaycee have a clue what she was letting herself in for?

"The more I think about it," Kaycee continued, "the more sense
it makes. I've gone back into analysis, by the way. My shrink says
I've got a lot of unfinished business to deal with—my mother, my
basic insecurities, all those abortions. But he agrees, it's every woman's right to have a baby."

"Well, of course it is but—"

"A basic right, whether they've signed some idiotic agreement
or not. More and more I realize that's what I truly want out of life.
I want a child, Dani, a wonderful beautiful baby. Now, before it's
too late. So, Dani, what do you think?"

They had come to the end of Central Park West. Snow was
beginning to fall. In the doorways of the Coliseum, dozens of New
York's homeless—the real homeless—had built a tent city of plastic
sheeting and rags.

"Is that a professional query, Kaycee?"

"Personal."

"Well, personally . . ." She sighed. "I can sympathize with your
situation, but the fact is, we don't always get everything that we
want in life. Did I? Does anyone? Why not look on the bright side,
as my mother would say. You're a lucky woman, Kaycee. You've
got a great job, a nice home, a terrific husband. I feel for you,
believe me, but I can't help feeling for Barney as well. Is it worth
jeopardizing a marriage for?" Suddenly she burst into tears. "At
least you've got a husband to go home to—be grateful!—whereas
I'm going home to nothing. To empty rooms! No Sam, no Ted.
No nothing!"

*   *   *

Dani went home and crawled into bed with a case of postparty depression. The apartment seemed to echo with emptiness.

If only Kaycee realized her good fortune! Why, at this very moment, she and Barney were probably sitting around the kitchen table, making small talk, picking on leftovers, rehashing the day's events: which guest had worn what, said what, which unlikely twosome had hit it off. Half the fun of throwing parties used to be in recapping them with Ted, Dani thought. She envied Kaycee that intimacy.

As for this business, this *fixation* on having a baby, Dani didn't know what to believe. Was Kaycee sincere? Or was this just another whim, a fancy comparable to so many in her friend's episodic life— like EST or the Cambridge Diet. Dani's bet was that it would all blow over in a few weeks. Kaycee would buy herself something extravagant and feel better.

Besides, Kaycee had given Barney her word, had given it freely, and one's word ought to count for something in marriage. Indeed— Dani grimaced—one's word ought to count for everything.

Which brought Dani right back to Ted.

Damn him damn him damn him! Even this new obsession of Kaycee's was all his fault in a roundabout way.

Amazing, really, that in little more than two months the fallout from Ted's bombshell should be so widespread. Not just among the principals involved, but all over the map. In an art director's Central Park West bedroom, a dentist's office on Park Avenue (and Dani didn't kid herself that Dr. Gessner was anything but a stand-in for her husband), even in a California bachelor's flat.

That very morning, her brother Kevin had called from Palo Alto, ostensibly to wish her a happy Thanksgiving.

"I did it, Dani. I called Mom and Pop yesterday. Since you'd already broken the ice, I figured it was time I got honest, too. I've been wanting to get square with them for years, but you know how they are—so grindingly conventional. But what the hell, if they can come to terms with a divorce in the family, they should be able to handle this. Anyhow, I told 'em as gently as I could."

"Just what did you tell them?" Dani braced herself.

"That I was gay. But you knew that, didn't you?"

Her heart turned over.

"Of course," she lied gamely.

In fact, she had not. Had Kevin dissembled so well? Or had Dani chosen to deceive herself? The latter, she realized. For whenever such a suspicion intruded, she had pushed it away. Not in *her* family, Dani's conscious will dictated. Her family had to be storybook perfect. That picture was inalterable.

And so Dani had managed to shut her eyes to the fact of Kevin's sexuality, just as she had done with Ted and the decay of their marriage.

Just as she was doing now—she felt a tremor of shock—with Samantha. Sam, who wouldn't make it home for Thanksgiving. Sam, with her snappy new haircut and her silences and her "secrets."

That the secret was a boy, Dani had no doubt, recalling her own freshman year at college. And though, in her hyperbolic fashion, Sam used to kid about being "the last virgin" in her class at high school, no one expected that status quo to last indefinitely.

Yes, Sam had met some boy. Had fallen in love and was having an affair. There was nothing shameful in that. Dani supposed it was more or less inevitable. But what a time for that first love affair! With Sam at her most vulnerable.

Inside her head, Dani felt alarm bells go off. Boys that age could be so macho. So eager to shuck their adolescence, prove their masculinity. They'd break your heart, often as not, and walk away whistling. How would Sam cope?

For despite her daughter's claim to adulthood, Dani found the idea that her "baby" had become sexually active most disturbing.

It was a measure of how far apart she and Samantha were drifting that her daughter felt constrained to be secretive about such a major event. Indeed, Sam had grown elusive to the point where Dani could rarely reach her on the phone. Out every night, it appeared.

Yes, a boyfriend, Dani concluded, though beyond that she could only guess. Was he good for Sam, bad for her? A fellow student? A kid from the area? Did he have a name?

Everybody has a name, she recalled Sam's disingenuous response to her question, and Dani had let it pass, intent on other matters. Now Dani made an effort to recall.

A nice voice, she remembered. Inferentially, a nice person.

Yet if he was so nice, why the secrecy? And if he wasn't . . . ?
Then Sam's evasiveness made sense.

Either way, Dani had to know.

And the only place to find out was in Oberlin.

17

MAKING THE DECISION to visit Oberlin proved easier than informing Samantha of her plans.

A dozen times that week, she had tried reaching her on the phone only to learn, at whatever hour she called, that Sam had "just stepped out," or was "not here right now," or "gone for the evening." No one ever knew when she'd be back.

"Well, be sure to give her my message," Dani said each time. Which was that, barring the outbreak of World War III, she would arrive in Oberlin late Saturday morning.

But by then, of course, Dani, too, had got the message: Samantha Sloane was spending her nights elsewhere.

Nonetheless, it came as a letdown when she pulled up at the residence house in a rented car to find, in place of Samantha, a scribbled note and a set of directions.

Welcome to Oz. Didn't know what time you'd arrive. Just follow the yellow brick road and we'll be waiting.
A toute à l'heure.
                    Us

The "yellow brick road" terminated several miles out of town in a lonely cottage half hidden in the woods. A '79 Mustang was parked out in front. Sam's ten-speed bike, propped against an un-painted porch railing, assured Dani she had come to the right place.

At the sound of the car, Sam popped out the front door.

"Hey, Mom!" She came down the steps followed close behind by a heavy shambling figure in a heavy sweater and cords.

Dani gaped in disbelief.

He was—*there must be some mistake*—late thirties? Early forties? In any case, old enough to be Sam's father. Surely this couldn't be . . .

She made a quick recovery.

"Hello darling." Dani gave her daughter a kiss. "Well, here I am. How about some introductions?"

"Yeah . . . sure." Samantha flushed, but whether out of an-noyance or embarrassment, Dani couldn't say. "Mom, this is Mel . . . actually, Melville Landrum."

"Melville?" Dani said. "What an unusual name."

"So everyone tells me. My mother was reading *Moby-Dick* when she went into labor and Melville was the first name that came to mind."

Dani smiled. "Good thing she wasn't reading *Crime and Punishment*."

"Dostoyevski Landrum. I love it." Sam turned to Mel with a brisk laugh. "Then I could call you Dusty."

They were standing on the wooden steps of a country porch. Were they going to ask her inside? Dani wondered. But Sam made no move toward hospitality; instead, she placed her hand on Mel's sleeve and launched into a kind of résumé.

No, Dani rationalized while Sam ticked off his academic honors. This man couldn't possibly be her lover. ("Dr. Melville H. Landrum, Ph.D.") Perhaps her student adviser or simply a mature older friend. Given his appearance (the paunch, the receding hairline, the general aura of middle age), it seemed unlikely that Sam would find him sexually attractive.

Landrum specialized in some obscure cranny of French lit, Dani deduced from Sam's introductions, but she was too confused to absorb details.

". . . gave a paper at the last convention of the MLA—the

Modern Language Association, you know, Mom?—on the mor-
phology of gender in Froissart. It was extremely well received."

"Yes . . . Froissart . . . ," Dani mumbled. "I see. I'm sure I'd
like to read it."

"I doubt that, Mom. It's very arcane."

Dani stiffened, but Sam continued unabashed. "Anyhow, I guess
you should know, since it seems to be the object of your visit—
Mel and I are living together."

Dani found it impossible to miss the unspoken *So there!*

An awkward silence ensued, then Mel Landrum jumped into
the breach.

"Well, what do you say we go out for lunch, Mrs. . . . ."

"Call me Dani," she said, still smarting from Samantha's rebuff.
"I think we can dispense with the formalities, especially since you
and Sam are living *en famille*. I trust I've pronounced that correctly?"

"You have a natural accent."

Dani turned to her daughter. "Don't you want to put on some
lipstick before we go?"

"I don't wear lipstick anymore," she announced. "Mel says why
ruin a beautiful complexion with chemicals. *Un peau de velours*."

Dani forced a smile. "Let's go and eat, please. I'm tired and
hungry."

And heartsick.

Throughout lunch at the Wagon Wheels restaurant, the conversation, though civil, was clumsy. Mel did his best to be agreeable.
Dani struggled to hide her dismay. As for Samantha, she said hardly
a word, her eyes moving from one principal to the other with an
anticipatory air. Mostly her glance came to rest on Mel. When she
did speak, her conversation seemed limited to Mel-this and Mel-
that.

The restaurant didn't serve liquor, and Dani, who could have
used a drink to grease the social wheels, wondered if the choice
was deliberate. Mel had ordered a vegetarian special for himself,
and Sam, the inveterate carnivore, had followed suit. Did Landrum
disapprove of meat and alcohol as well as lipstick? Dani wondered.
In any case, his influence over Samantha seemed profound.

While they ate, Dani learned the pertinent facts of Mel Landrum's life. He was thirty-eight, the child of academics at a Tennessee state college. Most of his adult life had been spent pursuing grants and various degrees at a string of colleges in the United States and France. He had finished his doctorate the previous year at Berkeley. Never married ("Never stayed in one place long enough," he said with a smile), Mel Landrum appeared to have made no major commitments in his life, except to the advancement of French lit.

"Mostly I've been researching the impact of the Hundred Years' War on lyric poetry," he said. "One year for each decade, as Sammi says."

Had circumstances been different, Dani might have found the topic interesting and Mel himself a decent sort. But the only circumstance she could focus on was: *This man is sleeping with Samantha.* Or "Sammi," as he called her.

Yet Landrum didn't strike her as a seasoned seducer; if anything, he seemed unwordly in a manner that belied his years, and Dani was beginning to shape a picture of a life spent in student digs and furnished rooms.

"Problem is," he explained, "as an academic specialty, French lit of the fifteenth century is both narrow and overcrowded, and there are only so many tenured positions."

"In other words, you're an instructor," Dani mused.

And likely to remain so, she thought, for by now she had sized him up as an intellectual drifter—likable enough, perhaps, but essentially a man with no real home, no responsibilities, no prospects.

Yet Dani could understand that in her daughter's eyes, he cut a far more dashing figure: mentor, teacher, voice of authority. No good dwelling on the fact that the man was old enough to be Sam's father; presumably, that was part of the attraction.

Dani was about to ask him how long he planned to stay at Oberlin when Sam, who had been largely silent, interrupted.

"Oh, Mo-ther! Stop grilling Mel like he's Public Enemy Number One. He's a scholar. A gentleman and a scholar."

Dani excused herself, went to the lady's room and threw cold water on her burning face. The last thing she wanted was to lose her temper, although she could cheerfully have wrung Mel Landrum's neck. Why couldn't he pick on someone his own age and leave her daughter alone?

When she came back, the two were chattering away, heads to-gether, in rapid French.

"Sorry about that," Samantha said after a moment, and Dani sensed that the snub was deliberate. The rest of the meal limped along accompanied by small talk. The weather, recent books, plans for the remainder of the weekend. Maybe they'd go to a movie that evening. Or stay home and play Scrabble. "Mel's got a fabulous vocabulary," Sam added.

Now and again, when she wasn't holding his hand beneath the table, Sam would finger a little jade heart she wore around her neck.

"Mel gave it to me for my birthday," she explained, with a secret smile.

When the bill came, Dani reached for it out of habit.

"Allow me," said Mel.

"No no. My pleasure," she said, handing her credit card to the waitress.

They drove back to the cottage, which proved to be as grubby inside as out. The sense of isolation was suffocating. In the manner of cheap rentals, the furniture ran to faded chintz, a tired Axminster rug and coil-sprung upholstery. Through the living room door, Dani glimpsed a rumpled double bed and Sam's belongings strewn about like autumn leaves. The place was funky with the smell of sex.

Mel followed her gaze and closed the bedroom door.

"Can I take your coat, Dani?" Mel asked.

Dani shook her head. "No thank you, but I tell you what I would like. If you've got some brandy . . ."

"I can get some. I'll just run down to the liquor store."

"I'll go with you." Sam popped up like a Jack-in-the-box, but Mel sounded a more prudent note.

"I think your mother would like some time alone with you, Sammi. Be back in twenty minutes."

The door closed. Dani sank to the sofa amidst a billow of dust. Samantha, perched on a Morris chair, observed the dust cloud.

"I guess I flunked the white-glove test," she said with heavy sarcasm.

Dani felt immensely sad. She searched her daughter's face looking for a scrap of warmth, a flash of humor. But Sam's eyes were
dark and angry, her mouth set in a sullen vise.

"Mel seems like a very pleasant fellow," Dani said. Sam folded
her arms and studied the pattern on the carpet.

"And such an interesting background. Still"—she kept her voice
low and even—"I wish you had told me you were living with
someone."

"Well, now you know."

"You could have confided in me, Samantha."

"Why?"

"Why?" Dani echoed. "Because I love you, that's why. Because
I care about what's going on in your life, and when I don't hear
from you from one week to the next, I get anxious. I start wondering, are you sick? are you unhappy? is something wrong?"

Sam fell back to the contemplation of the rug. Even the crown
of her head gave off angry vibes.

Proceed with caution, Dani told herself. *But proceed.*

"Please, Sam, look at me when I'm talking to you. Believe me,
I'm not sitting in judgment. I just want to understand."

"What's to understand?" Sam raised her head, eyes glittering.
"It's simple. Mel and I are in love, and we've decided to live together."

Dani swallowed. "I appreciate that," she said. "But you don't
have to be so secretive. I'm not the enemy, Sam. I didn't fly a
thousand miles to start an argument. All I ask for is some clear idea
of what's been happening, why you decided to move out of the
dorms—"

"Right! I should be as frank and forthright with you as you were
with me about you and Daddy splitting up. You lied to me." Sam
sprang to her feet and began pacing. "Yes, you lied. You tried
to make the whole thing sound like a walk in the park instead of
which . . ." She spat out the words. "Daddy left you, didn't he?
He found someone he liked better and left you. What did you
think?" Her voice trembled with rage. "That I was too dumb to
figure out what was going down? You didn't respect me enough to
tell me the truth. . . ."

Dani shook her head, vehemently.

"I was trying to spare your feelings, Sam."

"Fine!" Sam shot back. "I'll buy that if you like. Now you buy this. I didn't tell you about Mel and me to spare *your* feelings. I knew you'd hate him—"

"I don't hate him," Dani protested, "I hardly know him. I'm simply trying to under—"

"Oh yeah, sure. You don't hate him. And I'm supposed to believe that? I saw your face, Mom, the way you looked when he came out of the cottage. Your jaw dropped a mile, like he was something out of *Nightmare on Elm Street*. You made a good recovery, I'll grant you that, but first impressions never lie. You despise him."

"I was surpri—" Dani started, but Sam barreled on.

"Why surprised? By your own admission, you came out here to spy on me, so why should you be surprised at anything you found? Anyhow, there's no point discussing Mel and me, since I know what you're going to say. All you want to do is put him down. You should have seen yourself, flashing your American Express Gold Card in the restaurant—the big New York lawyer rubbing it in."

"Samantha!" The accusation caught her off balance. "What difference does it make, who paid the bill?"

"Because you did it to humiliate him, to make us both feel like shit. You can't stand the fact that I'm having a love affair without your written permission." Her cheeks were bright with rage. "Well, tough! Ever since I can remember, you've been telling me what to do. Clean up your room, Sam. Stand up straight. Wear your overshoes. Don't mix plaid with stripes. Even this morning, Put on some lipstick, Samantha. Like I'm a baby or a retard, and Mother always knows best." She gave a mordant laugh. "Dani Sloane, attorney at law, the world's greatest authority on love and marriage and whether I should wear lipstick or not! Well, you didn't do such a great job on your own life, did you? You drove Daddy away and now you're jealous of me! Because I have a lover and you don't! That really bugs you, doesn't it, that you can't run my life anymore." Samantha took a deep breath, then, to Dani's astonishment, veered off on a dozen other tangents. "Like when I wanted to take up the saxophone, or that time I went to camp and had to bunk with Katrina Baines. . . ."

For the next ten minutes, Sam continued scattershot. Ancient grievances were aired, recent injuries, a list of complaints both serious and trivial, real and fancied.

A dozen times Dani yearned to interrupt, to shout that "No, it wasn't like that" and set the record straight. Instead, she bit her tongue and dug her nails into her palms. Argument would only aggravate the situation. This was not, Dani realized, and must not become, an adversarial proceeding, for there would be no winners. Losing her husband was jolt to the system enough; she had no intention of forfeiting a daughter as well.

So Dani sat quietly and listened, especially to what went on beneath the words. Throughout Sam's diatribe, she heard a single common theme. *I will not be treated like a child.*

And the realization began to sink in: Her "baby" wasn't a baby anymore.

The Sam who now stood before her, eyes hot with indignation, was a different figure indeed from the girl who had been so conscientious in high school, so compliant, so *sweet*.

All those years when Sam's classmates were at the height of adolescent revolt, experimenting with drugs and alcohol and sex, Dani and Ted had simultaneously congratulated themselves and crossed their fingers. *Their* daughter, thank God, had escaped the craziness, her rebelliousness running more to hot-fudge sundaes than to six-packs. And as for the televised question "It's ten o'clock. Do you know where your child is?" the Sloanes could answer with a hearty "Yes."

Now, with sinking spirits, Dani realized that their self-satisfaction had been premature. Sam's youthful rebellion hadn't been bypassed at all. The inevitable had merely been postponed.

At last, Samantha ran down, more out of breath than out of anger, for she had balled her hands into fists.

"May I say something now?" Dani asked.

"No."

"Look, Sam. I hear what you're saying. Can't we discuss this reasonably?"

But Samantha was in no mood to be reasonable.

"No! *You* look. I didn't invite you here. That was your own bright idea. Well now that you've satisfied your curiosity, you can take the next plane back. Just go, Mother. Get out of my home. Get out of my life!"

Then she clapped her hands over her ears.

That night, Dani slept for twelve hours, then woke up Sunday morning feeling numb.

What to do? Ought she to call Ted, tell him their daughter had got herself involved in this unsavory romance? Let him take over the reins, for a change? After all, it was Ted's fault—not so much that Samantha was embarked on her first love affair, but that the object of her affections should be not some nice young boy, but Mel Landrum.

Excuse me, Dr. Melville H. Landrum, Ph.D.

And Father Figure.

Dani winced. There was a slight physical resemblance between the two men. Not that Mel Landrum had Ted's good looks, but both were on the heavy side, tall and broad-shouldered. Mel, Ted: even the construction of the names was similar.

In her list of wild charges, Sam was right about one thing: Dani *did* detest Landrum. Almost as much as she detested Ted Sloane.

No, she couldn't bring herself to phone Ted and have to listen to his voice. Instead, she spent most of the day drafting a long anguished letter.

Dear Ted . . . She crumpled the first sheet, threw it out. No, not *dear*. Never *dear*. There would be no greeting at all.

To Ted Sloane:, she typed, as though it were an interoffice memo.

First off, she outlined the situation vis-à-vis Sam—*This is all your fault*—but once having found her voice, Dani was unable to stop. Her anguish overflowed onto the paper. Every slight, every minor sexual failure, every injustice, real and imagined, of the last twenty years was set down in vivid detail. Each word was an arrow designed to wound, draw blood. The sheer passion of this letter would break his heart, she pledged. Would leave him helpless, guilt-ridden, aware that he alone was responsible for the wreckage of two lives.

All day long she rewrote, revised and expanded the tract, fleshing it out with more half-forgotten injuries, eloquent in her own cause.

By dinnertime her "indictment" had swelled to half a dozen typed pages. Any jury worth its salt would find him guilty.

Then she read the letter through once more and shuddered. Decent people don't send hate mail. Anyhow, what was the point of such a missive, other than the perverse pleasure of letting off steam? Ted would either tear it up or laugh over it. Or worse—pass it on to his lawyer, whose communications continued to pile up in her desk drawer at work.

Dani bundled up in her winter coat, and headed downstairs, tossing the letter in the trash compactor on the way out. Then, feeling curiously purged, she walked all the way to Union Square and back, brow furrowed, unconscious of the cold. She returned close to midnight, fingers numb but head clear, then sat down again to compose another letter, this one hand-written. And far more important.

My darling Samantha,

Words can't express how much I regret what has happened. Not just between your father and me, but between you and me too.

Sam, I was wrong to lie to you, to fob you off with soft-soap stories about the circumstances of Daddy's leaving. At the time, I thought I was doing it out of a desire to protect you from unecessary pain, but looking back on it, I think it was as much to protect my own pride and self-esteem.

No, my darling, you're not a child, and I was foolish to treat you as one. From my heart, I apologize. I do want to be honest with you, though I admit I bumble sometimes.

About yesterday. I would be less than honest to pretend that I'm happy with your decision to move out of the dorm and in with Mel. I've always believed that one of the best things college has to offer is a variety of social experience. It's a place to meet new people, date different boys, get involved in all kinds of activities. In short, I hoped you would enjoy the mainstream and bustle of campus life. That's how I feel.

However, Sam—and this is what I most want to say—it's not what *I* feel that matters. It's what *you* feel, whether it's about Mel (whom I hope to get to know better) or living off campus or wearing lipstick or whatever.

I've thought a great deal about what happened yesterday. It's your life, you said. So it is, though the idea takes some getting used to. I realize

I can't lead it for you. It goes without saying that if I can help, if you want my advice at any time, you have only to ask. And I suppose I'll continue to volunteer it.

That said, I respect that you will make your own decisions. My darling Sam, believe me, I understand that you're the only one who can decide what you want in life, and I appreciate that it may not always be what I would have wanted for you. You're an adult. I respect that.

But though I can't lead your life for you, Sam, I can't walk away from you either. There are bonds between us that nothing can break. Nothing! not what has happened between me and your father, or what is happening between you and Mel.

Dani paused and blew her nose.

I want you to know, and I can't put this too strongly, that whatever you do, Sam, whatever choices you make or however you choose to live, whether or not I "approve," doesn't matter. What matters is this: I love you, Sam. I will never love you one milligram less than I do at this very moment. Which is with all my heart and soul. And that I will always be . . .

She wiped her streaming eyes. How odd, how unspeakably odd that the very phrase that she jeered at when it had come from Ted's lips now sprang onto the page in all its sincerity.

And that I will always be there for you.

18

"WELL, HELLO STRANGER!" Marian Barstow bumped into Dani in the cheese aisle of Food Emporium late one evening. "Why don't we see you at the poker club anymore?"

"Sorry 'bout that." Dani pressed a smile into service. "I've been so busy."

"Don't I know it," Marian said. "The Christmas whirl. Who has time to breathe with all the entertaining?"

While they chatted, Marian loaded her wagon: a wedge of Emmentaler, two ripe Bries, a Bel Paese, a massive chunk of mascarpone. "My in-laws are coming over tomorrow for dinner," she explained. "How about joining us sixish for some cheese and wine? My refrigerator runneth over."

"Thanks," Dani said politely. "I wish I could."

"Another time, then. Anyhow, we'll be seeing you at the Melmans' on New Year's Eve."

"Actually," Dani said. "I'm afraid not."

Marian looked surprised. "Going to Florida or what? Well, have a merry . . . ," she said.

"Yes, you too."

Dani selected a three-ounce packet of sliced Swiss, added a pint of skim milk and headed for the express checkout. Christmas, she thought. Parties. *Bah, humbug.*

No matter that the invitations were piling up on the coffee table:

cocktail parties, open houses, the usual rounds of Christmas hospitality and New Year's Eve blowouts.

Dani scarcely glanced at them. Never had she felt less festive. The mere idea of dressing up and venturing forth by herself left her feeling exhausted. And upon arrival, she mused, you were obligated to glitter and be gay. She hadn't the strength.

Besides, whose lips would she kiss at the stroke of midnight? *Bah, humbug. Humbug and bah.*

Anyhow, she was busy busy busy, she told herself, too much on her plate; in fact she had fallen into a kind of lethargy. The visit to Oberlin had left her drained of emotional energy. Work, worry, sleep: those were the basics, and they absorbed a full twenty-four hours each day. Even the sending out of Christmas cards struck her as a monumental task. What was there to say, anyhow? SEASONS GREETINGS FROM LIMBO.

The one friend she saw sporadically was Kaycee. They met for drinks at the Plaza a week before Christmas. Kaycee arrived late, framed in Canadian lynx and laden with packages from Bendel's and Bergdorf's.

"You look gorgeous, duckie," Dani said admiringly.

"And you look—well, *fraught*."

"It's this business with Samantha," she confessed. "It's wearing me down."

"Then maybe a pair of martinis will pick you up."

Over the drinks, Dani poured out her heart.

"I'm not sure if I did the right thing," she agonized. "Maybe I should've tried Tough Love. Or complained about Landrum to the school authorities. But the thought of losing her was more than I could bear. Maybe there is no right thing," she added.

"Well, at least you two are talking now."

"We're talking nonsense," Dani said with a shrug. "All euphemisms and blather. *Well that's fine . . . that's cool . . . how's Mel? . . . have a nice day . . . thank you for calling.* Like a couple of airline stewardesses trying to put on a happy face. I'd hardly call it a dialogue. In fact, she's still furious with me. More pissed off with me than she is with Ted, which makes you wonder if there's any logic in the world. After all, who dumped whom?" Dani sighed.

"But he was always the family Good Guy, and she was Daddy's Girl."

"So what does Daddy say about her living with this guy?"

"We haven't discussed it. I doubt he even knows. Or wants to. He's too busy playing Peter Pan. You want to hear the ultimate craziness? Sam has asked me not to tell him. 'Daddy will go bananas if he finds out,' she keeps saying, and I'm not going to blow the whistle, especially since I made a point of promising to treat her like an adult. Besides," Dani added, "I'd just as soon not have to talk to the bastard. Ted, I mean. Not that other bastard out in Oberlin. To Bastard Number Two, I'm always scrupulously polite."

"Maybe you'll grow to like him," Kaycee said helpfully.

"Who . . . Mel? Maybe I'll grow to like sumo wrestling and ingrown toenails. I suppose it could be worse, though. Sam might have taken up with a drug freak or a bike boy or—"

"—or a PR man," Kaycee interjected. Both women laughed.

"Though I find it instructive," Dani remarked, "that Sam considers Ted too delicate to deal with unpleasant facts."

"Well, you might take that as a back-assed compliment. Like you can handle it, he can't."

"That kind of compliment I can live without." Dani stirred her drink morosely. "I sometimes wonder if it's worth having children at all. You knock yourself out to ensure that they grow up as civilized human beings with healthy bodies and decent values. The best schools, finest pediatricians, the Brownies and ballet class and ski holidays and museum trips and flute lessons—though it seems in retrospect that Sam had really wanted to play sax. You worry about their making nice friends or having problems with their algebra teacher or whether heavy metal music will injure their eardrums or are they going to get mugged when they go biking in Central Park. Which has happened twice, you know.

"Funny, now that I think of it. We were always so concerned about New York's being so dangerous. At least, I figured, Oberlin was safe. Anyhow, you make this huge emotional investment year after year, and for what? So your kid can walk out of your life the day she reaches eighteen and shut the door behind her. Slam bang. So long and good-bye.

"I'm so conflicted, Kaycee. One part of me wants Sam to be independent, the other is in total panic. She could be heading straight for the abyss with this guy, and there's not a damn thing I can do. First Ted, now Sam. I feel so fucking powerless." Dani drained her glass and checked her watch. "Anyhow, end of bitching session. You're a heroine for listening. Time I was getting on home."

"Yeah, me too." Kaycee signaled the waiter. "So will we see you at Pat and Betsy's on Saturday?" She tapped a Bendel box at her feet. "I got the most incredible little panne velvet chemise."

"I've decided not to go."

"We'll miss you. What about the Carneys' open house?"

Dani shook her head. "They were Ted's friends more than mine. I'd feel uncomfortable."

Kaycee frowned. "Next thing, you're going to tell me you're skipping New Year's Eve at the Melmans'. But you *always* go to the Melmans', Dani. Everybody does. It's a tradition. You can't put your life on hold indefinitely. When is this hibernation going to be over?"

"I don't know. Maybe I'll emerge for Groundhog Day. I just need time. Sorry to be such a Grinch, Kaycee, but I'm not in a holiday mood. I'll have to muddle through in my own way. Anyhow, I'm leaving my Christmas plans open. Samantha's coming home Tuesday and I want to be available for her."

"Which means she didn't walk out of your life and shut the door, slam bang," Kaycee remarked.

"Not totally," Dani admitted. "Though she may be bringing the boyfriend, which makes for a problem. I won't condemn, but I won't condone. Anyhow, I made it clear to Sam on the phone yesterday, if he comes, he'll have to sleep on the living room sofa. I mean, it *is* my home, after all, and I'm entitled to some measure of control."

"Did she agree?"

Dani nodded, then Kaycee went on.

"Which means you're not so fucking powerless either."

"I guess not."

"So count yourself lucky. She's a good kid at heart. I know it will work out. Yes, lucky. I wouldn't mind getting a Samantha of my own for Christmas. . . . But Barney's still giving me a hard time."

Kaycee's recent obsession with motherhood left Dani feeling ambivalent. For though she wanted Kaycee's happiness, she doubted if her friend had really thought the proposition through.

Kaycee was a thoroughgoing romantic, which made Dani wonder if she hadn't succumbed to a romanticized notion of motherhood—all smiles, no tears, a luscious dream from a Victorian valentine.

When Samantha was small, Kaycee used to blow into town with the most extravagant presents: immaculate white Italian knit babywear that had to be washed by hand, crisply pleated Alice-in-Wonderland dresses that took an hour to iron. "Oh, isn't that a picture!" Kaycee would exclaim when Sam was dolled up in the finery, then clap her hands. And Dani would look at the two of them and think, *Two children.*

Because that was at the crux of Dani's doubts. Kaycee was kind and generous and warmhearted and loving—and willful. A brilliant beginner, but with a short attention span.

And like many another beautiful woman, she was accustomed to getting her own way. *Must have* was her favorite phrase. Yet although Kaycee usually got what she wanted, she rarely managed to hang on to it.

She wanted a child now, she said, a lovely infant to nestle in her arms. Yes, that appeal was irresistible. But a few years down the line, would Kaycee want to keep pace with a roisterous toddler? Or a messy ten-year-old? Kaycee would then be in her fifties. Age was a factor.

Not that it couldn't be done—but was Kaycee the one to do it? More to the point, was she willing to do it alone? Not the Kaycee Dani knew—with her flawless nails and Bendel boxes and one man or another always at her side.

The Christmas break had arrived, Sam along with it, minus Mel, who was visiting his family in Tennessee. Dani looked forward to long evenings tête-à-tête.

Sam has lost weight, she noticed, and the first night at home actually bypassed Dani's veal marengo. "We all eat too much meat in our society," she remarked with a bright shallow smile. It was a smile Dani was to see often over ensuing days.

"Are you becoming a vegetarian?" Dani asked, which elicited a superior smirk.

"I'm considering it, like most caring people. Besides, I want to get down to a size fourteen."

On the surface, Sam was chatty. College was fine, she was working hard, either going to do a double major (French poetry and poli sci) or maybe transfer to the University of Michigan. But on a more intimate level, Dani couldn't get through. At the most tentative probe concerning her feelings about either Mel or her father, Sam's face would compose itself into a mask of empty cheerfulness.

Everything was "fine"—*smile, smile*—or "most excellent." Behind the mask, Sam had withdrawn into some interior hiding place.

Much of the time, Sam was out shopping or visiting her father in Greenwich Village or getting together with high school friends. When home, she usually appeared in equable spirits, though always with an ear cocked for the phone.

"I'll get it!" Sam would holler and was halfway across the apartment before her mother could blink.

If the call was for Dani, she would hand over the receiver with a sigh; if it was for her, she would take it on the bedroom extension and disappear for up to an hour. No point in asking who called.

"Well, I hope Mel has stock in AT and T," Dani observed at one point, which elicited the now familiar shallow smile. All told, Dani preferred the old days when she and Sam would have their shouting matches complete with verbal pyrotechnics. At least they were communicating; it was a two-way street. Messy, to be sure, but better than the pasted-on grin.

Every now and then, Samantha would drop casual remarks about her father's new living arrangements, usually interspersed with sly digs.

Though consumed by curiosity (What was the household like? Was it a nice apartment? What kind of furniture? Did Jennie cook? Was she working? Did Ted say anything more about their plans?), Dani refused to ask pointed questions, reluctant to put Sam on the spot. Instead, she gleaned such crumbs as fell at her feet.

"Wow! It's chaos down there," Sam said one day.

"Oh?" Dani's heart skipped. Lovebirds singing out of tune already? Chaos? Discord? *Tell me more, more!*

"Yeah . . . boxes, cartons, no one knows where anything is. Dad said I could have his sheepskin jacket. He won't be needing it."

Ah! The happy kind of chaos. The lovebirds were migrating south after all.

Another time Sam came back from the rink at Rockefeller Plaza and volunteered that "Jen's okay. In fact, she's kind of fun. She's teaching me how to ice-skate, last chance. They're leaving Friday. Did you know she was figure-skating champ of eastern Iowa?" *Dig dig.*

It quickly dawned on Dani that these references were deliberate, teasing, taunting. Sam's method of keeping her off balance. A kind of revenge, perhaps, for the scene in Oberlin. A way for Sam to preserve the upper hand. Dani fought to keep her cool while extracting as much information as she could.

"Figure-skating champ," she said. "Imagine that! Leaving Friday, hmmmm? Well, I don't imagine there'll be any rinks down in . . ."

Dani let the phrase hang, and this time Sam obliged by filling in the gap.

"In St. Thomas? I wouldn't think so. She says she'll probably take up water-skiing instead. You know, they have mongooses there, or is it mongeese?"

Aha! St. Thomas. At last, a concrete fact. Dani and Ted had once spent a weekend there when he was training for the Peace Corps in nearby St. Croix. Paradise. Sapphire beaches, coral sand, palm trees—paradise!

"Wonderful," Dani growled.

"Yeah, maybe I'll go visit them in spring break." *Dig dig.*

Dani's jaw dropped. "Spring break? But I'm expecting you here!" Then the phone rang. Sam dashed to get it. Clearly, it was HIM, the Demon Lover of Oberlin, for when she came out of her room a half hour later, her cheeks were flushed, her eyes dancing.

"Mom, I know you're gonna say I'm an awful shit,

and you'd be right, but I'd really like to leave tomorrow, be back in college in time for New Year's Eve. It's a very special occasion . . ."

Dani felt outfoxed.

"Why, I don't even know if you can change your air tickets," she said. "And besides . . ."

"I can! I called already. Oh, Mom! Excellent! You're a real heroine. I'll never forget this. Hugs and kisses!" And that big shallow smile.

And then she was gone.

And then Ted was gone.

And the two people who mattered most in the world had slipped far beyond Dani's reach, beyond her control. And Dani was alone at the butt end of the very worst year in her life, facing a pile of bills and a larger stack of worries.

Conceivably, she might have made an issue about Sam's staying on, but it wasn't a fight she wished to tackle by herself. Playing Family Cop was nasty business.

It was Ted's fault. Naturally. Ted's fault that their daughter had gone off the deep end. Ted's fault that Sam was so needy.

Even now, as Dani sat slumped over the kitchen table alone, a new year close at hand, Ted was gamboling with his lover in the tropical night—carefree, happy, well fed and well fucked.

She wished him—no, not dead. That coy suggestion of Chris Evans ("Get a hit man") was absurd. But if not dead, then not happy either. No Happy Rest-of-Your-Life for Mr. Theodore Jay Sloane, that rat!

She wished him ill. She wished that his Caribbean paradise would prove his nemesis, a Devil's Island where fate doled out just deserts. She wished him—no, not dead, but heir to any and all of those unpleasant conditions for which the tropics were notorious. She wished him ticks, dysentery, ringworm, sunstroke. May he step on a sea urchin, may he be stung by jellyfish. May he be visited with scabies and plagued by boils. Let him choke on a dish of tainted lobster. Be bitten by a rabid mongoose. She wished him small, mangy ailments that would disgust his little Jennifer. May he be cursed by impotence! Ah, poetic justice indeed!

And while she didn't wish to see him dead and buried (after all, this creep was the father of her child), if something untoward *should* happen to him during his sojourn in paradise (the Virgin Islands having gained a reputation for violence), she could accept his demise with composure.

Here Lies the Late Theodore Sloane. R.I.P.

Roast In Pain. Rotten Insensitive Prick.

Momentarily, the thought lifted her spirits. And she would bar Jennifer MacDougall from the funeral. So there! Serve 'em both right.

Yet even as Dani cursed, something within her was changing, reshaping; without conscious effort, a new creature was emerging from the chrysalis of pain.

She was beginning to shake off the paralysis that had held her captive all these months. Words, wishes, verbal venom, sick fantasies: those were the weapons of the blowhard. She had been too blinded by anger to function. But what had those savage daydreams accomplished? Nothing. They had neither eased her suffering nor wounded her adversary. Such passivity was alien to her nature.

Little by little, old instincts asserted themselves anew. All her life, Dani had been a doer, a fighter, a risk-taker. She still was, by God. The time for empty talk was over. The time for action, drawing near.

On New Year's Eve, Dani stayed home to watch the ball go up on TV. She prepared for the moment by opening a bottle of Veuve Cliquot that had been stowed in the wine rack ages ago, awaiting some significant event. Well, this was it. A few seconds more and the 1980s would be history.

In Times Square, motley thousands had gathered to kiss the decade good-bye. Drunks, kids, merrymakers, Bridge and Tunnel folk, pickpockets, out-of-town gawkers muffled against the cold, mounted cops with an eye out for mischief: a great, seething, rollicking, pushing, shoving, thieving, laughing, shouting, vibrant mass of energy.

"Hi gang!" An exuberant teenager had jumped into camera view and was waving wildly, to be drowned out by a cacophony of horns. It was the great American ritual, the annual rebirth of New York, and Dani watched, fascinated. In her veins she could sense the crowd's raw power, its zest for life.

And there was Dick Clark counting down the seconds on television, milking each one.

TEN! . . .

My God, the whole world is out there, crowding, pushing . . .

NINE!

fighting for space and air. . . . Not sitting home,

EIGHT!

drowning in self-pity. What's with you, Dani?

SEVEN!

Are you such a lump . . . a stone . . .

SIX!

letting life roll over you as if you had no will?

FIVE!

Shape up, woman. You've played doggo long enough. Time

FOUR!

to join the living. Take control. Don't let the bastards

THREE!

grind you down. You're going out there a total marshmallow,

TWO!

like they say in the movies but . . .

ONE!

You're coming back a champ!

"HAPPY NEW YEAR!"

The ball went up, and with it, the roar of the crowd.

"Happy New Year!" she yelled back to the TV.

Then everyone was joining in—hoarse baritones, piping sopranos, noisemakers, sirens and horns.

Should auld acquaintance be forgot . . . a thousand voices were raised in song!

Most likely it should. Fuck auld acquaintance. What had it ever done for her! Because Danielle Sloane, Esq., was ready to move on. The Eighties were dead. Long live the Nineties.

Midnight. Time for resolutions. Time to act, to pounce, to grab the world by the balls.

She hoisted her glass.

Resolved: I, Dani Sloane, refuse to be helpless. I will not let circumstances roll over me.

From now on, she would take charge of her life. Of her career. She was sick and tired of playing Fido. If anybody imagined for one instant that she was going to lie down comatose while Ted waltzed off unscathed, that someone was in for a nasty shock. What did Ted think? That a couple of routine legal noises from some tinpot lawyer would make her, Danielle Sloane, Esq., panic into instant surrender? That he could jerk her around left and right?

Well, it was about time Ted got real. Time he learned that this was war. She couldn't regulate any other aspect of his life, but this one she could. When it came to divorce, she knew her stuff. There were dozens of delaying tactics available—countersuits, depositions, interrogatories, endless motions motions motions—and Dani would employ them all. She'd make Ted dance to her piper, pay for his play, make him wait till love ran cold. Grant that bastard his freedom so he could marry Miss MacDougall? No way. Not till she was damned good and ready, not till he was down on his knees begging for mercy.

Resolved: I, Dani Sloane, shall prevail!

She finished the bottle with ease. Revenge is a dish, she decided, best washed down with Veuve Cliquot at thirty bucks a bottle. High time she started being good to herself.

The first business day of the new decade, Dani closed what was left in their joint account and blew most of it on a full-length Blackglama mink. Sleek, smooth, and glistening. Luxurious. A coat fit for a female tycoon.

It was a wacked-out purchase, one that left her nearly broke yet feeling glorious, and in direct contradiction to the advice she gave clients. "Be prudent," she warned them. "Don't go on a spending spree. It counts against you in court." But Dani would rather be bold at this moment than prudent.

Besides, she had yearned for years to swathe herself in furs but always squelched the desire, knowing how thoroughly Ted disapproved on moral grounds. Moral grounds, indeed! she snorted. Look who's talking morality. Mr. Candidate for Sainthood himself!

Then she repeated the oath that had become a bedtime ritual. *Over my dead body will he marry Jen MacDougall.*

No reason why Ted should be the only one permitted a measure of self-indulgence. The fact that his money had paid for half the coat made buying it even more pleasurable.

So she was close to penniless. So what! Had she not read somewhere (in her mother's Norman Vincent Peale, most likely) that poverty acts as a stimulus to the strong? Well, Dani was strong and next month's mortgage would provide incentive enough. She'd collar Jack Pruitt first chance she got and demand a hefty raise. It was due her, overdue her, in fact. All that was required was an aggressive stance. *Think positive,* she told herself snuggling into the fur. *Think mink, not mouse.*

"Beautiful!" Kaycee said when Dani modeled the coat for her. "Is it made from female pelts?"

"No." Dani smiled. "I prefer to wrap myself in the skins of dead males."

Part Three

Part Three

19

"DIVORCE . . ." Dani folded her hands on the desk top and assumed the grave expression she kept for newcomers. "Divorce is such a painful measure. . . ."

"Save your breath, honey," came the impatient rejoinder. "You're not talking to a bleeder."

In fact, Dani knew perfectly well whom she was talking to. The face, smile, the lithe muscular body could belong to no one but "That Girl Sherle," the exercise queen who, a dozen years earlier, had blitzed the airwaves in a series of TV spots for a chain of health clubs.

"Hi, I'm That Girl Sherle from the Lean Machine"—she would chatter on even as she limbered up or lifted weights or gyrated a pelvis—"so, let's get skinny. It's easy as one, two, thureee!"

The commercials had a low-budget look. No sets, no extras, just a cute blonde in an exercise suit—moving, spieling, selling, Yet, though crude, they were effective. The secret was in the spokeswoman: friendly, bouncy, irrepressible Sherle, exuding vitality and health. And who could resist that glorious smile and the promise that "I'm gonna make you beee-yutiful!"

Sherle Nelson wasn't smiling now, however. She was taking a quick inventory of both lawyer and office, the bright eyes darting from Dani's face to the filing cupboards to the prints on the wall to the no-frills bookcase to the new mink on the coatrack, then back to Dani.

Dani, closeted for the first time with a celebrity, also took stock. What she saw was impressive.

In her mid-thirties, Sherle Nelson still appeared as limber and energetic as the girl in the old commercials, though now she reeked of Giorgio rather than gym mats, and the black leotards had given way to couture clothing. In a plum-colored Chanel suit and Hermès scarf, she emitted the kind of panache that Dani, who read fashion magazines intermittently, recognized as consistent with price tags ending in three big zeroes. You wanted to feel the fabric, study the seams. She had small shapely hands, beautifully kept, with long sharp plum-colored fingernails, the better to impale you with, my dear. On the ring finger shone a huge emerald solitaire; on the wrist a gold Patek watch. God is in the details, as Mies van der Rohe said.

At last, both women having completed their inventories, Sherle Nelson leaned back and crossed her legs, then produced the famous yard-wide smile.

"My dentist tells me that his about-to-be-ex stripped him bare. Practically down to his fillings." She spoke with her hands, punctuating key words with jabs and stabs. "So naturally, I asked for the name of Mrs. Gessner's lawyer." Jab. Stab.

"Ah, I see. . . ." Dani laced her fingers judiciously and tried not to smile. "Yes, Linda Gessner is a valued client of mine. I was happy to be of service. So, Mrs. Nelson . . ."

"Call me Sherle. Everyone does, even total strangers."

"Sherle it is. And I'm Dani. Now, what can I do for you?"

"That remains to be seen, but for a start, get out your yellow pad, clear your desk, and cancel your appointments for the rest of the day. I got a lot to say. You got a lot to digest. Basic problem is, I want to skin my husband alive."

Dani laughed. "Don't we all!"

She was born Shirley Judd some thirty-five years earlier in a trailer park near Tucson, the oldest of six children. Her father was a part-time mechanic at the nearby airbase. She had matured young. At twelve, she could have passed for twenty.

Quick and self-reliant but, by her own admission, not much of a one for book-learning, she dropped out of school at sixteen and headed for Las Vegas, hungry for glamour. With the help of a fake ID, Sherle found work at a small casino, dealing blackjack, becoming adept at the trade. It was while working as croupier aboard a Bermuda-based cruise ship that she met Laszlo Nelson of New York.

She was eighteen. Lazzi was forty-plus and married, which didn't trouble Sherle one whit. She was swept away on the spot. "He was so suave, so continental. It blew my mind." They became lovers before the week was out.

From his father, Lazzi had inherited a shabby East Side gymnasium that had served as training grounds for generations of second-rate boxers. No sooner was the property in his hands than Lazzi shut it down. The location was too valuable to be wasted on a handful of pugs; it stank of sweat and jockstraps rather than nice clean money.

By switching from punch to paunch, as it were, and converting the premises into a unisex health club, he cashed in on the booming exercise craze. His motto was *When You Lose, You Win*. The first Lean Machine was born.

By the time he met Sherle, the Lean Machine had expanded to four sites in the New York area and Lazzi had dreams of going national. What he needed was a spokeswoman, trim and appealing, a personality to put his company on the map. Sherle fit the bill.

The sole obstacle to their happiness was the then-Mrs. Nelson, who intended to make him pay for his freedom. The final arrangement granted her a percentage of his earnings, a conventional settlement in those days.

Like any good entrepreneur, Lazzi's faith in the future was unbounded, but the thought of handing over progressively bigger and bigger sums to a woman he no longer lived with struck him as an offense against nature. He began restructuring the business, arranging matters so that almost no cash passed through his hands. On paper, Sherle would be the earner. She would draw the salary, pay the household bills, have sizable funds at her discretion, while his own wages, a meager three hundred dollars a week, were supplemented with a generous expense account.

Sherle was thrilled. It was more money than she had ever dreamed of, and when Lazzi asked her to sign a prenuptial contract forfeiting all rights in the company in return for a magnificent salary, she did so gladly. "What did I know!" she explained to Dani. "I was nineteen years old and an executive vice-president in charge of public relations, having fun, pulling down a hundred grand a year. Like, yippee!"

What she hadn't realized was that all real property was in the company name. Lean Machine Inc. held title on their cars. Their homes. Their significant collection of American paintings. And she had signed it all away.

"Dumbnuts me, I didn't even know what a P and L statement was. How could I? I never went beyond tenth grade."

What evolved was a division of labor. Sherle's role was to publicize, to inspire and motivate sales while Lazzi took care of the financial end.

Like Lazzi, she was a perfectionist—obsessed with achievement, energized by rising graphs and growing membership. Fourteen-hour workdays were the norm, during which Sherle ate, drank, and dreamed Lean Machine. What interested her most was the problem of marketing.

"The company needed a focus, a symbol. And I was it."

The idea for the TV spots was exclusively hers, and she drove everyone crazy from start to finish. "I wrote the scripts," she said, "developed the routines, drew up the budget. I would have cranked the cameras if the goddamn unions had let me. That campaign represents my personal best."

When, in the campaign's second year, Sherle became pregnant, she saw it as an opportunity.

"Everyone said I'd have to lie low until after the baby was born. Like who wants to see fat ladies in leotards? But I had a brainstorm."

Sherle Has a Baby, the new campaign was called. Each week, a fresh commercial was shot. Millions watched as Sherle—five months pregnant; six months pregnant; big as a house, for God's sake!—continued to work out with her customary cheer. Occasionally she'd pat her stomach and declare that "Exercise is good for both of us." Right up through the ninth month.

Then, after a two-week hiatus, Sherle was back on screen in a bright pink leotard, a postpartum miracle inviting you to track her progress as she got her old figure back.

"If I can do it, you can too—with a little help from the folks at Lean Machine. And oh, by the way, 'It's a girl!' "

The baby, named Precious, was now eleven years old and in boarding school, but it was already apparent to Dani that Sherle's real "baby" was the company.

For some years, the Nelsons had enjoyed an open marriage, personal considerations having given way to professional ones. And it was professional conflict that had put the marriage in jeopardy.

By the late '80s, "fat" as an issue was beginning to lose its potency. "Fit" was the word on everyone's lips. Sherle felt the time had come to phase out the Lean Machine concept and start a new kind of enterprise.

"The Health Habitat," as she designated it, would be a total, controlled environment. In its precincts, members might not simply work up a sweat, but experience fitness in the round. They would breathe filtered air, drink purified water, eat a supervised diet, have heartbeat and blood pressure monitored, relax on orthopedically correct divans while fountains plashed.

"You know what a week in Main Chance costs? Thousands! Well, ordinary people don't have the time or the bucks, and ordinary people have always been my clientele. So what I want to do is offer real spa living at city prices in city locations, on a drop-in basis."

Sherle began working out the details. She consulted architects, doctors, designers, dietitians, commissioned a feasibility study, found a location in the midtown area. "Lend me five million for seed money," she told her husband, "and I'll do the rest."

Lazzi thought she was crazy. He should give his wife money so she could set up in competition? No way! Anyhow, he told her, Lean Machine didn't have that kind of capital on tap. He had a cash-flow problem. She knew that.

But she knew nothing. She had never really troubled herself about the financial minutiae of Lean Machine. She'd been content with her salary.

"Then I got smart," she told Dani.

Six months ago, she'd hired a CPA to teach her the principles of accounting and tax law. Simultaneously, the marriage began to

disintegrate. Last month, Lazzi had moved into a suite at Trump
Tower; then came the cruncher. On Monday morning, Sherle had
arrived at work to discover she'd been locked out of her own office.

"You can't do this to me," she shrieked at Lazzi in front of a
dozen staffers. "I'm executive vice-president."

"Not anymore," he said. "This is my company, this is my decision. Now get off my back."

The next day Lazzi's lawyer made her a proposition.

"What it amounts to is," Sherle told Dani, "I get the apartment
outright, child support, plus a cash payout of sorts. The amount
would be negotiable, depending on whether I'm a good little girl
or not. In other words, I don't go into business for myself. But I
want my due. Half the value of Lean Machine. I'm talking serious
money, and Lazzi has it, in spite of his hollering poverty. I'm talking
paintings, my friend. Great paintings."

She was talking Nolands, Rosenquists, Jasper Johnses, Larry
Poons, Ellsworth Kellys, "plus some Schnabels that will knock your
socks off. . . ."

With a thrill of pride in her voice, Sherle reeled off the names,
not all of which were familiar to Dani, who kept mum. ". . . and
three of the most gorgeous Basquiats. You know, that Haitian kid.
Lazzi's got taste, I'll grant him that. He's been collecting for years,
plowing in almost all the firm's profits. Plus he bought cheap, when
a lot of those guys were nobody. Yeah, . . . the man's got an eye
for talent. After all, he picked me, didn't he?"

The paintings, Dani learned, were housed in the upper floor of
their duplex and could be reached either through the living quarters
or by a separate entry on the floor above. However, the day after
he left, Lazzi had the locks changed on both doors.

"I should've done it myself first," Sherle said, "but I'm a schmuck."

"What are they worth?" Dani asked.

"That's a toughie," Sherle said, rubbing her nose thoughtfully.
"Maybe fifty, fifty-five million, maybe more. Almost everything's
museum quality. I helped collect a lot of them, Dani, which ought
to make it as much mine as the company's."

"And your daughter?" Dani asked. "How's she taking the
breakup? That's a very sensitive age and it might be a help if she
got some therapy pronto."

"Precious is no problem. She's busy with her own life, couldn't care less. You know what kids are, all wrapped up in themselves."

"And have you thought about custody?"

"We could share it, I suppose. Again, no problem. Anyhow, your job isn't worrying about Precious, it's worrying about me. Seeing that I get mine. Pictures, money, the whole bit. Did I mentioned the Picasso plates . . . ?"

As she enumerated the rest of their possessions, Dani listened, amazed. The Nelson child appeared to be the sole item in the estate whose ownership was uncontested. However, that was a matter that could be discussed at a later date.

"So there we are," Sherle concluded the catalogue. "Or there I would be if not for that goddamn agreement I signed."

Dani sat still for a moment, her mind racing.

"Prenups aren't always binding," she said.

"When are they? When aren't they? And what do I do next?"

"Next, Sherle, you file for divorce." Dani glanced at her watch. "Well, we missed our chance today by about four hours," she said humorously, "so within the next couple of days. Look, I'm not saying that it matters legally who files first, but this way we can put a temporary freeze on Lazzi, prevent him from selling pictures or squirreling assets away. If things work out, you can always drop the suit. If not, any deal we make will be retroactive. So what have you got to lose?"

"Sounds good to me. All I'm asking for is my share. Half the business or the cash equivalent. And if that chiseling little lowlife has to sell the paintings, which would break his fucking heart, that's tough!" She paused to catch her breath. "Don't get me wrong, Dani. This isn't about revenge or injured pride or getting even or any of that wounded-ego crap. It's about money, pure and simple." Then she got to her feet. "Christ, I'm stiff."

Having shed her jacket earlier, she now divested herself of shoes, watch and scarf, then bouncing back to her feet, began a series of calisthenics.

"You work out much, Dani?"

"A little sailing now and then."

"That's not working out, that's escapist stuff. On your feet and we'll do a few simple exercises that are terrific when you've been sitting on your ass all day. Okay, chin up, hands above your head. One . . . two . . . thureee. . . ."

The cleaning woman looked in on her rounds to discover two silk-shirted shoeless women doing knee-bends. She blinked in puzzlement. Dani winked back.

Workout over, Sherle prepared to leave, while Dani fell into her chair, winded but exhilarated.

"So . . . !" Shirle was slithering her fingers into butter-soft leather gloves. "What's your take on my situation, Dani? Legally speaking, am I asking for the moon?"

Dani slid back into her business mode, feeling remarkably sharp and able. Oxygen in the system, she supposed; it quickened the mental processes. It also made her wary. The thought crossed her mind that she might be getting romanced for free advice—Dani, along with God knew how many other lawyers. Sherle's exposition had been so lucid, so well rehearsed, if ungrammatical, that it had probably gone a few laps around the track already. Unbilled time was one thing, unbilled legal advice another. She chose her words cautiously.

"You understand, it's much too soon for me to commit to an opinion on such a complex matter. In any case, you haven't retained me as yet. Let me explain our fee structure. . . ."

Sherle listened, nodded, then broke in with "You want a check now as a sign of good faith?"

"Tomorrow would be fine."

"No problem. But if you're with me, pal, it's gotta be all the way, one hundred and ten percent. I expect that of everyone who works for me, from my dry cleaners to my accountant. One hundred and ten percent. No chickening out or getting mushy about the head or putting your personal life ahead of my interests. *Capisce?*"

Dani looked her in the eye. "This *is* my personal life," she said.

Yet for a fraction of a second, Dani had hesitated. Not only would she be dealing with one tough cookie, but she'd also be up against her biggest professional challenge to date. One part, the sensible part perhaps, longed to run for cover. The other part jumped at the chance.

Think mink, not mouse. Think mucho bucks. Think Chanel suits. Think power. Think clout. Think self-respect. Think how bare-boned clean you would like to pluck Ted Sloane had he but Lazzi Nelson's assets. She felt a rush of adrenaline.

Dani seized Sherle's outstretched hand.

"You have just hired yourself one hundred and ten percent of the toughest, meanest, drivingest, hardest-working lawyer in Manhattan."

Sherle laughed. "That's the spirit. By the way, you got a beeper? Nope? Then get one. I like to keep in touch."

Dani gathered her notes. "I'll take these home tonight and review them. Then I think we should get cracking right away. One question, though. Ira Gessner's recommendation aside, what made you decide on me? Naturally I'm delighted, but I presume you've—"

"Comparison-shopped? Honey, I've done the rounds. Felder, Cohen . . . all the heavy hitters except for Willi Shannon. My husband beat me to it and hired him first."

The name sent a flutter through Dani's heart. Willi Shannon. The King of the Bombers, the flamboyant Mr. Split of the white Rolls-Royce. He usually represented the wives of the rich (some said he slept with them as well) and was an artist at extracting large sums. When you see his name on your Mrs.'s divorce papers, the joke went, stash a subway token in your back pocket; you'll need it to get home from court.

"Very interesting," Dani said to Sherle. "I look forward to meeting Mr. Shannon. But you still haven't said why you chose me over a host of such . . . ummm, very able competitors."

Sherle snapped her handbag shut.

"Because you and me are a lot alike, hon," she said. "We're both stand-up broads. I feel it in my bones. I've got an instinct for such things."

"Thank you . . . I think."

As she did each morning, Dani checked the weather in the *Times* (38° in New York, 87° in St. Thomas—where it was raining, she noted with satisfaction), then prepared for her meeting with Jack Pruitt. It was the first order of business that day.

The "stand-up broad" (Sherle's description both amused and annoyed) dressed for her assault on the corner office with unusual care: best suit, silk scarf tied with a rakish flip, highest heels. For once, she'd use her height to tower over Jack physically. Let him think of her as a "big lady" in every sense. She'd been gearing to ask for a raise in any case, but the acquisition of Sherle Nelson as a client had thrust her into a shakedown position.

Dani liked Jack and he in turn was fond of her, but his affection was impersonal, unthinking, the kind of casual goodwill awarded a pair of comfortable shoes or a lapdog. A born hustler, Jack was a "rainmaker" in law firm parlance, dedicated to beefing up the client list. Wherever he went, whether for business or pleasure, he was always on the lookout for prospects. More than once, Jack had boarded an airplane (he traveled First Class only), sat next to a stranger, and landed with a signed retainer in hand. He expected comparable efforts from every lawyer in the firm.

"Socialize, socialize," he harangued new associates. "Every dinner party, every wedding, every PTA meeting is a business opportunity in disguise."

For years, Dani ignored his injunctions. When she went home at five-thirty, she left the office behind her. As a result, of the fifty-odd lawyers on the Pruitt-Baker staff, she found herself relegated to the sidelines. Her name never came up at partnership discussions nor did it figure in the annual reorganizational charts. Her forty-hour week was considered part-time employment. Even office gossip skipped her desk.

Yet what had held her back, she knew, was not ability, but attitude. Had she worked weekends and holidays, wangled, pitched, scrambled, socialized, she might have had a shot at partnership. Partners made big money at Pruitt-Baker, but only high-flyers ever made partner.

You could tell which lawyers had the potential. The Boy Scouts, Dani dubbed them; they never walked when they could run. You'd see them racing down the corridors as though it were a triage ward, always late, always pressed, working hard, playing harder—not that there was any difference between the two. After hours, you could catch them up at Smitty's Bar and Grill, where they gathered nightly to booze, swap war stories, cement bonds.

But by that hour, Dani was home having dinner with Ted. That scum!

All those years, she though ruefully, those opportunities lost while she had striven to achieve harmony, balance. The "greater good." She had traded off worldly success for the felicities of married life. And wound up with neither.

Now, however, that balance was gone. It had walked out the door with Ted Sloane, and with it went a host of restraints.

Another Dani was beginning to emerge from the wreckage. A primal Dani, ambitious, competitive. The Dani who had fought her way to be head of the class. The teacher's pet, the high school valedictorian, the college student making Dean's List year after year—and how sweet the taste of victory had been!

What she had once done, she could do again.

To win, to prevail, to have her name stand for something, to kick ass on occasion. What better way of proving her worth, not just to onlookers but to herself. She refused to be—dear God!—a dishrag, a whiner, an object of pity. Not an object at all, but a Somebody, envied and admired and, truth be told, feared.

Like a Mafia don, Dani craved respect. *Rispetto.* She wanted the world to kiss her ring and tremble.

Since Ted's departure, the only happiness she'd known had been on learning that she had clobbered Dr. Gessner. That triumphant day, Dani had walked on air and felt that she could walk on water as well. You could bet Ira Gessner had come to respect her. Leo Margulies, too, poor slob. It was Jack Pruitt's turn now. After six years on the back burner, Dani Sloane was ready for success.

At nine sharp, she marched into Pruitt's office and stood before his desk.

"I am about to bring in a client," she began without ceremony, "who is involved in a multimillion-dollar action. We're talking mucho mucho bucks, to quote the lady. Fifty, sixty, conceivably more. If you doubt my assessment, look 'em up in Dun and Bradstreet. My client is Sherle Nelson of the Lean Machine Inc."

Swiftly, Dani outlined the ABC's of the situation, while Jack Pruitt listened with astonishment, as if that pet lapdog had suddenly sprouted ten-foot fangs.

"So," Dani concluded her précis, "she'll be sending over a thirty-thou retainer by messenger as soon as I give the word. Now you realize, Jack, that this is a woman who's accustomed to doing business with principals, not foot soldiers. . . . Hell, the retainer agreement ran three pages."

"Sit down," Jack said. "Stop hovering over my desk like a goddamn King Kong. You make me nervous."

Dani savored the moment, then took a chair.

"As I was saying, Sherle naturally expects to be dealing at the highest level, and while I didn't tell her I was a partner in this firm, I didn't tell her I wasn't. You follow?"

The hint could hardly have been broader, but Jack, frowning, was following another line of thought.

"Willi Shannon." He frowned. "That's heavy-duty stuff. You think you're up to handling it? Maybe we should call in an outside co-counsel."

Dani narrowed her eyes. "Let me make one thing clear, Jack. Sherle Nelson wants to hire *me!*"—how splendid that sounded!—"me personally, not Pruitt-Baker. She'd never even heard of this firm, so if you give me a hard time moneywise, I'll simply take her business with me and rent space elsewhere. Not a half-bad idea, anyhow. At least I'd get to keep a nice healthy chunk of that two fifty an hour you bill for my services instead of the pittance I actually receive."

Jack studied her for a moment, trying to discern if she was bluffing, and apparently decided she was not, for he began speaking in conciliatory tones.

"Now now Dani, I meant no offense. Never for one moment did I doubt your ability to handle complex issues. I have the greatest respect for your talents. My only worry was the physical toll these cases take. However, I'm sure we can work something you can live with. I'll have to take it up with the other partners. . . ."

When he called her back around quitting time, it was all Dani could do to refrain from letting out a relieved "Whoopee!"

She had been granted, if not everything she asked for, still far more than she'd expected: a raise big enough to get the wolves off her back, a nifty bonus arrangement, plus the honorific title (well, it would look good on business cards) of Director of Matrimonial Litigation, and the prospect of a partnership if all went well. Meanwhile, she could enjoy the full-time services of the secretary she had previously shared with two other associates.

"So you're mine all mine," she told Annabel Lozack, "starting as of now. I'm just delighted."

"Will you be staying late tonight?" Annabel asked with a glance at the clock. "I gotta know."

"I don't think so, honey. I'm about done for the day."

"Leaving around six, would you guess?"

"Maybe six-thirty, thereabouts."

She waltzed home close to seven to be greeted by her doorman Mikhail's announcement that "your ladies are waiting in the lobby."

"My ladies?" Dani furrowed her brow and went in.

"Well, this is quite a delegation," she said, thoroughly confused. It wasn't her birthday—she checked a mental calendar. So how come the surprise party?

There was Gloria Melman, whom she hadn't seen in months. Marian and Carole from the poker club. Martha Winograd, whose daughter had gone to Dalton with Samantha. Ellen McCroy, from the East Side Democrats and one of Dani's favorite people. Angie Beckwith, her good friend who lived upstairs in 27G. Billy Ann Grissom whom she's known since Barnard . . . Allie Winters . . .

Someone had gone to a lot of trouble to get this group of disparate women together. For though they weren't particularly close to each other (she wasn't aware that Angie even knew Billy Ann), they were all old and good friends of hers.

"Girls' night out," Ellen said.

"No men."

"Who needs men?"

"We've made reservations at the Dynasty Palace," Martha said. "For seven-thirty."

"Angie booked one of the big round tables."

"When did you think up all this?" Dani felt a thrill of delight. "You guys have been plotting behind my back."

"Well!" Gloria Melman hooked her arm through Dani's elbow. "Since you didn't come to my New Year's Eve party, for which I shall never forgive you, we figured it was time to smoke you out. By the way, I love your coat. . . ."

And Dani was pretty sure who the chief conspirator was: Gloria, she'd bet. That woman was such an organizer. Unless it was Marian. Or Angie, that pussycat. With—definitely—a tip-off from Annabel Lozack. She felt a rush of love.

"Listen," Martha Winograd suggested. "Maybe Dani doesn't want to pig out on Chinese food. Maybe she'd rather go to somewhere else."

"Like where?"

"Chippendales? You know, the male-strippers club."

"You've got to be kidding."

"Okay, Dani, the choice is Chinese banquet . . ."

". . . or Chippendales and all those gorgeous hunks."

Dani laughed. "I don't think my system could stand it. Chinese is fine. I'm starved."

More for companionship than food.

Ellen McCroy squeezed her hand. "Welcome back to the land of the living."

She returned around eleven, high on MSG and the laughter of friends. Then, still on a roll, she called up Samantha to share the day's triumphs.

"What a coup!" she said. "I've got a raise plus my own secretary and this fantastic new client. You know who she is, toots? That Girl Sherle from TV."

"Gee," Sam said pointedly. "Mel will be thrilled. Or he would be, if he ever watched cheap commercials."

Dani ignored the barb. She was feeling too good. "Anyhow, things are easing up financially a bit, so if you want to come in for a weekend—just you—then the two of us could go shopping, maybe catch a couple of shows . . ."

"Is that meant as a bribe?" Sam asked warily.

"Absolutely," Dani said.

"Absolutely not," Sam said. "I can't be bought."

Suddenly, Sam giggled. And Dani followed suit. It was the first time they'd laughed together in months.

20

THERE WERE DAYS when Dani likened her lot to that of a short-order cook in a busy busy coffee shop: taking orders, juggling dishes—all of them hot—operating on a dozen different burners at once. The demands were incredible. No one ever shut up. One BLT on a seeded roll, hold the mayo! Gimme a couple of sunny-side-ups with bacon, toasted English on the side. Five burgers to go, two rare, three medium. Yeah, with fries. Hey, bud, watch your back! I got hot fat going here! Pronto pronto!

One misstep and you were flat on your ass, a menace to yourself and everyone else within striking distance. For like hot-fat cookery, high-powered divorce was dangerous work. No time to breathe, no margin for error, and if you couldn't stand the heat, then damn well get out of the kitchen.

Unlike the short-order cook, however, Dani's work conferred status. "All that *agita*, I don't envy you," Chris Evans remarked, green with envy. Dani grinned. "There'll be enough work in this for everyone," she said.

Lazzi was ingenious, a tax man's nightmare, a "creative" accountant's dream. He had structured his life so intricately that it would appear he personally had no assets. Those two hundred Italian suits and six dozen pairs of Gucci loafers were a business expense, ergo company property, as was the food he ate, the air he breathed. To say nothing of the paintings. A poor man who owned a rich business. Believe that, and you can believe anything.

Jack Pruitt had given her a fresh-out-of-law-school associate to do the grunt work. Lanky and casual in an oxford shirt and denim skirt, Marsha Lowe looked like a throwback to the sweaty '60s. Straight hair and wire-rimmed glasses completed the picture.

"I'm gay," she announced her first day at work. "Is that a problem?"

"No," Dani said. "Though I'd rather you come into the office looking more businesslike. Is *that* a problem?"

Marsha shrugged. "Jack hired me to help with research, not client contact. However, I've got a blue suit somewhere."

Marsha proved to be as advertised: tenacious and shrewd, great with figures, an excellent drafter of memos, never happier than when digging out some obscure point of law. She lived in Queens with four cats and a lover who taught kindergarten. Within a week, Dani knew she had a gem.

"Wow!" Marsha said, picking through papers on Dani's desk. "I wouldn't let any guy fuck me over like that."

"Hey!" Dani barked. "That's my personal file."

But the best thing about Marsha was that she came in early, left late and was available weekends.

"So I've got myself not only a full-time secretary but a terrific associate," Dani told Kaycee over a hurried lunch at the Brasserie. "Plus which, I'm providing employment for half the professionals in New York." Did that sound arrogant? Probably, but the role of Boss Lady was still a novelty.

"You should see the army that marches in and out of my office," she continued. "Auditors, assessors, private detectives, paralegals. Even Sherle's press agent is in on the act. Thus far, though, it's been preliminaries. On Wednesday, we buckle down to serious business. That's when we get the art collection appraised. It'll be a mob scene. Our experts, their experts, mavens from the auction houses. I wish I knew more about contemporary painting. The fact is, I'm a word person, not a thing person. Maybe I should ask you and Barney to give me a crash course. . . ."

Dani stopped her patter. Her friend seemed to be listening with only half an ear. "But enough shop talk," she prodded gently. "What's new *chez* Feldman?"

"What can be new?" Kaycee picked at her *salade niçoise*. "Barney's giving me a hard time. More intractable than ever. And suspicious? You wouldn't believe! We hardly have sex anymore, he's so petrified of making babies. Last night, middle of the night, I woke up and found him going through my medicine chest—checking to see if I was still on the pill. And when I confronted him, you know what he said? He said he was a Pro-Choicer and not having kids was his choice. Nothing like having the feminist arguments thrown back in your teeth. We had a rousing argument, let me tell you. The upshot of it was that he feels that I haven't been honest with him. 'You gave me your word,' he kept saying, like it was some kind of business deal. Barney and I are hardly talking anymore. As far as he's concerned, we signed a contract and that's it. But I've had a change of heart. I can't be bound by my name on a document. Or can I? What about my rights as a woman?"

Dani sighed sympathetically. "The contract isn't the issue, sweetie. Contracts get broken every day of the week. In fact, I'm busy trying to break one now. But what's between Barney and you—that's something else. We're not talking legal paper. We're talking flesh and blood and feelings. Sure you have a right to have a baby, Kaycee. That's not the question. Every woman has that right. It's the greatest thrill, the most powerful experience there is. You know, even with all my bitching about Samantha, am I glad she was born? You bet. And we seem to be patching things up. If you were to ask, could I picture life without her, I'd say, no. No way. She's part of myself. I wouldn't want any one to miss out on those rewards. But"—she swallowed the lump in her throat—"Barney has rights, too. And if he feels that strongly, it might come down to a very basic choice: marriage or motherhood. And that's a very tough call."

"I love Barney, but I also want what I want." Kaycee pulled a wry face. "What are you trying to tell me, Dani? That we can't have it all? Coming from a woman of our generation, that's heresy."

"I've got a suggestion," Dani said.

She was an excellent negotiator, she reminded Kaycee, skilled

in moving situations from Point A to Point E with minimum friction. "I'm better at mediating other people's problems than my
own," she added wryly. And before the lunch was over, Kaycee
agreed that the three of them would sit down together, informally,
and try to work out a compromise.

"My bet," Kaycee said with a nod, "is that he'll come around.
Barney has never denied me anything, and I can't see us breaking
up over this. He's basically a good husband. To change the subject,
though not really since he's husband material, I hear you went out
with Lou Morrison."

"Lingerie Lou." Dani grinned. "We had brunch Sunday, and
very pleasant it was. Thanks for giving him my number."

"Yes, Lou's a pussycat. Besides which, he's loaded. Loaded and
lonely, the ideal combo, especially for someone in your situation."

"Gee!" Dani said. "All we had was Bloody Marys and an omelet,
so don't start publishing the banns."

"You could go farther and do worse. Jews are terrific providers,
you know, and he's a member of that generation that looks after
women. Dewlaps and all, Lou's a catch."

Dani looked at her, astonished. "I realize I'm no chicken,
but . . ."

"I was only trying to be helpful, Dani. You're the one who
makes such a big deal out of age. You know what my mother says—
marrying well is the best revenge."

Dani walked back to the office in a quirky mood. Kaycee's hint
that Dani should be grateful for the attentions of any man, even
some sixty-plus grandpa, had set her teeth on edge. The very idea!

She liked Lou. He was eager to please, easy to talk to. But the
chemistry wasn't there. And the age difference was.

It was ironic. No one queried that Ted, at forty-five, was entitled
to a lovely woman twenty years his junior, while Dani should be
happy to "settle" for a member of the truss-and-dentures set. So
much for equality between the sexes!

And as for Kaycee's promoting such a romance, that, too, was
ironic. Or perhaps there was a subtext involved.

Dani had long been conscious of an ancient rivalry between
Kaycee and herself, a rivalry no less profound for its being unstated.
Theirs was a contest not so much between two individual women,

she felt, as between different visions, opposing values, two lifestyles that never converged.

Dani would have been less than human had she not, on occasion, envied Kaycee's travels, the wealth of lovers, the reckless affairs. Were it possible to lead a double life, then admittedly Dani might have relished some riotous interludes. Or at least, a few more years of youthful independence. But of course she had married right out of school, and no one can have it both ways.

The day of Kaycee's wedding, as Dani stood by her side at City Hall, she had felt a quiver of triumph. *See*, she had addressed Kaycee mentally. *My way of life has prevailed. East, west, wedded is best.*

But now (Dani had a swift vision of Ted on the beach, coral sand between his toes), now it was Dani's turn to ask herself—Oh yeah? What's so hot about marriage?

Wedged into breathing holes on the Nelson case, Dani did some legal chores on her own behalf. After four months of unanswered notices and within an inch of Ted's being granted an uncontested divorce, she called his lawyer and said she was thinking of filing for a legal separation.

Whit Rollins was puzzled. "Why a separation? You're not Catholic, are you?"

"Nope, but I may plan to convert."

The next day, she filed her own suit for divorce along with a request for complete financial disclosure.

"That takes us back to square one," Rollins said.

"Well, before I could accept any settlement, I'd need a complete rundown of my husband's assets. . . ."

"Assets!" Rollins groaned. "He's practically broke."

"And to that end, I've prepared a detailed set of interrogatories. Extremely detailed—concerning his current lifestyle, sources of income, recent expenditures. Did his air fare to St. Thomas derive from the marital estate? And the costs of entertaining Ms. MacDougall while living at home? Surely I can't be expected to pay half! In short, I want documentation on every item that might conceivably have bearing on the case, down to and including what happened to our recording of Sinatra's Greatest Hits. There were three records in the set, now there are only two and it was joint property as I recall."

She hung up feeling gleeful. Her move was a nuisance action, pure and simple, but it would keep him occupied for weeks. And there were dozens more to come.

Oh, the paperwork—she gloated—the growing mountain of costs. Postage and notarizations and messengers and affidavits and secretarial charges, to say nothing of his lawyer's fees. Dear God, play it right and Ted could wind up owing thirty, forty thou to good ole Rollins. Have to get a JOB (dirty word!) to pay it off.

No more sitting on the beach and letting the tide run through his toes. Ted would become a waiter or a clerk in a liquor store. *Yes ma'am, no ma'am. Thank you, call again.* The very thought of it warmed the winter air.

On the morning of Valentine's Day, Dani put on her mink coat and fur-lined gloves (18° and blustery in New York City, 85° and sunny, dammit! in St. Thomas), then taxied to the Park Avenue home of the Nelson Collection of American Art. She took the elevator direct to the penthouse.

Dani had been in the apartment several times on business, but Upstairs (Sherle spoke of it in capital letters) had been locked since Lazzi's departure. In contrast to the opulently appointed rooms that constituted Sherle's home, Upstairs was for looking, not living.

Today, both Nelsons, Willi Shannon and a team of experts would be on hand for the appraisal. Dani had prepared for the event by reading up diligently in the hope that her self-inflicted cram course would familiarize her, at least, with the major artists of recent decades.

Okay, she drilled herself: begin with Pop and Op. Then Neo-Expressionism which was not to be confused with Abstract Expressionism. Don't forget Super-Realism, which was a response to Minimalism, to say nothing of Post-War, Post-Modern, Post-Painterly. Every block in SoHo seemed to have its own School. The mind reeled. The eye went numb.

Like most lawyers, Dani considered herself a generalist, at ease in all kinds of circumstances. Beyond her bailiwick of law and liberal arts, she spoke good Spanish and restaurant French; had a solid grasp of politics, sports, music and travel; and knew enough of more exotic subjects, say, computers or ballet, to fake her way through a conversation. She was a fast study and a voracious reader, proud of her ability to grasp the basics of a client's field, be it veterinary medicine or wholesale groceries.

But modern painting was something else: a foreign language written in unfamiliar characters. She found it impossible to relate to the content. For unlike the philistine who boasted that he knew nothing about art but knew what he liked, Dani didn't even know what she liked. She was not a particularly visual person.

The Sloane apartment was decorated (if the term were not too strenuous) in a style best described as nondescript: some Scandinavian blond wood furniture, a Mediterranean bedroom bought on sale at Macy's, and a living room dominated by a monstrous black Barcalounger. Ugly but comfortable, Ted had insisted when he ordered the piece, though he later admitted that the color was a mistake.

Occasionally the two of them would discuss spiffing up the decor, but their efforts rarely went beyond buying a few sets of coordinated sheets. As Kaycee Feldman once put it, their apartment had all the panache of a college dorm. As for artwork, with the exception of the Ecuadorian hanging, they owned nothing original. The walls were decorated with bright prints and museum posters.

Now, as the elevator delivered her Upstairs, Dani vowed to look and listen and keep her mouth shut. If experts saw fit to place an incomprehensibly high value on the paintings, that was their business. She'd stick to hers.

At the door, her name was ticked off the list by one of three security guards Dani had hired for the day.

"It may sound excessive," she told Sherle, "but we don't want anyone walking off with as much as an ashtray."

In this, she was reflecting the views of Judge Murtagh, who had ruled that until such time as ownership was determined and a settlement made, the collection be put in storage beyond the reach of either litigant. Today, therefore, was Dani's sole chance to see the pictures that had provoked such a brouhaha.

She checked her coat, then followed the conversational hum into what she recognized from Sherle's description as the Long Gallery.

The room which housed the largest works was not so much long as large, perhaps fifty feet by forty, high-ceilinged, multiwindowed and blindingly lit. Both floor and walls covered in stainless steel. It was like being inside some gigantic appliance. Her heels clacked as she entered.

Most of the invitees were already on hand, studying the pictures, making notes, taking an occasional sip of the champagne offered by a maid in a crisp black uniform.

The paintings dazzled. Too big, too bright, too much. Dani's instinct was to shield her eyes and turn away until her pupils adjusted to the glare. In the center of the room, a huge circular copper table was set with the most mundane of articles: a brown paper bag and a plate with four oranges. Dani walked over to it, drawn by the comfort of the familiar. Except it wasn't a paper bag and dish of oranges, but a sculpture of metal and ceramic, the articles ten times larger and somehow realer than real life.

Slowly, Dani turned to the paintings, trying to soak up the ambience. She wanted to understand, to feel.

A dozen feet away, Sherle was deep in conversation with Lazzi. She raised her head to wave a casual hello.

Amazing, Dani thought, that the two of them could be within spitting range of each other and not come to blows. *If it were Ted, I'd be throwing hysterics*. And speaking of hysterics . . .

For that was the word that came to mind as she occupied herself with the glowering canvas before her. The thing was half the size of Samantha's bedroom and twice as messy: a dense concoction intermixing brushstrokes with wood fragments and broken crockery in what appeared to be a random pattern. Dani was perplexed. What was the artist trying to say? Was he saying it? Or was the purpose expressly to befuddle and unnerve?

"Overtones of Gaudí, eh?" someone said close to her ear. "That distinctive mosaic texture, the use of shards. Almost sculptural."

Dani swiveled her head.

She didn't know anything about art, to be sure, but she knew a great-looking man when she saw one. Her interlocutor had olive skin, black eyes, dark hair tipped with silver. The face was much younger than the hair. A very handsome face indeed. Not terribly tall, but tall enough, and elegantly dressed in a gray cashmere suit.

She smiled. He thrust his hand out.

"I don't believe we've met. I'm Steve Haddad from Wetherings."

"The auction gallery?" Dani said, then winced. Wetherings the auction gallery? Rolls-Royce the car? Tiffany the jewelry store? What must he think!

Sheepishly, she introduced herself as Sherle's lawyer. "Forgive me for sounding naïve, but I suspect I'm the only layperson present, excepting the hired help." He nodded encouragingly, then Dani blurted out: "This painting! What does it mean, can you tell me?"

He smiled, displaying white even teeth, then paid her the courtesy of behaving as though she were a fellow sophisticate who might enjoy sharing his perceptions. As he squired her around the room, he talked about the paintings and artists in terms that were comprehensible yet not condescending. Dani felt grateful enough to go down on all fours.

"You're very kind to take the trouble."

"Not at all. It's a superb collection. Not a false note anywhere. And don't neglect the smaller pieces in the back rooms. You'll find some real gems there."

"I'll make a point of it, Mr. Haddad, and thank you."

He dipped his head and moved off.

She studied the plate painting awhile longer, trying to absorb the points when Willi clapped a hand on her shoulder. With the other, he was gobbling caviar.

"Marvelous stuff, eh?" he said. Dani could swear she saw him wink.

"The experts seem to think so," she said.

"Yeah . . . well, this whole appraisal is nothing but a charade, you know. Lazzi has no intention of selling. Though I don't blame Sherle for wanting to take a last look. Once he has 'em back, maybe she could apply for visitation rights. You know, every other Sunday from two to five."

Dani laughed and they traded off small talk, leaving business for the session next week.

Adversary or no, Willi was amusing. She liked him. What the hell, all else aside, they were lawyers together, which, in present circumstances, formed an adequate bond.

Close up, the renowned Bomber looked less like an attorney

than a regular in a Third Avenue saloon—ruddy, tweed-jacketed, full of Irish bonhomie. He limped slightly and sported an ivory-topped walking stick. "War wounds," he said. "Korea." Though gossip had it that the limp derived from his having been kneecapped by an outraged husband.

Willi made a point of treating Dani with an old-fashioned chivalry, as though their encounters were purely social. He flirted, pulled out chairs, which Dani took as an indication of professional contempt.

Indeed, what grounds did he have to think otherwise? Presumably Willi had done his research. He knew her reputation to be that of a conciliator rather than a combatant, a midlevel lawyer with limited experience. He must have written her off as a pushover.

But Dani had done her research too, and after careful analysis of "Willi's Biggest Hits" had arrived at some shrewd conclusions.

The Shannon career had been built by representing the wives of the wealthy. When it came to extracting large sums from rich husbands, no lawyer was more aggressive. In all likelihood, Lazzi Nelson had hired him as a preemptive move, thus beating Sherle to the draw.

Yet Dani was struck by the fact that Shannon's strategies were more geared to attack than to defense. He was a bomber, not an anti-aircraft device. In this, she perceived a slim advantage.

Willi was used to getting his way. A man who enjoyed the sound of his own voice, he bossed his staff, his clients, his adversaries (his family, too, was Dani's bet), and tended to dominate conversations through sheer volume.

Once, during a meeting, Dani had put forth a suggestion of Sherle's when Willi cut her off in midsentence.

"Why are you letting yourself get pushed around by clients? Can't have the loonies taking over the bin, you know."

Dani bit the bullet that day, and said nothing. Playing dumb, though hell on the ego, could serve a larger goal. Her hope was that Willi would let down his guard, coast on his charm.

When he flirted, Dani flirted back. And if he was led to believe that Sherle had engaged Dani's services out of naïveté or some quirk of feminine reasoning, that was all right too.

She cultivated the sense of fragility, dressing for their meetings in pastel suits, with soft blouses and strappy shoes. She was wearing them now, those spindly Italian heels, and they were killing her.

"Hey, over here!" Willi called to the maid, who came around with caviar and toast points. His eyes glittered. "Genuine beluga. Better than Ma Shannon used to make. Can I help you, Dani?"

"No thanks. I'm going to find myself a quiet seat somewhere. These floors are murder on the feet. Enjoy the pictures."

She made her way through a smaller series of art-filled rooms, chatting briefly with Sherle, nodding to Lazzi, past a kitchen where caterers were setting out more trays, finally coming upon an unlit den at the end of the corridor. The room offered a comfortable sofa and a relief from the glare.

"Ye gods!" Dani pulled off her shoes and massaged her feet. What a relief just to sit. And not to see.

Gradually, as her eyes adjusted to the gloom, she realized she was not alone.

The girl was sitting primly with downcast eyes in a small gilt chair in the darkest corner of the room. Her lips were pursed, hair neatly combed, hands folded in her lap. She was dressed in a starchy white blouse and blue pleated skirt. She wore immaculate white cotton gloves.

"I'm sorry," Dani said with a sense of having stumbled into the preserves of a shy forest creature. "I didn't mean to disturb you. You're Precious, aren't you?"

The girl inclined her head.

"Well, I'm . . ."—*Mrs. Nelson's lawyer* sounded too ominous— "I'm a friend of your mother's. My name's Dani and I have a daughter just a few years older than you. How come you're not in school today, Precious?"

Precious mumbled something, which Dani took, correctly, to be half term. Conversation was like pulling teeth.

"Ah yes, so it is. You enjoying school?"

A shrug, then the shyest, faintest nod.

Dani wondered if she should go, when Precious piped up.

"Do you have any candy?"

"Why, haven't you eaten? There's beluga caviar. . . ." Then

Dani realized how foolish that sounded. The child was eleven, for heaven's sake. "I think I have some Life Savers in my bag. Yup, Tropical Fruit flavor. Here you go."

Precious came over, peeled off one glove, popped half the roll into her mouth, then put the glove back on.

"Thank you," she said.

"You're welcome." Dani was curious. "Tell me, it's so warm in here, Precious, why are you wearing gloves?"

"So I won't touch the paintings and get them dirty."

Precious returned to her chair, folded her hands and sucked on the sweets.

21

HE SMILED and cupped her face in his hands. She buried her lips in his palm.

"Beautiful Dani. So lovely. So soft." His fingers played with the hollow of her throat. "My sweet sensual darling. I wanted you from the moment we met. And you wanted me. . . ."

Oh God, yes! She ached for him as she had never ached for any man. "Yes," she murmured, lay back on the satin-sheeted bed. "Take me. Take me every way you want."

Eyes shut, she could feel his lips against the tangle of her hair, gliding down the length of her naked body, closing about her breasts, kissing the soft flesh of her belly, moving on . . . moving down. . . . Her nipples tightened. Her mind floated free. The warm tongue slid between her legs seeking out her moistness. . . .

. . . *three-car pile-up on the George Washington Bridge. This is shadow traffic on 1010 WINS.* . . .

Strong smooth fingers pushed apart her thighs. She could bear no more. "Oh Steve my darling, take me now. . . ."

. . . *a drive-by shooting in Bedford-Stuyvesant* . . .

Every nerve cell strained for the touch of his flesh, every orifice was open and lubricious. "God! . . . Yes! . . . Now!"

. . . *will be seven-fifteen. Now here's Gabe Winters with the basketball results.* . . .

Dani jerked up in bed. Forehead sweaty. Eyes open.

She was all alone, she realized with a jolt. In her own familiar bedroom. No satin sheets or dark-eyed lover in sight. The hands that had been caressing her so pleasurably, so intimately—were they her own as well? Dubiously, she lifted her fingers to her face and sniffed. Christ! She hadn't done that since she was a kid in high school mooning over Steve McQueen.

Only the man in her dream had been that other Steve. Steve What's-His-Name, of all people!

She shook her head to get rid of the cobwebs.

What day was this? What time?

She stared at the clock-radio until the numerals came into focus. Seven-fifteen A.M. Monday morning, had to be. A conference at Willi Shannon's less than two hours away. Wash. Eat. Dress. Join the real world. Stop thinking like a horny adolescent and start thinking like a lawyer. Today promised to be a very big day.

Having showered and laid her clothes out, Dani put on coffee and tried to anticipate what the morning might bring. This once she should have a decent breakfast. Fruit, cereal, the works. Fuel for going *mano a mano* with Willi Shannon.

But sitting at the kitchen counter with a bowl of Grape-nuts (could anything be more mundane?) and a sliced banana, she found herself slipping back into the aura of the dream. She could almost smell it.

Weird, she brooded, that the object of her first erotic fantasy in all these months alone should be a man she'd spent all of ten minutes with a week ago. Weird and disturbing, so much so that she could hardly eat.

Sex and Steve Haddad? Yes . . . that was his name. How could she ever have dreamed up such a thing? The very idea of sex with a stranger was bizarre. To Dani, sex was that complex blend of feelings and actions she had reserved for her husband these twenty years. Sex had meant Ted, and vice versa.

"I'm flattered," she said whenever a male acquaintance threatened to turn serious, which was, frankly, not all that often. "But as it happens, I'm already married to the most attractive man I know."

Throughout those years when she'd been at the height of her youth and good looks, years when so many friends were taking lovers, enjoying escapades, Dani had been a faithful wife. A woman who made the distinction between flesh and fantasy.

Fantasy was what lay between the covers of books. Erica Jong and her zipless fuck, Rossner's sex-driven women looking for Mr. Goodbar, *The Hite Report*, the *Cosmo* findings, the women who revealed their kinkiest desires to Nancy Friday: fascinating reading, whether as fiction or statistics, but it had nothing to do with Ted and Dani Sloane.

Ted, love, sex, happiness: In her mind, those factors were inextricably bound. Then one fine September day, Slam! bang! and he was gone, leaving Dani feeling neutered as a house cat. Until this morning.

Gingerly, she placed her fingertips on her face, her throat, her breast—to be rewarded with a rush of sensuality. It was a long-forgotten sensation.

But as to what had triggered this emotional onset (surely not a few minutes with a stranger!), Dani fixed upon Sam, whose situation was never far from her mind. Sam, and that dank cottage with its rumpled sheets and scents of lovemaking. The glow on Sam's face, a glow of utter satiety, was about as subtle as a Times Square billboard.

To be fair, Dani read more in her daughter's expression than mere sex—assuming sex can ever be mere. She had seen there the joy of being loved, being cherished.

Dani sighed. Sam was right. She was jealous, just a bit. Maybe even a lot. And though Dani had never believed in the prophetic nature of dreams, it was foolish to deny their significance. Dreams nudged you in the ribs. They revealed your fears, your feelings. This dream, for instance, had told her that she wasn't ready for the boneyard yet.

She was a normal, sexual woman. She had needs, desires, like anyone else. The nights were so empty. She missed the warmth of another human body.

It had been so long since anyone had shared her bed or body, she thought, awash with yearning. How splendid it would be, to snuggle in a man's arms once more. To cuddle, to sweet-talk, to make love, to feel ecstasy, to bask in the afterglow, to awake feeling cherished and replete.

Perhaps a casual affair was the answer. She ought to take a lover, have a fling.

Be faithful? To whom? For what?

Ted had found himself a sex partner. Samantha as well. Why should Dani be the odd one out?

That morning, she put on her makeup with a bit more dash and added a dollop of Giorgio for good measure.

"Mmmm . . . ," sniffed the cabdriver. "Very nice."

"Thank you," she said. "Feeling good."

It was 82° in St. Thomas, 21° and snowing in Manhattan when she arrived at Willi Shannon's town house.

Nice!

The Rolls-Royce insouciantly parked at the hydrant. The freshly polished brass plate. The Mexican houseboy who answered the door and took your coat.

Very nice indeed. If you had to live above the shop, then this East Sixties limestone was the kind of shop to live above.

She climbed the marble staircase to the first-floor conference room with a renewed respect for what money can buy. No dust on these banisters. No dust at all on Willi Shannon. Crisp and clean. He was standing in the doorway, all smiles.

In a bay-windowed office, the Nelsons sat facing each other. Sherle was wearing a boxy Chanel and looking ladylike. Lazzi, dour and swart in a silk double-breasted suit, took his tonsorial cues from John Gotti.

Yet disparities of age and style notwithstanding, the Nelsons resembled each other in the basics. Both were wiry, muscular, cold-eyed.

Dani shook hands, then sat down and sopped up the Shannon milieu. Very very very nice, from the burled paneling to the hunting prints to the suede Saporiti sofas. On the mantel a bronze of Greek wrestlers locked in a death grip abutted a bowl of fresh roses. Brutal tactics, big bucks, the juxtaposition declared. By now, Willi was doubtless richer than most of his clients. Let that be a lesson, Dani Sloane!

While a secretary poured coffee into porcelain cups, Dani buttered a croissant and thought of Leo Margulies's "matched Styro-foam" and Dunkin' Donuts.

The Limoges service, Willi informed, had belonged to the Duchess of Windsor, and the coffee was a custom blend from Kenya. Dani hummed. Sherle and Lazzi looked stony. Then, the niceties over, they got down to business.

The secretary handed around a set of bound folders.

"My client is not a mean-spirited person," Willie began, "and we prefer seeking the peaceful solution. You'll find this a generous offer. Let me walk you through the highlights."

Sherle was to get half of all personal property, Willi said. Her legal fees. Joint custody of Precious. Child support.

Dani nodded. So far, routine. And insufficient.

"Where's the beef?" she asked.

Willi grinned. "It's in here. It's coming. Be patient."

In addition, the lawyer said, Sherle would receive the living quarters in the Park Avenue apartment. Her choice of the Corniche or the Testarossa. One painting from the corporate collection to be selected from the following (Willi read off a list). ". . . and finally, the sum of six million dollars," he announced with a flourish. "Which happens to be a great deal of money."

The first million was to be spread out over five years, the balance being given as a balloon payment at the end of that period. Provided that certain conditions had been met.

The two women exchanged quick glances. Willi continued.

"Sherle will have to relinquish all future claim in Lean Machine Inc. Also, during that period, she may not undertake any work that might be construed as competitive. Nor may she use the name or image of That Girl Sherle, such being the trademarked property of Lean Machine Inc."

He ran down a list of businesses he deemed competitive—health clubs, athletic wear, exercise videos—then assumed his most persuasive tone. "You appreciate, I'm sure, that the cars, the pictures, et al., are company assets, not marital property. Ditto the six million dollars. If we were to stick to the letter of the prenuptial agreement, you wouldn't see a penny of it. You knew that, Sherle, when you waived interest in the business in lieu of salary. However, rather than get bogged down in litigation, which is a tiresome and costly procedure, Lazzi is willing to make a handsome settlement. Let's call it an *ex gratia* payment for Sherle's services to Lean Machine. Technically we don't owe you, but we're nice guys. Accept the offer, and we can all part friends. Here are the details for your perusal," he said, handing out the folders. "However, there is one small stipulation."

Dani placed the proposal on her lap. It required serious thinking, but it was an excellent launching pad.

"And that is . . . ?" she asked.

"I want to make it clear. This is a one-time-only offer. It expires at five P.M. Take it or leave it."

"That's outrageous," Dani started to argue. "This is a complex proposal. Sherle and I need time to consider and we'll want to make counterproposals. Didn't you ever hear the word *negotiate?* Or isn't that in your lexicon?"

"You have exactly"—Willi checked his watch—"six hours and eight minutes left. You'd better get cracking."

For privacy's sake, they rented a suite at the Plaza, sent for sandwiches and a coffee urn, then spent the rest of the day examining Shannon's proposal in detail. Toward four, Sherle flopped on the sofa.

"What do you think, Dani?"

"I think maybe we could squeeze another million up front. Five years is a long time to pay out."

Sherle made a face. "When I told you half, I meant half. What's the whole deal worth? Ten million? Why, that business must have a book value of close to a hundred million. The paintings alone . . . Plus, you know what really frosts me? Not being able to capitalize on That Girl Sherle. The motherfucker's trying to rob me of my identity along with everything else. I want my half."

"Forget half, Sherle. It won't happen. New York is an equitable-distribution state, which means, essentially, that you get out in proportion to what you put in. Let's face it. Lean Machine was a multimillion-dollar enterprise before you two ever met. It was Lazzi's concept, founded on his inheritance. So even if you hadn't waived all rights, he'd still get the lion's share. Unless . . ." She brooded.

"Unless what?"

"Unless we can find a way to show that over the years of marriage, your contribution outweighed his, that you personally were responsible for most of its growth. . . ."

"You bet your ass I was," Sherle broke in. "My life's blood went into that company and I want my due. Come on, counselor. Make it happen."

Dani chewed for a minute. She hadn't spent those years living with Ted for nothing. She knew the value of research, opinion polling, of proving whatever proposition happened to be convenient. The idea had been bubbling beneath the surface all last week.

"Let me propose a scenario, Sherle. One requiring patience and nerve. First, we have to get the prenups set aside, but I'm hopeful for various reasons, enough reasons to have Shannon really worried. Let's call that Round One. Round Two, we lay the groundwork for your claim of half, shaping our strategy around the influence of the TV spots. We'd have to establish that the campaign was your brainchild, yours alone. We'd need affidavits from everyone who worked on it."

"No sweat," Sherle said. "They still have scars."

"Next, we do a study. A poll of patrons who signed up during the years that you were involved. Which years, we hope to prove, produced the company's fastest growth. We'll want to identify the single most compelling factor in attracting in new business. Was it the ad campaign? The personality of That Girl Sherle? Okay. Assuming we get the desired response, that your work accounted for, oh, maybe seventy-five, eighty percent of all growth, we now examine two sets of figures. One, the company's worth when you got married, and two, its current value. Then, we hire management consultants to project what the company fortunes might have been without your input. Would it have grown so fast? Would it be currently worth—let's throw in round figures—fifty million rather than a hundred? That way, we arrive at the cash value of your contribution. You follow?"

Sherle's eyes blinked like a calculator. "Oh, do I ever!"

"It's a path filled with hazards," Dani cautioned, "and there's no guaranteeing what the research will prove. We'll have to hire a reputable firm. Yankelovich, for instance, or OPR or Data-Depth. It won't come cheap."

"Can you give me a ballpark figure?"

"Not between now and five o'clock. Which is when Willi Shannon expects his answer."

"Maybe we can stall him."

"I doubt it. Wisely or not, Willi's put himself on the line, and this is one macho guy. For him to back off would be an admission of weakness. So it's now or never, war or peace. And don't kid yourself. It we turn this down, things'll get mean."

Sherle looked thoughtful. "So what do you think, Dani? Do I grab the money and run—or go for broke?"

"I can only recommend."

"And you recommend I do the prudent thing."

"I recommend that you consider the risk. Weigh the factors, Sherle. A six-million-dollar-plus sure thing against a long shot."

"I like long shots, going back to when I was shooting craps in Vegas. Give me ten minutes to think it over."

Dani looked at her watch.

"We're not that pressed for time. Take twelve."

Sherle set the alarm on her wristwatch, stretched out on the sofa and shut her eyes, motionless as a snake in the sun.

When the buzzer sounded, she sat up slowly.

"Okay," she said. "We go for it. Start pulling together the research project. And apropos of public opinion, I'm calling in my PR firm for extra help. I think the best way to play it is like Ivana's doing with The Donald. 'I gave him the best years of my life' kind of stuff, accompanied by hearts and flowers. Can't you see the story in the tabloids—'Slim Pickin's for Lean Machine Gal'? With a photo—me, gracious and smiling, while maybe brushing away a tear? Good press never hurt anybody, and judges read the papers too."

Sherle smoothed down her jacket, brushed away microscopic lint. She looked as fresh now as she had six hours earlier.

"God," she said. "I can hardly wait to see the expression on

Lazzi's face, that gorilla. Anyhow, up and at 'em. And if we bomb"—
she faked a roll of the dice—"I can always work the tables in Vegas."

And I can always shoot myself, Dani thought.

Minutes later, they were back in Shannon's town house. A bottle
of champagne rested in a bucket on the glass-topped table, waiting
to be popped. Dani remained standing.

"I'm afraid, gentlemen, we'll have to postpone the celebration.
I regret to say your offer is unacceptable on each of the following
points. Firstly—"

She was set to enumerate, when Sherle interrupted.

"What Dani really means to say is—fuck you!"

Dani worked till almost two in the morning, roughing out a plan,
then headed home exhausted.

She had long since stopped begrudging the hours. Late nights
were the best cure for insomnia. You worked till you dropped, then
fell into bed. It was better than lying awake worrying about personal
problems.

At home, the red light of the answering machine was blinking.
Routinely, Dani checked her messages.

Kaycee. *Business Week* wanting to know if she renewed her subscription. The dry cleaner; he'd found her houndstooth jacket.
Then:

"Hello, this is Steve Haddad. We met at the Nelsons' last week.
I wonder if we might get together one of these days, perhaps have
dinner. I'll call again."

Dani played the message twice, then went to bed.

Steve Haddad, she thought wryly. The man of her dreams that
very morning. Was she prescient, or psychic or what?

22

AT FIFTEEN, he won an Olympic Gold medal.

Years of intensive training, of denial and self-discipline, of building muscle and learning breath control: all culminated on that one glorious afternoon in Mexico City as he clutched his prize while thousands cheered. Just as everything in his life had led up to that moment, everything since fell away from it. He never swam competitively again.

By the time of the next Olympics, the nineteen-year-old medalist was at Harvard, studying art history.

"Swimmers peak early," Steve Haddad explained. "I knew I'd already achieved my personal best, so what was the point of continuing? Nothing's quite as pathetic as an athlete who's over the hill."

Dani was impressed. To have achieved so much so young, to relinquish fame with scarcely a sigh: that argued the most extraordinary will. Yet there was no hint either of boasting or of self-pity in Steve's recital.

"So you're still an undefeated champion," Dani said. A line of poetry sprang to mind. " 'And early though the laurel grows, it withers quicker than the rose,' " she quoted, then flushed. "I didn't mean to sound pompous."

But Steve nodded thoughtfully.

"That's from 'To an Athlete Dying Young,' isn't it? A powerful image. Though at the time, my old man put it a bit less poetically. 'So, kid,' he said, 'what do you do for an encore?' "

His father was a top Hollywood agent, and Steve enjoyed the distinction of having had Joan Crawford stand godmother at his baptism and being baby-sat by a young Marilyn Monroe. "Which has got to be some sort of primal curse," he said with a laugh.

He was one of a kind, Dani concluded. He had that well-maintained glow that she associated with expensive European cars and best-of-breed setters. Well dressed, well spoken, well mannered, small boned and medium height, he possessed the athlete's grace and carriage.

An athlete's appetite, too, for he ate simply and heartily. And although he had ordered a splendid bottle of Bordeaux and kept her glass assiduously filled, he hardly touched the wine himself.

Why book a table at Les Miroirs, she mused, only to order rump steak and spinach? Unless you dined at such places as a matter of routine.

Dani plowed into her cassoulet.

"I gather you don't care for Hollywood," she said, speculating on what kind of baby-sitter Monroe had made.

"I found it narrow. As long as I'd live there, I'd be known as Mike Haddad's son, Joe Haddad's grandson. For me, it's a one-industry town. I suspect I took up swimming as a way of hiding out from the movie folk who cluttered up our lawn every weekend swinging croquet mallets. It's such a clannish milieu. Though my sister's in the industry now, and both my brothers. Third-generation picture folk. Whereas my great-grandfather Selim . . ."

Steve speared his steak with gusto and explained that the originator of the family fortunes, a Lebanese immigrant, had come to California around the turn of the century and peddled sewing notions off a tray to farmers' wives. "The last honest Haddad. We've been downwardly mobile ever since."

He chatted on, brisk and entertaining, regaling her with tales of scams and skulduggery in the film industry and also in the more "esoteric" world of fine arts. The two fields sounded akin; neither was a place for amateurs, he implied. "Although I imagine in your line of work, Dani, you hear stories far more scabrous every day. It must be fascinating."

Dani listened with delight. Such a treat, dining with a man who was amusing, attentive, attractive. She'd almost forgotten how exhilarating the experience could be. He made her feel feminine. Sexy.

Several weeks had passed since Steve had left that first message on her machine. He called back, she was in court. She called back, he was in London. There were times, given their schedules, when she despaired of their ever getting together. But he appeared to be worth the delay.

Lately, she'd been getting a lot of advice from well-meaning friends, all of whom seemed to agree that the only cure for a broken heart was to get herself paired. Don't sit on your duff, everyone said. Join a singles club. Take an ad in the *New York Review of Books*. Meet and mate. "After all," as a neighbor pointed out, "Ted's been gone over six months. You can't stay in solitary forever."

She didn't need others to tell her she was lonely. Why, there were nights when she felt she would have cheerfully gone to bed with Jack the Ripper. Even Lou Morrison had begun to look good. Or if not good, at least feasible.

But an image of herself, tenaciously held—the notion that she was proud, feisty, independent—prevented her from acting upon her urges. The singles scene was a meat market. She didn't go to bars alone. And just imagine if Ted should discover she'd taken out an ad! It was too demeaning for words.

Tonight, however, none of those sentiments obtained. Tonight was male and female in the classic sense: a proper date, and he had done the asking.

She glimpsed their reflection in the smoky mirrors that gave the place its name and felt euphoric. What a smashing couple Steve and she made! Glamorous. Well dressed. An onlooker would be justified in assuming that this handsome pair was involved in a romantic tête-à-tête. It was a scene out of a brandy ad or shampoo commercial.

She ached to be spotted by someone she knew (ideally someone who knew Ted and would report back), but her circle of friends rarely patronized Les Miroirs. Which merely proved she knew the wrong people.

All day long at the office, Dani had been absorbed with the

image of Steve Haddad, and as she dressed for dinner, she dabbed L'Air du Temps between her breasts and on her thighs, just in case they wound up in bed.

Nothing heavy, mind you. Dani wasn't looking for an entanglement, let alone a commitment for life. Merely a marvelous affair, sans tears and regrets. She owed herself an adventure, by God! All she asked of a partner was that he be straight, presentable, and under sixty. Steve certainly met the requirements. Exceeded them.

He was witty. Worldly. A reader of Housman. A Hollywood aristocrat. Rich, too—which was not to be held against him. And, apparently, keenly interested in the life and times of Dani Sloane. What was her background? he wanted to know. How had she become a lawyer? What were her career goals? her tastes in music? her favorite places?

If Steve had set himself out to seduce, he was succeeding admirably. Mentally Dani was already bridging the gap from table talk to morning after. His place or hers? Hers, she decided. He'd see her home, she'd invite him up for a drink, after which nature would doubtless take its course. Meanwhile, she smiled and chattered.

"You mean all you've seen of California is Disneyland?" he remarked at one point.

" 'Fraid so," Dani said. "We made a trip there with our daughter when she was nine. Grand Canyon, Yosemite and Disneyland. She liked Disneyland best."

"And what did you make of the place?"

Dani grinned. "I know all intelligent adults are supposed to hate it on sight, but . . ."

"It's fantastic, isn't it?" Steve broke in, beaming approval. "Nothing like it."

Dani giggled. "Way too good for kids! Although I'm sorry we didn't see more of the Coast. Next trip I make, I'd like to . . . ummm . . ."—she groped for a more prestigious frame of reference—"visit the Norton Simon museum."

"When you do, let me know. The director is an old friend of mine. I'll see he gives you red-carpet treatment."

"I'd like that!"

"It would be my pleasure, Dani."

He leaned toward her. Dani glowed. The beeper buzzed.

"Oh damn!" she declared.

It buzzed a dozen times a day now, one minicrisis after another. It might be Sherle. Shannon. Pruitt. Marsha. Anyone, really, since Sherle had a way of shooting her mouth off to reporters, then climaxing it with "Call my lawyer to verify."

But why must they call during her first romantic rendezvous in months!

As she made her way to the phones, a well-dressed man glanced at her admiringly. She knew why. She looked great. She felt newly desirable.

On the phone, Sherle Nelson was bubbling over with excitement. "Wait till you catch me on *Live at Five* tomorrow! I can't tell you more, except to say I'm giving Liz Smith the exclusive."

"You mean," Dani said, "you had me beeped at dinner just to tell me you can't tell me?"

"I like to keep you informed, counselor."

Dani scurried back to the table, where Steve had sprung to his feet. How flattering. Ted, that asshole, hardly ever got up when she entered a room.

"Sorry about the interruption," she said. "The business day never ends."

"No problems, I hope?"

"No," she said, not wanting the conversation to degenerate into shop talk.

Steve signaled the waiter to bring dessert.

"I took the liberty of ordering you a soufflé. They're a specialty of the house."

"Mmmm . . ." She inhaled. "Grand Marnier, no less. Smells gorgeous. Can I offer you a taste?"

He shook his head. Smiled. "I don't eat sweets. Tell me, Dani, what do you think Mrs. Nelson's chances are of getting a substantial part of the collection?" The smile was fixed.

Dani poked her spoon into the soufflé. It collapsed instantly, along with her spirits. Was this why he had asked her to dinner? The motive behind all that charm?

She took a bite, burned her tongue, framed a response, forced her face into a semblance of sociability.

"It's too early to say, though naturally we have high hopes. Nor can I answer as to what she'd do with her share of the pictures. I presume your firm is interested in handling the auction, should there be one."

"Yes, indeed," came the enthusiastic reply. It was a marvelous collection, he said. And while it would be a pity to break it up, nonetheless (the eyes sparkled, the voice sang), should such a circumstance arise and Mrs. Nelson decide to sell her share, he would assist in every way possible. He talked briefly, careful not to bore or get technical. He spoke of price flux, of catalogue production, publicity, of the complex services involved in a major sale. All of which led, naturally enough, to the topic of Wetherings.

To say he trumpeted his firm would be misleading, for Steve never stooped to anything as crass as a sales pitch. He implied, he hinted, seduced.

Dani stiffened. He had provided her with two clear messages. First, that Wetherings was well equipped to handle such a sale, more accommodating than Sotheby's or Christie's. Second, that Steve Haddad was on the job.

This "date" was simply one of the tools of his trade, utilitarian and tax deductible. So much for romance! She lowered her eyes, vaguely humiliated. And yet . . . and yet.

Yet she found him sexy, and sensed a reciprocal spark. So what if he'd asked her out for mundane reasons? Where was there a law against having an affair with a business contact? Maybe he was one of those men who combined business with pleasure. Maybe she should be one of those women. It wasn't as if there was a conflict of interest. Dani had her head on straight. She pushed the soufflé away, as though to say, *I can't be bought for a dinner.*

"I gather you'd like me to use such influence as I have on Sherle Nelson to recommend Wetherings' services."

"I'd be delighted!" he said. "But only if you feel comfortable doing so. However, I sincerely believe it would be in Mrs. Nelson's best interests."

"I must tell you, my client calls her own shots," she said crisply. "Anyhow, any such recommendation at this point would be wildly premature. However . . ." Inadvertently, a note of promise had crept into her voice. She was unwilling to close doors just yet.

"However, I'll keep what you said in mind. Is that why you asked me out tonight, Steve—to lobby for Wetherings? We could have had this talk during office hours."

"I asked you out because you're an interesting woman and I thought we'd enjoy each other's company."

Dani mulled his statement over.

"What makes me so interesting, other than my being Sherle's lawyer? I'm curious. It certainly couldn't have been the brilliance of my conversation the day we met. Looking back, I don't recall saying anything at all, other than the fact that I know zip about art."

If she had thought to disconcert him, she failed, for he answered without missing a beat.

"I admired your candor, Dani. Then and now. I found it refreshing. You know the first question people ask an auctioneer about pictures? They ask—what is it worth? What will it fetch? Forget the jargon you hear in the galleries, the yammering about schools and techniques and so on. It all comes down to that one nagging conundrum: What's it worth? If it's a de Kooning, the answer is millions; if not, haul it out with the trash. Hardly anyone ever asks, What does it mean? You did, though, about the Schnabel. I liked you for it. Makes for a change from all the grabbers and self-styled experts."

"In other words, I'm an unjaded palate."

"Something like that."

Steve got up and helped her on with her coat. His arm brushed her cheek. She inhaled his warmth. Business and pleasure. But mostly pleasure.

"Shall I take you home?"

"Please," she said.

It was after eleven when the cab pulled up at her building. Dani was grateful for the dark. The dark was full of possibilities.

"Come up for a drink, won't you?" she said. "Or perhaps some of my very good coffee?"

He reached across her body to unlatch the door.

"That's very sweet of you, Dani. Perhaps another time. I have to get to Grand Central by half past."

She stared at him. "You're a commuter!" she exclaimed.

"Mmm . . . hmmm. I have a house in Pound Ridge, northern Westchester," he said, while images swirled in Dani's head. Westchester. House. Rosebushes. Kitchen curtains. The whole catastrophe. Who commuted, after all? What man in his right mind would make that schlepp every night if not for . . .

"Omigod! You're married, aren't you?"

He stared at her with an ambiguous expression.

"Why? Does it matter?"

She was dumbstruck. Did it? She didn't know. Could she do to some unknown unnamed woman what Jennifer MacDougall had done to her? Or was she the only woman in the world still dumb enough to have moral scruples?

What scruples? What morals? What did she owe anyone?

"Why . . . why. . . ," she spluttered, but Steve spared her further agony.

"No, I'm not married. I just don't like city living, that's all. By the end of the day, I need to escape."

Dani exhaled slowly, clammy-handed with relief.

"Thank you for dinner," she said. "And call me. Please. Or else I'll call you."

"THAT GIRL SHERLE A BATTERED WIFE." The *Post* had picked up the ball from *Live at Five* and was running for a touchdown. Eyebrow cocked, Dani skimmed the story, picking out the choicest tidbits as they popped from the page.

" . . . used me as a punching bag . . . in front of our daughter . . . said nothing because I loved him . . . broke every bone including my heart. . . ."

The story was illustrated with a photo of Sherle looking cute but weepy in a sequined dress cut so low you could practically see that broken heart.

"Looks like the Garbage War has begun in earnest," Marsha commented. "Fabulous PR, though. Especially that picture of her brushing back the tears. Ah . . . the glamour, the glitter, the heartbreak—what a combo! Dynamite."

Dani tugged at her ear. Not that she countenanced Sherle's antics, but all's fair in love and divorce wars. As for Lazzi's sensibilities, well—that's how the game was played. May as well feel sorry for the Late Ted Sloane (which is how she now referred to him), who was, according to his lawyer, crying poverty. Boo-hoo.

In fact, Sherle's grandstand play was shrewdly timed. The woman had a flair for publicity, and what better time than now, to keep That Girl's image thrust before the public, with Dani's research project about to begin?

The day after the Liz Smith story broke, Sherle appeared in Dani's office accompanied by a pair of six-foot gorillas.

"My bodyguards," she explained. "I don't dare go anywhere without them. Like I told the gal from the *Enquirer*, I fear for my life."

They were blond-haired black-belt karate experts with monosyllabic names, interchangeable hulks in white T-shirts and Arnold Schwarzenegger suits. By contrast, Sherle looked almost fragile. A neat visual touch, Dani acknowledged with a sigh. Sherle called them the Schwarzie Twins.

While Sherle was busy grabbing headlines, the real struggle was taking place behind the scenes—in conferences, offices, meetings with expert witnesses, law libraries and courtrooms, with Dani working at full throttle to have the prenuptials set aside.

As expected, Willi moved for summary judgment, claiming that the agreement had been made in good faith. Had Dani lost that round, the ballgame might have ended right there, but luck had been with her (luck and hard work), and at last the date of a hearing was set.

"This could be it," she told Sherle. "It's like a full-fledged trial. Our witnesses, their witnesses, oral arguments on both sides, all going to the question of whether or not the original contract should stand. You'll be expected to testify, of course."

"Just tell me when to turn on the waterworks and I'll oblige."

With or without waterworks, there was a compelling case to be made. True, Sherle had been represented by her own lawyer at the time, but the lawyer had previously done work for Lazzi's firm. Conflict of interest? Conceivably. A setup? Harder to prove. But enough to plant the seed of doubt.

An even stronger card was Sherle's youth at the time. Only nineteen, she would stress, which was young indeed, especially in the eyes of a seventy-two-year-old motions judge.

But strongest of all Dani's arguments was the Woman-in-Love doctrine.

It was a commonplace, recognized in numerous rulings, that when a woman fell in love, her brains turned to mush. She became irrational, quick to relinquish her rights, easily duped. Love, it might be argued, was a debilitating disease, at least for women. (There was no comparable Man-in-Love doctrine.) Hence any contract negotiated while in that pitiable state was bound to be unfair.

Woman in Love. Such would be the thrust of Dani's argument. Feminists might scoff, but she for one knew the hard truth of that tenet. Had not love blinded Dani herself to Ted's deceit and betrayal? All those months she had been oblivious to his infidelities. Perhaps all those years.

For what a man will do once, he will likely do a hundred times. In which case, their entire marriage had been a farce.

Thus she prepared the oral arguments, picturing Sherle as a vulnerable child and Lazzi as a wily Lothario. Then, riding the crest of her emotion, she shot off a call to Ted's lawyer.

"He wants a divorce, he can come back and fight it out. I have a ton of additional questions to ask."

"Gimme a break," Whit Rollins groaned. "You're talking a fortune in legal fees. These games of yours are just eating away at whatever joint estate you guys have left."

He called her back an hour later, apparently having got in touch with Ted. "Look, Dani. He's willing to let you have his share of the boat. All he asks for is his equity in the apartment. Twenty thou will do it, and you're over and out."

Suddenly, from the depth of her being, a spear of anger shot through her, forced her lips apart.

"Over my dead body will he marry Jenny MacDougall!"

Then she slammed the receiver down, trembling, startled that she had behaved so improvidently. She was behaving like a client, not a lawyer. Yet she could, and did, derive satisfaction from the hint that Ted was having trouble paying Rollins's fees. Well, that was tough. Let him eat sand. Time and skill were on her side.

Oh yes! once she too had been a woman in love—frail and foolish—but no more.

*   *   *

"There you go!" She handed the Nelson plea over to Marsha to check citations a few days later.

"That's true, you know," Marsha said, handing back the papers. "Women in love are total assholes."

Dani made no comment. Her outrage had since dissipated. At the moment, she was too busy daydreaming, waiting for Steve Haddad to call.

23

ALL TOLD, it had been a week of sweet and sour.

On Monday, Judge Lewis B. Murtagh set aside the Nelson prenuptial contract and granted Sherle temporary maintenance.

On Wednesday, Samantha called home with startling news.

On Friday night, Dani and Steve became lovers.

In retrospect, Dani Sloane would have been hard put to say which event would have the greatest impact.

"It was bound to happen," Jack Pruitt said the day Murtagh's ruling came down.

"I made it happen," Dani replied, a surge of confidence sweeping through her. She was on a roll.

That evening, she joined a dozen of the regulars in their nightly postmortem at Smitty's Bar and Grill. "And I'm buying."

She'd grown to like the scene at Smitty's and often dropped in for an hour or so when working late. The conversation was sharp, the atmosphere clubby. There was a sense of "us and them": *us* being the bedeviled lawyers of Pruitt-Baker, *them* being the rest of the world. And for all the horseplay and bitching that went on at these sessions (or perhaps because of them), they engendered a kind of family feeling. What the hell, Dani thought. This was just about the only family she had, these days.

"You done good, kid." Chris Evans thumped her on the back.

"Feelin' good," she said with a sisterly glow.

From the moment Sherle had launched that first unguided missile on *Live at Five*, the public battle of Nelson versus Nelson took on a course of its own, one over which Dani had little control.

The Garbage War, as Marsha had termed it: a mixture of slapstick and savagery to be played out daily in full view of millions of delighted New Yorkers.

Charge followed outrageous charge. Petty complaints escalated into full-blown outrages, for the benefit of whoever would listen and rush the latest tidbit into print. She drank, he cheated. She was a druggie, he was a swindler. He said . . . she said . . . he hinted . . . she implied. . . .

The details were often lurid enough to make a Roxanne Pulitzer blush.

The morning after Judge Murtagh's ruling, Lazzi told a roomful of reporters that he had serious doubts concerning Precious's paternity. The story made "Page Six" of the *Post*.

Dani exploded.

"Leash in your dog," she told Willi Shannon, while Sherle sat in her office looking homicidal.

"Look who's crying!" Willi jeered. "And remember it was your mutt who took the first bite."

Dani slammed down the phone.

"Tomorrow we go to court," she told Sherle after a moment's consideration, "and apply for sole custody of Precious. Biology aside, that man's not fit to be a father."

Sherle began to fidget. "Is that a good idea? I was figuring, joint custody. I mean, a kid needs both parents."

Dani stared at her. Was it conceivable Sherle was begging off? She shoved the notion aside. The woman was a mother, after all.

"In theory I agree, Sherle, though in fact I'm never happy with joint-custody arrangements. They're for the convenience of judges, not children. Besides," she argued subtly, "think of the polls we'll be doing. It'll be good public relations."

"Yeah. . . ." Sherle nodded gravely. "When you're right, you're right. Okay, do whatever paperwork is needed."

"Good. And where is she now?"

"Where is who?"

"Precious!"

"Sweet Jesus!" Sherle thumped her forehead with the heel of her hand. "She's been sitting in the limo all this time!"

That night, Sherle and Dani dined in public as a mark of confidence and solidarity. When they left the restaurant, a TV crew from Channel 4 was waiting, hungry for comments.

Sherle smiled sweetly. Dani chatted good-naturedly with the reporters, nominating Lazzi for the Baron Munchausen Award. "Little man, big mouth," she said. "We're sending him a box of Burger King Whoppers in the morning."

Then she dashed home to catch a glimpse of herself on *The 11 O'Clock News*.

Sam called the next day. "I saw you on TV," she said, and just as Dani was about to preen, knocked the air right out of her. "Yeah, it was on this program called *Lowdown USA*. And there you were, my mom—right alongside Marla Maples and some guy who trains dogs to sniff cocaine. Congrats! You're in great company."

"It was also on NBC News here," Dani said stiffly. "Somehow, I thought you'd be pleased . . . ," but Sam talked right through her.

"Now for my news," she said. "The real gen, as Hemingway put it. Mel and I have decided to get married next Christmas."

"You've . . . what?" Dani's jaw fell slack. Was Sam saying this merely to get back at Dani for hogging the spotlight, or could she possibly be serious?

"Well, don't I hear congratulations?" Sam continued.

"You are kidding, aren't you?" Dani couldn't conceal her panic.

"I'd hardly joke about something as solemn as marriage, would I? We've been thinking and I've decided, I'd like an old-fashioned church wedding. . . ."

Dani was mute. *Over my dead body will you marry.* . . .

Was Sam doing this to shock? she wondered. To hurt? To tease? And just when they'd been beginning to communicate.

But Sam was rattling on merrily, oblivious to the silence on the other end.

". . . a Victorian theme . . . mistletoe . . . strawberries out of season . . . Mozart quartets . . . antique lace. After all, you and Dad had a big church wedding. . . ."

And now we're having a great big divorce, Dani was tempted to say, but held her tongue, determined to hang in there and keep cool.

"Well, aren't you proud of me?" Sam said. "You're always telling me to think for myself. Be decisive, independent."

Dani struggled for a noncommittal response. "Well, I'm not sure that getting married is a declaration of independence. Possibly the opposite. You might want to think about that. We'll talk again later in the week."

She hung up, hands trembling. Her immediate instinct was to phone the Oberlin police and swear out a warrant against Melvin Landrum. Child abuse, white slavery, contributing to the corruption of a minor. Except, of course, as Sam was at constant pains to remind her, her daughter was a legal adult.

Calm down, Dani told herself. Sam wouldn't see it through. It was a tactic, a weapon, a means of getting back at her parents.

Yet supposing she was serious, how could Dani dissuade her? This was a two-parent job.

Ted Sloane, goddammit! Where are you now that your daughter needs you?

In the tropics, scrunching sand beneath his toes.

On Friday, it was 72° in New York and 81° in St. Thomas, which evened out a few of life's inequities.

At six-thirty, Dani slipped into the ladies room and changed from her suit into a peacock blue silk jersey dress.

"Well, look at you!" Marsha said when she came back for her coat. "All this glory for Lingerie Lou?"

"Actually, I'm going to a dinner party with Steve."

"Off with the old, on with the new, huh, Dani?"

"Off with the old, on with the young is more like it." Dani laughed and fished in her bag.

"Which earrings should I wear, Marsh? The silver drops or the pearls, which do you think?"

Recently Dani found herself confiding in Marsha. You couldn't spend ten, twelve hours a day in somebody's company without achieving a certain intimacy. Marsha wore well. Her perspective was fresh and unromantic, especially when it came to sizing up men. She was now scrutinizing Dani with a quizzical eye.

"You really want my opinion?" Marsha asked.

"About the earrings?"

"About you. I think you're in the market for Husband Number Two . . ."

"Come off it!"

". . . and that Mr. Breaststroke's a bigger prize than old Lingerie Lou."

Dani crimsoned. What made Marsha's flippancy even worse was that she had so nearly hit bone.

In theory, the very notion of marrying again was off-putting. Dani had a fascinating job, money in her pocket, independence. After years of anonymity, she was making a name for herself. Marriage? Who needed it! One Ted Sloane was quite enough for a lifetime, thank you kindly.

Yet periodically, she had bouts of total panic. Anything could set her off: a minor legal setback, a snatch of Puccini, her monthly credit card bill, the sight of young lovers in the park holding hands.

At such moments, and they were frequent, she ached to be married again. Safely married, as the phrase went. She missed the status, the security. The intimacy of family life.

"When you're ready, you'll meet him," her sister Sally assured her. "It all has to do with state of mind."

And Dani nodded agreement. Impossible to believe she would never be a Mrs. again. That the uncertain status quo might continue forever. Of course she would marry!

But if her heart shouted yes, her brain knew better. Dani had seen the statistics. She knew precisely what her chances were of lucking out, of meeting anyone with even half of Ted's merits. All she had to do was picture the appropriate ad as it might appear in *New York* magazine.

> *Divorced mother, 42, seeks cultured, youthful, healthy, successful, attractive, unencumbered male with an eye to matrimony. The line forms on the right.*

On the practical front, Lou Morrison was a live prospect. Lou was gallant, generous, good for the ego.

"Such a smart girl you are!" he'd say with near-fatherly pride, though his intentions proved to be other than paternal. More than once, he'd tried to tempt Dani with a holiday in Barbados. "A little sun, a little sand—it'll do you good."

A little sex, too, for that was implicit. Dani put him off gently. The vibes just weren't there.

Whereas Steve . . . !

The man was a puzzlement. In the Eligible Man sweepstakes, he was Grand Prize: amusing, thoughtful, well connected and well informed. Dani was wildly attracted and assumed the feeling was mutual.

During the past month, they'd had wonderful times together. Steve had taken her to the theater, the ballet, several gallery openings. Yet came the witching hour, this dashing male Cinderella would disappear into the bowels of Grand Central, leaving her with nothing more substantial than a brush on the cheek.

Was he gay? she wondered. Or asexual? Was Dani being used as a front to mask a darker side of his life?

In fact, she knew little more about him than she had learned that first evening at Les Miroirs.

Whereas Steve had by now heard most of Dani's woes. She had told him about Ted, Samantha, about the breakup of her marriage. He always listened politely yet remained detached.

Tonight, however, he was taking her to the home of a former Harvard classmate, her first-time invitation to meet his friends. Did this indicate a commitment, she wondered, or was it, more likely, an audition?

Their hostess was a large personable woman, black-haired and gypsyish in an elaborate caftan studded with great chunks of ethnic jewelry. Steve effected the introductions.

"I loved your book on the Arapaigo Indians," Dani said with a throb of pleasure. "You *are* that same Hella Klein!"

"You actually read it?" Hella broke into a cascade of laughter. "And you're not even an academic? Where did you find this won-

derful woman, Steven, and why haven't you brought her round
before?"

The book was an oddity. Dani had picked it up years ago in a
secondhand bin at the Strand and been entranced. It augured a
good start for the evening.

"I didn't know you were an anthropology buff," Steve remarked
over sherry.

"There's a lot you don't know about me."

Behind her shoulder, someone was saying, *sotto voce*, ". . . woman
with Steve Haddad is the lawyer in the Nelson divorce." Dani
glowed.

They were ten at dinner, a varied yet convivial group with Dani
seated between a world-famous cellist and a documentary filmmaker
from the BBC, and across the table from an undersecretary of state.
Conversation was sharp, topical, with a premium placed on wit,
and Dani had a keen sense of being at the center of things: that
locus where trends were set, decisions made, policies formulated.
The talk touched upon politics, books, current events.

"Did you hear the latest ploy in the Globexx-*Gargantua* affair?"
said the woman sitting next to Steve. She was a columnist with
Newsweek magazine. "They've filed to change the name of the tanker.
To the U.S. *Columbia*, no less."

"I know," Dani said. "My husband was the man responsible."

Steve's eyes flashed an SOS. Was Dani going to start in on her
marriage?

But Dani smiled and said sweetly, "He used to work at Globexx.
He was a writer in the duplicity department."

The columnist did a take. "Surely you mean the publi—" but
Steve broke in with a laugh. "Dani always means exactly what she
says."

"Love it!" said the cellist, and poured her more wine while Steve
beamed. She had passed her audition.

By evening's end, she had garnered two invitations to lunch, a
tennis date at the East Side Racquet Club and an offer to tour the
BBC studios "next time you're in London."

"We'll get together before I go out in the field again," Hella Klein
said, squeezing her hand.

She was planning a tour in New Guinea next winter, to study

the cargo cultists. "You'd find them interesting, Dani. They're a Stone Age culture who believe in the divinity of things that have fallen to earth out of airplanes. The goods are the gods, so to speak."

"And vice versa. But why go to New Guinea for your research? Just be outside Bloomingdale's when the doors open each morning. All the cargo cultists you could ask for, lined up in a row."

Hella roared. "Thank you, love. You've just saved me six months of eating unspeakable food."

"Wonderful party," she said to Steve as they left. "I like your friends. Are you in a rush to catch your train?"

"I brought my car in."

"Then how about coming back to my place for a drink?"

Perfect, she thought. *Tonight will be the night.*

It wasn't until they were riding up in the elevator that she had misgivings. Steve had never been to her apartment before. What would he make of it? The man was such an aesthete, a perfectionist, and her apartment wasn't exactly a color spread from this month's *HG*.

"I'll get us coffee and brandy," she said. "Just make yourself at home and maybe put on some music."

When she came back with the drinks, he was sitting on the sofa, while some easy Harry Connick jazz played on the stereo. Suddenly, Dani could see the room through his eyes.

That Barcalounger, for instance! Big, black, hideous. What in God's name must he think of a woman who could cohabit with such a monstrosity. Of course he hadn't commented. He was too much of a gentleman.

She took a deep breath. "My husband had this thing about comfortable furniture, hence the eyesores. But now that I'm living alone, I thought I'd redecorate. I'd love your advice about what to keep, what to throw out."

"Why, Dani! I wouldn't presume to say."

"Why not? You advise people all the time. That's half your job, you told me—matching people with possessions. Well, I'm people!"

"You're a friend. That's different. Besides, taste is such a personal matter."

"Get personal," she pleaded.

He looked uncomfortable. He must have hated everything in

sight. But Dani wouldn't let up. The brandy had made her bold. She began tickling his neck. "Ve heff vays of making you talk!"

"Please, Dani . . . !" He laughed, then grabbed her hands. "Don't do that. Tickling drives me bananas. Okay, you win . . . I'll talk. What do you want to know?"

"That Barcalounger, Steve. What should I do with it? The truth, Steve."

He hesitated. "Give it to the Smithsonian."

Dani crimsoned.

"My Ecuador hanging?"

"Very charming."

"And my prints?"

He paused. "Well, I could hardly fault you for wanting to look at Van Gogh but . . ."

"They're posters . . . prints, right? And copies are for philistines. Well, I wish I could afford original art."

He smiled, noncommittal. Then he stood up. "What are the other rooms like?"

"There are only two more. My daughter's, which is what you'd expect of a teenager. And . . ."—she opened the door to the bedroom—"and this is mine," she murmured. She stepped inside, rapped her knuckles against the huge mahogany highboy, with its matching headboard and dresser and night tables. "I'll have you know this bedroom set is genuine Macy's Mediterranean Provincial Gothic. What can I do with this room? I wouldn't know where to begin."

In the distance, Harry Connick was teasing them with soft and twisty convolutions.

He put his face close to hers, so close she could feel his breath.

"Let's begin with a kiss and see where it leads."

She wound her arms around him. "What a fantastic idea."

Amazing! Amazing that two men could be as utterly different as Ted and Steve. In the first phase of their lovemaking, his body was alien to her: different tastes, touches, textures. She was terrified of failure. "Relax," he kept saying, but for the longest while she couldn't. She felt dry, uncomfortable, apologetic.

"I'm sorry. I can't. It's just that I've never made love to anyone but my husband in twenty years. . . ."

"Then I'm doubly flattered."

He got to his feet, pulling her up against him gently until they stood together thigh to thigh, nipple to nipple. He slid one hand around her waist. In the next room Harry Connick was making love sound easy.

"Nice music," he said. "Let's dance."

She rested her head on his shoulder and half shut her eyes. He had an athlete's body, well muscled, slim hipped and graceful, unfamiliar. As they moved to the slow, insistent rhythm, she felt herself caught up in a dream. The past fell away to infinity.

Love with a stranger. The idea thrilled. Dani raised her head and sought out his mouth. He tasted of cloves and vanilla ice cream. And as they danced, his firm smooth fingers discovered her body, tangling her hair, exploring the small of her back, the shape of her buttocks. She felt him grow hard against her, felt herself grow moist with desire. The music stopped and they danced on, arousing, caressing.

He drew her down on the bed, only this time she was ripe.

"Is this good for you?" he would say, exploring, probing, experimenting. Yes, she would murmur . . . yes . . . no . . . then suddenly it was nothing but yeses. She shut her eyes, mind going white, and gave herself over to his art.

He was a phenomenon: luxurious, sensual, tireless, responsive to every pleasure point, yet exerting the most extraordinary physical control. When it was over, Dani was on the verge of collapse.

"Oh God," she panted. "You're wonderful."

"We're wonderful," he said, stroking her hair. "It takes two."

They lay in the dark for a while, side by side, decompressing, dozing lightly. Then he folded her in his arms. She felt him quicken against her. Yes, amazing. "So what would you like, Dani—something different or more of the same."

"Both!" she sighed.

If only Ted could see me now!

She awakened to hear him moving about in the dark.

"What are you doing, Steve?"

He came over to the bed and kissed her on the nose. He was fully dressed. "Sorry, Dani, I have to push off."

"At three in the morning? Anyhow, tomorrow's Saturday. We could have a leisurely breakfast. Fool around. Spend the night, darling."

But he couldn't. He had to change his clothes, take care of chores at home. Feed the dogs.

Dani rolled over sleepily.

"I didn't know you had dogs."

"I keep Basenjis. Splendid creatures. All bite and no bark." He kissed her on the forehead and was gone.

She waited until the door closed behind him, then pulled the covers around her. Imagine! she thought just before drifting off. All the hours they'd spent together and he'd never once mentioned having dogs.

Extraordinary! Here she was, just coming down from the most intimate, most intricate experience a man and woman can share, and the details of his daily life were still a mystery.

The following morning, she banished the Barcalounger into Sam's room.

24

KAYCEE , who never wore black, was wearing black.

"I am in mourning for my life," she said. "Forty-three years of
it. Like Nina in what's that Russian play? *The Wild Duck?*"

"*The Sea Gull*," Dani said. "Chekhov. Though speaking of birds,
the edible variety, they do a very nice duckling here, garnished
with pears. And of course, we must have champagne. It's gorgeous,
by the way. Not the duckling, I mean, but your outfit. Simply
stunning."

"It ought to be," Kaycee said sourly. "It's my consolation prize
from Barney. Eighteen hundred bucks' worth of Missoni sequins
and spangles, so I can wear it to dine out with a girlfriend."

It was Kaycee's birthday, a ritual occasion in a friendship full
of rituals, and Dani was taking her to dinner at the Café des Artistes.
The previous year, Sloanes and Feldmans had celebrated the occasion jointly with a bibulous party aboard the *Fairweather Friend*,
but tonight was dinner-for-two, female style. Barney was in California shooting TV commercials.

Dani hadn't seen him since that night, some weeks back, when she
and the Feldmans had sat around her dining table drinking coffee
and wrestling with the "what-ifs."

"Let's begin with the premise that everything's negotiable," Dani said, "then go on from there." But though she did rack up a few compromises during the course of the evening (Barney would give up smoking, Kaycee would keep a closer eye on household bills), there was no meeting of the minds on the principal issue. When it came to parenthood, each Feldman peered into the future and saw different scenarios.

"I don't want to commit the next eighteen years of my life to bringing up another child," Barney said. "I'll be seventy before I'm a free man again."

"And I," Kaycee said, "don't want to go to my grave without having experienced motherhood."

Despite goodwill on all parts, irresistible force had met immovable object, and Dani's efforts were for naught.

At one point, temporarily out of steam, the three fell silent. Dani poured another coffee. Barney lit a cigarette and snuffed it. Suddenly Kaycee sat up.

"Do you hear that?" she said.

"Hear what?" Dani was puzzled. The sirens on Second Avenue? Next-door visitors saying their good-nights in the hall? The usual noises.

"That!" Kaycee said, wagging her index finger from left to right. "It's the ticking of my biological clock."

It was ticking now, in the Café des Artistes, as the two women ordered first champagne, then wine and the most opulent dishes on the menu. Throughout the meal Kaycee picked at her food. Her mood was as dark as her dress. "Forty-three," she muttered. "I can't believe it's happening." Or, "Birthdays suck."

From the gravlax on, Dani chatted away in an attempt to lift her friend's spirits. While the waiter cleared for dessert, she launched into an account of what was, at least to her own ears, a hilarious custody battle over a pet named Fangs.

"So the judge orders Fangs brought into the court, and it turns out to be this ancient Irish wolfhound, the size of a horse. My client Laurie is on one side, her husband on the other, they're going to put Fangs in the middle, see which one he'll go to. Like a Tug-of-Love. Well, first thing he does, naturally, is pee on the bailiff. But what I didn't know was that Laurie had hidden a piece of rump steak in her bra. . . . Oh Kaycee, don't cry," she pleaded, for tears were streaming down her friend's cheeks. "I know it's a dumb story, but I didn't think it was that bad."

"I hate growing old." Kaycee made a fist and pounded the table. "I fucking hate it."

Dani sobered. "Forty-three isn't old."

"Spoken from the vantage point of someone who has yet to hit forty-two. I'm growing old old old—inside and out. You know what the first signs of aging are? In the hands. Look, Dani. Look at the liver spots."

Dani felt for her. For someone who prized beauty as much as Kaycee, the passage of time must be particularly hurtful.

Gently, she took Kaycee's flawlessly manicured hand in hers, inspected it. "Pure driven," she said, then turned the hand over to scrutinize the palm. "What I do see is a long happy future, plenty of good times, good friends, a loving husband . . ."

"And children?" Kaycee asked with asperity. "Do you see children?"

"Oh Kaycee." Dani couldn't think what to say. "That much of a fortune-teller I'm not."

"You're a lousy fortune-teller." Kaycee withdrew her hand and reached for the dessert menu. Over her head, Dani gave the waiter a high sign.

"Why must they put so much glop on everything?" Kaycee said with disgust. "And nothing is less than a million calories. I'll just have coffee."

At that exact moment, their waiter marched to the table, bearing a lavishly frosted birthday cake.

"Sorry about the glop," Dani apologized, as he set it down with a flourish. "But it's the most fabulous mocha-rum with strawberry, and worth every one of those calories."

Kaycee, however, was intent on counting the candles.

"Thirty," she said. "Didn't they teach you any math in Hupperstown High?"

"Never could count straight. Anyhow, you know the routine, love. Blow out the candles before and make a wish. Who knows? maybe your wish will come true."

"I wish . . ." Kaycee scrunched up her eyes, leaned over. "Fuck! I can't blow out that many candles."

Then she took a breath worthy of a pearl diver and extinguished them all.

"See?" Dani said triumphantly, while the waiter served them both generous slices.

But Kaycee, a smudge of frosting on her nose, was fighting back tears. "No, my wish will never come true. I didn't tell you before, didn't want to spoil your treat, but Barney went and had himself a vasectomy last week. Without even consulting me. I think he was afraid I'd talk him out of it. What was the rush? Another year or two and it would probably have been a moot proposition. So there we are." She swiped at her eyes with a napkin. "It's out of my hands, and I'll just have to resign myself."

"Oh, sweetie." Dani's eyes welled. "I'm so sorry. I had hoped it would work out in a way that would make you both happy. Anyhow, what's done is done, so if you can, put it behind you and you can get on with your life. You still have Barney and all that other stuff I read in your palm. As my mother would say, look on the bright side."

"And as my mother would say,"—Kaycee studied the plate before her—" 'I have been rich and I have been poor and believe me darling, it's better to be skinny.' " Then she plunged her fork into six inches of frosting.

All that spring, she and Sam spoke at least once a week, with her daughter issuing bulletins from the front. "We've decided on country instead of Victorian," she would ramble. "Laura Ashley gown . . . spun-sugar apples . . . wildflowers . . ."

Dani refused to be sucked in. It was talk talk talk, designed to rile. "Well," she said after hearing a description of various veilings. "I just hope you're spending as much time with your textbooks as on bridal magazines."

Their most recent conversation, however, could not be sloughed off.

"What do you mean, you're not coming home this summer!" she found herself yelling. "I expect you . . ."

Stick? Carrot? Dani was flummoxed. Start with the carrot.

"I thought we'd take a place in the Hamptons for a couple of weeks, get all tanned and gorgeous. . . ."

"I told you, Mom. Don't you listen? I can't leave. Mel's working on an important paper and I want to be here with him. You've never taken my engagement seriously. Never!"

"I take it very seriously that you think you can escape from your problems by hiding out behind this flurry of activity. What do you think—that marrying will solve all your problems for the next hundred years?"

They bickered for twenty minutes, then Dani reached for the stick.

"Just don't expect me to support you out there. Not a penny! Your Mr. Wonderful can pick up the tab."

"Fine!" Sam shrieked. "I don't need your goddamn money. I can get a job, in a bookstore, waitressing . . ."

"You do that!" Dani slammed down the phone.

"Talking to that girl is like talking to the wall," she said to the wall. *Get a job . . . !* She had never worked a day in her life, if you didn't count baby-sitting. Maybe a stretch in the real world would shake some sense into her, and if not . . . Dani was mad enough to eat nails.

Since Sam felt that way, what Dani really ought to do was turn her bedroom into a home office, which would serve the girl right. "And God knows I could use the space."

She spent a busy hour in Sam's room, measuring, planning— the fax would go here, a computer terminal there, down would come the poster of Sting—then walked out, leaving the space unchanged. She couldn't do it, couldn't bring herself to close the door on her daughter. Instead, she phoned Oberlin the following day.

"Look," she said, "I hope you'll change your mind, and if you do, you know your room is always ready."

Never, not even in law school, had Dani worked so hard as during that spring and summer. Now, Round One behind her, she plunged into the discovery phase of *Nelson v. Nelson*.

"Before we can slice up the Lean Machine pie," she explained to Sherle, "we have to measure it accurately, which is the hard part. So be prepared for the long haul."

By law, all the books should have been available to Dani. In fact, each scrap of paper was a struggle. Time and again, she was forced to go to court for the most mundane documents, only to wind up receiving a fraction of what was requested.

"What do you mean, you're missing all canceled checks for May of 'eighty-five?" She waived a subpoena beneath Willi Shannon's nose. "I've got a court order here!"

Shannon shrugged. "May . . . May . . . I believe that was the month there was a fire in the office."

"A fire!" Dani snorted. "Why not a flood?"

It was trench warfare with each side dug in, every inch of ground contested as a matter of routine. Dani pressed, Willi dodged, Dani persisted, Willi played dumb.

Items were lost, Willi claimed in mock-bewilderment. They were misplaced, stolen, wrongly filed by stupid secretaries. One crucial document had been eaten up by silverfish.

"God's truth, Dani. You know what the plumbing's like in those old buildings."

"So the silverfish came out of the pipes and made their way into the filing cabinets?"

"Yeah . . . remarkable creatures. Here's a report from the exterminator."

One afternoon, she and Marsha were in the office when two men from Federal Express arrived with a shipment of cardboard boxes.

While Dani was trying to figure out where to put them, the fax machine clattered into action.

DON'T EVER SAY I NEVER GAVE YOU NOTHING. HAVE FUN.
WILLI

Marsha opened the first carton and removed a handful of what looked like supermarket tapes in different colors.

"Receipts." She held one up to the light. "This one's for fifty cents. I think it's a coffee bar chit. Yeah, in fact all the yellow ones are . . . the white ones seem to be for customer towel rentals in nineteen seventy-seven. Dollar. Dollar thirty-five . . . Fuck, there are thousands of 'em."

Another carton was revealed to hold twenty years' worth of laundry bills on paper so flimsy that it crumbled when touched.

"You can bet your ass there's nothing substantive here," she said. "Still we'll have to check it out."

They would never, she knew, reach a precise evaluation, for the company was too large, too amorphous. Ultimately, two sets of experts would arrive at two sets of figures. Lazzi's people would give estimates at the low end, Sherle's would be predictably high. The court would likely settle on a compromise figure, then decide what share was Sherle's.

The key word was equitable. But what was truly equitable? Shannon had hinted at twenty percent of total value, Jack Pruitt thought with luck they'd squeeze out thirty, but Dani was convinced she could make a powerful case entitling Sherle to a full forty percent. And if she did, she'd be the star of the bar.

"If you had asked my opinion a year ago," Dani told Marsha, "I would have summed Steve up as 'interesting, but not my type.' Which shows how little we know about ourselves. Of course, a year ago, I thought I was happily married. Anyhow, he's a total change of pace from the Late Ted Sloane. In build, temperament, preferences. And he knows such interesting people. Last night, for instance, we had dinner at the home of an investment banker friend of his, and it was a fascinating group—Tony Randall, Gloria Steinem, Pat Moynihan, the Chancellor of NYU. Well, we got into a fairly heated discussion about the best way of dealing with the city's fiscal crisis. Where do you cut? On public theater? On day-care centers? How do you balance cultural goals against the needs of the poor? What are the priorities? Somehow it turned into a working dinner. I mentioned that my local library is only open three days a week, which to me is a problem that addresses both issues. The upshot is, Marsha, that then and there I got drafted into the Mayor's Volunteer Advisory Task Force. I'll be working on the Library Committee alongside Norman Mailer. . . ." Dani grinned at a memory; Ted Sloane used to say that he would kill to meet Mailer. "So it turned out to be an extraordinary evening. And to top it off—total change of pace—Steve and I went to the Rainbow Room, danced till one, whereas I could never coax Ted onto the floor. God, it was fun! But Steve sure keeps me on my toes, literally *and* figuratively."

Marsha arched an eyebrow. "Why don't you just get cats?" she said. "They're easier."

A week after they became lovers, Steve brought her a framed drawing of a girl seated beneath a plum tree.

"How lovely!" Dani exclaimed.

"It's a Jean Charlot. He was a French-American artist who lived in Mexico. . . ." He went on to point out the drawing's merits. As he spoke, his eyes glittered. He looked like a man in love.

Notice, he said. Notice the curve of the girl's cheek . . . the echoing line of the tree . . . the ripeness of the fruit. . . .

As he explained the significance of Charlot's choice of a plum tree, Dani began to perceive that the drawing was not merely "lovely" (that garden-club word), but also tender, sensual, moving.

"Let's put it there." Steve pointed to the spot where a framed poster from the Botanical Gardens was hanging.

Dani took the poster down, put the Charlot up, stepped back to admire the effect. Off with the old, on with the new. She was very pleased.

As always, she found herself intrigued by the contrast between old love and new. The disparities went far beneath the surface. Steve was major league by any yardstick, and Dani delighted in the notion that she was "a big girl now," finally liberated from Ted's smothering (and provincial) clutch. Yet not all of the differences between the two redounded to Steve's benefit.

Where Ted was cozy, Steve was cool. Where Ted was laid-back, soft and easy as an old shoe, Steve was tough-minded and exacting, and Dani sometimes felt as though she were dancing barefoot on a hot plate, never quite sure if she was measuring up to his standards.

The Charlot drawing set a pattern of giving. Whenever he came, he brought some item of interest: an ivory netsuke, a lithograph, a bit of Delft, a Georgian thimble. On one occasion, he arrived with fifteen yards of Scalamandre fabric for her sofa, which he was having recovered as a birthday present.

She didn't know how to repay his generosity. Financially, a quid pro quo was out of the question, and once—when she bought him a book of Ansel Adams photographs—he was quick to protest.

"It's very generous," he said, "but far too expensive. I really wish you hadn't."

"It's only a book." She felt embarrassed, but it was clear to her that Steve would rather give than receive. Perhaps he was afraid of being beholden.

They frequently did the galleries together, and she was thrilled to discover that heightened familiarity with modern painting bred, not contempt, but a desire for ever more familiarity. Steve was encouraging.

The eye was like any other organ, he said. Use it or lose it. Given time, he guaranteed that she would come to love the Nelson paintings, right down to the last Ellsworth Kelly. "You might even want to buy one at auction."

"A very small one," she said.

Steve himself was an inveterate collector, and it was impossible to walk down 57th Street with him, or even pass a church rummage sale, without his poking around and coming away with something. It might be an expensive Chelsea snuffbox or a cheap piece of Carnival glass. Much of what he bought he gave away. It was the process of acquisition he loved.

"I think you'll like these," he announced one evening, handing Dani a package to unwrap. "They're quite fine."

Inside was a set of hand-painted Japanese pillows. Dani blinked. Each pillow portrayed a man and woman copulating, though the sexual positions varied from one to the next.

"These are marriage manuals," Steve explained. "A kind of Japanese version of *Everything You Wanted to Know About Sex*. They were given to brides on their wedding day so they could learn how to please their lords and masters."

Dani giggled and picked up a pillow in which two bodies were linked in the most improbable coupling. The woman's face bore an expression of rapture.

"Good Lord! This is straight out of a porno flick. Look where her legs are! Is that position physically possible, do you think?"

He laughed. "Only one way to find out."

It was indeed possible, but she felt sore for days.

They saw each other one or two evenings during the week. They went to parties, and sometimes spent Sundays together. When she was with him, life was divine. She could only wish it were divine on a daily basis, but Steve steered shy.

Anything that smacked of domesticity put his guard up. He rarely stayed overnight at her apartment, either timing their love-making so he could catch the last train home or, if he'd come in by car, rising well before dawn to make the long drive back. On the plus side, he usually sent flowers the next morning.

Dani couldn't understand this insistence on going home. Was it the dogs? Clean clothes? A desire to sleep in his own bed? The latter, most likely. Maybe he couldn't rest easy on other people's turf.

"How come you never married?" she asked him once as they lounged in bed, naked and happy in the afterglow.

"I never got around to it."

"But you must have met some terrific women," she probed. "Haven't you ever been tempted? I mean, surely—"

"Dani," he broke in, uncharacteristically. "I don't grill *you* about your past."

"I'm not grilling, it's natural curiosity. Come on! You must have had some serious involvements over the years. I just wondered—"

"At the risk of sounding rude, this has zip-all to do with our relationship. I'd never ask about you and your ex-husband. You'd say it's none of my business and rightly so. Now be a good girl and make us some tea. I think I'll catch the eleven twenty-two."

But Dani would not be outflanked. She wanted to let Steve know that she might one day be eligible.

"Ted's not my ex yet," she said carefully. "But it may not be long. It all depends." She waited for Steve to say—on what? But he propped himself up on his elbow to study her with museum-goer eyes.

"You're handling the litigation yourself, you once mentioned. Is that usual?"

Dani shook her head. "It's called *pro se*. Acting on one's own behalf. They say the lawyer who represents himself has a fool for a client, but I like maintaining control. Besides, who else could I find who's as tough?"

He laughed, and Dani, suddenly afraid of appearing harsh in his eyes, gentled her tone. She began fishing.

"What do you suggest, Steve? I value your opinion. Should I retain somebody else and get it over with?"

"Why, Dani, I wouldn't presume to advise."

It was a typical Haddad response: polite, elusive, avoiding anything that might be construed as a romantic declaration. It drove Dani up the wall.

She was curious about her predecessors, but when she quizzed him again, some nights later, he was fully on guard. The best reply she could get was "Ancient history. You wouldn't be interested."

She would! she would! every bone in her body cried out. She was convinced that some woman somewhere had broken his heart.

Yet despite his secretiveness, Dani felt he had already made a commitment of sorts, simply by sleeping with her.

The morning after their first night together, she had phoned Lou Morrison to say she couldn't see him anymore.

"Is there someone else?" he asked.

"Yes," she said.

"And it's serious?"

"I think so," she replied, forfeiting the bird halfway in hand for one that was still very much on the wing.

No sooner had she hung up than she felt ashamed. Amazing the speed with which her imagination had made the leap from the exchange of bodily fluids to the exchange of marriage vows. It was far too soon to think of remarrying. The savvy thing would be to relax and enjoy it, this first fine flush of romance. And if, on occasion, she speculated on the possibility of some day becoming Mrs. Steven Haddad (no! no! make that Danielle Sloane-Haddad, Esq.), that was perfectly normal. He was a man who appealed to the fantasy. At present, however, it didn't bear serious consideration. Maybe later, when the Nelson case was over. . . .

So she accepted Steve's trinkets and relished his sex and his company. More would have been better, but given the exigencies of two high-powered careers, it was a marvel they had any time together at all.

The bulk of Steve's energies went into his career. He was a man of surpassing ambition, determined to carve out a realm of his own as surely as his father and grandfather had done, and to do so without using "connections."

To this end, he brought the self-discipline that had once forged the Olympic champion. Now, still shy of forty, the firm's youngest vice-president, he was second-in-command of the New York salesrooms, overseeing sales worth hundreds of millions each year. His short-term ambition was to be put in complete charge of a major branch ("ideally New York, though London or Geneva would be great"), rounding out his experience in such a manner as would eventually lead to his becoming managing director of Wetherings International.

"On top by the time I'm fifty."

"And if not?"

"I'll go home and breed Basenjis."

Like Dani, he put in eighty-hour weeks and it was hard to determine which aspects of his life were social, which professional, so seamlessly did the two flow into each other.

Much of his time was spent in the cultivation of the rich: cosseting old customers, attracting new ones, persuading collectors either to buy or sell or (ideally) both. And when major prospects moved on to the Salesroom in the Sky, Steve pursued their heirs with equal vigor. When he opened the *Times*, he turned to the obituaries first, the art news second—which amused Dani greatly.

His social circle was immense—architects, historians, doctors, horse-breeders, bankers, journalists—and she was pleased to observe that he valued wit and accomplishment at least as much as money. But if Steve had countless acquaintances, he had few intimates and apparently no bosom buddies, a fact that Dani found puzzling. He made it a rule never to discuss personalities, either his own or anyone else's. Rather, he looked upon life with the wariness of a gambler in a high-stakes poker game, holding the key cards close to the vest.

What did he think? Feel? She could only guess.

For though by now Dani had explored every inch of his body— knew the feel of his teeth, the taste of his semen, the way the cords of his neck stood out at the moment of climax—yet his innermost thoughts remained obscure.

*   *   *

In early June, Deirdre Carlson Greaves had died after eating tainted mussels in Namibia.

Barney had flown out to Windhoek, escorted the body home, made the funeral arrangements, notified friends and the handful of relatives, and written the obit for the *Times*.

Dani was touched by his devotion.

Barney shrugged. "We never took to each other, Deirdre and I. She took great pains to let me know I'd married into the superior race and should be accordingly grateful. Still. . . ," he rationalized his efforts, "my wife's mother, it's one of those things you do. Poor Kaycee! She's distraught. But what the hell . . . the old babe had a fabulous life and died in hot pursuit of a childhood dream. I should be so lucky."

"But she only got to the N's," Dani said.

"Better than halfway through the alphabet. And how many of us have achieved most of our goals?"

A few dozen people showed up, mostly fellow ancients from the fashion world. Dani recognized some once famous faces. The editor of *Vogue* sent a wreath.

As Deirdre had wished, the body was placed in an open coffin, looking as perfect in death as in life. She was buried in a pleated silk Fortuny gown the color of molten gold.

Kaycee took the death very hard. "Gone . . . gone . . . ," she said at graveside. "Now I'm the last of the line."

Deirdre's estate, which had been destined for her daughter, turned out to be considerably less than anticipated. Her journey through the gazetteer had forced her to dip into capital at a perilous rate.

"I guess Mother figured, See Zimbabwe and die!" Kaycee said ruefully. "Still, she left me enough."

"Enough for what?" Dani was suspicious.

"Enough to do what I want. Which is—now don't give me that there-she-goes-again look, Dani—nothing indecent or illegal. Certainly not as wacko as pissing away a fortune because of a coloring book you had when you were a kid."

The two women were sitting in the Feldman living room, sifting through boxes of the dead woman's personal papers while Kaycee decided what to keep. There were snapshots, love letters, ancient dance cards—memorabilia dating back to Deirdre's debut in the Kansas City cotillion.

"In nineteen twenty-eight," Kaycee observed. "She always lied about her age." Then she sighed. "Of course, the money was hers to spend as she chose. Hell! She'd earned it. My mother spent the first seventy years of her life trying to please other people, so I'm glad she was able to please herself at the end. And she was good to me—the best prep schools, the greatest clothes. Plus which she bailed me out time and again. Still, when it comes down to it, who did she have left but me? I'm the only heir, Dani, except for a bequest to the lady who did her alterations. Look."

She handed Dani a portfolio photo by Avedon. Deirdre in white satin and pearls.

"Pure poetry, huh? Those bones, those genes. And I'm all that's left of her grace and beauty. I'm it!—the sole survivor. These are my mother's pearls, by the way. The ones in the picture." She fingered a double strand around her throat, then pushed the box away.

"What do I do with this stuff, Dani? Keep it? Dump it down the garbage compactor? Her clothes were easy. I called up the Met Museum to take their pick and gave the rest to Spence Chapin. But these things—they're so personal. They're meaningless to anyone but me."

"You have the space. Why not hang on to them for now?"

"As a way of keeping her memory alive? But I do that by the mere fact of my existence. So why save this stuff? Who will care? Who will treasure them when I'm dead and gone?" She fell silent for a moment, then spoke with an intensity that went straight to Dani's heart.

"I feel like that character in *Under the Volcano*. We read it in college, remember? He's wasted his life on booze and mindless fucking, and at some point he says, 'Where are the children I might have had?' Drowned in a thousand douche bags, or something grisly like that. Well, you know Malcolm Lowry—a bundle of laughs. But I've had eleven abortions, Dani, and I ask the same question: Where are the children I might have had? My oldest would have been twenty-five by now, the youngest, nearly six. My flesh and blood. I think of them often, those might-have-beens, those snippets of tissue left in clinics and doctors' offices all over the world. I know I can't change the past, but I can control the future. A few months ago I thought I'd resigned myself, but my mother's death changes everything. I'm going to have a child if it's humanly possible. I have the financial means now, thanks to mother's will, and I have the motivation."

"But a child by whom?"

"I haven't decided. Maybe a sperm bank, or else I'll find a lover. I don't even know if it will take. Either way, I'm through discussing it with Barney. I know how you feel about fidelity, Dani, but I have to be faithful to myself first."

"And what happens to your marriage?"

"If I don't get pregnant, probably nothing. Barney will never know. But if I do . . ." Kaycee expelled a long slow sigh. "I'm not setting out to wound him, believe me. I still love him in my way. But at my age, men are expendable and children aren't. You once said if I really wanted a baby, I should have one, that there are plenty of single mothers around. At that time I couldn't see it. I was totally dependent on having a man in my life, that's how I knew who I was. Then Ted left and you were so devastated, Dani. That's when my perspective began to change. Maybe we've lived in a men's world too long, both of us. In any case, I have no qualms about bringing up a baby alone. I know what you're going to say, Dani. That raising a child is such a precipitous course, even with two parents. That this is just another one of my flaky whims."

But Dani wasn't going to say that at all.

"Samantha called me last night," she murmured. "She wanted to know if she can borrow my bridal veil, which I have stored at my sister's house in Richmond. And I said sure. You know how I feel about this Christmas wedding she's got planned. Already they're talking about starting a family. It breaks my heart to see what Sam's doing with her life. But she has to be happy in her own way, so what difference does it make whether I approve or disapprove? She's my daughter, I love her and if that's what she wants, she has my blessing. I love you too, Kaycee, and I wish the same for you. . . ." Dani's voice cracked. "But I feel so torn. Because I love Barney as well, and it hurts."

Under Steve's aegis, Dani had entered a glittering new world.

"My Filofax runneth over," she said to Marsha. "There aren't enough hours in the day."

With Steve by her side, she passed through unfamiliar gates and in the process discovered Thoroughbred racing at Saratoga, what really went on backstage at CBS News, how to walk through an art gallery with an air of total insouciance and which, proverbially, were the best seats in the house in all the New York theaters. She met people—his friends, many of whom soon became hers—and perhaps the high point of his bounty came when he proposed her for membership in the Metropolitan Club. It was a sweet day for Dani when, across the club's luxurious lounge, she caught the eye of Jack Pruitt. *What are you doing here?* his expression seemed to say, then he came over and pumped her hand.

It was a new life and she was becoming a new person. Little by little, in light of this fresh self-image, she began fixing up her apartment. The Barcalounger made its way to the Salvation Army, followed, after due consideration, by the blond oak Swedish china cupboard and the outsized umbrella stand, on the principle that less is more. In the living room Dani had the old carpeting removed, the floors scraped and polished and set off by a small but lovely Kilim rug whose muted shades of peach and raspberry and greens made her think of a latticed garden. Then she broke the bank with a pair of Chinese Chippendale side chairs from the Place des Antiquaires (even though Steve saw that she got the trade discount), after which she called it a day. "At least for this year."

And though the changes weren't radical, the total effect of these few new touches was one of grace and elegance.

On Midsummer's Eve, Dani threw her first solo party with a catered buffet from Balducci's. It was about time, she decided, to return some hospitality. The guest list ran to fifty-plus, mixing old friends, new acquaintances and a handful of colleagues.

"It's the shortest night of the year," she told everyone, "so stay till dawn." More than a dozen people did. At five in the morning, she went to the kitchen to scramble eggs. Gloria Melman followed her in.

"He's gorgeous, your Steve," she whispered in Dani's ear.

Dani flushed with pleasure. Through the doorway, "her Steve" was discussing game fishing off Bimini with Chris Evans from her office. She paused in midscramble to beam on them both.

In that instant, she had a delicious sense of her worlds coming together, fitting, meshing. It would never have happened without Steve.

But the greatest perk of this wondrous new love affair came from the least expected quarter.

The first time Steve invited her to his house in Pound Ridge, she was apprehensive. Given Steve's exacting nature, Dani expected a museum in miniature, not only exquisite, but flawless in every detail.

"A gem of classic Federal architecture, seventeen ninety-four,"— his exact words—"with most of the original timbers intact. One might say it's the total antithesis of Beverly Hills."

The sole concession to his California upbringing was an Olympic-length pool. "But it's out of sight, around the back of the building."

To Dani, it sounded like a place where God forbid you put your feet up on the furniture or bumped into the artwork. Maybe she should don white cotton gloves, à la Precious Nelson. Maybe she shouldn't go.

Instead, Webster House turned out to be the happiest disappointment of her life.

"I think I'm in love," she said the moment she set eyes on the clean white house with black shutters. "I know I am," she said when she crossed the threshold. "It's paradise."

How full of surprises Steve was! In New York, always proper and formal, immaculately dressed. But Pound Ridge was another story. It was bare feet and shorts and easy chairs.

Like a restaurant critic who dined so lavishly on the job that at home he contented himself with boiled eggs and tea, Steve, too, had opted for the creature comforts after hours. However, Dani hesitated to push the boiled-egg analogy too far. Webster House was still a rich man's home.

The house was small, on six acres of land, and furnished in an artfully casual way. Nothing "went" in the decorators' sense, yet everything worked. Steve had mixed contemporary art with English chintzes and period wallpapers and fresh tulips in blue-and-white china jars. Almost every room held a cozy nook or sunny corner where one might curl up in an armchair and doze off.

Wherever one looked, there was an abundance of "things": small, charming items that cried out to be picked up and fondled. Each came with its own minihistory: bought at a local estate sale, on the Portobello Road, a gift from the artist, discovered at an auction on the rue Drouot or on a fishing trip to Guatemala. "I can resist everything except pretty objects," he said, a remark that set Dani glowing.

"You know about the Shakers," he remarked, when Dani had picked up a small wooden box for inspection. "They married, but they didn't reproduce."

"Only boxes," Dani said.

Usually she would arrive late Saturday, then spend Sunday poking around the property. Steve swam first thing each morning, a hundred bulletlike laps, while Dani made breakfast or slept late. Sometimes they played tennis with neighbors, sometimes they gardened. For a change of pace, she would sit on a wicker settee by the pool with a detective novel, and throw sticks for Rosie and Max to retrieve.

They were graceful creatures, these lean-limbed Basenjis, who managed to combine aristocratic bloodlines with a playful temperament. Rather like their owner, she thought. One was brindle, one was black. The brindle turned somersaults when you whistled do-re-mi.

According to Steve, they were bred for hunting lions in Africa, and he had bought them for watchdogs, only to discover they lacked proper vocal cords. "But by that time, I was hooked." He himself was never happier than when romping with them in the pool or stretching out on the grass while they slobbered over him with hot moist tongues.

"Silly creatures," Dani said, as they stole her heart.

Inevitably, her return to the city Monday mornings was marked by a sense of anticlimax. Surfacing at Grand Central, assaulted by the heat, Dani would stand there for a moment in a state of culture shock, inhale the fetid air and groan. Ted was right. New York stank.

And one morning, covered with instant grime, beating off panhandlers while trying to flag down a cab on 42nd Street, it came to her that yes! she might indeed live happily ever after in a pretty Federal house in Pound Ridge. With Steve and Rosie and Max.

"Taxi! Taxi!" she hollered. Christ! She was going to be late for work.

Yet all that day, sitting in the office, papers piled high, she was haunted by the vision of herself as the chatelaine of Webster House. Cooking. Gardening. Swimming. Playing with the dogs. Entertaining neighbors. Away from the screech of horns and hectic pace of Manhattan.

Which was funny, come to think of it. Ted's craving for precisely that mode of life had been a major source of friction in their marriage.

"Better death than dandelions," she used to say.

How ironic, she mused, that she could so easily picture herself with Steve leading the suburban life she had begrudged her own husband.

Not that anyone was proposing, mind you. Not that she was desperate to get married again. Still, if she should manage to land a catch like Steve Haddad, wouldn't that frost Ted!

25

TO DANI'S ASTONISHMENT, Lazzi caved in instantly to Sherle's request for sole custody of Precious. To her even greater amazement, Sherle didn't view this concession as a victory.

"But Sherle," Dani argued, "whether he shares custody or not doesn't minimize his financial obligations. He'll still have to shoulder his fair share of the costs. You won't lose by it, I assure you!"

"It isn't that."

Sherle's eyes grew moist, the shoulders trembled. But Dani, who knew her client's ability to weep on cue when useful, remained skeptical. *Save me the crocodile tears,* she thought as Sherle reached for the Kleenex box. *You're talking to your lawyer, remember?*

After a couple of minutes of silent weeping, Sherle honked her nose, then looked Dani in the eye. Her face was set and grim.

"I never bullshitted you, Dani. I won't now. A lot of what Lazzi's said about me is true. Not the smear stuff—the drugs and all that crap; you know me better—but statements he made about my life before I hooked up with him.

"I didn't exactly 'leave home' when I was sixteen, like it says in my press releases. My old man threw me out with nothing but the clothes I stood up in. He was a drunk and a brute and a wife-beater. And I was fifteen, to set the facts right. Those first years in Vegas—well, what could I do? I turned tricks. I picked pockets.

I'd hang around the casinos, not the fancy ones either, and if I couldn't find a john, I'd steal half-eaten food off plates. I ate garbage, Dani. Hell! I *was* garbage. But I survived.

"When Lazzi came along, it was everything I dreamed of—good clothes, security, a chance to make something of myself. And then I got pregnant. It's not that I didn't want Precious, Dani. I thought it was going to be wonderful—this sweet lovely baby to care for, someone all my very own. But when she was born—I don't know, it wasn't there, the feeling, the instincts. I tried to love her, I swear to God. I wanted to love her, to care, get involved, but I couldn't find it in me, then or now. It was like trying to speak in a language I never learned." She shook her head sadly. "I didn't have the vocabulary. I'm sorry, Dani, but you can't give what you haven't got. And that's the truth."

Periodically, Dani would regale Steve with her troubles. Mostly concerning Samantha, who was working as a vegetable chef in a busy health food restaurant. "For this we sent her to prep school," Dani wailed, "so she can peel potatoes!" while Steve nodded politely and made appropriate sounds. He really wasn't interested, she knew, but that was the price of sharing Dani's bed.

"At least, she's going back to college in the fall," Dani said while they were getting ready to turn in. "Which is a kind of relief. She claims she's not doing it because I want her to or even for her own sake, but so Mel won't marry a dummy. Some logic, huh? Although I don't suppose I should complain about her too much, she's trying to find her way. On the other hand . . ."

The recent conversation with Sherle was still fresh in her mind. She felt full of undischarged emotion.

"This business with Sherle and Precious is really getting to me." She gave a heartfelt sigh. "Can you imagine what that kind of childhood must be like?"

"Sherle's?"

"No, her daughter's."

Steve started peeling off his clothes. "Let it be, Dani. I don't feel like hearing all this."

He unplugged the phone and climbed into bed.

"But Steve, don't you—"

"A, I'm not interested in the Nelson's marital wars. B, I may have to do business with these people. And C, we're on our own time now, Dani," he said, sliding a hand up her leg. "My, you smell good."

Just then the beeper sounded on the night table.

"Bloody hell!" He picked up the offending instrument and for a moment Dani thought he was going to heave it out the window. Instead he got out of bed and jammed it in the depths of a dresser drawer. Something within caught his eye.

"Now what have we here? He drew out a handful of feathers and held them to the light. "Why, Dani, have you been keeping peacocks?"

Dani giggled. "Just some lingerie I bought last year. I know it's tacky . . ."

But Steve was intrigued. "Very sexy. And decidedly un-Dani. Model it for me, will you?"

She changed in the bathroom and emerged feeling more un-clothed than had she been totally nude. All that was lacking were high heels and dangling earrings. Then, wondering if she didn't look half a fool, she strolled across the room like a runway model.

Steve was sitting up, chin on his elbow, bright-eyed, with a huge erection, just as the girl in Felinda's Fantasy had guaranteed. Dani did a half turn and struck a pose.

"Your bird of paradise."

"Very nice, my fine feathered friend. Too bad I'm not an or-nithologist. Do birds fuck, do you think? They must. There's that Cole Porter tune, how's it go?—Birds do it, bees et cetera, though I'm damned if I know how."

"In flight, I imagine, with both feet firmly in midair, rather like airplanes refueling."

"I bet we could do that." He got up, circled around her as though to take some measurement, then locking his hands around her hoisted her up off the floor, like an Atlas raising the world. His arms were like iron.

"I bet we could have one right royal fuck without your ever coming down to earth. Think bird, Dani. Think of being weightless . . . free. . . ."

God, what a splendid body he had, clean-limbed and virile! His lips brushed her navel, then he slid her down into position, manipulating until his cock was thrusting through the thin fabric of the panties. With a wrenching move she tore the scrap of feathers aside to grant him untrammeled entry. As he entered her, she felt airborne, feather-light, floating in defiance of gravitational law.

They began a slow waltz. This was what it must be like to be a dancer, not a peacock but a swan, an exquisite Odette being borne aloft by her prince. Never once did his arms tremble, his absolute control of her body diminish. She wanted the sensation to last forever, to fly away with Steve into some never-never land of blue skies, white clouds, blind rapture, infinity.

When it was over, he fell to the floor laughing, Dani on top of him. She shut her eyes and waited for her breath to return.

"Wow!" he said. "This stuff is more strenuous than the four-hundred-meter freestyle. I'm bushed." He stifled a yawn. "And I'm afraid I wrecked your outfit into the bargain."

Dani rolled off him and stumbled to her feet.

"That's a spectacularly unromantic remark."

He was stretched out on the floor, hands behind his head, looking content. "That wasn't romance, Dani. That was fantasy. Be careful next time you don't bring home tiger lingerie, complete with claws. I wouldn't want to be responsible for the outcome." Then he grinned. "My God, Dani, you are fabulous in bed. Or out of bed, as the case may be. That was terrific."

By the time she'd washed up, he was under the covers, fast asleep. Dani crawled in beside him, physically replete but less than happy.

Fabulous sex. Steve was a virtuoso, though she hadn't much cared for that four-hundred-meter remark. This was not a sporting event. It was lovemaking with something left out.

She leaned over and picked a peacock feather out of his hair, and began tickling his nose. He grunted, scrunched further under the covers.

"Say something, Steve."

"How about—'Let's go to sleep.' "

Dani pulled up the sheets, close to tears.

"I can't. I'm feeling blue."

"What is it in Latin?" he mumbled. *"Omne animal post coitum triste sunt.* Birds, too, I expect. Now go to sleep."

"Thanks a lot."

She knew, of course, exactly what was missing. Words. She craved words. The kind of words she'd always associated with the act of love. Not the cries made in the heat of passion, nor the grunts or ecstatic shouts, but the little silly tender words you traded in the afterglow. Idiot small talk, foolish endearments. *Honey sweetie darling baby love angel.* It was a kind of verbal fondling, love's small change, and Steve never indulged in it. Not even tonight, when they had been so very good together.

The difference was, tonight it bothered her. Steve had drifted off again. She woke him up.

"How come you never use endearments, Steve?"

He rubbed his eyes. "What do you mean?"

"Well . . . honey, sweetheart. That kind of thing. You never call me anything but Dani."

"Because," he said, suddenly wide awake, "that kind of thing, as you put it, is the cheapest sort of currency there is. Worse than meaningless. False. Where I grew up, everyone was sweetie darling honey baby sugar. People you loathed. Most particularly them. *I love ya, baby. Trust me.* That was when you knew to check your wallet. Personally, I find that whole terminology so . . . so sleazy, so Hollywood. Now if I had called you by another woman's name, then you'd have every right to be annoyed."

But Dani wasn't satisfied. "It's not just endearments, Steve. It's that you so rarely show physical affection."

He stared at her in amazement. "It seems to me I've just shown you a good deal of affection. Give me a half hour to recoup and I'll do the same again."

Dani felt defensive. "Well, you're affectionate but not demonstrative."

"By demonstrative, I gather you mean to convey that I'm not a public backslapper or a glad-hander or a bottom-pincher or one of those jokers who routinely kiss all the women at dinner parties. In which case, you're correct. I don't care for certain forms of sentiment. They're not my style."

"I'm not talking about pawing total strangers, Steve. I was talking about our strolling Madison Avenue hand in hand, like normal
couples."

"Well, I don't know what the law is concerning normal couples.
I only know what I'm comfortable with. I am what I am, Dani—
and at this moment what I am is dead tired."

With that, he rolled over and went back to sleep.

Steve drove her crazy. She couldn't get a handle on him. In his
absence, she was able to whip up the most marvelous domestic
fantasies, complete with rosebuds and white eyelet curtains flapping
in the breeze, but in the flesh he remained elusive.

A few evenings after their bird game, Dani invited Hella Klein
to her apartment for dinner. It was a pleasant meal, and afterwards
the two women settled in the living room over brandies. Hella
talked about her plans for New Guinea, giving Dani just the opening she desired.

"Speaking of cargo cultists, Hella, I'd like to ask a few questions
about my favorite auctioneer, who's a bit of a cargo cultist himself,
you have to admit."

Hella laughed. "Are these personal questions, or are you solic-
iting my opinion as an anthropologist?"

"Either . . . both. The problem is, I can't get a fix on what
goes on inside his head. He hardly ever speaks about himself, let
alone any other women in his life. Still, I can't believe he was
celibate all these years."

"Good Lord, no!" said Hella. "Although I wouldn't call him a
swinger, either. But Steve always has a woman on tap."

There had been, until recently, Dani learned, a long-term affair
with a Princeton art historian. Monica Storrs was, according to
Hella, "a fabulous woman. Smart, funny, from a top New York
family. They were together for years. He'd go down there every
weekend."

"So what happened?" Dani pressed.

"Nothing. That was the problem. Monica wanted the usual—
marriage, kids—till finally she got tired of waiting. One Saturday,
Steve went to Princeton as was his wont to find she'd put his shaving

things out on the doorstep. Then she turned around and married somebody else the next month."

"Ouch! He must have been crushed."

"You think so? I think he felt relieved. I'm very fond of Steve. He's a wonderful friend. You want to borrow money? Steve's your man. You need some contacts? He knows everyone. But he never lets anyone really know him."

Some years earlier, a flashy women's magazine had included his name on a list of "New York's Ten Most Eligible Bachelors." Furious, Steve had threatened to sue for invasion of privacy.

"That was when he bought that nest of his in Pound Ridge and got an unlisted number. But the article had it wrong. Steve may be a bachelor, but hardly eligible. You could say avoiding marriage has become his religion. That's why he likes independent women, at least for as long as they stay that way. You, for instance. You're ideal. Smart. Respectable. With a grown child, so you won't be clamoring for motherhood. And still legally married, did I hear you say? Well, don't get a divorce on his account. I know he's fond of you, but you also happen to be—this sounds awful—a kind of insurance policy. Protection from the ravening mob."

"Maybe he's just never met the right woman," Dani said.

Hella frowned. "And maybe you are? My dear, there is no right one. I know his routine. I bet when you met him, he gave you a prefab bio, being wet-nursed or whatever by Marilyn Monroe. Which is probably true; his father's a powerhouse. Still, it's a typical Haddad ploy. What Steve does, you see, is get the obvious truths of his life up front quick, so it appears he's being forthright about himself, his family. But overstep the line and down comes the curtain."

"Why? Is the family so dreadful?"

Hella shrugged. "I met them a few times and they struck me as about par for Beverly Hills. Hustling. Sleek. Lots of teeth. Lots of marriages. Except for Steve, of course. The Lone Ranger." Hella paused. "Ever wonder what lies beneath the tip of an iceberg, Dani? Ninety percent more ice. So I wouldn't even try to get too close to Steve Haddad. Remember what happened to the *Titanic*."

Dani tabled Hella's warning for future reference, yet she remained convinced that Steve's reticence stemmed from an unhappy love affair. Some woman, somewhere, if not this Monica, had done a job on him. Still, as Dani knew herself, nobody dies of a broken heart. There's always a little bit left that you can build on.

Nelson v. Nelson was going well, and Dani enjoyed almost every minute of it. The research had begun to come in on the That Girl Sherle study, with results even better than anticipated. That the ultimate beneficiary of all this effort should be a woman about whom Dani had such mixed feelings was simply irrelevant. She had fallen in love with the challenge.

As one law professor once put it: If you can think about a thing inextricably attached to something else, without thinking of the thing it is attached to, then you have a legal mind.

Dani had a legal mind, and at this point, grounds for cautious optimism.

"Law would be a ball if it weren't for clients," she kidded Marsha, who agreed absolutely.

Kaycee called during the dog days of August and mentioned that Lou Morrison had just got engaged.

"A lovely woman," Kaycee said. "In her thirties, very attractive, a psychologist. They're both happy as clams. You missed your big chance."

Oddly, Dani felt a twinge. "Well, give him my warmest best wishes."

Thoughtfully, she hung up the phone.

Perhaps she would have an announcement of her own one day. Meanwhile, she had a career to attend to.

Her practice was booming, with new clients rolling in on an unbroken tide. Several had come through Steve's connections, still others attracted by the Nelson notoriety. All of them looked to be profitable. Jack Pruitt was pleased.

Only one new piece of business aroused reservations. Should she, should she not, offer her services on his behalf?

He looked so agitated, so haggard, as though he'd never been inside a lawyer's office in his life.

"Divorce," Dani said solemnly, "can be hell."

"I know," Mort Ketchell said, wringing his hands. "It's killing me. I'd do anything to keep our marriage alive."

Dani stared. His face was a map of suffering. This man—El Swino, The Prince of Pricks, The Goon of Globexx—this man whose demands and humiliations played such a major role in the destruction of her own marriage—this monster was now asking for help.

But sitting in the chair across her desk, tense and unhappy, El Swino looked like nothing more than yet another candidate for Misery Lane.

Dani took a deep breath.

"My husband used to work for you," she said. "Ted Sloane? Public relations?"

Ketchell furrowed his brow. "Ivy League type with a ponytail?"

"Ted had a beard."

"Can't place him. Those guys come and go. Now about Selena, I don't want to do anything that would hurt her. . . ."

Amazing, she thought. How time changes the shape of the landscape. And yesterday's Hitler is today's high-paying client.

Yes indeed, Dani said a half hour later. She would be delighted to represent him. What did it matter really whether Ketchell was the greatest threat to conservation since the inchworm or merely another wounded spouse? Business was business. Grief was grief.

The week before Labor Day, Samantha surprised her mother with a call from JFK. She was on her way back to college from St. Thomas where, courtesy of her paternal grandparents, she had been spending a week's holiday. Her ticket permitted a stopover in New York.

"So if it's okay with you, I thought maybe I'd come home for a couple of days. . . ."

"Of course it's okay, love!" Dani whooped with delight. "Grab a cab and I'll meet you there in an hour."

She scarcely recognized Sam. The tropical tan was to be expected. But the slim figure, the firm athletic arms and legs—no baby fat on her baby these days.

Dani threw her arms around her. "Why there's nothing to pinch anymore. You look fabulous, cookie, just fabulous. Like the models we used to cluck over in the fashion supplements."

"Oh, Mo-ther!" Sam flushed with embarrassment. "You sweat-work eight hours a day in an overheated kitchen, you lose weight. It's no big deal."

She looked around the living room, noted the new art, the old sofa reupholstered in Scalamandre silk. "Place looks different," she observed. "You had a decorator in?"

"Nope. Just a paint job and a few fresh touches. Your room's the same, though. So why don't you unpack and freshen up, then we can go out to dinner. How about Indian?"

"I'm kinda tired," Sam said, "so if it's all the same with you, I thought I might slice up a few veggies, make a salad. Busman's holiday." She laughed. "I've really become an artist with the vegetable knife."

In an unfamiliar reversal of roles Dani sat on a stool watching Sam chop and slice and dice with quick deft motions. Yet she felt a sadness behind her daughter's eyes. Problems with her father? With Mel? With her December marriage plans? To probe or not to probe, that was the question. But she and Sam had been over the ground so often on the phone, she decided to let it rest for the present. They ate, washed up and decided to make an early night of it.

"I'm taking tomorrow off," Dani said, "so if you'd like, we can go shopping."

"God, yes!" Sam said fervently. "I'm down to size ten and all my old clothes simply swim!"

Then she went into her bedroom and switched on her favorite rock station, while Dani left her door open to catch the rumbling *VOOM VOOM VOOM*. Not that she liked rock any better, mind you, but it was nice having life in the house. This once, she didn't complain.

By late afternoon the following day, Dani had pretty much outfitted Sam from head to toe. All that remained was to find a good pair of wool slacks.

The two women were in a dressing room at Lord and Taylor,

clothes piled high, while Sam wriggled out of one pair and into another.

"What do you think, Mom?" She undressed again, looking troubled. "The gray or the navy or the black-and-tan check?"

"Well, the navy's the most practical, but I prefer the checks. However, it's not an earthshaking problem," she added, for Sam, in a tie-dyed T-shirt and panties, was staring at herself in the mirror, her mouth taut in a paroxysm of anxiety. She looked so naked, so vulnerable. "Maybe we'll take them both and you can decide later."

Sam's response was to burst into tears.

"He was so mean to me!" she sobbed. "So goddamn mean!"

Dani caught her breath. "Mel?" she whispered, "or . . ."

"Daddy! All the time I was there, he was just so nasty and unfair." She paused to wipe her eyes on a corner of the navy slacks, then started crying again. "It's like, he kept lecturing me how I was throwing my life away, how Mel was old enough to be my father ya ya ya . . ." Dani paled at the diatribe, for what had Ted done except make the same points that Dani herself had believed from the start. Except, of course, that in the Sloane family tradition, Ted was always called upon to play the Good Cop and Dani the Bad One. Now Sam couldn't stem her rage.

She pulled the corners of her mouth down and mocked Ted's rich basso. " 'Now you listen to me, young lady, I won't have it. I won't have my baby getting involved with a man twice her age. It's indecent.' " Sam gave a bitter snort. "Like Daddy's so smart, like he knows what's best for me, 'young lady.' He's telling me that men like Mel ought to be locked up and put away somewhere. And all the while I'm getting this moral guidance, she kept hanging around in the background. . . ."

She. Dani felt a thrill of indignation. *She*—who was scarcely older than Samantha.

"Oh Sam, darling . . ." Dani took her hand, but Sam continued.

". . . Little Miss Match Girl, sort of peeping out of the kitchen with those big blue eyes. For Crissakes, who the fuck is Daddy to talk about what is suitable and what isn't! What gives him that authority!"

"Oh Sam! You know he loves you and all he wants is—"

"Don't interrupt!" Sam snapped. "Jesus, Mom! For months you've been bugging me to talk things out and now when I'm trying to, you keep interrupting."

Dani shut her mouth, while Sam, the gates of speech unlocked, spewed out a year's worth of anguish, fear, rage, anxiety, gave voice to an overwhelming sense of loss. "I don't think I would have made it without Mel's support. He was a rock. I could tell him everything, pour out my heart. I talked to him in French, would you believe? Like it was easier that way. And then, to hear Daddy dump on him. It just pissed me off. Anyhow, I was so mad when I left St. Thomas I didn't even tell him . . ."

Sam paused, then began putting on her clothes. She had run out of fire, and Dani, who had listened without comment for the last half hour, knew in an intuitive flash exactly what Sam was about to say.

. . . *that you and Mel have split up?* Dani almost jumped in. Don't interrupt. Let her talk.

". . . that Mel and I have split up. Well, not like we split up exactly. I mean, I'll always feel very special about him but . . . Well, he's going to Oklahoma U. next semester. There was a sudden opening in French lit. Seems the guy who had the post dropped dead of a heart attack last month. Anyhow, Mel will have tenure, which is neat for him, but I've decided not to go. I mean, like, you know that Cyndi Lauper song I used to drive you nuts with—'Girls Just Wanna Have Fun'? I'm not sure I want to feel tied down just yet. Running a house, all that stuff. Well, Mel's the best of the good guys, but, I mean, I'm only eighteen and he's—you know, like a lot older."

Sam flushed, faintly embarrassed. Dani swallowed the lump in her throat.

"Besides," Sam added, "there's a course I want to take next semester on Chinese history, from Ming to Mao. Sounds interesting, doesn't it? In fact, I'm thinking of doing a double major, maybe French and poli sci. A lot of the kids are doing double majors. Though I may decide to switch from French to Middle English." She lowered her eyes, then began getting dressed. "I guess what I'm saying is I'm not exactly sure what I want except that I'd like to poke around and try out a few different things for a while. So if it's okay with you, I think I'll live in the dorms this term."

In Dani's heart, the five-hundred-pound vise, which for so long had been clamped about that portion reserved for Samantha, finally loosened.

"Yup," Dani said, while offering up a fervent prayer of thanksgiving. *No, I'm not going to cry, not going to cry.* "It's okay with me." She was about to add a few more thoughts, threatened to get absolutely fulsome, but she knew enough to quit while she was ahead.

The saleswoman knocked on the door of the dressing room.

"Nearly closing time, ladies."

"We'll be out in a minute," Dani replied.

Sam wiped her eyes and tried for a laugh. "And we still didn't decide, the navy pants or the check."

After Sam left the next morning, Dani checked out her room to make sure nothing had been left behind. Nothing had, but on the wall, Dani noticed, the poster of Sting had come down, replaced by a big strident blowup of Madonna.

"You know," she said to Marsha one morning, "Today is exactly one year since my husband left me."

"You actually remember the date?"

"The day, the hour, the minute. September ninth, eleven fifty-two P.M., to be precise. Like it's engraved."

"Happy anniversary."

"And it could be another full year before he gets his divorce."

But one night in late October, an extraordinary event occurred.

It had been a hectic day. A breakfast meeting at the Hyatt, an early-morning court appearance, a hot-dog lunch from a stand in Foley Square (obeying the maxim that "Real lawyers eat fast food"), a session with Ketchell's tax attorney, a phone conference with Willi Shannon, a client meeting at 5:15, then time for one quick drink at Smitty's before joining up with some new people named Hetherton for a press party at NBC and a latish dinner at Le Refuge.

It wasn't until she fell in bed at half past eleven, bone-tired, that

she realized what was wrong, and the revelation came with a sense
of utter shock.

Believe it! She hadn't thought about Ted Sloane once all day.
Not one single moment! She had been remiss in her duty.

Dani yawned, reached for the light and said her litany.

Over my dead body will he marry Jen MacDougall.

But this once, her heart wasn't in it.

26

"SO THERE!" Kaycee quoted the red-slipped grandmother of Barney's lingerie ad. "I did it and I'm glad!"

"Oh, Kaycee . . . I don't know what to say."

"How about congratulations?" Kaycee said in an uncertain voice, but Dani couldn't. The word stuck in her throat.

The two women were squeezed into a cramped sitting room, cotton cabbage roses and heavy-duty carpet, at the Shelmore Arms Apartments ("suites by the day, week or month"), the room made even smaller by a clutter of boxes and luggage of every size. "Part of my inheritance," Kaycee said of the Vuitton suitcases, which had once cost a fortune but now looked the worse for wear. *As who did not?* Dani thought.

She walked over to the window, pushed the curtains aside and gazed down on the Third Avenue traffic, trying to get a grip on her feelings.

At heart, Dani had never believed that Kaycee would go through with a dream that could only be attained at the sacrifice of her marriage. Now, in the face of this *fait accompli*, her loyalty to Kaycee rubbed up against her affection for Barney.

He had called her the night before in a paroxysm of pain. "I feel betrayed," he said. "Not just betrayed, but dumped and shit upon."

They were feelings Dani could identify with. She had been down that road herself. But Kaycee seemed miraculously calm.

"So will you be staying on here?" Dani said, merely to have something to say. "You going to look for an apartment?"

Kaycee shook her head. "I've had it with New York, Dani. This is not the greatest place to bring up kids. I think Arizona, or maybe New Mexico. I'm leaving next Monday for Santa Fe."

To Dani, it was the old sad familiar pattern. When the going got rough, Kaycee simply packed up and moved on. But this time, she was leaving heartbreak behind her.

"I don't understand," Dani found herself saying. "How could you do this to Barney?"

Kaycee sighed. "Ah Barney Barney Barney. I know you're going to find this difficult to accept, Dani, because you were always rooting for us to have this terrific marriage. You were so glad when I finally settled down. But I sometimes got the impression that our making it was almost as important to you as it was to me. From the day you stood up for me at City Hall, you were always there, cheering us on, for which I'm grateful. But it wouldn't have lasted, Barney and me."

"Kaycee . . . !" Dani reared back in dismay.

"It's true. If we didn't break up over this, we would have broken up over something else. One way or another I would have made it happen. I would have been unfaithful, or he would have. More likely me, though. Sooner or later I would have hurt him, Dani, so perhaps sooner is best. You should know me by now. When it comes to men, I'm not built for the long haul. I start feeling antsy, restless. Only what's new is this—that at last I know why. You see, my whole life I've been looking for happiness in a hundred different places. With this man or that. Well, now I've found what I'm looking for—and it wasn't a man after all."

Kaycee sipped a pint of skim milk from a cardboard container while Dani contemplated the rings in the carpet, Kaycee's admission astonished her, yet it bore the unmistakable ring of truth. She found herself struggling to adjust to this new image.

"There's a kitchenette here," Kaycee said. "Would you like coffee? Myself, I'm giving it up for the present. Caffeine, alcohol, secondhand smoke, even aspirin can affect the fetus, it seems. Especially at my age."

But Dani was shaking her head in confusion. "Who's the father, Kaycee? Did you go to a sperm bank?"

"Now don't throw a fit, Dani." Kaycee put down the milk carton. "You remember my client Bo Antonelli?"

Dani remembered him well from Thanksgiving dinner. The blue-black hair. The Sicilian cheekbones. The tight jeans bulging with maleness. Beef on the hoof.

"Mr. EverReady, isn't that what you called him?"

"Yes . . . well, Bo and I have had an affair, though that's probably a bit of hyperbole. More like a few rolls in the hay. But it did the trick. Of course he doesn't have a clue that I'm pregnant. Frankly, I can't picture Bo in the maternity ward passing out cigars. No matter. I didn't select him for strength of character. It happens he's excellent breeding stock, healthy as a horse. Plus this will be one gorgeous child. Actually, I did consider artificial insemination at first, but then I thought—it's so cold-blooded, turning motherhood into a commercial transaction. Besides, I was curious how Bo would be in the sack. You don't work with a guy on a daily basis and not speculate, especially when he's always flaunting his prowess."

Dani turned away. It was as though they were back in the dorms, with Kaycee set to recount yet another tale of physical rapture, of being swept away. But Kaycee was frowning.

"Actually, the sex was lousy. No foreplay, no fantasy. Strictly slam bam, thank you, ma'am. What can I say? Just one more punctured balloon in my eternal quest for the perfect fuck." She finished her milk, then looked Dani in the eye.

"If you want my opinion, the sex act is vastly overrated. In fact it's one of life's biggest hypes. For me, anyhow. I think anticipation has always been nine-tenths of the pleasure, and talking about it afterward the other one-tenth. D. H. Lawrence was right. Sex is all in the head. Love, too, for that matter. I sometimes think I've never really loved anyone. Not in the way you used to feel about Ted."

"Kaycee!" Dani stared at her. "I can't believe my ears. For twenty-five years now, I've been listening to these tales of un-

bounded rapture, those fabulous love affairs that were to die from.
I have to admit, you used to make me envious. . . ."

"And I envied you, too, so now we're square."

"But I don't understand. Do you mean to sit there and tell me
it's all been a fraud?"

"Oh the affairs were real enough, but the rapture wasn't. And
the person I defrauded most was yours truly. When I think of how
I tortured myself about being beautiful and feminine and chic. And
for what? For something I didn't really enjoy."

"I'm simply boggled, Kaycee. It's like I'm sitting here talking
to a total stranger."

"And that's another thing. I don't want to be called Kaycee
anymore. My name's Katherine. That's what it says on my birth
certificate, and I've decided to start using it. It's part of the new
life I plan to build for myself."

"Katherine!" Twenty-five years of friendship rolled itself into a
blinding fuzzy ball and began spinning dizzily before Dani's eyes.
She struggled to focus. "How can I possibly start calling you Katherine after all this time? We've known each other too long. To me,
you've always been Kaycee."

Kaycee, alias Katherine, grew thoughtful.

"You know what's wrong with our friendship, Dani? We came
into each other's lives with our roles already set. Like some mas-
termind in central casting ordained that I was cute flighty Kaycee,
the incurable romantic on a perpetual merry-go-round, and you
were Dani, the sensible one. Who would naturally make the sensible
marriage. We accepted it all without question. Don't you see, Dani,
I never really questioned myself until these past few months. I
think I was brainwashed."

"How? By whom?"

"It's true, going back to when I was yea big. God didn't give
you those looks, my mother would say, so you could become a
nun—which just happened to be my earliest dream, but no matter.
There was only one game, one scorecard. Men. They made you
rich, made you happy, they were the measure of all things. And I
was going to be just like Mother—glamorous, sexy, chic, narcis-
sistic, a breaker of hearts, surrounded by men, flinging myself into
storybook love affairs, half Rapunzel, half Zelda Fitzgerald. A man's

woman. The ultimate compliment. It's taken me all these years to figure out that I was a dumbnuts romantic who'd been sold a bill of goods. Simply because I wanted to be like her. Which goes to show," she concluded, "we're both our mothers' daughters."

"Bullshit!" Dani said. "I'm nothing at all like my mother. Why, my mother's the world's most conventional person whereas I'm—"

"What? A liberated woman? Get real, Dani. You're one of the most traditional people I know. Somehow you manage to hang on to the same values you grew up with, experience notwithstanding. You've always been into the virtue of hard work, the sanctity of marriage. A place for everyone, everyone in his place. I think that's why you were so shattered when Ted cut out. You couldn't fathom that he might be triggered by a completely different set of stimuli. And I used to think you were so perceptive. In fact, I was always jealous of you."

"Oh please!"

"Of you and Ted. What you had, or what I fantasized you had. You guys loved each other, you were the ideal couple, at least on paper. Because I thought your roles were cast in stone, too. Wise clever Dani, whose life was always perfect. Ted, who loved her so. Then when Ted left, you went to pieces and I was furious with you."

"With *me* . . . !" Dani gasped.

"More with you than with him. I mean, what kind of behavior can one expect from a man, realistically. But you! All of a sudden, you were like a beached whale, thrashing around in every direction, not knowing which end was up. Completely out of character! You weren't playing your role anymore. And I was so angry I could spit. For a while there, I was absolutely bitchy. My God, I thought, this isn't the smart savvy capable Dani I've always looked up to. How dare you! How dare you not subscribe to the image I assigned a zillion years ago? It was a revelation, Dani, and it made me rethink everything. You. Me. Our clichés about ourselves. About our friendship, which has always been a kind of knee-jerk affair."

"Genuine enough on my part . . . ," Dani said, stung.

"On mine too. But unexamined, from then until now. You stopped seeing me a long time ago as anything other than the same old Kaycee. In retrospect, I wonder if your image of Ted wasn't fixed in stone, too, solidified way back in college, with no stretch, no allowance for change. Maybe that was part of the problem, that you didn't know him anymore."

"If you mean, I didn't know he was fucking around with Jen MacDougall . . ."

But Kaycee had meant more than that. "I'm not supposed to be the one offering advice. It's against our appointed roles. However, let me put a proposition to you, Dani, which is that it's very difficult to actually perceive people you've known for donkey's years. You never step back and try to adjust your perspective, to see them afresh. Why bother? Because in your head, they are what they always were. Well, I'm not the girl you went to school with, Dani. I've changed. Grown some, I hope. Out of old attitudes and into new ones, for better or worse. This baby I'm having, it's not a whim, a caprice as you seem to feel. I made the decision out of a fundamental need. *My* need, not yours or anyone else's. And I'm not the same pretty little Kaycee who lives by men's lights. I'm not your ditzy roommate from Barnard. Forget the old images, Dani. Time passes, people change. Make allowances." She came over and took Dani's hands in hers. "Look at me now, Dani. And really try to see me accurately, without your vision being obscured by the past."

Dani looked. Cleared her mind, looked again. Gone was the ditzy roommate from Barnard, the endearing exasperating ever-girlish Kaycee Carlson. And in her place stood a pale middle-aged woman, brow furrowed, still handsome, very serious, utterly sincere. A woman of presence and dignity.

Yes—changed almost out of recognition. Much as Dani herself had changed this past year. Her throat seized up with emotion: the sense that an era was coming to an end.

"Oh my dear dear Kaycee!" Dani put her arms around her old-new friend and hugged her tight in a great shuddering embrace.

"No." Dani's voice broke. "Not Kaycee. You've become . . . Katherine. Yes, Katherine." She repeated it, and the second time the name came more easily to the tongue.

She started crying. "It looks like we're going to have to build our friendship all over again, doesn't it? Katherine. But next time

it will be better, because I've changed too. The new *us* . . . !"
Suddenly, the idea took hold, burst forth with a sense of revelation.

"We're newborns, Katherine. Just like newborns. Ready to start
life over."

The two women embraced for a moment in wrenching silence,
then Kaycee/Katherine pulled away gently. And nodded.

Dani swiped at her eyes.

"Though I still have a lot of good memories of the old us. And
I'm going to miss you. What is this we're saying at this juncture—
is it good-bye or hello?"

"Whichever. Just wish me well, Dani," she breathed.

"I wish you . . ." The words sprang to Dani's lips. "I wish you
all the happiness, the joy . . . yes, the sheer wonderful joy—even
with all the heartaches—that I've had from Samantha. And more
than that, my love, I could never wish anyone."

"Fuck all this paperwork, Dani." Sherle Nelson tapped the floor
with a stiletto heel. "When do I get my money? I'm sick of waiting."

"There are problems," Dani said, secretly pleased the discussion
had taken this turn. "The discovery process is slowing everything
down. When you're dealing with a business this size, getting all
the details can take a lifetime."

"Well, I don't have a lifetime," Sherle carped.

"No, you don't," Dani leaped in. "And that's why I've called
this meeting. The fact is, Sherle, Lean Machine's been hurting
lately, missing your magic touch, I suspect. As you know, Lazzi
is into the banks. He might be tempted to declare bankruptcy."

Sherle's antennae shot up.

"And if he goes down the tubes, do I get to pick up the pieces?
After all, I'm entitled."

"You'd have to get in line to collect. Along with Willi Shannon
and Citibank and the linen service and everyone else."

Would Lazzi do it? Dani wondered. Would he surrender control
of his own company in order to screw his wife? More to the point,
would Precious Nelson survive another two or three years of this
ordeal?

"Sherle," she said with an air of concession, "you're right. You
don't have a lifetime. Yes, we could try to hang in there forever,

and, yes, you might get your fifty percent. On the other hand, it might be fifty percent of zilch. Is it worth it? Another four, five years in limbo? Can you wait that long to start your spa? I think the time has come to settle."

Sherle nodded slowly. "Okay, I'm game. Yeah, . . . let's get it over."

Dani pushed a yellow pad across the table to Sherle.

"Write down a figure, bottom-line. The kind of money that you could walk away with and still feel good."

Sherle hesitated briefly, scribbled a number on the sheet and passed it back.

Dani studied it.

"I think we could both live with that."

"But can we get it?"

"Only one way to find out."

For all its thousands upon thousands of pages of documentation, *Nelson v. Nelson* would probably never come to trial. War-weariness pervaded both camps. Now, with Dani's research complete, the time had come for working out a deal. She called Willi Shannon that afternoon.

"As you know," she told him, "I've got a deposition scheduled for the eighteenth with the woman who cleans Lazzi's office."

Willi laughed. "Jesus, Dani, you're really scraping bottom."

"Well, she might have some interesting things to say about the contents of your client's wastebasket. However, as a courtesy to you, Willi, before I add another few inches to the paper mountain, I'd like to show you a little movie we've made. Come here Monday at ten; I've booked the conference room. Bring Lazzi if you like and any or all of your associates. Sherle won't be here. She's seen the picture. You could say she has the starring role."

She hung up the phone and turned to Marsha.

"Well, toots. Here we go. Lights . . . camera . . . action!"

She and Steve dined at Trosti's that evening, an evening during which nothing went right.

Steve had arrived a half hour late, edgy and full of complaints. The traffic was terrible, the soup cold, the restaurant drafty, the people at the next table were making a racket. When the bill came, he found a six-dollar discrepancy. Furious, he called over the captain.

"I'm sorry, sir." The man was all apologies. "The waiter must have read a one as a seven. You know how it is with Europeans."

"Fine," Steve said grimly, leaving a quarter tip for a hundred-and-fifty-dollar meal. Dani was humiliated.

"For God's sake, Steve," she said when they hit the street. "The waiter made an honest mistake."

"And I should reward him for gross incompetence? The last time I eat in that place, you may be sure." He set off at a brisk clip down Central Park South. "Come on, Dani. I need some exercise. I'll walk you home."

The weather had turned crisp and Dani felt cold in a woolen suit. She should have gotten her fur coat out of storage. Steve's chilly mood only added to her discomfort. Twice over dinner, she had asked what was wrong, only to be rebuffed. Now, as they marched along in semisilence, Dani felt called upon to make peace, or at least conversation. There was no shortage of topics. It had been a day full of newsbreaks.

"God, this business in Kuwait scares the hell out of me. We had the radio on in the office all day. And now Bush is calling up the reserves. Looks like the White House has thrown in the towel vis-à-vis sanctions, but I don't know that they've been given a fair test. What do you think, Steve? You think we're headed for a war?"

"Looks that way," he said, tight-lipped and preoccupied. Then he expelled an angry sigh. "Christ, that's all we need to scare off Arab buyers."

"I don't believe my ears!" Dani wheeled round to face him. "Arab buyers? Here we are on the brink of what could be another Vietnam and that's all you can say? Well, fuck the Arab buyers. I find it extraordinary that all you can think of at a time of crisis is how it'll affect sales at Wetherings. For shame, Steve! And you part Lebanese! How callous can you get!"

He sucked in his breath. A pulse had begun to throb in his neck.

"Don't you dare tell me what I think, Dani! You haven't a clue what goes on in my mind. You take a single offhand remark and feel free to extrapolate it to an absurd conclusion. What do you know of how I feel about the situation in the Gulf? Or about my being Lebanese, for that matter? Who provided you with special insights?"

They were standing on the corner near the Plaza, a hairbreadth away from a shouting match, when Dani stuck out her arm to hail a cab.

"If I want to be dumped on," she said, "I don't need your help. I have a husband who serves that function admirably." Then she stepped into the taxi and slammed the door, leaving a white-faced Steve on the curb.

She leaned back in the cab, still trembling with rage. No, she didn't have a clue as to the workings of his mind, and at that point, she didn't give a damn.

All those months they'd been together, all the sex, the dinners, the entertainments, yet never once had he uttered a word of genuine concern about her life; never had he struck a note of commitment. Months when she herself had been engaged in a hopeless endeavor to uncover the essential Steve Haddad, the warm human being beneath the dazzling exterior. Beneath the tip of the iceberg—Hella Klein's warning reverberated. And you couldn't cut through an iceberg with a butter knife. The man was hopeless. The situation too, if she dared be honest.

"Let me off at the video shop on the corner," she told the cabbie, then went in and rented two Mel Brookses and a Monty Python. What did people do for relief before video? she wondered.

Halfway through *Blazing Saddles*, Steve phoned.

"I'm sorry I was such a shit," he said. "We had a major sale fall through today, and I'm afraid I took it out on everyone else."

"You should have told me that over dinner," she said. "We could have talked it through. I'd have understood."

"Well, I don't like being probed."

Dani felt a flash of anger.

"And I don't like having a No Entry sign shoved in my face every time the conversation gets personal. It's not just what's happened tonight. It's the whole pattern of our relationship. What are we, anyhow? Friends? Lovers? Or just casual acquaintances who happen to sleep with each other a couple of times a week? Christ, that makes me feel like a convenience store. I had hopes for us, that we could build something together, make something of our lives. I must have been crazy! You know, Steve"—she blurted it out, astonished by the depth of her rage—"maybe it would be better if we didn't see each other for a while."

He must have been stunned, for there was a brief gasp on the other end.

"As you wish," Steve said coolly.

27

"What you are about to see," Dani informed Willi Shannon, "is a short film based on our research. It's merely a synthesis, mind you, but it will illustrate, in graphic terms, the extent of Sherle's contribution to Lean Machine. Okay, Marsha. Run it."

Lights out. And there she was, That Girl Sherle, popping off the screen large as life and twice as animated.

> SHERLE: Hi . . . I'm gonna make you bee-yoootiful. . . .
> MUSIC UP

Instinctively, Dani crossed her fingers.

The videotape had been a sensational idea, expensive but potent, based on the notion that one picture of Sherle was worth a thousand briefs.

If necessary, Dani could use it in court as a kind of visual aid, a supplement to a mountain of data, but if all went well, this would be the first and last showing. *Sherle and Company*, as it was called, had been created for an audience of one. Willi Shannon. The piece was quick, clever and well cut, interspersing snippets of classic Sherle commercials with slice-of-life testimonials, each segment culminating in a simple statement of fact.

> SHERLE (*wiggles her rump*): . . . and you can too. Ah one, ah
> two, ah three. . . .

FAT WOMAN: I never woulda joined a health club except she
made it look easy. I figured, maybe I could do it too.

ANNOUNCER (*voice-over*): Fact: In St. Louis, Missouri, three-
quarters of all current Lean Machine patrons still remember
this nineteen eighty-four campaign.

SHERLE (*touches toes*): Because keeping fit can be fun.

TRUCK DRIVER: I saw her on a local talk show. The dynamite
kid. Both me and the wife joined up.

ANNOUNCER (*voice-over*): In Pittsburgh, Pennsylvania, eighty-
six percent of Lean Machine members . . .

The entire tape took less than fifteen minutes. But Dani wasn't
watching the movie. She was watching Willi, who had come alone.
And his eyes were glued to the screen.

"Just to reiterate," she said when the lights went up. "We have
compelling evidence which proves that Sherle Nelson was responsible for eighty-two percent of Lean Machine's growth between the
years nineteen seventy-seven and nineteen ninety, which works out
to an equitable distribution of sixty-one point five percent of the
total marital assets at the time of separation. However, since judges
like round numbers, we're willing to round it down to sixty."

"Ha ha," Willi said. "You ladies get the Academy Award for
the year's most original screenplay."

But he was pale. The results had stunned him. Dani took a quick
read of the situation. He was more than surprised. He was shocked.
She stifled a desire to say, *Outside of that, Mr. Shannon, how did you
enjoy the show?*

"You ladies get the Academy Award . . ."

You ladies . . . !

You members of the inferior race.

For there was the secret of Shannon's success—and his failure. He
had built his reputation championing pampered society women, winning huge judgments for the wives of celebrities and rock stars. He
had come to see such women as appendages. Ornamental and delightful baubles, to be sure, but ill equipped for the rough and tumble
of the practical world. Refusing to take any guff (who listened to these
broads?), Willi appointed himself as their guide and guru.

He had made divorce into a morality play: the frail damsel, the

ogre husband, and chivalrous Sir Willi to the rescue. When it came
to portraying women as victims, Willi was in his element.

"I never met a woman I didn't like," he was quoted as saying,
but that liking was essentially the affection of a dog owner for his
favorite Pekes. Women were warm furry creatures, prone to tears
and confusion, wanting to be guided, coddled, instructed, "pro-
tected" by the likes of Willi Shannon. With cotton batting where
their brains ought to be.

From the start, he had discounted Sherle's contribution to Lean
Machine. He had discounted Dani as well, and for the longest while
she had let him. But the time for dissembling was past.

"So there we are," she said softly. "I think it likely that, on the
face of it, the court will reasonably award us sixty percent of all
marital assets as they stood on the day Lazzi left. The question is,
sixty percent of how much? Look, my friend,"—Dani poured him
fresh coffee, for Willi appeared shaken—"you and I can spend the
next ten years in the discovery stage of this suit while both the
Nelsons keep their lives on hold. However, my client is willing to
make you an offer. She's decided she'd prefer less cash now than
more later, after inflation eats it away."

Dani scribbled a figure, put it in Willi's hand.

"This is her bottom line, not negotiable. We either do it quick
and clean or it's back to the drawing board for the next few years.
You'll find the details in this folder, including payment schedules,
but I must point out that this is a one-time-only offer." She couldn't
help grinning. "However, I'm nowhere near as hard-nosed as you.
I don't expect an answer by the close of business day. Nine A.M.
tomorrow will be fine."

Willi scoured her face. Was she bluffing? He decided she was
not. He took the folder, didn't open it.

"The problem is, as you well know, that Lazzi will never agree
to anything that permits her to set up a business in competition
with Lean Machine. We've been down this road a hundred times,
Dani. It's a key issue. Every bit as crucial as the money."

"I know, and I respect his feelings, but I think I've devised a
solution that will suit them both."

She told him what she had in mind.

"Fifteen percent," Willi came back.

"Let's split it. Twelve and a half."

"I'll have to check. And we're both agreed, joint custody of Precious. A month with her, a month with him, alternate summers."

Willi contemplated the tops of his Guccis. You could see the ceiling reflected in the shine.

"That's a lot of dough, Dani. Lazzi's not so liquid as you think. It would mean selling most of the collection."

Dani inclined her head.

"I realize that and I'm sorry. However, the pictures aren't giving anyone much pleasure locked away in a warehouse. And he gets to keep what's left after the sale."

"I'll have to discuss this with my client." Willi got up to leave. "You'll have your answer tomorrow." Then he paused at the door, put his hands on his hips and peered at her. "You turned out to be quite the Lady Bomber, didn't you?"

"Thank you, Willi." She smiled.

The moment he left, Marsha burst out.

"Are you serious? You really won't negotiate? You asked him for—"

"I know what I asked him for," Dani said. "And it's totally outrageous. Of course I'd be willing to negotiate."

"In other words you were bluffing."

Dani laughed. "Ah . . . but Willi Shannon doesn't think so. He doesn't think I'm capable of bluffing. You know, years ago, when I first started playing poker at this little club over on the East Side, there were mostly men in the game. We used to play a form of draw poker called 'Guts.' I found that I could bluff all the time and get away with it, with the result that I'd win on the damnedest hands. You know why it worked? Because I exploited their macho. A lot of guys have it in their heads that women are either too soft or too timid to put up a ballsy front. Guts. Men have guts. Women have luck, intuition. That's their mind-set, with the result that they almost never called my hands. Of course, you can't pull that number indefinitely, but by the time my fellow players caught on, I'd changed my tactics. Fortunately, Willi Shannon has not quite reached that advanced stage in our acquaintanceship. Anyhow, we'll see what tomorrow brings."

*   *   *

"Thirty million dollars!" Sherle squealed with delight. "Three oh big ones, do I hear you right? But I only asked for twenty."

Dani laughed. "I can grant him a rebate if you find it's too much. . . ."

"No no. . . . Hey, Maria!" She yelled for the maid. "Bring us a bottle of champagne. The good shit. And tell my secretary to hold my calls." She turned to Dani, beaming. "I still can't believe it!"

"Why not? You always said I was a stand-up broad. There is a catch, though, one major stipulation. You'll be allowed to use the That Girl Sherle name, which as you know is trademarked, in return for giving Lazzi a piece of the action. He's entitled. He backed you up all those years, taught you the business and then got worried that you'd eat into his market. It was a reasonable fear. Anyhow, the deal I cut is that Lazzi will get a royalty of twelve and a half percent of your net profits, which supplies the both of you with an incentive to make the new company go. I admit it's not a conventional setup, but . . ."—Dani paused before continuing—"it's equitable, in the real sense of the word."

"So Lazzi and I wind up partners after all." Sherle rubbed her nose thoughtfully. "Yeah, I can live with that. Jesus, I can't wait to get rolling. I'm gonna need a lot of legal work these next few months, getting my corporation set up. I want you to help me, Dani. I trust you all the way."

Dani beamed. "We'd be delighted. Our firm is superbly equipped for organizing start-up companies. I'll introduce you to Jack Pruitt tomorrow. He'll get an experienced team going."

"No, not Pruitt. I want you to personally handle my affairs."

"That's very flattering, Sherle, but I'm a divorce lawyer, a specialist."

"Bullshit," Sherle said. "You're a specialist like I'm just a tenth-grade dropout. Dani, you know what I came from, what I've made of myself . . . from zilch. But I pulled myself up out of the gutter by my own fucking fingernails. I created a somebody. And I didn't do it on so-called credentials. Smarts! Guts! That's what I had. You've got 'em too. They're all that really count in this world. Everything else, you can pick up as you go along. So if a two-bit hooker can parlay herself into a multimillion-dollar entrepreneur,

just think what you can do. The sky's the limit, babe. You could
be major league."

Could she? The prospect made her heart leap. Sherle was right,
anything was possible. And one thing for certain: With an account
like Sherle's in her pocket, Dani Sloane could write her own ticket.
Either a name partnership at Pruitt's or get a bank loan and start
her own firm. New challenges. New horizons. Powerful clients left
and right. Sky's the limit, babe. Scary, but exciting.

That was the plus side. The down side was years and years
more of Sherle. She admired Sherle, respected her will, even in a
crazy way almost liked her. When things went well, Sherle could
be an angel. But she wasn't sure she wanted to go down that long
path hand in hand.

"I'll need some time to think it over," she said.

"No rush," Sherle said. "Can't do anything much between now
and Thanksgiving. Listen. I'm going to get the paintings out of
storage and get them installed Upstairs for the time being. It'll be
nice having 'em around, even briefly. Then I'm throwing the biggest, noisiest party that ever hit this town. Thanksgiving. Yeah!
Thanksgiving would be perfect, since I got thirty million reasons
to be thankful. Come on, Dani. We'll celebrate."

"Thanks," Dani demurred, "but I'm tied up on Thanksgiving.
I promised to dine with a very dear friend of mine."

"Then bring him along!"

Dani shrugged. "I think not. His wife just left him, so he's not
in a particularly festive mood."

"No problem. You and I will have lots of other occasions. And
I'll call your friend from Wetherings for an appointment. I want
to start moving on that auction."

"Frogs' legs in peanut sauce." Barney toyed with a spicy morsel.
"Nothing like those old Pilgrim traditions."

The dinner had been Dani's idea. Her original plan, spending
the holiday with Steve in the country, had gone down the chute.
Presumably, so had Steve. She hadn't heard from him in over two
weeks. At the last minute, she called Barney.

"I guess you won't be doing your usual blast this year," she said, "so why don't we go out and have Thanksgiving dinner in a nice restaurant?"

"Every decent place will be booked," he said gloomily. "Probably weeks in advance."

"Only if you're hung up on turkey. But there's this great new Thai place on Second Avenue. . . ."

So here they were in a mostly deserted restaurant, eating frogs' legs and drinking Bangkok beer while canned gamelan music played in the background.

"I'm not going to grill you, Dani," Barney said, picking at his food. "I don't even want to know the name of Kaycee's lover, in case I happened to kill the guy. Jesus, I loved that dopey woman!" Then he pushed his plate away.

"My father should see me now, eating Siamese frogs' legs. On Thanksgiving, yet. He'd plotz. He was strictly kosher, and that's how I was brought up. Your average nice Jewish boy from the Bronx. Go figure I'd wind up an old fart with three failed marriages behind me.

"Oh Barney! Fifty-five isn't old."

"Right. And three marriages is par for the course. Well, maybe it is among your clientele, but that's it for me and marriage. Three strikes and you're out. My father stayed married to the same woman for forty-eight years. And when my mother died, he passed on a few months later. Out of grief, is my bet." He rubbed the bridge of his nose as if to relieve an unbearable pressure. "Now let's go see a funny movie."

They caught the new Woody Allen and were out by nine, then Dani said she had to make an early night of it.

"Why? You working tomorrow?"

She groaned. "The old paper chase. How 'bout you?"

"Yeah, me too, I'll probably die in harness, chained to the drawing board at Marsden. And on my tombstone they'll inscribe 'Here Lies the Man Who Wrote REAL UNDERWEAR FOR REAL PEOPLE.' Some epitaph, huh? Kaycee and I should have been cruising the islands this time next year. So much for crazy dreams. I think I'll take the crosstown bus home."

Unaccountably, Dani recalled her father on the balcony in Florida. Youthful dreams, pretty dreams, all gone astray.

Outside Bloomingdale's, the first Santa of the season had set up his business. Sam would be coming home for Christmas.

"By the way," Barney said as the crosstown bus was coming. "Ted called me last week. Wanted to know if I could lend him money against his share of the boat. He sounded kind of down. I got the impression that his girlfriend is getting kind of antsy with the current setup."

Then the bus doors opened and swallowed him up.

Dani walked home slowly.

28

THE OFFICE was deserted, the switchboard turned off. In the distance, a door opened and shut.

A fellow masochist, Dani thought wryly, who doesn't know it's the Friday after Thanksgiving. Then she immersed herself in *Ketchell v. Ketchell*.

In the corridor, footsteps reverberated. Drew near. Dani raised her eyes. Steve Haddad was silhouetted in the doorway.

"Steve! What a surpr—" Then her amazement turned to horror. "Oh my God, you look like death."

He staggered into the room, collapsed into a chair. For a moment Dani thought he had fainted.

"The paintings!" he rasped. "Gone . . . all gone!"

He moved his mouth, but nothing more came out.

Dani sprang to her feet and loosened his tie. The man was in shock. "Don't move. I'll get you something hot to drink."

She came back a minute later juggling two cups of coffee and a pitcher of water.

"Here!" she ordered. "Coffee first. It's strong and loaded with sugar. Now drink up."

He sipped. "Too sweet," he murmured, but he finished one cup, then the other. "Don't know why I came here," he said between gulps. "Nothing you can do. All so goddamn awful. . . ."

Gradually, Dani pieced the story together.

At nine that morning, he had gone by appointment to discuss the forthcoming auction. A tousled Sherle greeted him at the door. "Excuse my appearance," she said. "We were partying till five A.M."

They chatted for a few minutes, then Steve asked to be taken Upstairs to check over the pictures. "Sure thing," she said. She mentioned having thrown open the rooms the previous night for an hour or so, while the staff served cocktails and canapés, after which she'd shooed the guests downstairs and locked the premises.

"Couldn't resist showing the collection one last time. So it may be a bit of a mess up there. I'll get the key."

Steve followed her up the spiral staircase, Sherle unlocked the door and they stepped into the anteroom.

The place reeked of stale smoke and flat champagne. It made his eyes water. Then he heard a kind of mewling sound.

"At first we didn't see her," Steve said.

She was huddled in a corner, crouched on her haunches like an animal. Her knuckles were crusted with blood. Sherle shrieked and ran over.

"Oh fuck! You poor kid! You been locked in here all night? Jesus, what happened!"

Then Sherle shrieked again, a banshee howl that pierced Steve to the bone. "MY GOD!"

She began racing through the rooms, crying, shouting, cursing. "Precious, goddamn you! What have you done? Omigod! The paintings! The paintings!"

Steve could hardly bear to look. "In my life," he told Dani, "I've never seen anything so horrible."

He could only guess at what had taken place. Precious had been hiding from the company. Perhaps she had fallen asleep in a corner and awakened to find herself alone in the dark, locked in and forgotten.

What then? Had she cried out for help? Banged on the door unheard? Had her screams been drowned out by the din of the festivities downstairs? Who could say?

Alas! not Precious Nelson, for by the time Steve saw her she was far beyond speech. Catatonic. Meanwhile, Sherle was tearing through the rooms like a woman possessed.

"My Jasper Johns!" she was yelling. "My gorgeous Schnabel.

My Basquiats! That lunatic child! crazy . . . crazy . . . crazy! How could you do this to me?"

There was an upstairs kitchen, Steve reminded Dani.

At some point during the night, Precious must have gone there and found an arsenal. Carving knives honed to sabre sharpness, poultry shears that could cut through flesh and bone. Ice picks, cleavers, skewers, scouring pads, bottles of bleach, tins of lye.

Precious had gone berserk. The damage was immeasurable; no painting had escaped unscathed.

"I wouldn't think it possible a child that size would have had the physical strength, the stamina," Dani said at one point, but Steve was quick to disabuse her.

"Oh yes, Dani. Believe me—it's possible. I know. You'd be amazed what children are capable of."

He buried his face in his hands, while Dani struggled in an effort to grasp the dimensions of the tragedy.

It was too immense, too grotesque. The paintings, the child— both destroyed beyond recognition. A tragedy to break the hardest heart. She could see that Steve was suffering too.

"Is there anything we can do?" she whispered.

Steve lifted red-rimmed eyes. He didn't seem to understand the question.

"Do? For God's sake, Dani, how do you salvage—"

"Salvage?" she screamed. "Even now, all you can think of is the goddamn paintings!"

"No, no . . . !" He raised his hands as though to fend off a blow. "Fuck the paintings. How do you salvage a child's life? That poor demented kid, God have mercy." He stood up abruptly. "I feel rotten. I'm going home. We'll talk later."

For some time, Dani sat at her desk, numb and empty and helpless. Then the beeper sounded.

Sherle. Who else?

Wearily, she dialed an outside line.

"Something awful's happened!" Sherle whispered.

"Yes, I know," Dani said.

"Well, come on over, I need you. I'm going nuts."

Sherle opened the door, a jangle of nerves and silver bracelets, then

ushered Dani into the room that served as her office. The floor was
strewn with papers.

"How's Precious?" Dani asked.

"The doctor is there with her. A psychotic episode, he calls it.
Twelve years old and having breakdowns. Anyhow, we're putting
her into a clinic, poor thing, where she'll get tip-top care. The
ambulance is coming at three." She shook her head, profoundly
puzzled. "What foxes me, Dani, what I absolutely can't get through
my skull is—why? Okay, she got locked in accidentally, that's
scary, but all she had to do was call out or pick up a phone."

"Didn't you miss her at any point in the evening?"

"For Chrissakes, Dani, I had over a hundred guests, and by the
time the party broke up, naturally I assumed she was tucked away
in bed. And even if she was trapped, even so, she could have let
us know. Worse come to worst, she could've broken the glass in
the fire alarm system, you would've heard it up in the Bronx.
Instead . . . Jesus!"

Sherle paused for breath. Dani was silent.

"Well, what's done is done. Meanwhile, you can help me with
a problem. I've been going through the insurance policies. Thank
God everything's covered up to market value, and some of the
paintings can probably be restored, but go try reach anybody on
a Thanksgiving weekend. . . ."

"I know," Dani said.

"Some timing, huh? You know, if not for the holiday, Precious
would've been away at boarding school. The whole catastrophe
would never have happened."

Dani made an effort to steady her voice.

"May I go Upstairs?" she asked.

"Go ahead," Sherle said. "See 'em and weep."

Dani cleared a place on the floor in the middle of the Long Gallery,
then sat down, legs tucked beneath her.

Beirut, she thought. Or Berlin after the war.

Impossible to look through these rooms without a wealth of
images piling up. Images of destruction, of riot and war and mad-
ness. For a massacre of sorts had taken place here. Only the corpses
here were those of paintings, not people. She was witnessing the

death of beauty, the mindless annihilation of what had once been fine and pure.

A few feet away, a black-handled knife, its tip blunted, lay amid the debris. A Sabatier vegetable knife, Dani noted. She had its twin at home. And suddenly, she was treated to a swift memory of Sam in the kitchen slicing carrots with quick capable hands.

Two knives. Two daughters. Two different outcomes.

She could look no more. Instead, she shut her eyes to conjure up once again the lofty rooms as they had been on the day of her first visit. Sunshine streaming through high windows, the glitter of steel and copper, vivid bursts of color on the walls. She could recall the excited hum, the tinkle of champagne glasses.

In memory she walked down the long corridor again, past the paintings, past pristine sculpture and gleaming ceramics, into the small dark den where Precious had sat.

Precious with her folded hands, white gloves and sober mien. "Do you have any candy?" she had asked, and Dani had handed her a roll of Life Savers.

That was the only time Dani had seen her in the flesh. Now it was seared in her memory.

True, Precious's name had crossed Dani's desk on numerous occasions. The name had figured in a mountain of paperwork, was mentioned in countless motions and hearings, had cropped up far too often in the newspapers.

But the name was an abstraction, one more thorny factor to be reckoned with in a complex proceeding. So easy to dissociate the name from the actual child.

Could Dani have altered the course of events? Could this have been foreseen? Forestalled? She scoured her conscience.

In candor, what could she have done? There had been no physical abuse here, no obvious maltreatment, no grounds for court intervention. The only abuse had been the absence of love.

Poor Precious. Poor invisible inaudible Precious.

Hear me, see me, touch me, love me. She had cried and no one had listened.

But Precious had their full attention now.

Dani opened her eyes and looked about her at the mutilated paintings. What rage it had taken to wreak this much havoc. What blind frenzy. The rampage must have gone on for hours—the slashing, defacing, destroying, the meting out of vengeance—so grand was the scale.

And yet there was a poetic justice in this holocaust, a kind of lunatic fairness. Her parents had cared for the paintings more than they had cared for her.

Well, Precious had shown them, once and for all.

Downstairs, Sherle was pacing, restless and edgy.

"Something else, huh? Well, we may as well be practical and get on with it."

"What precisely do you expect me to do, Sherle?"

"First, I want a fast read on my situation. Not everything has been deep-sixed, thank God. A lot of it looks to me like surface damage. But the big-money crunch is going to be the insurance. These are awfully complicated policies. Here"—she handed a sheaf of papers to Dani. "Let's start going through—"

"I'm a divorce lawyer, not a claims adjuster," Dani said. "This has nothing to do with me."

"What the fuck is that supposed to mean? You were going to handle all my business, matrimonial and otherwise, remember? We sorted that out a couple of weeks ago."

"No we didn't." Dani headed for the door. "I said I'd think it over and I have. I'm sorry, Sherle. My job is done."

"Hey! Don't you dare turn your back on me now!" Sherle was yelling. "You can't just walk out, Dani. You have an obligation! You're my lawyer, for Chrissakes!"

"Not anymore," Dani said.

Dani started for home profoundly depressed. The weather had turned cold. Probably in the 80s in St. Thomas, but here in New York it looked like snow. She pulled up her collar. Cold without, and cold within.

Poor Precious.

"That poor demented kid," as Steve called her.

Poor Precious. Then, through a trick of mind, she found herself thinking—Poor Steve!

Suddenly, the tumblers began to fall into place, engage and spin freely. Yes! Her instinctive conclusion had been the right one. "Some woman" had indeed done a job on him, put a lock on his heart. But now, shivering beneath her fur coat, Dani knew who it was.

The insight almost took her breath away.

At a phone booth on the corner of Third and 71st, she fished out a handful of coins. He should be home by now. Poor Steve.

"I have to see you," she said. "This is not a good time for either of us to be alone. I'm taking the next train up. Don't bother to meet me, I'll get a cab from the station."

He was swimming, the strong arms plowing through the water with the mechanical certainty of a scythe slicing through wheat. At the completion of each lap, he lifted his head and his breath turned steamy in the cold November air.

Such weather. Raw and gray with the threat of snow. Even Max and Rosie had the good sense to stay on dry land. They came to greet Dani, eager for company.

Rosie nuzzled Dani's fur coat as if to inquire what kind of beast is this. Then, having satisfied herself, she hunkered down to resume her voiceless vigil over Steve. Dani stood for a while, watching. Breaststroke out, Australian crawl back. Back and forth, back and forth.

Had it been anyone else, she might have been alarmed, but Steve swam every day, he told her, no matter the weather. "It keeps me sane."

He swam with the single-minded dedication of a monk or an artist or a baseball player, someone for whom the world beyond his immediate milieu had no meaning.

Why not? Some men drown their sorrows in booze. Steve preferred to drown his in a seventy-five-foot pool.

It started to snow.

Dani walked around to the shallow end and knelt down. He swam up to her, panting lightly.

"Had enough?" she asked.

He nodded, got out of the pool and raced into the house barefoot over the frozen ground.

Dani followed him in and, while he showered and dressed,

busied herself in the kitchen. She scrounged through the near-empty refrigerator, found a salami and some cheese, cut sandwiches and made a pot of coffee. Real linen napkins. He liked real linen. Then she brought the meal into the living room on trays.

With a bit more self-confidence, she would have built a fire, but her Girl Scout days were over. She was afraid of burning down the house.

Steve came down presently, dressed in a soft gray track suit, still pale but in better spirits.

"Oh, doesn't that look nice," he said, stretching out on the sofa. "That's very kind of you, Dani."

She recognized his tone straightaway. The polite compliment, the gracious smile. Business as usual. But she wasn't going to let him get away with it.

She watched him closely. He was nibbling a salami sandwich, eyes fixed on his food. His hair was still wet from the shower. The dogs had settled about his feet in worshipful silence. Steve rumpled Rosie's fur and gave her a piece of salami. She licked his hand.

"When you came to my office this morning, I was stunned," Dani said softly. "I'd never seen you before with your guard down. You have a reputation, you know, for being very cool and aloof. The Iceberg, people call you, but for a long time I couldn't bring myself to accept that definition. He's not really cold, I'd tell myself, just wary, bottled up. But I was never sure of actually what went on beneath the surface. You play everything so close to the vest. Then lately, I began to think, well, the iceberg definition is correct. There was no getting through to you. I began to think you weren't capable of real emotion. But today, I got a glimpse of the other Steve, the human Steve, and it was a kind of epiphany. You were so profoundly touched, so full of compassion."

She paused for breath, then moved in on her target. "Those feelings about Precious didn't come out of nowhere. They came out of you, your past. Something like that happened to you once, didn't it? It had to, for you to identify that closely with a twelve-year-old girl. A terrible loss? A grief? Was it your mother, Steve? Something she did? Did she abuse you? Abandon you? What hurt you so? Tell me. You can trust me. It *was* your mother, wasn't it?"

He shook his head. "My mother died in a car crash when I was a year and a half old. I don't even remember her."

But Dani persisted. "Then someone else really close."

He put down his sandwich with a suspicious air.

"What do you want from me, Dani?"

"The truth."

"I've never lied to you."

"Truth is more than the absence of lies. I'm asking you to be open with me. I'm not the enemy, Steve. I want to help."

He stretched out on the couch and put his hands behind his head, brooding, daydreaming. The only sound was the tick of the coach clock on the mantel.

"You're a very astute woman, Dani," he said finally, "or else intuitive, I hesitate to say which. Your guess about my mother was halfway there, though I assure you my childhood is nowhere as lurid as Precious Nelson's. But you're right. There was a woman and we were close. Very close."

Her name was Pam.

She was fresh, warm, affectionate. A pretty Englishwoman so full of charm and vibrancy that he fell in love with her at first sight.

To be with Pam was to be kissed by the sun, blessed by all the good fairies. Pam was magic. She knew all kinds of secrets: how to tickle the soles of your feet, how to fill a room with flowers, how to play marbles, how to plan the most lavish picnics and marvelous birthday parties. She knew how to make a small boy feel that he was King of Creation. She was the second Mrs. Mike Haddad.

Pam came into his life when he was three years old, amidst fanfare and flourishes. "Stevie, I'd like you to meet your new mom," Mike said.

He could still recall being dressed as a page in white knickerbockers for the wedding and Pam bending down to hand-feed him the first slice of wedding cake. To this day, he could recall how it tasted, lemony and sweet all at once.

His new mother was lovely, with red hair and fine English skin, but very different from the other women who came to the house. She was neither actress nor director nor scriptwriter. Wasn't even in the industry. This exquisite creature, this living, laughing Good

Fairy incarnate, had been put on earth for no other reason than to make him happy.

Over the next few years, she provided Steve with a little brother and a baby sister and he was so naïve, he didn't know he was supposed to be jealous. He loved Alex and Amy, not just because they were kin, but because they were Pam's. The Haddads were a proper family now. "But you," Pam would tell Steve with a hug, "you're still my great big boy."

She bought him a pony, taught him to ride and play croquet. She let him win at Fish and Casino. She refurbished the pool that his father had built largely as a backdrop for cocktails, and Steve's happiest memories were of swimming lengths alongside Pam each morning.

In his mind's eye, those years were cloudless, blissful, serene, varied only by delightful surprises.

One night, when Steve was ten, Pam came into his room and sat down on his bed. She told him that she and his father were separating. She was very sorry.

"I want to go with *you!*" he cried, "I want to be with you forever," but she explained why that was impossible. A week later she had moved to Malibu, taking Alex and Amy with her.

Why? Why? He would never comprehend. Never as long as he lived. How could grown-ups do such a thing? They picked you up, these Olympian beings, as if you were a jackstraw or a pair of dice or a deck of cards, then they flung you this way and that. One day you were a member of a family, cherished and spoiled; the next day you had ceased to exist. You were helpless, powerless. Go beat your fists against the wall until they were sore, but you could change nothing. No explanation could ever fill the void.

Steve was ten years old, and the world as he knew it had ended.

"It's not like she was your real momma," the housekeeper tried to console him. "Don't worry, your poppa will marry again. Someone just as nice."

A boy at school had told him that if you held your breath underwater for more than two minutes, your lungs would burst and you'd die. He decided to kill himself in this manner, then Pam would come back for his funeral.

Every day Steve would dive into the pool and hold his breath until he thought his body would explode from sheer agony only to discover that this was a near-impossible form of suicide. The instincts rebel against it. The lungs, the heart thrash for life, regardless of what message the brain might send. Then too, as Precious Nelson had proved last night, children have extraordinary physical stamina.

Yet he kept at it, timing his efforts on the underwater watch Pam had given him for his birthday. Two minutes, then two minutes ten . . . two minutes fifteen seconds . . . up up up . . .

"My God!" His father observed Steve's performance one day. "The kid's a regular porpoise. If you're really serious about swimming, Stevie, I'll get you a coach. Let's see what kind of talent you have."

"So," Steve, told Dani, "the act that was supposed to take my life actually saved it."

All through junior high, he lived only to swim.

Then came that glorious day in Mexico when he won the Gold Medal. His father and new stepmother were in a box applauding wildly, as thousands more cheered. "Remember to smile for the TV cameras," his father had cautioned him. "People all over the world will be watching."

And as he stood there radiant, honored, flushed with victory, his only thought was, "Pam will be watching, too."

"And was she?" Dani asked.

"Oh yes. She sent me a lovely telegram. She was living in Palm Springs, she'd remarried. For a while, I'd see her during the summer holidays, when we'd go down to visit Alex and Amy."

"And where is she now?"

"Oh, married a third time. Making someone else happy. Her current husband's a Canadian who owns department stores. They live in Toronto, last heard. No, I don't see her anymore, though we still exchange Christmas cards."

All through his recitation, Dani had held back her tears, even as her heart went out to him. Poor Steve. He was suffering enough without having to deal with a weeping woman.

She rubbed her eyes. Steve wiped his. Then he sat up and poured fresh coffee.

"I've told you this, Dani, not because I'm looking for sympathy, God forbid! but only so you'll understand. I decided early on that I'd never marry, have children. I didn't want to be responsible for anyone else's happiness, or for their misery, either. You can see that, can't you?"

Yes, she could. She understood that he had been emotionally violated, yet even so she refused to despair. The fact that he could finally speak about it was grounds for hope.

"People overcome childhood traumas," she said. "There are ghetto children who have suffered the worst of circumstances, who've known physical abuse, hunger, deprivation. And they survived. There's a fellow in my office, both his parents died at Auschwitz, can you imagine anything more unspeakable? But now Ben's a married man. He has children, grandchildren. He has a life! If anything, his friends and family matter that much more to him because of what he lost. Think, Steve! With all that behind him, he managed not just to survive, but to triumph!"

She began to choke up. Steve handed her a napkin and waited till she blew her nose.

"This is not a competition, Dani. I'm not claiming I've suffered more than others in the agony sweepstakes. I'm just trying to explain who I am, why I behave the way I do. That business this morning, it was terrible. It opened up all the old wounds. There was a moment there . . . one moment . . ."—he swallowed, then forced himself to continue—"when I looked at Precious Nelson and I saw myself, Dani. Shut up . . . cut off . . . catatonic . . . estranged from life . . ." He began gulping for air like a drowning man. "It was horrible, Dani! It was—a glimpse of the abyss!"

"Oh Steve!" she burst out. "You can't compare—"

Impulsively, she moved to embrace him, to grip his hand and bring comfort, when Rosie let loose with a dull menacing growl. Steve jumped. "Stop!" he said, and for a moment Dani didn't know whether he was addressing her or the dog. "Calm down, Rosie. Good dog . . . good dog." Then he managed a grim laugh. "My protector. Big emotional scenes upset her. What the hell, Dani, they upset me too." He sat there for a moment, soothing the dog with easy strokes, then turned to gaze into Dani's eyes. His own were soft, troubled.

"I don't want to live that life anymore, Dani. It scares the hell out of me. You see, you're not the only one who had an epiphany today." He paused to marshal his thoughts, and when he spoke again it was in a firm clear voice. "These months we've been together, I was fully aware that you had certain expectations of me. Two, in particular. First, you wanted me to be more open with you, to confide my feelings. And second, you expected me to make a serious commitment. As for the first item, I've been franker with you this afternoon than I've been with anyone, including my shrink. It hasn't been easy, but not quite as hard as I'd feared." He placed his hand on hers, circling her wrist. "So now for the second part. The part that deals with our future. We've both been alone too much, too long. I would like us to live together, Dani, to care for each other and be close. I'm ready to make that commitment if you are."

Dani's mouth went dry with incredulity.

"Steve? Are you saying what I think you're saying?"

He nodded. "I guess so. I've never proposed to anyone before, never even considered it. But all of a sudden, it makes such terrific sense. We could have a glorious life, but you know that already. Wonderful sex . . . well, we've always been great in bed, but so much more, so very much more. What a couple we'd make. . . ." His eyes sparkled, he began to amplify, embroider, spilling over with plans and schemes. "We could—my God!—what couldn't we! We'd keep this house, of course. I know how you love it. And then, since you're so keen about the city, we could get a co-op on the East Side so we wouldn't have to commute during the week. But something nice, Park Avenue or Beekman Place. The best of the best. We could furnish from scratch. We'd travel, entertain, maybe take a place in the Hamptons in the summer. Which one do you prefer, Southampton or East? Think about it. South is more elegant, East is more fun and Samantha would probably like it better. We'd both have our careers, of course. Naturally I wouldn't expect you to compromise your ambition. And if, for instance, you ever want to strike out on your own, set up an independent practice, Danielle Sloane and Associates, I'd be happy to . . ."

He was selling, she realized, selling his vision of their future together as though it were an incomparable work of art. She was too stunned to answer sensibly. This was the moment she had dreamed of time and again, the ripest of plums in her lap. It was too much, too sudden, too confusing. And in his inventory of luxuries and pleasures on offer, he had omitted the key word.

"Oh, Steve!" she broke in. "Don't tempt me with moondreams. Just tell me honestly, why do you want to marry me? What is it you're seeking? Is it love? Companionship? Devotion? I'm touched and grateful by everything you offer, but I have no picture of what you expect out of marriage. Why me, Steve? What can I give you in return?"

Her question took him by surprise, for his face grew grave, his voice fell to a whisper.

"I want your strength, Dani. I want your warmth. I want you to illuminate my life. I want you to . . ."

And in that moment she knew what he sought. He wanted her to save him from the abyss. It was more than a proposal. It was a cry for help.

And then the tears she had been fighting off since the morning refused to be stemmed. She cried. He held her fast and still she cried until her face ached and her eyelids were swollen, till his jersey was clotted with her tears.

"Oh da . . . da . . . dar . . ." Even as he comforted her, he struggled, his tongue stumbling around the simple yet unfamiliar endearment, until at last he was able to say it. "My darling. My darling Dani. My darling darling darling. . . ."

Even now, it sounded alien on his tongue. But he was trying, Dani knew, and it wrenched her heart.

"Ah, Steve, sweetheart!" She disentangled herself. "It's been a harrowing day. You . . . Precious . . . I'm sorry, I can't take it all in. At this point, I just want to go home, be by myself for a while and think things through."

"Of course, darling." This time, the endearment came a bit more easily. He would one day be fluent. "I understand. Take as much time as you wish."

She picked up her coat, groped her way to the hall mirror. "God, to look at me, you'd think I'd gone ten rounds with the heavyweight champ. Plus I have a wretched headache. If you'd just run me over to the station . . ."

She blotted her eyes, put on fresh lipstick. It didn't do any good.

"Of course, Dani. And when you get home, lie down for a couple of hours with an ice pack. Pam used to put these beefsteaks on, I recall. She said it was good for the eyes."

Dani stared at him, then sighed.

"I always heard it was veal cutlets."

29

SHE WEPT all the way home, wept on the train, in the cab ("You all right, lady?"), in the lobby ("Can I help you, Mrs. Sloane?"), went upstairs, cried some, fell into bed, slept a bit, woke up and wept some more.

Then she straggled into the bathroom only to be visited by an apparition that lurked in the mirror above the medicine chest. Bloated, blotchy. Looking about a hundred years old, into the bargain.

Dani shuddered, then patted down her face in cold water, which only aggravated the situation.

Pam recommended beefsteaks. Deirdre said veal cutlets. Take your pick.

Not that you'd find either in Dani Sloane's freezer. The cupboard was bare. Who ate at home anymore? Who shopped? Who cooked? Who had the time? And if she did manage somehow to get her hands on a nice pair of veal cutlets, she'd probably devour them raw on the spot.

God, but she was hungry. Starved. As ravenous as Sam on one of her adolescent binges. Which was instructive. Here was Dani, in the midst of one of life's seminal moments, reduced to the level of a single monstrous appetite. Extraordinary that at such a juncture, the stomach should take precedent over the heart.

Still—she had had nothing to eat since breakfast, except two bites of a salami sandwich at Steve's, and that had been hours ago. Seemed more like years ago, in the longest damnedest day of her life.

Correction, make that second longest damnedest et cetera. September ninth still held the record.

Dani threw on a shirt and jeans, then called the all-night Italian deli on Third to order a hot sausage sandwich on a hero, a side of potato salad, eggplant parmigiana, fried peppers and two pints of Häagen Dasz vanilla ice cream. When the delivery boy came, she almost snatched the bag out of his hand. "Oh, that smells great!" Then she went into the kitchen and began on the hero sandwich, tomato sauce dripping down her fingers.

"Never been so hungry in my life," she said with a touch of self-consciousness. Living by yourself, you talked aloud sometimes, she'd come to recognize. No harm done. It broke the silence.

She bit into a sausage, which was hot enough to open the sinuses and clear the brain. Good, hearty, simple food. The kind of meal Steve would have appreciated.

Poor Steve. Poor dear Steve whom she would never marry, after all that heavy wishing. Even at the very instant of his proposal, Dani had known instinctively what her answer would be. She would tell him no, "with regrets." And the regrets would be sincere.

She was sorry to disappoint him, but the fact was, she didn't love Steve Haddad. She had never loved him. What she had loved was the abstract idea of him. He was an image, a symbol. She had loved his house, his clothes, his cars, his dogs, his manners, his Shaker boxes, his status. She had loved a vision of herself as the possessor of the beautiful home, the brilliant husband. Best of all, she was in love with the triumph that would come of landing such a catch. New York's Most Eligible Bachelor. Brought to his knees by Dani Sloane.

"So there!" as Barney's lingerie lady might say.

She had wanted to love him, at least that sentiment was true. Even more, she had wanted him to love her. Oh my, yes! That was crucial. For in her daydreams, theirs was going to be the most notable, most romantic, most prestigious coupling since Mark Antony forfeited an empire for Cleopatra.

Mrs. Danielle Sloane-Haddad, Esq. Eat your heart out, every-body. What better proof could there be of Dani's beauty, of her worth and powers of seduction? What greater slap to Ted Sloane? That rat. That loser.

For how could Dani pass up the chance to play Lady of the Manor combined with the opportunity of getting back at *him*, the architect of her anguish? Of showing her husband the full-market value of what he had tossed away?

Marrying Steve would make Ted sit up and take notice. Like Precious Nelson, she had found a way to say, "Now do I have your attention?"

Looking back, Dani now perceived that her "love affair" wasn't concerned with Steve Haddad at all. It been about Ted Sloane from the start.

Love Steve? How could she? She hardly knew the man. All those months he'd been little more than a fantasy figure, about as real as the giant poster of Sting that Sam had kept in her bedroom. An object for pretending. For pleasant dreams and pretty fancies.

Not until today had Dani glimpsed him in the round, perceived the flesh-and-blood man behind the idol.

The funny part was, she reflected with a wry smile, that she had never liked Steve quite so much as she did at this very moment, when she was about to reject him.

Poor Steve. He wanted someting from her other than love. His words came winging back to her. *I want your strength, your warmth.* He wanted her to heal him, save him from despair. It was an enormous undertaking, one that would conceivably absorb her to the exclusion of much else.

Marrying him—indeed, marrying at all—had lost its allure. At present, she didn't wish to be Mrs. Dani Anyone.

She had lived that life: soothing hurts, drawing out thorns, placing the happiness of others ahead of her own. She planned to lead another life now. Fine. And free. And independent.

With certain regrets, and equally certain satisfactions.

For even though this much-wished-for marriage was not to be, she and Steve had served each other well. In retrospect, she could see that their affair had been therapeutic for them both. Steve, the iceberg, had begun to thaw, and she suspected it was a nonreversible process. Dani had a shrewd notion that some other woman might one day make Steve whole.

As for Dani, she had emerged from the crucible as her own woman at last.

She had made a life for herself.

Right now (and one lived in the now), she relished being her own mistress. Alone, but by no means lonely. She was busy, mostly happy, enjoyed a broad and lively acquaintanceship (much of it Steve's legacy) and plenty of friends—most of them women, to be sure. Yet with or without Steve, she could always round up a presentable man for a bar association dinner or the theater. She had close colleagues at the office—an extended family of sorts— and only last week Jack Pruitt had told her that she would make partner on the first of the year.

She loved her work. She enjoyed the fruits of success.

Marry Steve? Marry anyone? At this stage, the last thing she needed was having her life turned upside down by yet another man. Maybe someday, some other man as yet unimagined would make her reconsider, for the future was unknowable. But at this particular moment, it wasn't worth it.

She recalled having a conversation with Steve when a baseball trading card had gone at auction for over $300,000. How can it be worth that? she asked, and Steve had replied that things were worth whatever people wanted to pay for them.

What was marriage worth? Or love or romance? What was she willing to pay? Once upon a time, she would have deemed it perfectly proper to shelve her career, her ambitions, her friends, to follow "him"—that proverbial *him*—to the ends of the earth.

That chapter in her life had closed; the next one had yet to be written—by the new-born Dani Sloane.

She would call Steve tomorrow and tell him of her decision. And who knows? He might even feel relieved. Perhaps they would remain lovers. They would certainly remain friends.

She finished her dinner and opened up a carton of ice cream. Plain vanilla. The very best accompaniment for plain thinking.

It had been, what . . . ? One year, two months, how many weeks, days, hours, minutes? The mathematics were too random to be symbolic.

By rights, there ought to have been some symmetry about the interval, some pattern to indicate the grand scheme of things. A significance in the date, perhaps. One year exactly. Or two. Or five. Their wedding anniversary would have been appropriate for such an occasion. Or a birthday (his, hers, Sam's). Or else, a meaningful formula: say, one month of misery to pay for every year of happy marriage, which would have carried her into next May.

But the heart keeps an independent timetable, and so it came to pass that in the early afternoon of the Saturday after Thanksgiving (she didn't bother to check the calendar), Dani Sloane's marriage came to an end.

Ted's had ended some time before.

And if the date was unremarkable, the circumstances were even less so. Dani was sitting at the kitchen counter at the moment of severance, wearing an old shirt and jeans with a half-empty dish of ice cream before her. It was as good a vantage point as any to survey the wreckage.

Such appalling behavior! Not Ted's, but her own. For a smart lady, she had done everything wrong. The *pro se* lawyer with a fool for a client.

She had torn up subpoenas. Looted bank accounts. Made scenes in public. Alternately browbeaten and bribed her daughter. She had refused to talk, to compromise, to deal, to settle, to face reality. In short, she had ignored all the sound advice she offered others.

Which was mystifying.

Because Danielle Fletcher Sloane was (as those who knew her could testify) a strong, superior woman. Learned. Capable. Adept in matters of marriage and divorce.

Yet every emotion that she had hitherto observed in her clients (from a certain distance, let it be said), all the messiness, the anguish, Dani had since endured firsthand. Shock, denial, pain, paralysis, rage, fear, hatred, self-loathing: she had been spared nothing. So much for theoretical knowledge.

If the experience hadn't been so devastating it would have been comic. Danielle Sloane, Esq., reduced to two dimensions, like a figure in a kiddies' cartoon. A Bugs Bunny, zapped by a steamroller,

flattened to the thickness of a thousandth of an inch. Except Bugs
Bunny picked himself up in the following frame and waltzed off
to fresh mischief.

Not Dani. When it came to the crunch, the so-called smart,
savvy lady had reacted no differently from Linda Gessner, to pick
an extreme.

Except Linda Gessner could avail herself of a single neat alibi.
My husband left me for another man. Whereas Dani . . . Ah, clever
Dani had a multitude of scapegoats.

Blame?

Where to start? There were candidates aplenty to explain Ted's
defection, enough to fill every line on a legal pad. Blame the eco-
nomic situation. Blame Globexx. Mort Ketchell. The birds on the
beach at Kennebunkport. Blame the apartment—too small. Manhattan—too frantic. Mortgage payments. Bank loans. The IRS.

And let's not omit noise. Boredom. Stress. Tension. Traffic.
Crime. Male menopause. Definitely male menopause.

Which brings you to the Calvin Klein ads with their sybaritic
promise. Woody Allen with Mia Farrow on his arm. Fear of bald-
ness. Fear of dying. Sweet memories of Ecuador.

Peripheral? Then the world is peripheral.

Except to blame everybody was to blame nobody, and Dani was
too scrupulous for that. So she had narrowed down the list to get
on with the serious fault-finding. Bottom line, there were three
principal culprits in *Sloane v. Sloane.* The heavy hitters, each of
whom had dominated the Hall of Blame spotlight at one time or
another.

First, Ted Sloane, that rat.

Then Jennifer MacDougall, that bitch.

And finally Dani, prime fool among fools.

Did that cover all possible root causes? All except one.

For the one villain she hadn't factored into the dissolution of
their marriage was the passage of time. Time and its mutations.
The clock, the calendar, moving forward relentlessly even as you
begged it to stay. Slow corrosive time, altering circumstances, re-
shuffling dreams, nibbling away at the edges of old convictions,
transforming Dani and Ted into new people, other people, unrec-
ognizable from that young couple who had stood up in St. Mat-

thew's Church in Hupperstown and sworn to love and to cherish two decades past. Till death us do part?

Till change us do part.

Only in Dani's mind had that young couple remained fixed, preserved under glass, like the framed wedding photo that used to sit on the bedroom dresser.

Kaycee/Katherine was right. Dani's conceptions had gelled years ago. They had declared Ted to be the sum of one particular set of characteristics, Dani of another.

Her husband was (it was engraved right there in stone) Ted who loved tennis, Verdi, Hawthorne, his wife, his job, the Mets, Szechuan food, playing poker on Wednesdays, putting his feet up on the big black recliner, taking his little girl to the zoo in Central Park to watch the seals get fed.

And she was Dani: loving wife, devoted mother, so-so housekeeper, middling-to-good cook. Who went on to become a lawyer, but not really. Not *seriously*. Because work was what you played at. Home was where you lived.

Given that perspective, you arrived at that conclusion. The fact that you might be in error was incidental.

Once when Samantha was small, Dani had brought home a picture book. On the right side of each page was an extremely tight photograph, so simple as to be indecipherable, and the challenge lay in figuring what the object was. Was that wavy line a vast river snaking through the desert? Or a coil of hair on a barbershop floor? Or a cowboy's lasso?

Then you turned the page to discover that your vast winding river was actually a close-up shot of the stitching on a baseball.

Poor Sam would become frustrated.

"I didn't see it," she'd say, pounding the table with small fists. But not for lack of looking; her perspective was wrong.

Thus with Dani.

For how many years had she looked at Ted Sloane without seeing clearly? Two? Three? More? With the benefit of hindsight, Dani had almost perfect vision. She could interpret the clues, see where Ted had drifted, thrashed, flailed, panicked, grasped for fresh meaning in life. Read the stitching on the baseball, so to speak.

But not then. Then she had been blind. Was that because Ted

was too close, and she was too incurious? Or had she dreaded what a clear-eyed appraisal might show?

It was a question she often asked herself of clients. How could they not know? How could intelligent people be so dumb?

The day Linda Gessner first came to her in a state of shock, Dani's reaction had been—*But she must have known in her heart!* None so blind as those who will not see, Dani had quipped to Leo Margulies.

But who would choose to see and acknowledge such awful truths, no matter how visible? Not Linda. Nor Dani, either.

Another image of that summer day came to mind—vivid, painful. The image of a carriage horse running amok outside the Plaza Hotel. A superstitious woman would have viewed the incident as an omen, a prophecy of dire things to come. A less superstitious woman should have seen a parallel.

The runaway horse. The runaway man. Both frenzied, panicked by external pressures, stressed beyond the capacity to endure. Had Dani grasped the depth of Ted's turmoil, she might have tried to grab the reins and wrest control. And if that proved impossible, at least she should have had enough sense to get out of the way.

But by then, by that summer of his discontent, he had ceased to be the good old Ted of Dani's set vision. She was dealing with a different man. An intimate stranger. So close. So far apart.

And yet . . . and yet . . .

And yet they had been happy once upon a time. Another Ted. Another Dani. It was immensely sad. And very long ago. Only now did she feel able to take that last bit of advice she offered clients. Remember the good times. And there had been many. Then say your farewells.

Yesterday morning—it seemed a lifetime ago—she had sat on the floor of the Long Gallery, amid shards of glass and tatters of canvas, moved to tears by the wanton destruction, and by the darkness of Precious Nelson's soul. For what could be more hellish than the death of art? Of beauty? Of a child's tender life? It was enough to break your heart.

But Dani also had been intent on darkness. Like Precious, she had been caught in a loop—of anger, spite, hatred, of revenge.

She, too, had tried to vent her sense of futility by destroying what was rare and beautiful.

That something beautiful was the past, the good years of their marriage. And they were beautiful. And they would stay beautiful in memory, unless she chose to trash them.

No more!

For in all this struggle, her sole consolation had been the knowledge that she was making someone else's life at least a fraction as miserable as her own.

Let Ted have his freedom, his money, his sweet young Jennifer MacDougall.

Was there no justice? Correct. There was no justice. But at least she could cut her losses.

Dani didn't have the stuff saints were made of. She could never fully forgive Ted Sloane, not so much for what he'd done, but the manner of his doing. Wounds heal. Scars remain.

But no matter. The time had come to get off the loop. For her to do as Ted himself had done the year before. To choose health over sickness, change over stasis, the future over the past. And the hell with what the scorecard said.

Barney Feldman liked to tell the story of two feuding merchants who approached the rabbi to arbitrate some dispute. The rabbi hears the first one out. "You're right," he says. Then he listens to the second merchant's case. "You're right," he agrees. Afterward the rabbi's wife says to him, "That's ridiculous. How can they both be right?" The wise man considers. "You're right," he says.

So with Dani and Ted. The battle was over. And as it turned out it had never really been a question of guilt, of blame, of winning or losing. There were no perpetrators in the final analysis—only victims.

And so Dani wept. Not the sharp stinging tears she had shed so many times over the past year, not tears of wounded ego and injured pride, but soft tears. Tears of mourning.

She wept for vanished youth. For vanished love. For happy days that existed now only in snapshots. For the trials that had been inflicted upon Samantha. For the loss of the paintings. For Precious Nelson. For Steve Haddad. For Ted Sloane. For herself.

Then she dried her eyes and packed up the past, carefully,

lovingly. Tied it round and round with silken ribbons. Stacked it up, memory upon memory. Then locked it away in the attic of her mind.

Monday morning, she called Leo Margulies.

"I want you to represent me," she said. "And make it as quick and painless as possible."

She would be sending around the relevant correspondence by messenger, plus a net worth statement.

"Not that there's a helluva lot to divvy up, but you can tell my husband's lawyer that I'll be putting the apartment on the market. Which ought to relieve some of the pressure. Plus I'm sure Barney Feldman will agree to sell the boat. And, oh yeah"—she gave a short laugh—"when you start totting up the figures, be sure and give Ted an offset of forty-five hundred dollars. I went and bought myself a fur coat last year."

Then her secretary came in with an inch-thick stack of messages and Dani buckled down to work.